Kingdom's Edge

Exiles of a Gilded Moon, Volume 2

Dustin R Cummings

Published by Shadow Spark Publishing, 2021.

KINGDOM'S EDGE

First edition. September 15, 2021.

Written by Dustin R Cummings.

Chapter 1

Darshima climbed the broad staircase amid the darkness, his leather boots thudding against its granite treads. His gaze lingered upon Tenrai, who ascended the stairs a few paces ahead of him. Powdery flakes of snow clung to his silky black hair, fashioned in a tail. Ice crystals covered the fabric of his black overcoat, glittering in the moonlight. Darshima looked past Tenrai and peered into the night. The sky glowed with subdued moonlight from Ciblaithia, its golden crescent glimmering amid the void.

An immense temple complex and its imposing silhouette stood against the night, framed by arrays of constellations. Darshima drew in a halting breath of chilly air, exhaling it in a puff of steam. His eyes wandered over the sweeping lines of the eight-tiered central tower, rising above a cluster of large, adjoined buildings. Chains of gems hung from the curved eaves, their graceful outlines partially obscured by the snowfall. Darshima shivered as a frigid gust blew through the dark fabric of his trousers. He dusted a fine layer of snow from his overcoat with a gloved hand and clenched his numb fingers for warmth.

On either side of him, rows of sentries dressed in pleated black trousers, knee-high boots, black overcoats with wide sleeves, and blue hoods stood at attention. Stationed at either side of the staircase, the tails of their coats fluttered in the wind. Silken black scarves shielded the lower half of their pale faces against the icy winds. Their sapphire eyes glowing softy, the sentries stared intently at Darshima and his companions as they walked. They extended wooden lanterns burning with white flame, illuminating the path ahead, and offered a deferential bow as they climbed the stairs.

Darshima peered over his shoulder and glimpsed the expressions of Erethalie, Sydarias, Shonan, and Khydius, all dressed in similar black overcoats, gloves, trousers, and boots. Trails of steam rose from their parted lips, awestruck as they beheld the unusual scene. Moments ago, Tenrai had led them into Chryshaihem, the capital of Tiriyuud. The murmurings Darshima remembered from his childhood about Iberwight and its hidden cities failed to capture the mysteriousness of this place. The sound of Tenrai's footsteps thudding faster upon the treads echoed amid the silence.

1

"We are nearly there." Tenrai pointed toward the soaring crown of steeples at the center of the complex.

As they neared the top of the staircase, Darshima's eyes unexpectedly met the gaze of a man standing atop the uppermost step. The man's narrowed azure eyes, reminiscent of a cloudless sky, cast a discerning stare as they approached. Appearing similar in age to Tenrai, a thoughtful frown graced his pale, smooth face. A pair of golden threads secured his silky black hair, fashioned in an elegant tail hanging down his back. Darshima noted a series of markings in gleaming blue and red ink curving behind his right ear onto his neck. A stiff black robe embroidered in vivid, golden geometric lines draped over his broad shoulders. He stood still amid the blustery winds, his blue woolen cape fluttering behind him.

Tenrai hurried to the top of the stairway, stood before the man, then offered him a deep bow. The man returned it with an even more profound bow. Tenrai's voice broke the silence, his foreign words coming out in puffs of steam. Darshima's ears pricked at the staccato rhythm of their sentences as they exchanged what he presumed were greetings in their dialect. Though he couldn't understand them, he felt the fondness in their voices and the eagerness of their words.

"Dydan Waike, wise Sage of Tiriyuud, I offer you my heartfelt gratitude for welcoming us," said Tenrai in clear Vilidesian, his voice rising above the winds.

"Guardian Tenrai Nax, esteemed Knight of Tiriyuud, I am thankful for your safe return," said Dydan, in lightly accented Vilidesian. He reached from beneath the folds of his robe and gripped Tenrai's gloved hands. "I can only imagine the perils you faced during the journey home."

"It was an experience that I will never forget." Tenrai nodded slowly.

"I look forward to hearing more." The corners of Dydan's eyes wrinkled as he listened to Tenrai. Dydan turned to Darshima and his companions.

"There are several more people accompanying you than I anticipated." Dydan bit his lip and stared past Darshima.

"You are right, Sage Waike. The circumstances of our journey made it necessary for these Vilidesians to join us." Tenrai glimpsed behind him and beckoned them all forward. "I present my nephews, Darshima and Khydius

Nax. I also present their companions Sydarias Idawa, Erethalie Danthe, and her brother Shonan."

"I am pleased to meet you all." Dydan offered Darshima a bow, then shook his hand. His expression softened and a reserved smile formed upon his lips.

"Thank you, sir." Darshima bowed in return. As the sage greeted him, Darshima felt his heartbeat slow noticeably. A sense of calm flowed through him, much like when he first met Tenrai. Dydan extended his hands and welcomed Khydius. He then moved over and greeted Shonan, Erethalie, and Sydarias.

"I must present you all to the council before we discuss matters any further. The other sages are expecting you at the temple." His cape billowing behind him, Dydan guided them past the flanking rows of sentries and through a soaring stone arch marking the complex's entrance. They walked across a vast octagonal courtyard and toward a pair of dark wooden doors embellished with arrays of golden polygons.

Darshima moved along the glistening black stones, his eyes tracing the radial web of golden lines etched into the pavement. The snowflakes hit the heated surface, evaporating into clouds of vapor that hung over the courtyard in a damp haze. A pair of uniformed sentries pushed the doors, which groaned open and echoed into the night. Tenrai looked over his shoulder at Darshima and his companions, his sapphire eyes gleaming.

"You must stay silent as Sage Waike presents us." Tenrai offered a reassuring nod as he saw their nervous stares.

"We are entering the Sages' Temple. Please, follow my lead." Dydan beckoned them through the parted doors.

Darshima and his companions stepped past the threshold. He drew in a breath of warm fragrant air, his nose tingling with aromas of charred wood and smoky incense. He removed his gloves and tucked them into his coat pockets, his fingers tingling as the coldness dissipated from them. Amid the warmth of the temple, Khydius, Sydarias, Erethalie, and Shonan loosened their coats and brushed the snowflakes from their shoulders. They followed Dydan and Tenrai across the gleaming black stone floor, their footsteps echoing throughout the cavernous chamber.

Darshima's eyes lingered upon the graceful lines of the temple's interior. Shafts of pale blue light filtered through rectangular arrays of stained glass windows set in the ceiling. Muted beams illuminated the floors and carved granite walls, chasing away the veils of shadow. Held aloft by a colonnade of immense stone pillars, the roof sat high above their heads. A crown of stone buttresses supported the large, cantilevered wooden rafters. The cylindrical beams met at the center of the octagonal, vaulted ceiling, opening to the starry sky in a giant, gilded oculus. Darshima peered up at the gleaming aperture, which seemed to float above an array of trapezoidal wooden struts. The oculus emitted a golden curtain of light that cascaded onto the floor, blending with the moonbeams.

Tenrai, Darshima, and the others followed Dydan through the staid interior. They walked along an arcing path between the columns, toward the center of the temple. Above the silence, Darshima's ears filled with the hushed drone of chanting, the words sounding like the same language that Tenrai and Dydan had spoken earlier. He looked around, trying to identify the source of the stirring voices, his ears guiding him to the veil of light shimmering before them.

Chapter 2

Darshima waited beside Khydius at the center of the temple. He peered over Tenrai's shoulder and tried to catch a glimpse through the luminous curtain. His pulse thudded with anticipation as he observed several robed silhouettes mingling amid the light. Dydan and Tenrai stood before the radiant beams, their faces bearing solemn expressions.

Dydan stepped closer to the light, the embroidery upon his robes catching the rays in brilliant flashes of gold. He uttered a series of phrases, and Darshima strained to understand the unfamiliar vocabulary. Dydan's voice came forth in a steady cadence, his clipped syllables echoing in the enormous chamber. As he finished his phrase, a chorus of voices greeted him in the same language. Dydan looked over to Tenrai, then turned back to the light and squared his shoulders.

"Fellow Sages of Chryshaihem, I come before you with extraordinary tidings," proclaimed Dydan, speaking in Vilidesian. His forceful voice resounded through the temple. Darshima's ears rang with the gentle rhythm of his formal speech. Though Vilidesian wasn't his native tongue, Dydan had mastered the language. Then, in one swift movement, Dydan genuflected, his robes rustling around him. "Guardian Tenrai Nax, distinguished Knight of Tiriyuud, has completed his journey and returned from distant worlds beyond our skies." Tenrai moved closer to the light. He knelt beside Dydan and bowed his head.

"Sages of Tiriyuud, I offer my salutations and profound gratitude. Please allow me to present my nephews Darshima and Khydius Nax," said Tenrai. "It is also my honor to present their companions, Sydarias Idawa, Erethalie Danthe, and her young brother Shonan."

Unsure how to proceed, Darshima fell to his knees upon hearing Tenrai pronounce his name. Erethalie, Sydarias, and Shonan did the same, hitting the ground with a thud. Khydius hesitantly lowered himself upon one knee and glared forward. As they waited, a chorus of voices responded to Tenrai in impeccable Vilidesian. Darshima's pulse thudded in surprise as he listened to them speak in unison.

5

"Greetings Sage Waike and Guardian Nax. We welcome you and those who accompany you." Their voices faded in the voluminous silence of the temple. Dydan and Tenrai rose to their feet and stepped into the light. Before he disappeared from view, Tenrai beckoned them forth with a wave of his hand. Darshima and his companions stood up and followed Tenrai through the glowing curtain.

As his eyes adjusted to the brightness, Darshima looked around him. He squinted as the surrounding temple faded into a seemingly distant, pale image. He looked down at the polished stone floor and glimpsed his reflection, tinged in gold. Complex patterns of inlaid crystal arcs and tessellated octagons spread out before him. The intricate design converged upon a raised, circular golden platform positioned beneath the oculus.

Two dozen men and women sat in a semi-circle atop the gleaming, brushed metal surface. They wore stiff black and gold robes with hoods that partially obscured their pale faces. The assembled sages faced a woman dressed in shimmering red garments embroidered in rays of golden thread. She cast her narrowed sapphire eyes downward in a contemplative expression. The light gave her elaborate garments a subtle glow. Her black hair, fastened in a tail with golden cords, hung down her back. Behind the dais, the temple's thick stone walls gave way to an immense pane of glass, framing an expansive view of the moonlit lake and the surrounding mountains.

As Dydan led them toward the platform, the assembled group rose to their feet. Robes rustling amid the silence, the sages descended from the platform. Several of them approached Dydan, their white fabric, split-toed boots padding softly against the floor. The sage dressed in red stood before Tenrai.

"Most wise Aodren Ryte, Seer of Chryshaihem, I thank you for your welcome and beseech your grace." Tenrai bowed deeply in her direction.

"Welcome, Guardian Nax, Knight of Tiriyuud. I feel fortunate to see you again. I thank you for your valiant efforts." She returned with a polite bow and then turned to Dydan. "Sage Waike, thank you for personally escorting Guardian Nax and his party to the temple."

"Guardian Nax is an esteemed member of our Order and my dear friend. I could do no less for him." Dydan bowed toward the seer, then gestured toward Tenrai.

"I offer my apologies for disturbing your peace." Tenrai looked toward Seer Ryte and the sages gathered behind her. "I present my nephews, Darshima and Khydius Nax. They are the sons of the most revered, Rion Nax." Tenrai rested his hands upon their shoulders and ushered them toward her.

Darshima drew in an anxious breath as Tenrai mentioned their father's name. Latent questions stirred in his mind but settled as he felt the seer's intent gaze upon him. Darshima lifted his eyes and met her stare. Appearing slightly older than Tenrai, her smooth, oval face bore a contemplative expression.

"Against all odds, you succeeded in finding Rion's sons." She pursed her lips, trying to mask her evident satisfaction. Following the unfamiliar custom, Darshima, then Khydius bowed toward her in a polite gesture. Darshima looked toward the sages and studied their faces, but their stern expressions and deferred stares yielded nothing. The seer's gaze drifted past Darshima and Khydius. Her eyebrows arched in muted surprise as she looked toward Shonan. Tenrai cleared his throat as he read her expression.

"I would also like to present Sydarias Idawa, Erethalie, and Shonan Danthe." Tenrai beckoned them forward. "Like Darshima and Khydius, they are refugees who survived the invasion of The Vilides. They have accompanied us during our journey and seek to join the Order." Hushed murmurs rose from the sages, and they exchanged looks of incredulity.

"This is most unusual, Guardian Nax." Seer Ryte folded her arms across her chest, the rich fabric of her robes shimmering in the light. "I cannot recall a prior instance of outsiders being brought to Chryshaihem, let alone to the inner sanctum of the temple."

"Please forgive Guardian Nax for this transgression," said Dydan, his face growing flushed. "His intentions are pure." She abruptly raised her hand, and Dydan fell silent.

"Sage Waike, Guardian Nax, I have always placed my trust in your judgment. There must be some explanation for this most unusual aberration." Her brow wrinkled as she waited for their response.

"I have broken the council's tradition, and I offer my regret." Tenrai bowed deeply at the waist, his face bearing a look of contrition. "The circumstances we faced during the voyage made it essential for them to join us."

"Please enlighten me of these extraordinary circumstances." She glared at Tenrai, the sternness of her expression softening slightly.

Tenrai straightened his posture and cleared his throat. "I rescued Darshima and his friend Sydarias from slavery. They were captured in The Vilides and toiled together in a farming colony on the planet Navervyne. After our escape back to the invaded realm, we met Erethalie and her brother Shonan. She served as our pilot during our flight from The Vilides. Erethalie carried us back to Navervyne, where we rescued Khydius and Darshima's adoptive brother, Sasha Eweryn. They labored together under difficult conditions in a munitions factory in Stebbenhour. Upon rescuing them, we traveled to Gordanelle and returned Sasha to his parents. We then journeyed back to Iberwight."

"A most harrowing account." The seer's eyebrows arched in surprise. "It appears that these Vilidesians have given crucial support to Rion's sons during an undoubtedly terrible ordeal."

"Their help was essential, and we wouldn't have succeeded without their bravery and skill." Tenrai looked toward Erethalie and Sydarias as he spoke, his eyes narrowed in tacit recognition of their efforts. "They have shown intelligence, loyalty, and courage that would stand with the best among our Order."

Darshima listened to Tenrai's acknowledgment of his friends and silently recounted all that Erethalie and Sydarias had done for them. From Sydarias' resolve during their toil in Navervyne to Erethalie's unmatched skill as a pilot during their escape, Darshima knew that he nor Tenrai or Khydius wouldn't have survived without them.

"I humbly ask you to accept them into the Order of the Gilded Moon. We will train them in our ways as guardians." Tenrai faced the seer, a determined frown forming upon his lips.

She stepped back from Tenrai, her eyebrows arching in surprise.

"The Order has never considered such an unusual request." Seer Ryte shook her head in disbelief.

"These are unprecedented times. Our Order must make difficult decisions if Tiriyuud is to survive," said Tenrai.

"Please elaborate, Guardian Nax." Seer Ryte shot an inquisitive stare at Tenrai.

"The Vilidesian Realm was challenged and defeated by a previously unknown yet mighty nation. Within a matter of months, the Navervynish conquered Benai's four moons. They have not yet reached Tiriyuud, but we cannot expect our seclusion to protect us forever."

"The fall of the Vilidesian Realm and its effects are incalculable. We mourn the devastation and loss of life." Seer Ryte bowed her head. "We must have faith that Tiriyuud will avoid a similar fate."

"The Navervynish are unrivaled, and we must prepare ourselves in every aspect. Whether they are Tiriyuusian or foreigner, we must accept all who want to serve the Order of the Gilded Moon," said Tenrai.

"Guardian Nax, You have experienced more in your journey than most of us will ever truly understand. Your request is without precedent, and I must confer with the council. I will share your words of support." Seer Ryte stepped away from them and rejoined the sages.

Darshima's pulse thudded in his ears as he listened to the sages, their hushed voices rising and falling in conversation. He tried in vain to understand their unfamiliar words, but his feelings of frustration only grew.

Dydan lingered beside Tenrai, his arms folded across his chest as he watched the other sages conferring.

"As always, you have my full support Tenrai, but I will face difficulty in convincing my fellow sages to agree to your request." Dydan faced Tenrai.

"What more can I tell them?" Tenrai glimpsed over his shoulder at Sydarias, Erethalie, and Shonan. A look of concern spread upon Tenrai's face as he registered their anxious expressions.

"As you know, the seer and the sages have vast powers. The council has the authority to grant residence to anyone who seeks to live in Tiriyuud." Dydan gestured toward Seer Ryte and the sages surrounding her. "The council also has the right to banish anyone from the kingdom."

"We must accept them. Their homelands have been devastated. There is nowhere else for them to turn." Tenrai clenched his jaw in frustration. "They have sacrificed everything to be here with Darshima."

"The only foreigners Tiriyuud has accepted were rare Omystikai, centuries ago. They ventured from the dominions here on Iberwight and sought to learn our ways. We have no history of permitting any others." Dydan's lips curled into a worried frown.

"We must convince the council. Accepting them is the right thing to do," said Tenrai.

"I will do my utmost." Dydan offered a gracious nod and joined the seer and the other sages, who congregated near the dais.

Darshima and Khydius moved beside Tenrai and watched as Seer Ryte and her sages spoke among themselves. Khydius glared at the council, his brow furrowed in an intense expression. Several sages gesticulated toward Tenrai amid their deliberation, while others furtively stared in their direction.

"I don't understand what this means for us," whispered Khydius.

"They must decide whether to break with tradition. You and Darshima are both half Tiriyuusian. You are Rion Nax's sons and my nephews. I am confident that you both will be accepted." Tenrai solemnly bowed his head. "Sydarias, Erethalie, and Shonan have no Omystikai heritage whatsoever. Accepting them into the Order is a difficult decision without precedent."

"If the sages don't accept them, then I cannot stay on Iberwight," said Darshima, his voice catching in his throat. "I will do whatever it takes for them to stay." The possibility that his companions could be turned away because of their heritage left him stunned.

"This is preposterous," fumed Khydius. "I was a Vilidesian Prince. This entire moon was once my domain. Your sages mustn't forget that." Khydius clenched his fists, his growing frustration becoming evident. "Erethalie, Shonan, and Sydarias must be accepted without reservation."

"My nephew, circumstances are not as they once were. The era of Vilidesian rule upon the four moons has passed. Their realm is no more." Tenrai rested his hands upon Khydius' tense shoulder. "We must have faith that the council will make the right decision and accept your companions." Khydius fell silent at Tenrai's pronouncement, and a resigned expression spread upon his face.

His thoughts racing, Darshima glared at the floor. Tenrai had mentioned nothing of a formal acceptance into his Order when describing his plans for their exile in Tiriyuud. He hadn't even considered the possibility that the Order might reject them from the kingdom. Amid his frustration, he suppressed a sigh and scolded himself. Tiriyuud was the most geographically and culturally isolated territory among the moons. They were outsiders and couldn't expect an unconditional acceptance into this hermetic place. As Tenrai noted, they were no longer privileged Vilidesian subjects but refugees from a defunct realm.

After what felt like an interminable wait, the chattering among the sages ceased. Darshima lifted his gaze as Seer Ryte and the Council of Sages approached them. She stood before Darshima and Khydius, her eyes glowing softly.

"These young men are Rion's sons. I can feel his strength and spirit within them." She rested her hands upon their shoulders. "They are home, and they belong with us. We accept them." She then turned to Sydarias and Erethalie, who pulled Shonan closer to her.

"Per Guardian Nax's account, you both have achieved great feats under difficult circumstances." Her gaze shifted between them. Erethalie and Sydarias exchanged a stare, then faced the seer.

"We did our best to serve both Darshima and Prince Khydius," said Erethalie, turning to Sydarias.

"There is no previous instance of outsiders with no Omystikai heritage joining our Order." Seer Ryte stepped closer, peering intently into their eyes. "Do you believe you have the strength to submit to our training and learn our ways?"

"We have what it takes to serve your kingdom." Sydarias bowed his head.

"You must be willing to renounce your former lives and train with us. If you succeed, you will become a citizen of Tiriyuud and a Guardian of the Order. We will regard you as a fellow Tiriyuusian and an Omystikai in all aspects."

"We are willing to devote ourselves to Tiriyuud and its cause," said Erethalie.

"Your acceptance into our Order, into our kingdom is the most sacred commitment you will ever make. It is an unbreakable bond. If you harbor any doubt or hesitation in your hearts, you must not join our Order." A studied frown formed upon Seer Ryte's lips.

"We are ready," said Sydarias. He and Erethalie nodded in unison.

"I believe Guardian Nax. If what he says bears any truth, then you belong with us. Tiriyuud welcomes you." She rested her hands upon their shoulders, and her frown lessened some. Seer Ryte then faced Tenrai.

"While I trust you and your fellow guardians in the training of new recruits, I must insist upon a slight modification, given the extraordinary circumstance with which you have presented me." Her eyes narrowed with an unflinching seriousness.

"I do not understand, Seer Ryte." Tenrai's eyebrows wrinkled in confusion.

"You have requested that we induct these foreigners into the Order. Therefore I cannot leave their training solely to the guardians." She folded her arms across her chest.

"Training of recruits has always been the province of the guardians. Who else would be involved?" Tenrai shook his head in disbelief.

"Sage Waike will train these young recruits alongside you. He served with you as a guardian before joining the council. I believe that he will be of much help to you."

"My duty is to the Order, whatever the circumstance requires." Dydan bowed at the seer's pronouncement. Tenrai stared at both of them and drew in a measured breath.

"With regard to Sage Waike, I shall honor your request," said Tenrai. He offered a respectful bow to Seer Ryte and Dydan.

"I expect no less, Guardian Nax." Seer Ryte moved toward Shonan. "The boy is much too young. Training with the guardians entails rigors that are not meant for a child." She gently rested her hand upon Shonan's cheek. "We will find a family to care for him here in Chryshaihem."

"I understand." Erethalie pursed her lips in resignation.

"It's for the best." Sydarias rested his hand upon her shoulder.

"We are grateful for refuge in your kingdom, even if it means we must be apart," she whispered. Shonan looked up at his sister. A somber frown formed upon his lips, and he turned away from her. Seer Ryte whispered something in Tenrai's ear, and he offered a pensive nod.

"I know of a good home for him. The family will care for him as if he were their own son." She rested her hands upon Shonan's shoulders.

"Most wise Seer, let us spare you the trouble of traveling. I will gladly take them." Dydan stepped forward, gesturing toward Erethalie and Shonan.

"Given the extraordinary nature of this request, the seer should escort us." Tenrai leaned toward Dydan. "She is the leader of Chryshaihem, and the citizens will listen to her."

"You are right," said Dydan. "We shall travel together."

"Let us depart before the sun rises. The child needs his rest." Seer Ryte stepped past them, beckoning them to follow her.

The other sages resumed their seats atop the platform, their stares lingering upon Tenrai. Darshima and his companions followed Tenrai, Dydan, and the seer through the curtain of light. A sigh of relief escaped Darshima's lips as they walked through the shadows of the temple toward the entrance. He and his friends would find refuge in Tiriyuud, but they would have to earn their welcome.

Chapter 3

Erethalie and Shonan walked hand in hand under the pale morning sun. The snow showers had slowed, leaving behind cold grey skies. They followed Seer Ryte, Dydan, and Tenrai along the snow-covered roadway of a bridge. Giant stone pillars supported its arched span, meeting the dark, flowing waters of an icy river far below.

Khydius and Sydarias trudged beside Erethalie and Shonan, their boots thudding against its cobbled surface. Darshima lingered a few paces behind them, intently surveying the wintry terrain. They had set out from the Sages' Temple at dawn and walked through the labyrinthine streets of the capital. As they journeyed through the city, Darshima gazed upon the stately edifices of wood and stone, elegant temples with soaring steeples, venerated shrines with tiered roofs, and sanctuaries with their ornate arches. The city felt ancient, but he sensed a distinct vitality that he couldn't fully describe. Chryshaihem intrigued him like no other place.

Darshima and his companions crossed the bridge, which led from the capital's dense central island, toward a smaller outer island, further from the lakeshore. The terrain spread out before them in a series of snow-covered hills, verdant stands of coniferous trees, and gently terraced fields. Jagged outcroppings of crystal jutted through the snowdrifts at sharp angles, lining the road like bowing sentinels. The terrain sloped toward the rock-strewn shore, covered in fractured slabs of ice. Darshima's ears filled with the gentle sound of lapping water, interrupted by the crunch of their footsteps upon the powdery snow.

"We are almost there." Dydan glimpsed over his shoulder, his cape billowing behind him.

"It seems so far away." Erethalie squeezed Shonan's hand.

"It is not so far that you won't be able to visit him." Seer Ryte looked over to them. "I understand the importance of your kindred ties. This family will protect him."

His eyes narrowed against the gusts of wind, Darshima looked toward the mountain range encircling the lake. He eyed Benai's sphere through an opening in the clouds. Its halo of red and white rings dipped behind the jagged peaks, fading against the brightening sky. Amid the fields, Darshima glimpsed rows of neat, wooden multistory homes. The fluted, black ceramic tiles upon their roofs glistened with a fresh layer of snow. Billowing trails of white steam rose from their cylindrical chimneys, trailing into the sky. A square wooden arched gate marked each plot, its triple crossbeam supporting a large, cast bronze bell.

Darshima glimpsed over his shoulder toward the city. Soaring clusters of jeweled spires and temples greeted his eyes. An unexpected smile crossed his lips as he viewed the dense skyline rising above the surrounding snows and the lake.

"Chryshaihem almost reminds me of The Vilides," said Darshima. He recalled the striking skyline view during his trek through the Ciblaithian desert with Sydarias, days before the invasion.

"In some ways, it does." Sydarias followed Darshima's gaze, squinting as he looked upon the urban vista.

"Chryshaihem couldn't be any more different than The Vilides," murmured Khydius. "It is an isolated lakeside city presiding over a small, snowbound archipelago." He peered at the buildings and shook his head.

"Even so, it's beautiful in its own way. We have to adapt to life here." Darshima glared at Khydius.

"Listen to your brother." Tenrai turned to Khydius. "Tiriyuud is a part of your heritage. This place is your new home, and you must learn to embrace it."

"Try to find something familiar amid the unfamiliar," added Dydan. A resigned frown settled upon Khydius' face. He stared at the ground and trudged in silence ahead of Darshima.

Though they had arrived on Iberwight only two days prior, Darshima already saw the profound differences between Tiriyuud and the territories of the former realm. He yearned for the warmth and familiarity of Gordanelle but understood that those days were past. Growing accustomed to life in this strange land would be difficult, but Darshima was thankful to find refuge here. He and his companions would need to learn from the Omystikai if they had any chance at surviving in this harsh climate.

A sigh escaped Darshima's lips as he thought of his brother's unexpected reaction. Though Khydius no longer used his title, he was no less a prince in exile. Darshima shook his head in disbelief as he pondered how different their lives had been until the invasion. He had an unremarkable upbringing in Ardavia, with uncertain prospects. Khydius led a life of extraordinary opulence and realm-wide influence as the heir to the now-defunct Vilidesian throne. If the invasion had never happened, Khydius would have one day been their emperor and ruled the four moons. His thoughts swirling, Darshima caught a furtive glimpse of Khydius as they trudged through the snows. He needed to find a way to bridge the seemingly insurmountable chasm that separated them.

Darshima moved along the winding stone path, the intemperate gusts blowing through his uniform. The houses grew more sparse as they neared the shore, separated by large stands of towering green trees. Their spindly boughs sagged under the weight of snow and icicles. Darshima looked out over the lake, and his eyes darted toward a row of rapidly moving objects in the distance. He lifted his hand to his brow and made out the giant, blade-like silhouettes of a dozen ships. They sped in tandem across the shimmering surface, skimming above the waves. Sprays of water jetted from their paired rear fins, catching the sunlight in a refracted burst of color.

"Where are those ships going?" Darshima pointed to the sophisticated craft as they raced toward the horizon.

"They are freight ships traveling from Chryshaihem's harbor. They must be on their way to one of the southern islands of the archipelago," replied Tenrai.

"They don't look like they're from any Vilidesian firm." A quizzical frown formed upon Sydarias' lips.

"Those vessels are manufactured by an established Tiriyuusian enterprise. Their shipyards are on the kingdom's southernmost island," said Dydan. "We rely on our own means of transport." Impressed, Darshima stared at the ships. As he made out their details, he recalled the unique farming pyramids they saw on their journey to Foseidem, Tenrai's ancestral village. It was becoming clear to him that Tiriyuusians relied much less on the Vilidesians for their needs than the other peoples of the former realm.

Darshima looked toward the mountains in the distance, their peaks obscured by a layer of clouds rolling over their peaks. The sun dimmed, and the skies grew dark as the clouds moved overhead. He shivered as the temperature dropped and the snowfall resumed. His nose tingled in the biting air, thick with the scent of firewood. Darshima drew his overcoat tighter and shook his limbs, trying to stave off the unrelenting cold. He looked around him as the landscape faded into subdued, monochromatic tones beneath the swirling snowflakes.

A few paces ahead, Erethalie drew a shivering Shonan closer to her. Darshima's heart rose into his throat as he saw them trudge unsteadily through the surrounding snowdrifts. Memories of his last moments on Gordanelle with Sasha floated before his eyes, and he understood their sadness. Darshima moved ahead of Khydius and walked beside Erethalie.

"How are you and Shonan doing?" Darshima rested his hand upon her shoulder.

"As well as can be expected." Her eyes glistened with tears, and she cleared her throat. Erethalie pulled Shonan closer. "It seems like only yesterday we were living normal, hectic lives in The Vilides. Now here we are, struggling to survive on the furthest moon, at the edge of the realm. We are refugees in this kingdom." Her voice trailed off in a puff of steam.

"You aren't alone. We are all exiles here. We will only survive together." Darshima squeezed her shoulder. "We wouldn't have even made it here without you. Your skill as a pilot saved our lives."

"What right do I have to complain?" Erethalie's gaze drifted toward the grey skies. "You, Prince Khydius, and Sydarias experienced far worse as slaves on Navervyne."

Darshima drew in a sharp breath as he listened to Erethalie. Vivid images of his toil on Navervyne flashed before his eyes. For a moment amid the cold, he almost felt the oppressive heat of the farming colony envelope his skin. His nostrils filled with the sickly-sweet redolence of the ripening fields. Darshima put a hand over his stomach as it twisted into a queasy knot. He cleared his throat and tried to push aside the haunting memories.

"There is no use in comparing our suffering. You lived through a difficult period in the occupied capital with Shonan. Moreover, you risked both of your lives for us all back on Navervyne." An earnest smile formed upon Darshima's lips as he remembered their harrowing escape. "You're one of the bravest people I've ever known."

"I only did what was necessary." Erethalie shook her head as she dismissed Darshima's praise. "I will be fine, but my brother will have to adapt to life here."

"I can do it," said Shonan, his voice rising above the gusts of wind. He looked up at Erethalie and offered a timid smile, his face framed by his snow-covered hood. "But it's freezing here." Shonan's nose wrinkled, and a shiver coursed through his slender frame.

"I know you can." Erethalie patted his shoulder. "You always find a way."

"He will be safe, and that's the most important thing," said Darshima.

"I couldn't ask for anything more." Erethalie bowed her head as she trudged with Shonan through the accumulating snow.

Seer Ryte, Dydan, and Tenrai came to a stop at a paved walkway beneath the arch. Darshima and his companions stood behind them. Her bright red robes trailing in the powdery flakes, the seer moved under the sweeping structure of the gateway. The dark wooden crossbeams rose high above the glistening white snowdrifts. Beyond the arch stood a modest, multilevel dwelling perched upon a gently sloping hilltop.

"This will be your new home." Seer Ryte beckoned Shonan with her gloved hand, her eyes glittering in a sincere expression. She reached for a carved wooden rod resting against the sturdy post beside her and shook off the snowflakes clinging to it. In a swift motion, she struck the large bell hanging over their heads. Darshima's ears rang as a low, clear tone resounded through the chilly air. The peal stirred a group of birds roosting atop the gate into a frenzied burst of flight. The flock soared into the clouds, their black and white plumage fading amid the falling snow.

As the sound and the commotion dissipated, Shonan moved nearer to Erethalie. She pulled him closer, and he glared at the ground.

"You will be okay here." Erethalie tried to catch his gaze. Darshima's heart sank as he saw the Shonan's somber expression. He wished there was something he could say to put him at ease, but he realized that no words would make this circumstance any easier.

"It seems to be a very comfortable home," said Sydarias, his brow knit in concern as he observed Shonan.

As the bell tone faded, Darshima heard the crunch of footsteps upon the snow. He looked through the gate to see a man and woman, followed by a boy and a girl, walking toward them. The man and the boy wore loose-fitting black jackets that covered their pleated grey trousers. The woman and girl were dressed in patterned dark blue robes cinched at the waist by broad, folded grey cloth belts. They all wore split-toed leather boots and black woolen cloaks upon their shoulders that fluttered in the gusts of wind.

The man and woman approached Seer Ryte. They offered a bow and issued a greeting in the Tiriyuusian dialect.

"Greetings, Hezion Byx. I thank you, your wife Sera, and your children for welcoming us on such short notice," said the seer, transitioning into Vilidesian. She nodded curtly in their direction.

"Aodren Ryte, Seer of Chryshaihem, I offer you and your companions our sincere greetings," replied Hezion, in accented but clear Vilidesian. As he bowed in their direction, his shoulder-length black hair briefly draped across his pale face. His sapphire eyes glittered in surprise as he glanced at Darshima, Khydius, and the others.

"Greetings, most wise one." Sera stepped forward and bowed politely toward the seer, Darshima, and the others. The corners of her cerulean eyes wrinkled in a warm expression as she looked upon them. "I, my husband, and our children welcome you all," she said in impeccable Vilidesian. The porcelain skin of her face flushed against the cold gusts. Her shimmering black hair was fastened with a white silk ribbon and hung in a tail over her shoulder.

Appearing similar in age to Shonan, their children gazed curiously at Darshima and his companions. Their glowing sapphire gazes contrasted boldly against the glistening snowflakes clinging to their long eyelashes.

"I would like you to meet Sage Dydan Waike and Guardian Tenrai Nax." Seer Ryte gestured toward the pair.

"We thank you very much for your hospitality," said Tenrai. He and Dydan stepped forward and bowed toward Sera and Hezion.

"Accompanying them are Darshima and Khydius Nax, Erethalie and Shonan Danthe, and Sydarias Idawa." The seer beckoned them forward. "They are refugees from the fallen realm."

"Welcome, please join us." Sera ushered them through the gate.

They followed Hezion, Sera, and their children along the cobblestone path, up a curving stairway, hewn into the hill. They reached the top of the stairs, and Darshima eyed a comfortable, three-level home amidst a stand of mature, snow-covered trees. A fleeting smile crossed his lips as he thought of his childhood home back in Ardavia. Hezion slid open the large wooden door and ushered them past the threshold into the anteroom. They removed their outer garments and boots and followed him down a narrow hall into a bright central room.

Polished dark wood floors clad in bright woolen rugs, simple but elegant wooden furniture, and a blazing hearth in the center gave the space an inviting atmosphere. A spiral wooden staircase sat in the far corner, leading to the upper levels. Darshima's eye lingered upon its unique form, appearing as though it had been carved from a massive tree trunk. Panes of clear glass formed the room's opposite wall, giving a sweeping view of snowy fields and the city spires in the distance.

"Please make yourselves at home." Sera approached the hearth, gesturing toward a set of leather cushions surrounding a low-lying, rectangular wooden table nearby. Tenrai and Dydan took their seats beside Darshima, Sydarias, and Khydius. The seer moved toward Erethalie and Shonan and sat beside them, her robes ruffling about her.

"We will return with some tea and join you in a moment." A reserved smile crossed Sera's lips as she and Hezion excused themselves. The young boy and girl followed closely behind them, their footsteps padding softly against the smooth floorboards.

The seer's gaze lingered upon the family as they disappeared down the corridor. "Hezion and Sera Byx are dear friends of mine. We have known each other since childhood." Her eyes narrowed, and she appeared to sift through her thoughts. "They will take good care of Shonan."

"We thank you very much." Erethalie glared at the bright flames rising from the hearth, a restrained expression forming upon her face.

Moments later, Hezion and Sera returned with their children in tow. They carried lacquered wooden trays bearing translucent porcelain cups and an iron kettle of boiling tea. Hezion and Sera rested the items upon the table, then took their seats beside the seer.

"I see that your home remains warm and welcoming as always." The seer looked around her, then let out a contented sigh. "Aten and Ione are growing up so quickly." She gestured toward the boy and girl, her eyebrows arching in surprise.

"We do our best to raise our children and manage Hezion's workshop." Sera lifted the kettle and poured the steaming, milky brew into the cups. She offered the first cup to Seer Ryte, then one to everyone else.

"Thank you." Darshima held the delicate cup, inhaled the sweet, buttery aroma, and drank the rich brew. The seer took a sip from her cup and looked around the room.

"Hezion is a master carpenter. He learned the craft from his father, who learned it from his father. It is a skill that his family has passed on for generations. The Byx family produces some of the finest wooden furniture in the kingdom." The seer gestured toward the furnishings surrounding them.

"You are much too kind." Hezion bowed his head, his cheeks reddening at her compliment.

"I am quite serious." A polite smile formed upon the seer's lips.

The conversation lulled, and the seer narrowed her in a serious expression. "All pleasantries aside, I have come here to discuss an important matter with you." She rested her cup upon the table with a firm thud. Hezion and Sera exchanged a cautious glance, then looked toward her.

"As you are surely aware, a hostile foreign power invaded The Vilides and the four moons. Their realm has fallen." Seer Ryte's lips wrinkled into a somber frown.

"We have heard the reports of this unthinkable tragedy. It is hard to imagine how any nation could have vanquished the Vilidesians." Sera briefly closed her eyes in a saddened expression.

"I cannot fathom the terrible things that are happening out there." Hezion turned to Tenrai.

"The scale of the devastation to their realm is difficult to comprehend." Tenrai rested his cup upon the table.

Darshima listened to their conversation, his chest growing heavy as fiery images of the invasion clawed at the corners of his mind. A sharp lump formed in his throat as he relived the painful memories. Darshima turned toward Hezion and his family, and he tried to forget those difficult moments. His thoughts flashed with the realization that the Byx family knew little of the events apart from the invasion. Like countless other Tiriyuusian families, they were mercifully unaffected by the raging turmoil beyond the sheltered islands of their kingdom.

"Guardian Nax has returned from a harrowing journey to distant worlds in service to our kingdom." Dydan gestured toward Tenrai.

"He has succeeded in rescuing his highness, Khydius, Prince of The Vilides. He also rescued these Vilidesian subjects from the horrors of slavery and foreign occupation. For reasons I cannot fully disclose, the people seated before you are important to our kingdom," said Seer Ryte.

"I would believe no less, o wise one. You have personally escorted them here." Hezion bowed his head.

"They will be training with the guardians." The seer turned to Darshima, Khydius, Erethalie, and Sydarias.

"I imagine that the boy is far too young to train." Sera looked upon Shonan, a concerned expression spreading upon her face.

"Indeed, he is," said Seer Ryte. "Shonan is a young refugee and needs a good home."

"We would be happy to have him." An earnest smile formed upon Hezion's lips. He looked to his son and daughter, whose eyes glowed with excitement. "What do you both think about having a new brother?" He playfully tousled their shoulder-length, braided black hair and wrapped his arms around their shoulders. They giggled in response, smiling shyly at Shonan.

"He will have a good home here with us." The corners of Sera's eyes wrinkled in a sympathetic expression.

"As your friend, I give you both my eternal gratitude for your kindness. As your seer, I assure you the full faith and support of the Order for your generosity." She bowed toward Hezion and Sera, and they both returned the gesture.

Shonan turned toward Erethalie, then faced Hezion and Sera, the corners of his lips forming a subtle frown.

"Say hello to your new family, Shonan." Erethalie looked toward Sera, her voice wavering. Shonan rose from his seat, glared at the floor, and approached the Byx family.

"Welcome home, young one." Sera stood up and wrapped him in a warm embrace. Shonan hesitantly hugged her in return.

"We are glad that you are here, Shonan." Hezion joined his wife and rested his hand upon the boy's shoulder. Erethalie clenched her jaw and tried to stifle the expression of sadness spreading upon her face.

"I apologize for the brevity of our visit, but it is time for us to leave." Seer Ryte stood up from her seat, and everyone else rose to their feet.

"Be respectful to your new family, and stay strong. I will visit you soon." Erethalie stepped over to Shonan and wrapped him in a tight embrace.

"Be careful, Erethalie. Please don't forget about me," said Shonan, his voice wavering with sadness.

"I could never forget you, Shonan. You'll always be my little brother." Erethalie fought back her tears. "I will come back for you as soon as I can." She pursed her lips in a determined expression.

Shonan's eyes grew damp. "If you find our brother and sister during your journeys, please bring them back." He sniffled softly.

"I promise." Erethalie held onto Shonan for a moment longer as a shudder coursed through him. "Until we meet again, you have my love." She let him go, then gave him a nudge toward the Byx family.

"Do not worry, Erethalie. We will care for him as if he were our own son." Sera drew Shonan closer to her.

"I thank you from the bottom of my heart," said Erethalie, her voice catching in her throat. She bowed her head, then stepped back. Erethalie straightened her garments and moved beside Darshima.

Seer Ryte, Tenrai, and Dydan bid the Byx family farewell. They ushered Erethalie, Darshima, and the others toward the entrance. Darshima rested his hand upon Erethalie's arm as they approached the door. He didn't know what to say but wanted to offer his support. She glanced over her shoulder at Shonan, who stood with his new family.

"I don't want to forget him as he is right now," she whispered.

"What do you mean?" asked Sydarias.

"This place will change Shonan." She shook her head in frustration. "I won't be there to guide him."

"Tiriyuud will change all of us." A pensive frown formed upon Khydius' lips.

"I sense much kindness among the people here. Hopefully, it will change us all for the better." Darshima turned to Khydius, who avoided his gaze and glared at the ground.

"I sense it too," said Sydarias.

While the seer, Tenrai, and Dydan dressed, Darshima and his companions laced their boots and put on their outer garments. They stepped out of the dwelling, back into the falling snow. The door closed softly behind them, and Erethalie walked forward, dashing away her tears.

"This is so hard." She drew in a breath, then cleared her throat. "But there's no other way."

"I'm sorry," said Darshima, unsure what else to say. His thoughts raced to that moment in The Vilides when she beseeched him to be their pilot. He never would've imagined that her decision would have resulted in her separation from Shonan. "Your sacrifice will not be in vain." Darshima faced her, his chest tightening as he pondered the effects of her decision.

"They will keep him safe," she said. Her voice wavered with a note of uncertainty. Darshima rested his hand upon her shoulder and drew her nearer to him. They descended the stairway with Seer Ryte, Tenrai, and the others, back into the snowdrifts.

Chapter 4

Tenrai and Dydan followed Seer Ryte across the smooth pavement of a vast, octagonal courtyard. The falling snowflakes hit the heated black stones, evaporating into clouds of steam. Darshima, Erethalie, Khydius, and Sydarias walked closely together, shivering in the biting gusts of wind. Darshima looked around the imposing space, his gaze sweeping over its myriad details. Flanked by a quartet of immense, eight-tiered, square towers, the complex's courtyard gleamed under the afternoon light. A grand colonnade of pale stone arches encircled the space, abutting the chamfered, granite buildings. Chains of crystal hung from the sloping eaves, swaying with the wind.

The snow showers grew heavier, darkening the subdued grey skies. Darshima lifted his face toward the falling snow. He pulled his scarf closer as the icy flakes landed upon his cheeks in a fleeting sting of cold. Darshima looked above the roofline of the peristyle and glimpsed the temple complex where they met with the Sages of Tiriyuud earlier that morning.

Tenrai led them toward a pair of large bronze doors leading into the temple. Two uniformed sentries stood guard beside them, their long blue overcoats fluttering in the winds. As they approached the center of the courtyard, Seer Ryte and Dydan faced Tenrai.

"Thank you, Guardian Nax. "We must return to the Sages' Temple to prepare for our evening meditations. Sage Waike and I will take our leave." Puffs of vapor trailed from her lips as she spoke.

"Certainly, o wise one." Dydan bowed toward her and looked toward the Sages' Temple in the distance.

"Thank you, Seer Ryte and Sage Waike, for accompanying us to the Guardians' Shrine." Tenrai bowed toward them. "We have already taken enough of your time."

"You and Sage Waike have much work ahead of you in preparing these four Vilidesian subjects for life here in Tiriyuud." Seer Ryte gestured toward Darshima, Khydius, Erethalie, and Sydarias, a delicate layer of snow sloughing from her sleeve. Her eyes glowed as she appraised them.

"We won't disappoint you," said Dydan.

"I am putting my full faith in you. The Order and the kingdom are depending on your effort." A contemplative frown crossed her lips.

"You have our word and our resolve," replied Tenrai.

"Tenrai, I will meet you and your charges at dawn for the journey to the training grounds." Dydan looked toward Darshima and his companions.

"Though it has been some time since you served as a guardian, I am sure you will be helpful," said Tenrai.

"I haven't been a sage for so long that I forgot the important work that we did together as guardians." A smile crept upon Dydan's lips.

"I am thankful for your assistance. We will be expecting you," said Tenrai, as he tried to suppress a frown.

"Fare thee well." Seer Ryte waved to Tenrai, Darshima, and his companions. She and Dydan walked toward the colonnade and the temple complex in the distance. Darshima's eyes lingered upon their silhouettes as they faded beneath the falling snow.

"Let us continue to the shrine." Tenrai turned around and hurried his pace. They drew nearer to the doors, and Darshima jogged to match Tenrai's stride.

"What will we do there?" asked Khydius as he moved alongside Darshima.

"We are heading to the shrine's monastery, where we will rest until tomorrow morning," said Tenrai.

With a heave, the sentries pushed the doors, which yielded in a low groan. Darshima, Khydius, Erethalie, and Sydarias followed Tenrai across the checkered marble tiles of a vaulted, torchlit foyer. The doors slammed shut behind them with a booming thud. Tenrai slowed his pace, seemingly more at ease within the confines of the building. A fragrance of incense and aged wood suffused the warm air. Darshima drew in a deep breath and tried to forget the cold wind outside.

Darshima and his companions followed Tenrai through a long hallway, their footsteps echoing against the smooth stone floors and wood-paneled walls. Darshima's eyes adjusted to the softly lit space, illuminated by white crystal orbs hanging from the arched ceilings. His eyes traced the arrays of golden polygonal symbols and complex circular seals etched upon the imposing stone columns.

As Darshima walked through the halls of the monastery, he felt his tension ease. A sense of timelessness and peace seemed to emanate from every corner. He tried to imagine the events that happened within these walls over the ages, both insignificant and crucial.

"This shrine is immense," whispered Erethalie as she peered around the staid space.

"The Guardians' Shrine is one of the most important buildings in Chryshaihem. It is more than twelve hundred years old." Tenrai gestured around them. "Many distinguished guardians have trained in this sacred space."

"So this complex alone is centuries older than the Vilidesian Realm," mused Sydarias.

"Indeed it is." Tenrai drew in a contented breath. The corners of his eyes wrinkled as he looked around him, appearing as if he were sifting through his old memories.

"The Omystikai have lived upon this moon for a very long time," said Khydius. A studious frown formed upon his lips as he appraised the space.

"I hadn't realized," whispered Darshima, shaking his head in disbelief at Tenrai's description. Nearly everything he remembered learning as a child was about the Vilidesians and the Ardavians and their achievements. Though he had only been on Iberwight for a few days, Darshima was learning that the Tiriyuusians had a unique history of their own.

They followed Tenrai through another hallway, filled with groups of pupils returning to their quarters for the afternoon. Pale-skinned, with narrowed sapphire eyes and unshorn black hair that hung either loose or braided in a tail, they appeared similar in age to Darshima and his companions. Their uniforms consisted of simple black and blue robes with varied golden patterns, pleated grey trousers, and split-toed leather boots. Many of them wore wooden sandals with patterned stockings.

Darshima stared at the young men and women as they moved through the corridors, gripping their fabric satchels and leather-bound books. The stone floors reverberated with the sound of their footsteps as they milled about the staid space. Many of them entered and exited through the doors and passages lining the hallway. A few students briefly countered Darshima's gaze, turning away as they hurried to their destinations.

"There's no one like us here," whispered Darshima, his eyes widened in surprise.

"You are correct," said Tenrai. Khydius, Erethalie, and Sydarias peered around them, worried expressions forming upon their faces.

"What will they think of us?" asked Sydarias, his voice weighted with nervousness.

"We are so different from them. Will they even accept us?" Erethalie clenched her jaw as the crowds of students brushed past them.

"You are the only foreigners in all of Tiriyuud, but make no mistake, you are welcome here." Tenrai offered them all a confident nod. "Let us continue. We are nearly at your quarters." Tenrai ushered them down the hallway. Darshima stared at the crowds as they moved through the monastery, his thoughts drifting. During their journey from Gordanelle to Iberwight, he presumed that their presence among the Omystikai would be a rare exception. It was now abundantly clear to him.

Darshima and his companions followed Tenrai up a large, winding stone staircase and down another long hallway. They moved through the thinning crowds and stopped before a wooden door at the end of a dim corridor.

"Though our time in Chryshaihem will brief, you will share these quarters for the duration of your stay." Tenrai rested his hand upon its dark surface. "Make yourselves comfortable." Tenrai gestured past the threshold. He pressed a circular golden seal in the center of the door, and it slid open to reveal the bright interior of a spacious suite. Their footsteps creaked softly against the dark wooden floorboards as they entered.

Rectangular in shape, the suite contained four separate apartments and a common area in the center. A square window set in the opposite wall gave a sweeping view of the snow-capped spires and temples surrounding the shrine. A circular, sunken stone hearth sat in the middle of the space and crackled with soft flames. Low lying wooden furniture and woolen rugs gave the suite a simple yet inviting ambiance.

"Please take a moment to rest. I have a few matters to which I must attend. When I return, we will have supper together in my quarters." Tenrai peered around the room.

"Thank you, Tenrai," said Erethalie.

"How much time do we have?" Darshima's eyes drifted toward the hearth.

"I will return soon. We have a very long day ahead of us tomorrow. I advise you all to rest while you can." Tenrai offered a curt bow and closed the door behind him.

Darshima stared at the wooden panel as it slid closed. He listened as Tenrai's footsteps faded into silence.

"We should sit down and rest." Khydius pointed toward a circle of rugs arranged around the hearth. He slid off his boots and rested them beside the door. He then reached toward a wooden rack resting against the wall and grabbed a pair of split-toed, black woolen slippers.

"The Omystikai are strict about wearing shoes in their private quarters." He looked toward Darshima and the others as he put on the slippers. "They are quite fastidious and strive to keep their personal and sacred spaces protected from outside impurities." Khydius removed his gloves and overcoat, neatly folded them, then took a seat around the hearth.

"We must do as they do." Darshima slid off his boots and removed his outer garments, then put on a pair of slippers. Erethalie and Sydarias did the same. They all settled beside Khydius around the flames. Darshima let out a sigh of relief as he felt the warmth against his skin.

"It's unbelievably cold here." Sydarias stretched his hands toward the glowing hearth. "How does anyone manage to survive on this moon?"

"It's cold, but at least we're finally in Chryshaihem," said Darshima. His shivers abated as he acclimated to the warmth of the room. An unexpected smile formed upon his lips as he thought of their experience thus far on Iberwight. From their turbulent landing in Foseidem to their journey to the gates of Chryshaihem, everything here felt so unfamiliar compared to the other moons. Even so, Darshima was thankful that the sages had allowed them to stay in the kingdom.

"We are so far from home." Erethalie turned away from the flames and glimpsed through the window. The rectangular panes creaked as fierce winds and driving snows lashed against the glass. The city's shadows grew longer beneath the lengthening rays of the late afternoon sun. One by one, the numerous clustered towers illuminated their windows against the darkening grey skies. Their tiered roofs and glittering spires glowed softly against the snowfall. Darshima's eyes swept over the cityscape, his pulse thudding with an inexplicable feeling of familiarity.

"The climate here in Tiriyuud is particularly inhospitable." Khydius folded his arms across his chest and stared blankly into the fire. "I am accustomed to the way things are in Gavipristine. Fauridise and the other dominions are much closer to Vilidesian standards of living."

"Is Tiriyuud so different from the rest of Iberwight?" asked Erethalie.

"The culture here is best described as orthodox and somewhat antiquated." Khydius peered around the room, and his eyes narrowed in subtle resignation. "They've been under a self-imposed isolated from the wider realm for many centuries."

"Though it is different here, we must be no less thankful." Darshima glared into the flames, his pulse thudding at Khydius' terse assessment. He drew in a breath and tried to calm himself. "They have given us refuge."

"The Tiriyuusians could have turned us away, but they chose to accept us. I will do whatever it takes to earn my welcome here." Sydarias stared at Khydius. His eyes grew damp and glittered in the flames.

"I will do the same." Erethalie moved closer to Sydarias and nudged her shoulder against his.

"Tiriyuud is our home now, and we all must find a way to grow and to thrive here." Darshima stared pointedly at Khydius. "The people of this kingdom are placing their trust in us. We must embrace their way of doing things."

"I believe you are correct, Darshima." Khydius glared at the hearth, avoiding Darshima's gaze. "Forgive me, but I am finding it hard to adjust to our new lives here." He bowed his head, and a contrite frown formed upon his lips.

"You're not alone. We're all here with you." Darshima rested his hand upon Khydius' shoulder.

"Despite everything that awaits us, I'm thankful that we at least have warm beds for tonight." Erethalie rose from the floor and walked toward the door closest to her. "Let's go and see our rooms."

Darshima and the others joined Erethalie and looked at their accommodations. Darshima approached a door near the window and rested his hand upon the smooth wooden surface. He gripped the curved wrought iron handle and gently slid the door open. His eyes swept over a low-profile wooden bed, wardrobe, desk, and a pair of tall iron lamps flickering with yellow flame. A rectangular window set in the opposite wall gathered frost at its edges. The city spires and their hazy silhouettes were barely visible amid the snowfall. Darshima closed the bedroom door behind him and turned to the hearth.

"I wonder where the baths and latrines are," murmured Darshima.

"In Omystikai monasteries, the residents share those facilities," answered Khydius. "I believe they are at the end of the hallway." He gestured past the entrance. "The Omystikai also bathe in outdoor thermal springs from time to time."

"I don't think I could get used to that." Sydarias rubbed the back of his arms as a shiver coursed through him. "It must be cold."

Darshima looked toward his companions, who closed the doors to their rooms and resumed their seats around the hearth.

"What do you think tomorrow will be like?" Darshima settled beside Sydarias.

"I hear that training with the Omystikai orders is difficult." Sydarias drummed his fingers against his knees.

"The first few months are the most challenging, and Tiriyuud's tradition is the toughest of them all." Khydius rubbed his chin in contemplation. "If a recruit survives training with the Order of the Gilded Moon, they will be inducted as a guardian."

"What do you mean, survive?" Darshima shot a concerned glance toward him.

"I am only relaying what my counselors told me," said Khydius, speaking in measured tones. "Gilded Moon is, without a doubt, the strictest of the Omystikai orders."

"But we will survive, won't we?" asked Erethalie, her voice wavering with a hint of nervousness.

"Once a recruit begins training, they must complete it. Training with the guardians is physically and emotionally taxing. In ages past, Tiriyuusian recruits have perished during the exercises." Khydius glared through the window at the falling snowflakes.

"That cannot be true nowadays." Sydarias shook his head in disbelief.

"Their methods are tough, but most of the recruits they select are strong enough to succeed," said Khydius.

"We've survived much worse in The Vilides and on Navervyne." Darshima's brow wrinkled in contemplation. "We all have more than enough strength to survive and succeed."

"You're right, Darshima." Sydarias nodded confidently. "We are ready."

Darshima glared at the hearth, and his mind focused upon Khydius and his doubts. Tenrai had warned him of the dangers of the journey during their escape. Darshima had fully committed himself, and there was no turning back. He had already made it this far and had risked death more than once. Darshima wouldn't let the difficulty of training with the guardians discourage him.

As they relaxed amid the warmth of the flames, a soft knock at the entrance interrupted the silence. Darshima rose to his feet and opened the door to find Tenrai waiting patiently. Erethalie Khydius and Sydarias left the hearth and joined Darshima.

"Hopefully, you all have taken some time to rest. You will be training elsewhere for your first few months here in Tiriyuud. If all goes as expected, you will then return to these quarters." Tenrai beckoned them into the hallway. "Please join me, and we will go to my quarters for supper." Darshima's stomach growled at the thought of food. They had yet to eat anything for the day. He followed his companions past the threshold and joined Tenrai in the corridor.

Chapter 5

Darshima, Erethalie, Sydarias, and Khydius followed Tenrai up a narrow staircase toward a pair of doors at the end of the hallway. Their shadows loomed large against the walls as they followed the torchlit path. Tenrai stopped before the doorway and pressed a gold, octagonal seal at its center. The wooden panels slid apart with a muted whirr. He stepped forward as soft beams of light spilled into the hallway.

"Welcome to my quarters." Tenrai slid off his boots and placed them beside the entrance. He stepped into a pair of woolen slippers laying neatly beside the doorframe and walked past the threshold, his footfalls thudding against the floorboards. Darshima and the others followed him through the spacious suite, past a pair of closed doors. Tenrai led them toward a low, oval obsidian table, positioned before a large wall of windows. A glowing circular hearth set in the center of the room radiated warmth.

Tenrai gestured toward a set of dark woolen cushions arranged around the table, and they took their seats. His back against the window panes, Tenrai faced Darshima and his companions. Beams of waning sunlight filtered through the snow squalls, casting a subdued glow upon the surrounding roofs and spires. Darshima unfastened his collar amid the warmth of the flames.

"Please make yourselves comfortable. Supper will arrive shortly." Tenrai folded his legs and settled upon his cushion.

The room filled with the clear note of a chime, and Darshima looked over his shoulders to see the doors slide apart. A man and a woman stepped across the threshold. They wore simple black and gold robes, pleated black trousers, and sandals. Carrying covered lacquered wooden trays, they crept into the room, past the hearth. They deferred their glowing sapphire gazes and knelt beside the table. The woman set down a large iron tea kettle and a tray of porcelain cups upon the gleaming surface. She distributed the cups around the table, then poured a steaming emerald brew into each of them. The man placed a dinner tray before each of them. After they set the table, the pair offered a curt bow, then exited the room as quietly as they entered.

"Please eat. I am sure you're all hungry." Tenrai gestured toward them as he uncovered his tray. Darshima and his companions opened their trays and inhaled the savory aroma.

"Whatever it is, it smells delicious." Sydarias speared a morsel of flaky, seared meat with a wooden skewer and shoveled it into his mouth.

"This is a simple but typical Tiriyuusian meal. We usually eat steamed or boiled grains, roots, and creatures from the sea. This particular meat comes from one of the larger aquatic beasts that dwell in the open waters off the coast," said Tenrai in between bites. Darshima grabbed a ceramic spoon from his tray and ate a heap of the firm, opalescent grains.

"Tiriyuud is so different from anything we know. Can you tell us more about your homeland?" Darshima settled upon his cushion as he ate.

"You've all recently arrived, but soon you will see Tiriyuud as your homeland too." Tenrai set his utensils aside. "What would you like to know?"

"You refer to Tiriyuud as a kingdom, but I've never heard mention of a Tiriyuusian king or queen." Erethalie lifted her cup and sipped the steaming brew.

"We use the word kingdom, but our ruler is known as the oracle." The corners of Tenrai's eyes wrinkled in a thoughtful expression. "There is no precise word in the Vilidesian language to describe our homeland, so we use the term kingdom."

"Tiriyuud is unique among the territories of the former realm." Khydius cleared his throat between bites. "Despite acknowledging the Omystikai dominions and Vilidesian sovereignty over Iberwight, they have remained an isolated nation under the rule of their oracle."

"How have the Tiriyuusians manage to survive upon this frozen moon without Vilidesian expertise?" asked Darshima.

"Though we developed our own knowledge, Tiriyuud's isolation from The Vilides and its culture was not absolute. We maintained technical exchanges and broader economic engagement with the realm. With much trial, error, and time, our ancestors learned to thrive here." Tenrai gestured toward the expansive skyline, its myriad of spires and sloping roofs glowing against the darkening skies. Darshima's eyes wandered over the city's varied details as Tenrai spoke about the kingdom.

The islands of the Tiriyuusian archipelago were the first territories settled on Iberwight. Founded by the Omystikaiyn exiles from Ciblaithia, Chryshaihem was the kingdom's capital and largest city. Over the ages, the people of Chryshaihem developed a complex society whose customs and traditions reflected its importance as a center of faith, knowledge, and commerce.

"So the oracle serves as a political ruler?" Sydarias' eyebrows arched in curiosity.

"The oracle is far more important than a mere politician." A studied frown formed upon Tenrai's lips. "The oracle serves as both the ruler of Tiriyuud and leader of the Order of the Gilded Moon. The Order functions as Tiriyuud's religious, civil and military administration." As Tenrai explained, the Tiriyuusians viewed their oracle as the physical incarnation of their faith, the chief arbiter of religious enlightenment, and their kingdom's divine protector and ruler. The oracle was also seen as the source of Tiriyuud's stability and prosperity.

"How unusual," remarked Sydarias. "Vilidesian emperors weren't seen as religious figures."

"But they were nonetheless powerful." Erethalie methodically drummed her fingers against her cup. "They ruled over the four moons and held sway over billions of subjects."

"They were mighty figures, but they didn't inspire religious devotion in the same manner as the Tiriyuusian Oracle," said Khydius, his eyes narrowing in a thoughtful expression.

"Though we show our reverence and obedience, Tiriyuusians do not venerate the oracle like a deity," said Tenrai.

"How does one become an oracle?" asked Darshima. A shiver coursed through him as he pondered the fact that so much responsibility was vested in a single person.

"The sages use cryptic methods of divination to choose the oracle." Tenrai's eyes lingered upon the flames.

The oracle was consecrated in early adulthood and served as the ruler of Tiriyuud for an entire lifetime. The oracle's lineage was shrouded in mystery and did not follow any heritable pattern, like the monarchs of the Vilidesian Realm.

"So the oracle is chosen by prayer?" Sydarias shook his head in confusion.

"It is much deeper than prayer alone," said Tenrai. "We believe in the power of *kai*." He pronounced the last word carefully, his Tiriyuusian accent placing emphasis.

"Isn't *kai* is your word for strength?" questioned Khydius, a curious frown forming upon his lips.

"Yes, almost." Tenrai's eyes lit up in surprise. "You know more about Tiriyuud than you admit."

"Does the word *kai* have any relation to Omystikai?" asked Erethalie.

"Bearers of strength," murmured Khydius.

"I don't understand." Darshima turned toward them, shaking his head in confusion.

"It roughly translates to bearers of the sovereign strength." Tenrai peered at Darshima, his eyes glowing softly. "The sovereign strength permeates all existence." Darshima stared at Tenrai and pondered the unfamiliar meaning behind his words.

"Does *kai* have anything to do with the skills that you and Darshima used during our escape from Navervyne?" Sydarias rubbed his chin.

"It has everything to do with *kai*." Tenrai nodded, his voice bearing a solemn note.

Darshima peered through the window and avoided Tenrai's gaze. He struggled to comprehend how modern people could claim to feel or manipulate a force beyond human perception. He bit his lip as memories of Tenrai's and his own seemingly impossible feats of strength and skill came back to him. There was undoubtedly something more to the Tiriyuusians and their homeland than met the eye. Whether Darshima believed it or not, this kingdom was a mysterious, yet integral part of him.

"Though it may not make sense at this moment, you and everyone here will come to believe in *kai*." Tenrai rested his hand upon Darshima's shoulder.

"I want to believe," said Darshima. Erethalie and Sydarias nodded in agreement.

As Tenrai described, the Tiriyuusians believed that *kai*, in its ubiquitous presence and infinite wisdom, flowed through all living things. *Kai* imbued all humans and creatures with innate strengths and abilities. As compared to the other peoples and even other Omystikai, *kai* flowed strongest within the Tiriyuusians. Some Tiriyuusians manifested more extraordinary powers than others, but all showed some ability, both great and small.

"So does this energy choose the members of the Order, like guardians, sages, or even the oracle?" Erethalie turned toward Tenrai.

"Yes. Those in whom *kai* flows the strongest are destined to serve the Order. Through meditation, the seer, sages, and the oracle can interpret its will," said Tenrai. "The oracle is chosen based upon a divine pedigree that only the sages understand."

Tiriyuusians who demonstrated strong abilities with the sovereign strength were identified early in their childhood. Nurtured by their families and communities, they prepared themselves for eventual roles of prominence within the kingdom. These young Tiriyuusians received training and were inducted into the Order first as guardians. Some rose through the ranks until they joined the sages. Over the years of instruction and meditation, one among them was manifestly the wisest and strongest. This sage would be anointed as the next Oracle of Tiriyuud, when the previous oracle died and became one again with *kai*.

"So, what else about Tiriyuud makes it so different from the rest of the realm?" asked Darshima.

"You'll find that we are not so different from the Ciblaithians, the Gordanellans, or the Wohiimaians." Tenrai glimpsed through the window, his eyes wandering toward the other moons, which hung in a gleaming arc against the darkening sky. "Like the other parts of the former realm, we have civic institutions and industry. We pursue entrepreneurship and scholarship. We also seek a greater understanding of ourselves and the universe. We undertake these pursuits in our own time and way."

By the time Tenrai had finished, night had fallen, revealing numerous points of twinkling stars.

"The hour is growing late, and you all must rest for tomorrow." Tenrai looked over to them. Their trays cleared, Darshima and his companions sat contentedly in the flickering light of the hearth. Tiriyuud would be their home for the foreseeable future, and Darshima was eager to learn as much as possible.

"Thank you for inviting us here, Tenrai," said Darshima. They all rose from the table.

"I enjoyed the dinner and the enlightening conversation." Erethalie stood beside Darshima. Sydarias and Khydius nodded in agreement.

"I will see you all tomorrow." Tenrai led them to the door and bid them goodnight. Darshima followed Erethalie, Sydarias, and Khydius down the hallway toward their quarters. He peered through the shadows and focused his thoughts on what the next day might bring.

Chapter 6

Darshima gazed up at the rays of daylight streaking across the dawn sky. He shivered as the winds blew through the fabric of his black uniform. He dug his feet deeper into his boots, trying to find warmth. Khydius, Erethalie, and Sydarias stood beside him at the edge of a curving, rocky beach that hemmed the shore of the misty lake. Tenrai and Dydan waited on either side of them, their arms folded across their chests. They wore black trousers, split-toed leather boots, and embroidered black overcoats with gold and leather ribbons stitched upon the fabric. Darshima listened to the rhythmic sounds of water lapping behind them. He drew in a measured breath and looked beside him, his anxiety lessening as he saw his friends.

Darshima turned his gaze toward a trio of priests standing before them. They wore silken blue robes trimmed in golden tessellated patterns and long black coats with embroidered tails. Tall black headdresses folded in polyhedrons, adorned with hanging chains of glittering crystal, sat perched atop their heads. They waited patiently upon the broad landing of a richly carved stone staircase. One of several identical staircases positioned at intervals along the shore, it rose at a steep angle from the crystalline pebbles of the beach. Its pale granite treads rose alongside the immense, crenelated ramparts protecting the city.

Darshima looked up at the impressive structures, which encircled the island in an imposing, palisaded redoubt. He couldn't help but see traces of the Omystikai ruin he and Sydarias visited on Ciblaithia hidden in its details. The priests gazed out over the lake, their pale faces flushing in the chilly gusts. Their gloved hands held cylindrical wooden lanterns aloft, and a diffuse white light illuminated the space around them. The trio looked at Darshima and the others, their narrowed, sapphire eyes glittering in earnest expressions. The priests extended their arms in a gracious gesture and stepped forward, their elaborate vestments rustling against their lean frames.

The vast Chryshaihemese skyline towered behind the priests, framing them in a striking scene. Their lips trembled as they belted out rousing chants. Tendrils of steam rose from their mouths as their harmonies reached a crescendo. Darshima's heart rose with the unfamiliar words as he listened, the haunting tones conjuring a sense of mystery within him. The priests' voices grew softer until they faded into the wind. They concluded the ritual with a deep bow and departed in silence. They ascended the staircase up toward the city, the hems of their robes sweeping against the snowy treads.

Darshima and his companions turned toward the water's edge. They moved closer to Dydan and Tenrai, who beckoned them to follow. Darshima shivered amid the cold winds, tucking his hands into his coat pockets. He looked over to Sydarias, Erethalie, and Khydius, who huddled together as they walked away from the stairs.

As promised, Tenrai had come for them before dawn, and they met Dydan in the courtyard of the Guardians' Shrine. Together, they traversed the snow-swept streets of the city in silence and walked toward the beach. As Tenrai had explained, those who sought to train with the guardians needed to complete the journey to the training grounds in complete silence. Darshima appreciated the quietness as they moved along and tried to focus his thoughts on the moments ahead. Tenrai hadn't revealed much, but Darshima understood that he and his companions would face physical and mental tests that would push them past their limits.

Shaking off his fatigue, Darshima pushed himself to keep up with Tenrai and Dydan, who strode ahead at a brisk pace. They walked along the curving shore, their boots crunching against the rocky soil. In the distance, Darshima eyed a wooden pier jutting into the waters. He looked ahead, shivering against the winds, trying to glimpse the landscape beyond the swirling mists.

The snow showers grew heavier as they reached the edge of the pier. Tenrai led them onto the structure, their boots thudding against the bleached wooden planks as they walked its length.

Darshima eyed a large boat moored to a stone pylon at the end. The craft sat motionlessly upon the surface, seemingly unperturbed by the ripples. The polished black wooden hull gleamed in the early morning rays, its sleek, trapezoidal prow partially veiled by the mists. Dydan climbed aboard first and settled upon a carved wooden bench at the bow. Darshima and his companions followed Dydan and sat upon a wooden bench directly behind him. Tenrai stepped aboard and took a seat at the stern. He untied the thick fiber mooring cables and hauled them aboard the craft, gently bundling and stowing them at his feet. Tenrai reached toward a panel behind his seat and pressed a series of gleaming silver buttons. A quiet whir rose above the rippling sounds of the water. The craft shook with a gentle vibration as it launched itself from the pier. Darshima sank back into his seat as the ship sped away from the shore.

Darshima glimpsed over the side of the craft, his eyes widening in surprise when he realized that they were hovering above the surface of the lake. A white light emanated from the bottom of the craft, casting a subtle glow upon the water. He looked behind his shoulder and saw a twin-tailed wake of water arcing behind the vessel, glowing with the same white iridescence. He had never seen anything like it and wondered what type of engine propelled the craft. He looked over to Erethalie, Sydarias, and Khydius. They bundled their faces in scarves and squinted against the winds. He opened his mouth to ask them but remembered their imposed silence and stared into the mists. They seemed too preoccupied to notice.

Tenrai pushed a wooden lever beside him as they raced from the shore, and the paired jets of water tilted with the movements of his hand. Dydan leaned forward, the fabric of his uniform flapping in the steady breeze. He held an ovoid prismatic lens out in front of him and looked toward the horizon. Darshima steadied himself in his seat and peered over Dydan's shoulder. He glimpsed through the peculiar crystal, his eyes widening in astonishment as he saw a refracted but detailed image of the horizon with no mist.

Tenrai maintained his grip upon the leaver, making subtle corrections to their course across the lake. Darshima settled back into his seat and tried to relax, but anxieties about training tugged at the corners of his mind. He peered at the cascading line of waterfalls in the distance and glimpsed an immense shadow emerging from the fog. A large wooden gate with a broad, triple crossbeam loomed upon the horizon, seemingly floating above the waters.

Tenrai navigated the boat in a serpentine path across the lake. Darshima looked over his shoulder and saw the shore steadily drifting away from view. The spires and temples of Chryshaihem appeared as a glittering line in the distance. Darshima's heart thudded with a pang of sadness as the city slipped beyond the horizon. He stared out at the vast expanse of blue water, straining to see a trace of the capital. Though his time there had been brief, he yearned to return.

The outline of the floating gate loomed above them as they approached, and Darshima's gaze swept over its details. The immense, pale wooden structure rose abruptly from the lake. Foamy surf crashed against the gate's two massive beams, fashioned from tree trunks much larger than Darshima had ever seen before. Glittering spirals of golden Tiriyuusian script wound their way up either side, extending onto the crossbeams. The gate formed a striking frame around the line of mountains and the cascades in the distance.

Tenrai guided the craft beneath the structure, out into the open expanse of water. Darshima craned his neck upward and stared at the ornate crossbeam and its hanging chains of glowing crystals. His pulse thudded with a mixture of awe and curiosity. The structure looked mysterious to him. He blinked for a moment, then shook his head, reminding himself that it was not entirely foreign. From the arch towering above him to the city behind him, all of it belonged to his true heritage. He was coming to accept this new reality, but moments like these still took him by surprise.

The rugged trio of islands comprising the training grounds came into view. Tenrai guided the craft toward a row of wooden piers in the distance. Dozens of ships identical to theirs stood berthed in the narrow slips. Thick stands of conical trees rose above the rocky shore, their green, snow-covered boughs glistening in the sunlight. The line of cascades from the surrounding mountain range lay beyond the islands, shrouding the rock faces in a thin veil of mist.

The skies grew darker as they approached the westernmost island, and a steady shower of snow fell upon the water. Tenrai aimed the craft toward the shore, maneuvering it alongside the wooden piers into an empty slip. As he powered down the engines, Tenrai secured the boat with the mooring cables. Tenrai and Dydan disembarked from the craft and stepped onto the pier. Darshima and his companions followed closely behind them. Tenrai led the group along the wooden planks. Their footsteps crunched upon the fresh layers of snow, filling the silence between them.

Tenrai and Dydan guided them along a winding path that led deeper into the forest. Rows of trees flanked the worn cobbled stones, their silhouettes blotting out the sunlight. The gold ribbons upon their coats caught the rays of the sun in a flash, glittering brightly against the shadows. The chilly air grew still as they walked along the path, and the low, melodic call of a bird rose above the sounds of their footsteps. The dense canopy of trees gave way to patches of blue sky between the grey clouds. Darshima narrowed his eyes, and in the distance, he saw a large clearing. The sound of rousing chants echoed through the air. Tenrai looked over to Dydan, then beckoned Darshima and his companions forward.

Chapter 7

Darshima and his companions followed Tenrai and Dydan through a gate leading into the clearing. A dense line of trees with snow-covered boughs flanked the octagonal space. The snowflakes melted as they hit the glistening, heated stones, paved in a radial design of black and grey. Several dozen young men and women dressed in black trousers, overcoats, gloves, and split-toed boots waited in tidy rows. Their vivid sapphire gazes focused upon a golden ring inscribed at the center of the clearing.

Groups of guardians clad in similar attire stood at the head of each line. Like Tenrai and Dydan, they wore black fabric jackets decorated with gold and leather ribbons and embroidered lines of Omystikaiyn script. Facing the lines of men and women, the guardians issued rousing chants. The recruits responded with enthusiastic shouts, their breaths rising in puffs of steam.

Darshima and his companions made their way through the space, and Tenrai ushered them into a nearby line of recruits.

"What do we do now?" Darshima looked toward Tenrai, his ears filling with the unfamiliar chants.

"In a moment, you will follow the others out of the clearing and march through the forest. Have courage." Tenrai's lips curled into a restrained but reassuring smile.

"What are the other recruits doing?" asked Sydarias. He drew nearer to Erethalie, their eyes widening in curiosity as they looked around. Khydius glared at the crowds and rhythmically clenched his jaw.

"They are preparing themselves for the first trial." Dydan offered a reassuring nod. "All of the guardians speak Vilidesian and will give you further instruction. We will meet you all on the other side." Tenrai and Dydan bade them goodbye with a wave, then walked toward the center of the clearing.

Darshima looked past the other recruits toward the center and tried to focus upon the proceedings. The guardians issued another round of chants, the cadence of their words growing more rapid and insistent. At the end of each phrase, they clicked their heels in unison. The recruits repeated their words and clicked their heels in the same manner, the echo of their boots reverberating throughout the space. The recruits saluted the guardians with their right hands lifted to their brows, the powdery flakes of snow sloughing off the sleeves of their coats.

"What are they saying?" asked Darshima, his voice mingling with the chants.

"Their language is so hard to understand." Erethalie's brow wrinkled in frustration. "None of the Omystikaiyn phrases they taught us in school prepared me for this."

"We will find some way to learn." Sydarias offered her a reassuring nod. Khydius raised his hand, and Darshima stepped closer to him.

"They're giving instructions about the events of the day." Khydius' eyes narrowed in concentration. "The chants are meant to boost morale for the first trials."

"Hopefully, they'll give us a chance to acclimate." Sydarias stood upon his toes and peered over the other recruits toward the center of the clearing.

As they stood together, Darshima mulled over Khydius' explanation. One of Khydius' former imperial titles was Defender of Iberwight, and he had visited this part of the realm many times in the past. It was clear to Darshima that Khydius knew a great deal about this moon. Yesterday evening after their supper, Darshima, Sydarias, and Erethalie had pulled Khydius aside, and he explained what he knew.

Today marked the beginning of four months of conditioning with the guardians. All of the recruits would undergo weeks of intense exercise and training in large groups, led by teams of guardians. Once they were in proper physical and mental condition, they would separate into smaller groups and receive training in the Tiriyuusian martial arts. A pair of guardians would be responsible for teaching each small group of recruits.

After Darshima and his companions were properly conditioned, Tenrai and Dydan, along with a priest from the Order, would instruct them in philosophy, weaponry, and combat. After their training, the recruits would undergo a series of tests to judge their fitness and skill. If they succeeded, the Order would invite them to serve as guardians.

Darshima waited in silence, looking on as the ceremony continued. His heart thudded as he caught the curious, fleeting stares of the other recruits. He tried his best to ignore them. It was evident to Darshima that they were the only foreigners among the crowd. He tore his gaze away and stared ahead, the words of Seer Ryte echoing in his mind. Their presence as foreigners in the kingdom was a highly unusual circumstance. Even Khydius admitted to never having visited Tiriyuud in his previous travels on Iberwight.

Darshima's eyes wandered over the dozens of recruits, their determined expressions belying their palpable eagerness. As Khydius told them, the recruits came from Chryshaihem and the many towns and villages throughout the Tiriyuusian archipelago. Darshima imagined that they had waited much of their young lives for this moment to prove themselves to their kingdom and their Order.

The chanting subsided, and the guardians moved among the recruits. They arranged them around the clearing, separating them into smaller lines of a dozen. A trio of guardians approached Darshima Khydius, Erethalie, and Sydarias.

"These four will train together," said a woman in accented but clear, authoritative, Vilidesian. She led the group of guardians, and the two accompanying men stood on either side of her. They nodded in approval at her statement, their snow-covered locks briefly hanging before their faces.

Appearing slightly younger than Tenrai, the woman stepped closer to Darshima. A severe expression graced her smooth, angular face. Her pale cheeks flushed slightly amid the frigid gusts of wind. Her silky black hair was covered in delicate snowflakes and tied in a tail with golden thread. "You four must not worry. We will treat you no differently than any of the other recruits." Her narrowed azure eyes glowed as she looked at Darshima and his companions.

The pair of guardians beside her ushered Darshima, Khydius, Erethalie, and Sydarias into a nearby line with the other recruits, then walked with her toward the head of the group. Darshima's pulse slowed with a sense of relief, tinged with worry as he waited for further instruction from the guardians. He knew they would have to prove themselves to the other Omystikai recruits, but he was thankful that he and his companions would train together.

The echo of coordinated footsteps drew Darshima from his thoughts. He looked ahead to see the trio of guardians leading their group forward.

The recruits made their way out of the clearing, marching in time with the guardians. They moved through the clearing and across the golden ring. The guardians led them back into the dense cover of the forest upon a winding cobbled path.

"If we train like the other recruits, I know we will succeed." Darshima looked over toward Khydius, Sydarias, and Erethalie as they walked with him.

"You're right, Darshima." A pensive frown formed upon Erethalie's lips.

Darshima marched along the winding, snow-covered trail. His heart seemed to beat in time with their footsteps. He narrowed his eyes as the sun filtered through the snow showers, its subdued rays illuminating the shadowy path ahead of them. Hushed murmurs rose from the crowds of recruits as they moved deeper into the forest.

As he walked beside Khydius, Darshima kept his eye upon the guardians leading their group. He glimpsed behind him, making sure that Erethalie and Sydarias kept pace. The rhythmic crunch of his boots upon the snow lulled his senses, and he slipped back into his thoughts. When Darshima felt as if he was beginning to understand life on Iberwight, things had changed.

Though they had only left Chryshaihem earlier that morning, it was already feeling like a distant memory to him. The unfamiliar ways of the Order of the Gilded Moon, the nuanced customs of the Tiriyuusians, and the fact that these people made up half of his lineage were at times daunting. Darshima struggled to comprehend the extraordinary relation between himself, Tenrai, and his brother Khydius. On occasion, he dared himself to contemplate the history that had separated them. As his thoughts approached the unavoidable truth, they retreated to safer territory, and he focused on the immediate matters ahead of him.

His thoughts swirling, Darshima shook his head and glanced at his snow-covered boots. He tried to keep his footsteps in time with the other recruits. Despite his outward confidence, Darshima wasn't sure how he would perform during the coming weeks. Though he had grown stronger since their escape from Navervyne, he still wondered if he would be able to endure the physical trials that awaited them. He worried that he might disappoint Tenrai if he struggled. Darshima drew in a breath of cold air and tried to push aside his rising doubts. He knew Tenrai would be there for them, and they would succeed. He lifted his gaze and focused upon the path ahead.

Darshima felt the winds pick up around him. The tree boughs swayed in synchrony with the winds. He squinted through the snow squalls, which brushed against his cheeks in an icy flash. The din of falling water rose over the sounds of their footsteps. Darshima lifted his gaze toward a small clearing cloaked in a fine fog. The silhouette of a triple-beamed wooden gate marking its entrance loomed high above him. Darshima and his companions followed the recruits through the mist and into the circular space. His ears filled with the sound of water, which transformed from a steady whisper into a thundering roar.

Darshima walked with the other recruits across the slippery pavement. Droplets of cold water clinging to his face, Darshima blinked and looked past the other recruits. He swept aside his matted brown locks and tried to catch a glimpse through the fog. The assembled recruits stood in evenly spaced, radial lines around the clearing. Partially obscured by a column of billowing white mist, a large ring of gold lay at its center, glittering beneath the grey skies.

"Where are the guardians are leading us?" asked Erethalie, her voice rising in concern.

"I don't know, but everyone else is following them." Sydarias scanned the crowds ahead of them. He adjusted the hood of his coat, trying to shield himself from the icy spray.

"We must be passing into some other part of the island. Tenrai and Dydan said that they would meet us on the other side," said Darshima. He looked over his shoulder toward Erethalie, the roar of the water echoing in his ears.

"We must be near those cascades that we saw on our journey here." Erethalie swept aside her wavy, dark blond hair, dampened by the droplets.

The other recruits made it into the clearing, and the three guardians leading Darshima's group spoke in short phrases. The recruits stepped closer to hear their words over the sound of the rushing water. The woman leading them spoke at a rapid clip in the Omystikai language, and the recruits nodded vigorously in response to her words. Khydius' brow furrowed in a worried expression as he listened.

"What was she saying?" asked Darshima. Khydius shook his head, apparently unaware of Darshima's question. The woman finished her words, and the recruits stepped back in line. As Darshima moved beside Khydius, the woman walked toward them.

"This is the initiation rite." She pointed toward the column of swirling mist. "You must follow us to the center without hesitation or fear. Remember to hold your breath."

"I don't understand." A glint of fear flashed across Darshima's eyes as he tried to make sense of her words.

"Do not be afraid. You must trust us. More importantly, you must trust yourselves." She offered them a curt nod and walked back toward the head of the line. Darshima looked toward Khydius, whose lips had curled into a frown.

"What did they say?" asked Darshima.

"Abandon all fear as you fall." Khydius turned toward him, his eyes flickering with a glimmer of worry.

Before Darshima could ask any further questions, the sound of spirited shouting echoed around him. Darshima snapped his gaze toward a trio of guardians on the other side of the clearing. Barely visible through the mist, they sprinted toward the center. He squinted for a better look at the figures, and his heart skipped a beat when he noticed Tenrai and Dydan leading the group.

The recruits cheered them on as they rushed toward the column of mist. As they reached the center of the clearing, Tenrai, Dydan, and their fellow guardian launched themselves upward in a powerful leap. Their bodies vaulted gracefully, somersaulting through the air before tumbling into the thick shroud of mist. Their recruits let out a cheer, then sprinted forward. They dashed toward the center, leaping one by one into the air and falling into the mists after the guardians. Their shouts faded into an echoing, disembodied silence. Darshima felt his heart sink at the fearful sight. He now understood why Khydius had looked so worried.

Their shouts rising, another trio of guardians charged forward, leaping into the mists. Their recruits sprinted after them, following them into the unknown. The clearing steadily emptied as each group ran toward the center. Darshima's pulse thudded in his temples as he witnessed the ritual. He gazed in astonishment as the guardians and their recruits charged into the mists with serene expressions upon their faces. They jumped without hesitation, falling together into the abyss.

Darshima pulled his gaze from the mists and looked to the skies for courage. His chest tightened in fear as he heard the guardians ahead of them let out a hearty cheer. Darshima and his fellow recruits snapped to attention and readied themselves. The trio of guardians burst into a sprint, the embellishments upon their jackets glittering in a flash of gold as they ran. They reached the center and leaped upward, gracefully somersaulting into the column of mist.

Darshima felt the tug of Khydius' hand pulling him forward as their group surged forward. He glimpsed behind him to see Erethalie pulling Sydarias along with her. They ran together, their feet pounding against the pavement as they sprinted with the other recruits. Darshima approached the center and instinctively lengthened his strides. He drew in a deep breath as images of his harrowing jump onto the departing freighter over the skies of Stebbenhour filled his terrified mind. Those memories gave him little comfort. The icy spray soaked through his uniform as he rushed through the clearing with the others. As Darshima's toes touched the golden ring, he launched himself upward in an exaggerated leap. A sense of weightlessness filled him as he soared over the rising tendrils of mist. As he caught his breath, the tug of gravity pulled him down into the damp void.

His surroundings disappeared in a flash of white as he plummeted through the hazy, nebulous space. Darshima shut his eyes as the howling, humid atmosphere enveloped him. He fell faster, and his stomach rose into his chest. Darshima closed his eyes even tighter, seized by the fear of his impending doom. He let out an inaudible scream amid the whipping winds. His heart bounded against his chest, and his head spun in circles as he somersaulted through the emptiness.

"Abandon all fear!" shouted Darshima, the translated words Khydius had shared suddenly coming to mind. The winds tore the words away from his lips as he fell faster. His heartbeat unexpectedly slowed, and his eyes fluttered open against the driving mists. The howling whistle diminished, and it almost felt as if he were slowing down. He looked around him and saw the falling bodies of the other recruits. Underneath the sounds of wind, he heard the distinct sound of splashing water.

Before Darshima had the time to locate the source of the sound, his body slammed into the cold, hard surface of the water. His chest heaved as the force of the impact knocked his breath from him. The muffled splash of water filled his ears, and he slipped beneath the turbulent, blue ripples. The surrounding mists faded as he sank deeper into the water. Disoriented, he flailed his limbs, his ears ringing amid the turbulent thrum. Darshima sensed a patch of light above him and oriented himself toward the surface. He swam upward, the cold waters sapping what remained of his energy. His lungs burning, he propelled himself upward through the water.

Darshima opened his eyes and looked around him as he swam. He saw the other recruits surfacing above him. He steadily narrowed the gap between himself and the surface, struggling to ignore the smoldering ache in his lungs. The water churned around him, and the rays of light grew stronger. He frantically pumped his arms and legs against the currents and through the wake of bubbles left by the other swimmers. His vision growing dim, Darshima swam upward, making his way around the other recruits as they plummeted through the water, tumbling past him. With one last heave, he forced himself up through the water's surface in a violent splash. Darshima drew in a desperate breath, pulling the cold, damp air into his aching lungs.

Darshima blinked, and his vision cleared. His head bobbing at the surface, he moved his arms and legs rhythmically, trying to stave off his shivers as he floated in the water. A layer of mist hovered above the ripples. The once deafening sound of the rushing water had faded. His waterlogged ears hummed with the echoing splash of other recruits plunging through the surface and into the frigid depths. Darshima peered around him, searching for someone or something to show him where he was. He felt as if he were in an enormous, light-filled cavern.

"Where am I?" whispered Darshima. His pulse bounded as a wave of nervousness came over him. As he opened his mouth to call out for help, a woman's voice rose above the sounds of the water.

"Take my hand, Darshima," she said, her distorted voice echoing all around him. Darshima looked ahead, his heart thudding in surprise as a pair of glowing azure eyes seemingly burned through the pallid fog. A shiver ran through him at the unusual sight.

"Who are you?" asked Darshima. He felt the waters move him toward a wooden pier ahead of him.

"You are almost there. Please, come with me." A delicate, pale hand emerged from the mists above him. Darshima swam forward, and as he gripped her hand, he felt an overwhelming force yank him out of the water onto the pier. He collapsed into a heap onto the wooden planks. He drew in a tired breath, then rose to his feet. He stood face to face with the woman and realized it was the same person who had led their group.

"Close your eyes." She stared at Darshima, her eyes casting a soft glow as she appraised him. Darshima obediently closed them and stood still. The guardian placed her fingertips upon Darshima's right temple and whispered a string of phrases in Omystikaiyn. Though he had been on Iberwight for only a few days, Darshima found himself acclimating to the rhythm of their language. He listened intently to her words, hoping to understand them.

"Your body is now pure and ready to practice our arts. Your mind is now clear and ready to learn our wisdom. Your spirit is now unbound and ready to understand and believe our ways. Come with us and be at peace." A solemn frown crossed her lips as she released her hand. Darshima bowed his head, his heart rising in his throat as he contemplated the meaning behind her words.

"What is your name?" Darshima opened his eyes and looked at her. He shivered as his damp clothes stiffened in the icy gusts.

"I am Eikan Faite. I am one of several guardians who will train you," she replied.

Darshima heard the sound of footsteps behind him. He looked over his shoulder to see Khydius, Erethalie, and Sydarias thoroughly drenched. Escorted by the two other guardians, they stood beside Darshima and waited. His friends drew in heaving breaths and shivered in their damp clothes. Eikan faced them, placed her fingers on their temples, and repeated the same phrases.

When Eikan finished speaking, her fellow guardians directed Darshima and his companions toward a cobblestone path at the end of the pier. Eikan and the other guardians then walked back toward the water's edge, slowly disappearing in the mists.

Darshima huddled beside his companions and looked around them, trying to gain a sense of where they were.

"What happened?" A hesitant smile spread upon Erethalie's lips.

"That was incredible," exclaimed Sydarias, his voice rising excitedly. "It felt as if we were flying." He vigorously shook his head, his black curly locks sending up a spray of water.

"They literally marched us off a cliff," muttered Khydius. He clenched his jaw and drew in a deep breath. His damp locks dripped down his collar. "It was more an exercise in fanaticism than bravery."

"It was terrifying, but exhilarating." Darshima looked ahead, his eyes narrowing as he focused his thoughts. "We have met them on the other side, and now there's no turning back."

"You're right, Darshima." Sydarias stepped closer to him.

"If this is how the day starts, I can't imagine how it will end," mused Khydius.

"If the other recruits can get through this, so can we." A determined look spread upon Erethalie's face.

"Let's keep moving. We have a long day ahead of us." Darshima pointed to the path ahead of them, and they walked into the mists.

Chapter 8

Arms outstretched, Darshima stood before the roaring flames of a large bonfire. He stepped closer to feel the warmth, his boots scraping against the ring of black stones surrounding the fire pit. He was a bit too close and felt the flames tease the tips of his fingers. Darshima ignored the intense heat. He was simply grateful to be near a source of warmth amid the driving cold winds. Growing up in Ardavia, the sweltering jungles of Gordanelle were never far from home. Darshima would've never imagined a day in his life when he would be so grateful for warmth.

The flames steadily dried his damp clothes, and he felt some of his vigor returning after their icy plunge.

"Where are we?" Khydius looked over his shoulder toward the waters of the lake.

"We're still on the same island, but it's very different here." Sydarias stared up at the line of imposing cliffs lining the beach and shrugged.

"We're nearly on the opposite side of the lake. The shoreline is facing in the direction of Chryshaihem." Erethalie lifted her hand to her brow and peered out over the water.

"How can you tell?" Darshima followed her stare but saw nothing but the rippling waters stretching toward the horizon.

"The angle of the sunlight and shadow indicates our location. If you look closely, you can see a trace of the city's reflection upon the water." She pointed into the distance, drawing an invisible arc with her finger.

"Whatever you say." Darshima nodded toward Erethalie. Her keen sense of direction had never failed to impress him. A memory of her expertly piloting them through the hostile skies of Stebbenhour flashed before him. Darshima knew that her abilities would be helpful during their training.

Amid the crackle of the flame and the murmurs of the recruits, Darshima peered around them. They stood upon an isolated, rocky beach. Hemmed in by a massive range of pale stone cliffs soaring skyward, the narrow strip of land curved gently away from the horizon. Rows of transparent crystals studded the jagged line of palisades, catching the late morning sunlight in a brilliant flash. His gaze alternated between the shore and the cliffs, and he saw more than twenty bonfires stretching in a line along the beach. He could make out groups of other recruits lingering around the bright tongues of flame.

The waters of the lake crashed against rows of neatly arranged polyhedral boulders lining the shore, sending up a fine spray. The morning mists had evaporated, leaving behind crisp, cold air. Mingling with the sounds of the water, Darshima heard the faint din of the cascades but no longer saw them. He presumed they were nearby, their view obscured by the cliffs.

Since escorting them from the pier to the beach, the guardians had observed the recruits but said very little to them. Darshima stood near the flames, looking to the guardians and awaiting their next task. He rubbed his hands together and tried to ignore the lingering feelings of doubt creeping up within him. He was unsure how he would adapt to training with the other recruits. They were Tiriyuusian, and this unique experience was a part of their heritage. For both Darshima and Khydius, Tiriyuud represented only half of their lineage. He didn't know how they would measure up to the other recruits.

He looked over to Erethalie and Sydarias, his anxiety only increasing as he thought of their predicament. They had no Omystikai heritage whatsoever. He wondered how they would fare here. The sound of snow crunching underfoot interrupted Darshima's thoughts. He lifted his gaze and saw several figures in guardian attire approaching him. Darshima squinted and made out Tenrai and Dydan. Eikan Faite and the two other guardians who led their group walked with them. They stopped before the bonfire and faced Darshima and his companions.

"Welcome to the other side. I am glad to see you all here, safe and sound." A genuine smile crossed Tenrai's lips.

"Guardian Faite tells us that you all managed to complete the task." Dydan nodded approvingly.

"We did our best with the dive." Darshima shivered as he recalled their icy plunge.

"They are new to our climate. Based upon this first trial, these four are behind the other recruits." Eikan cast a studied glance toward them. "This is only the first day, but if they show effort and dedication, they might succeed. Prepare yourselves for trials far more difficult than this one."

"We don't have Tiriyuusian heritage, like Darshima and Khydius." Erethalie shook her head, her brow wrinkling in frustration. "How will we ever match the skill of the Omystikai recruits?"

"Omystikai heritage is no guarantee for completing training and becoming a guardian." Tenrai rested his hand upon Erethalie's shoulder.

"It's obvious that Tiriyuusians have abilities that are beyond what average humans have." Sydarias pointed to himself and Erethalie. "We are willing to train our hardest, but what can we hope to accomplish here as Vilidesians?" Sydarias' voice wavered with a hint of uncertainty.

"No Tiriyuusian is born with any sort of strength or power as you Vilidesians may believe," said Dydan.

"How do you explain it then?" asked Erethalie.

"Tiriyuusians are not much different any other humans. Many are born with a disposition toward the strengths they display in adulthood. They must train like any other individual," said Dydan. "We are not so naive to believe that we are the only people of the realm with unique talents. We Tiriyuusians simply have developed special ways to hone our abilities, in tune with the sovereign strength." His eyes glowed intently as he spoke.

"You both have potential that you cannot yet see. I sense it." Eikan looked toward Sydarias and Erethalie. "Training with us in Tiriyuud will help you realize it."

"The seer and the sages saw something in you both. They have placed their faith in you. You must find the same faith in yourselves," said Tenrai.

"We will do our best." Erethalie bowed her head. Sydarias nodded slowly, the worried expression upon his face lessening some.

"We will be leaving you for now. Guardian Faite and her assistants, Guardians Lleidas Vowe and Seibu Reede, will guide your initial training. Until we meet again." Tenrai nodded toward them, and the trio of guardians politely bowed.

"You do not yet know our language or our ways, but listen and learn from your fellow recruits. They will teach you." Eikan gestured around them. Several of the recruits peered curiously at Darshima and his companions, then turned back to the fire.

Tenrai and Dydan bid them farewell, then walked along the beach toward the bonfires in the distance. As their silhouettes faded, Darshima felt his heart rise into his throat. He had grown close to Tenrai since their first encounter on Navervyne and his heroic efforts to rescue them. Learning about their kinship had only strengthened their bond. Darshima often wondered about their shared past. He drew in a deep breath and tried to suppress the questions swirling in his mind. He resolved to be stronger and ready for the next phase of training when they met again.

Darshima huddled with Erethalie, Khydius, and Sydarias and tried to stay warm. Lleidas and Seibu extinguished the flames, and Eikan issued what sounded like a command in the Tiriyuusian dialect. The recruits stood at attention and awaited her next orders. Darshima and his companions joined a single file line behind Eikan. They marched with their fellow recruits in lockstep along the beach.

Darshima rested a hand upon his abdomen, his stomach twisted in an aching knot from hunger. He trudged forward, trying to ignore the feeling. They hadn't eaten anything for the day. He followed the line of recruits as they marched along the curving shoreline, keeping his thoughts focused and his eyes upon the path ahead.

Darshima looked out over the water and stared at the mass of dense clouds gathering in an impending storm. He drew his coat against his shoulders, hunching them against the rising winds. He marched in time with the other recruits, the rhythm of their footfalls filling his ears. The sun moved across the skies, threading a path between the clouds. As the day progressed, the palisades' long shadows stretched out over the lake's choppy waters.

The skies opened in a shower of snow, and the winds whipped the powdery flakes against Darshima's face. He squinted amid the fleeting sting of the icy crystals. They trudged against the wind, the lake disappearing intermittently between the snow squalls. Darshima and the others changed course and headed away from the coast into the shadowy forests of the island's interior. The sun retreated toward the horizon, and Darshima hiked with his fellow recruits.

They marched upon the snowy trails and clambered over fallen logs. They trekked across frozen ponds and scrambled over boulders, their surfaces covered in icicles. Despite Darshima's fatigue, he kept pace with the other recruits. He wasn't sure where they were heading, but he pushed onward, trying to gain a better sense of the island's layout. He glimpsed over his shoulder to see Erethalie, Khydius, and Sydarias marching behind him, struggling, but pressing onward.

Darshima brushed the snowflakes from his brow and caught a glimpse of the lake through the dense line of trees, its surface lit by a twilight haze. He craned his neck upward and looked through the snowy boughs glistening in the fading light. Darshima stopped for a moment and gazed upon the countless swirling flakes in silent reverence. He was in a sacred space, and he felt it deeply.

As night fell, Eikan led the group to the trail's end and back to the beach where they began their day. The bonfires lining the shore had been relit, casting their light into the enveloping darkness. In the distance, Darshima could make out the silhouettes of the other recruits standing around the dancing flames. He rubbed his hands together to stave off the cold, a layer of snow sloughing from his gloves.

Darshima looked toward the flames and saw a group of tall, conical tents forming a large ring around the fire pit. Constructed of white fabric panels, metal steeples, and embroidered black rays, the tents loomed above the campsite. The inviting structures glowed with an inner luminescence that cast a warm light upon the surrounding snowdrifts. Enlarged silhouettes of cots and bedding projected against their circular walls.

Darshima's heart leaped as he eyed the tents. He was relieved that the guardians had prepared a sheltered place for them to sleep. During his days hunting on Gordanelle, sleeping outdoors in the humid forests without a tent was the tradition. He imagined doing the same here on Iberwight would be lethal.

Darshima, Erethalie, Khydius, and Sydarias walked past the circle of tents and toward the bonfire. With the steady winds swirling around them, they sat upon thick woven mats arranged around the fire and huddled beside their fellow recruits for warmth. Darshima eyed a group of assistants dressed in black robes and overcoats moving amid the recruits. Eikan watched as Lleidas and Seibu helped them carry platters stacked with lacquered wooden trays.

As they passed out the trays, Eikan said a few words in Omystikaiyn. The recruits clapped in unison and nodded politely toward her. Unsure of her words, Darshima clapped and nodded along with them. Erethalie and Sydarias looked to Darshima and did the same.

"These assistants will be with us during your time on the island. They will prepare your meals, and arrange your nightly accommodation, so that you may focus on your training." Eikan continued in Vilidesian, looking briefly toward Darshima and his companions. With empty platters in hand, the assistants offered the recruits a polite bow. They walked past the line of tents and headed toward the other bonfires in the distance. Eikan, Seibu, and Lleidas joined the circle of recruits and sat beside them. Darshima's ears filled with the low, staccato voices of the group speaking amongst themselves.

As Darshima settled on his mat, he felt a gentle nudge upon his right shoulder. He looked over to see a recruit passing a stack of trays over to him. Darshima handed them down the line to Erethalie, Khydius, and Sydarias, and they each took one. Darshima unhooked a silver canteen from his belt and took a sip of scalding hot tea. He cleared his throat from the bitter but pleasing aroma. He lifted the lid of his tray, and a welcoming cloud of steam greeted his nostrils. His stomach growling from hunger, he peered at the unfamiliar but neatly arranged meal of pickled roots, steamed grains, and grilled meat. He picked up a metal spoon and skewer and ate, the savory flavors spreading upon his tongue.

"What do you think of Tiriyuusian food?" A young man seated beside him carefully balanced his tray upon his knee. His heavily accented Vilidesian words came out in puffs of steam against the light of the flames. He took another bite, and his square jaw moved rhythmically as he chewed. The wind blew his unshorn black hair over his face, and he swept it back with a hand. He stared at Darshima, his sapphire eyes glowing softly against the firelight.

"It's delicious." Darshima pointed to the tray resting in his lap.

"I'm enjoying it," added Sydarias. "I'm grateful for a hot meal after today's hike." He took another bite.

"You are Vilidesian subjects. Why have you come to Tiriyuud?" questioned another recruit. She pronounced her words carefully, her pale skin flushing slightly. She turned her oval face toward Darshima and his companions, her delicate features made more striking by the glow of the flames. Her long black hair hung in a braided tail over her shoulder. She drew her coat against her frame amid the rising winds, her sapphire eyes widening in a curious expression as she looked at them.

"The Vilides was invaded, and we have come here as exiles." Erethalie lowered her eyes. Her voice was heavy with sadness.

"We seek refuge in your kingdom. We want to learn your ways and to train with you," said Darshima. His heart thudded as he pondered the recruit's unexpected question.

"We are sorry to hear what happened to your homeland." A somber expression spread upon another young man's face.

"There is severe devastation throughout the realm. It is as bad as one can imagine." Sydarias lowered his gaze and bit his lip. His bright grey eyes glittered with tears as he stared into the flames. Erethalie put her arm around his shoulder and drew him closer.

"We offer our gratitude for giving us sanctuary in your kingdom." Khydius bowed his head toward the other recruits, who returned the gesture.

"You are welcome here in Tiriyuud," said the young woman, a studied frown forming upon her lips. "We hope to learn from you as well."

"We will help each other," said another young man. He pointed to his heart and then to theirs. "Tiriyuusian or Vilidesian, we are all the same." A confident smile crossed his lips, and his eyes glowed warmly.

"Thank you," said Erethalie.

Darshima sat around the fire with his fellow recruits and finished his meal. He listened to their chatter, his ears picking up Vilidesian words interspersed in their unfamiliar dialogue. Several of the Omystikai recruits looked over toward Darshima and his companions. They spoke a few standard phrases, then read their expressions for approval. Darshima nodded in acknowledgment of their effort, impressed at how much Vilidesian they knew. Despite the isolation of their kingdom, Vilidesian culture had managed to reach these hidden shores in subtle ways. Though the realm was no more, he saw that its legacy endured.

The howl of the wind over the shore and the crackle of the flames rose over their fading conversations. The day's activities had taken their toll upon the exhausted recruits. They packed away their trays, rose from their mats, and prepared themselves for the night's rest.

Eikan walked over to Darshima and his companions as they rolled up their mats. "You four will share the same quarters." She pointed toward a tent in the circle, halfway between the cliffs and the shore. "Though our climate is difficult, you will remain warm and comfortable through the night."

"Thank you," said Khydius. He offered a bow, then walked toward the tent. Darshima, Erethalie, and Sydarias bid Eikan goodnight and followed Khydius.

Darshima lifted his gaze toward the clearing sky. Ciblaithia, Gordanelle, and Wohiimai's crescent moons hung in a line above Benai's faded grey sphere. The dormant planet's red and white rings glowed exceptionally bright against the starry void. Darshima's eyes drifted to the lake, and he saw their shattered reflections upon the rippling waters.

Darshima stepped past the tent's fabric flap and slipped off his boots, his feet sinking into the dark woolen carpet. Surprisingly large, the circular structure's stiff fabric walls and pale wooden beams offered a welcoming atmosphere. Four neat cots piled with blankets lay like the spokes of a wheel around the space. A conical white crystal lamp stood in the center, emitting subdued light and radiant warmth. Darshima removed his coat and sat upon the cot nearest the entrance, stowing his mat beneath its stout wooden legs.

"We made it through our first day of training." Darshima let out a contented sigh. The thought of this day had loomed in his mind since Tenrai had mentioned his plans. He was simply happy to have survived.

"What a day." Sydarias pulled off his coat and sank onto the cot beside Darshima's. "Tiriyuud is unlike any other place I've been."

"We will have to do our best to adapt." Darshima extended his hands toward the warmth of the crystal.

"The other recruits seem friendly." Erethalie removed her boots and reclined upon her cot, positioned on Darshima's other side. "I was expecting them to be more guarded toward us."

"If we give them a chance, they will welcome us." Darshima removed his coat and placed it beneath his bed.

As he lay down, Darshima looked over to Khydius, who had remained silent since entering the tent. Khydius settled upon the cot opposite Darshima, and a stoic expression spread upon his face. Darshima exchanged a brief stare with Khydius, who hastily looked away. As Darshima was about to speak, Khydius removed his outer garments and placed them at the foot of his cot. He lay down, drew his covers up to his chin, and closed his eyes.

His pulse thudding in surprise, Darshima looked toward Erethalie and Sydarias, who greeted him with concerned shrugs. This day had been challenging, and Darshima realized that Khydius needed time to rest.

"If we can make it through today, we can survive this training." Erethalie put her hands behind her head and stared at the ceiling, points of starlight glimmering through a transparent cone at its top.

"You're right, Erethalie." Darshima let out a sigh. "We will make it through this together." Darshima lay down upon his cot amid the warmth of the tent and drifted to sleep.

Chapter 9

A strong gust of wind blew around Darshima, and he pulled his coat against his shivering frame. A blinding shower of snow fell from the grey morning skies, covering him in layers of icy flakes. Darshima marched in lockstep beside Sydarias. Erethalie and Khydius followed closely behind them. Their boots crunched upon the frozen forest trail, filling the silence between them. A low wind whistled through the trees, rising and falling with each frigid gust. As they made their way along the winding path, Darshima peered over the shoulders of the recruits walking ahead of him.

Muted rays of sunlight glimmered through the snow squalls. Darshima eyed the dark forms of the enormous trees lining the trail. Their thick green boughs swayed rhythmically, forming an imposing, shifting tunnel. He trudged through the snowdrifts and rubbed his gloved hands together, trying to stave off the bitter cold. Powdery flakes spilled into his boots with each step, gripping his skin in a stinging chill.

"It's even colder today," said Darshima, through clenched teeth.

"It's like this every day." Sydarias turned toward him, his shoulders shivering.

"Though it's freezing, at least we're together." Darshima glimpsed over his shoulder to Erethalie and Khydius, who trudged along, their eyes narrowed against the intemperate gusts.

"Despite outward appearances, I'm getting used to the weather here on Iberwight." Erethalie looked toward the sky, her words trailing in puffs of steam. Khydius offered a terse nod. A layer of snowflakes sloughed from his neck-length curly black locks, which had grown since his rescue from Stebbenhour. Khydius glared at Darshima for a moment, then deferred his gaze as he walked.

His pulse thudding, Darshima turned back around. Trying to ignore Khydius' silence, he shook his head and continued marching. For much of the morning, Khydius had kept to himself, barely engaging in conversation with anyone. Darshima could see that Khydius was struggling to adjust to life in Tiriyuud. They all were struggling to some degree. Darshima wanted to help Khydius but wasn't even sure how to begin.

It had been more than a month since they had arrived on Iberwight. Though he was growing accustomed to the near-constant snowfall, Darshima had never seen such heavy showers. He squinted as he peered down the forest trail, the icy flakes swirling around them. Eikan, Lleidas, and Seibu led the recruits past the stands of trees. The trio of guardians periodically glimpsed over their shoulders, checking the line of recruits behind them, making sure everyone remained in order.

Eikan guided the group through the drifting snows. Unperturbed by the weather, she brushed the flakes from her collar with a gloved hand. They were on their way to their outdoor training space, secluded in the depths of the forest. The skies brightened as they moved along the winding trail. They passed through a wooden gate and entered a paved octagonal clearing amid the trees. Darshima walked across the heated stones and felt the warmth radiate through his boots. The falling snowflakes melted in a cloud of vapor as they hit the glistening surface.

Darshima looked toward the center and saw the guardians step inside a golden ring set into the pavement. With their backs together, they stood within the circle and faced the group. Darshima, Erethalie, Khydius, Sydarias, and their fellow recruits spaced themselves at even intervals around the clearing. They stood at attention and looked toward the guardians.

As Darshima settled into his position, the guardians clapped their hands in unison. They issued a shout, and their voices echoed around the clearing. Darshima watched as they deftly crouched toward the ground, lowering their stances in a defensive posture. Darshima and the other recruits did the same, the radiant heat from the pavement offering some comfort against the cold weather. The guardians then rose to a standing position. They moved in unison, their limbs and torsos gliding through a series of fast-paced, martial poses. His eyes focused upon the trio, Darshima did his best to imitate their moves.

Despite his initial worries, Darshima made progress with these exercises. He looked beside him to see Erethalie, Khydius, and Sydarias moving their arms and legs in synchrony with the guardians. The first weeks of training had consisted of exhausting marches along the snowy trails of the island, routine laps in the frigid waters off the coast, and these group exercises. From what the guardians told them, these routines would improve their endurance. They needed to strengthen their bodies to adapt to the unforgiving, perpetual Iberwightian winter.

During his first days of training, Darshima had struggled. He did his best to keep up with the Omystikai recruits but wasn't accustomed to the climate like they were. The guardians had shown neither him, Erethalie, Sydarias, nor Khydius any favor. As they did with the others, the guardians pushed them to the brink of their physical limits. When they struggled, Eikan, Lleidas, and Seibu encouraged them to continue, usually with a word of support or a stiff pat upon the shoulder. During the most challenging days, Darshima leaned on Sydarias and Erethalie for help, and they all did what they could to encourage Khydius. Though he made progress, Khydius had steadily become more withdrawn.

Darshima moved with the other recruits, following the lead of the guardians, who glided flawlessly through the series of stances. He felt himself growing stronger each day. He made mental notes of his progress and ways in which he could improve. Darshima was also managing to learn a few words in the Tiriyuusian dialect. Despite Khydius' disposition, Darshima had pried a few Omystikaiyn words and phrases from him and discovered that his vocabulary was surprisingly large. Khydius had learned to speak the modern dialect from his Omystikai counselors during his childhood in the imperial court. Furthermore, the guardians and their fellow recruits had taken it upon themselves to teach new words and phrases to Darshima and his companions during their exercises.

Darshima stood in the clearing beneath the falling snowflakes and moved his limbs in time with the graceful, precise motions of the guardians. From what he gleaned thus far from Khydius and the other recruits, these postures were the most integral moves of the Order's martial art, eneri-kai. The mysterious origins of this ancient fighting style traced back to the Omystikai tribesmen, who once ruled unchallenged on Ciblaithia. Though it had been practiced for millennia, the art had faded into obscurity after Benai's ancient conquest of Ciblaithia.

Darshima threw a sequence of kicks and punches in tandem with the guardians. As his muscles powered through the moves, his mind drifted back to the desert sands of Ciblaithia. Darshima imagined his Omystikai ancestors honing their craft amid the gilded dunes in an era long past. He let out an exhausted sigh, then positioned his feet into the next stance.

Darshima crouched into a defensive posture, then sprung to his feet in unison with the guardians. He looked around the octagon at the other recruits, his mind swirling with Khydius' descriptions of Iberwight. The Omystikai had formed separate factions early in their exile due to ideologic differences. They spread out upon the continents and mountain ranges of the moon and created individual orders.

With the rise of the Vilidesian Realm, the Omystikai organized themselves into semiautonomous dominions under the emperor's rule. Enerikai was all but abandoned during this period, as the orders acquiesced to the expanding Vilidesian forces on Iberwight and the other moons. The Tiriyuusians, however, cultivated eneri-kai and were the only Omystikai who practiced it to its fullest extent. The guardians were the custodians of this art and trained their ranks in its intricacies.

Darshima threw another series of punches in time with his fellow recruits. He clenched his jaw as a twinge of disbelief surged through him. A lump formed in Darshima's throat as memories of the invasion and his enslavement mingled with tragic recollections of the Omystikai's ancient defeat, dispossession, and exile to Iberwight. Darshima's eyes widened in astonishment as he came to an unexpected realization. He came from a heritage of not only survival amid defeat but of perseverance, prosperity, and civilization amid desolation. No longer hidden to him, the Tiriyuusians and their kingdom were an essential part of his identity.

The sun threaded an arc through the cloudy sky, and the recruits pushed through a challenging series of stances. Despite the frigid weather, most of them had removed their coats and shirts to avoid overheating. The men stood bare-chested, and the women kept on their vests, cropped at the midriff. The recruits moved their bodies in synchrony with the guardians, following an intricate series of steps around the clearing. Darshima, Erethalie, Khydius, and Sydarias were noticeably darker than the others and stood out boldly against the snowy scenery. In hues of brown, their skin color had initially garnered curious stares. The other recruits had grown accustomed to their presence and no longer made any distinction toward them.

They thrust their fists and delivered forceful kicks in complicated se-
quences, the falling flakes of snow melting as they hit their athletic frames,
sculpted by weeks of intense training. Darshima eyed the various intricate,
tessellated markings, adorning their arms, backs, and torsos. He smiled to
himself as he glimpsed the markings on the skin of his right forearm, and
the design inked upon Khydius' chest. For most of his life, his markings had
made him feel like an outsider, but here in Tiriyuud, he clearly belonged.

With a commanding shout, the guardians increased the intensity and
intricacy of their moves. The recruits let out a cheer in reply and pushed
themselves harder. As it was an early stage of training, the recruits were
learning the basic fighting stances. From what Darshima understood, they
would eventually learn the philosophy behind these moves and the ways to
invoke the forces behind them. As he raised his arms in a defensive posture,
memories of Tenrai's astounding physical feats during their escape came
back to him. A smile crossed Darshima's lips as he imagined the strength
these moves might one day wield.

Darshima threw his fists in time with the guardians, his heart skipping
a beat as an unwelcome memory flashed before him. With a mere wave of
these same hands, he had wrought such unexpected destruction in their escape from Stebbenhour. He vigorously shook his head, desperate to forget
the memory. He blinked, and the fiery images of burning soldiers evaporated amid the squalls of snow. With renewed effort, Darshima mimicked the
guardians' moves. He executed a series of punches and blocks in time with
the other recruits. His eyes lingered upon the intricate design winding its
way along his right arm, flakes of snow melting as they hit the glistening
blue ink.

Darshima tore his gaze from his arm and looked toward Eikan, Seibu,
and Lleidas. He drew in a deep breath, refocused his attention, then proceeded with the next series of stances. He needed to learn everything he
could from these guardians. These moves were the only way he would learn
how to control the unknown force that seemed to dwell within him.

The sky darkened, and the snow fell faster as the recruits made their
way around the clearing. They were exhausted, but the guardians urged
them on, pacing them through even more complex moves, exhorting them
to continue. Not wanting to disappoint their teachers or each other, the

young men and women pushed themselves harder. Darshima eyed the sun as it drifted between an interstice in the clouds, its muted glow fading beyond the tree line.

Their knees trembling from exhaustion, the recruits closed the day's training session with a rousing chant. The guardians left the center of the ring and led the recruits out of the clearing. Darshima and the others grabbed their items, put on their coats, and followed the guardians back into the forest. He walked with his companions along the narrow trail, the growing shadows looming around them.

Darshima lifted his eyes toward the sky and glimpsed Gordanelle's shimmering crescent. His heart rose into his throat as memories of home came back to him. His exhaustion and emotions getting the better of him, Darshima tore his gaze from the moon and focused upon the trail. He wanted to move on from his past life, but some days were more difficult than others. Wherever life took him, he realized that Gordanelle would always be an integral part of him.

Darshima trudged alongside Sydarias in silence. Both hungry and tired, he couldn't muster anything to say to him. Erethalie and Khydius walked behind them, their plodding footsteps filling his ears. It had been an exhausting day, but they had prevailed. There was still much to learn, but the day's training brought them a bit closer to becoming guardians.

Chapter 10

Darshima walked upon the snowy beach, the waters lapping against the lakeshore in a rhythmic murmur. He approached the camp with Erethalie, Khydius, and Sydarias, who walked alongside him. His eyes lingered upon the bonfire's glow, which cast a soft halo against the starlit sky. The other recruits sat around the fire, their silhouettes shifting against the tents. Darshima settled beside Khydius and let out a sigh. He turned to Khydius, who looked blankly ahead. Erethalie and Sydarias sat beside him and chatted with the other recruits, using some of the Tiriyuusian words they had learned thus far.

Darshima leaned toward the fire, grateful for its warmth. He shivered as the heat he worked up from their exercises evaporated from his damp skin. Eikan, Lleidas, and Seibu joined the circle of recruits, and the assistants handed out the evening dinner trays. Darshima opened his tray and ate a spoonful of the savory white grains. He opened his canteen and took a gulp of tea, the tendrils of steam brushing against his nose.

His ears filled with the voices of the other recruits, rising and falling in lively bouts of conversation as they ate. Like most evenings, they were sharing tales and recounting past events from their history. As the weeks of training progressed, Darshima found himself hearing familiar words and phrases from their dialect. His ears pricked when he recognized a particular saying that meant wisdom gained through struggle.

His eyes drooping with fatigue, Darshima ate his meal in silence. He looked toward the fire, and a satisfying sense of exhaustion filled him. Though the exercises had become more strenuous, he felt himself growing stronger. The feelings of anxiety that gnawed at him when they first arrived upon these islands had subsided. Darshima found himself looking forward to Eikan's instruction. Lleidas and Seibu helped them with their stances, pushing them all to work harder. His thoughts drifted as he mulled over the next steps of their training.

The sound of clattering utensils broke through the din of voices, and Darshima pulled himself from his thoughts. He looked beside him to see the other recruits packing away their items. Darshima ate the remaining morsels on his tray, then put it away. He looked over toward Khydius, whose food remained untouched. Darshima opened his mouth to speak but fell silent.

As Darshima contemplated what to say to him, the guardians and the other recruits rose from their seats. They bid each other good night, then shuffled through the snowdrifts toward the circle of tents. Darshima stood up and walked with Erethalie and Sydarias away from the bonfire and toward their tent. He turned around to see Khydius still seated, with his eyes fixed upon the flames.

"Are you coming, Khydius?" Darshima waved toward him.

"I'll join you in a moment." A frown formed upon Khydius' lips, and he momentarily pulled his gaze from the fire. Khydius drew his coat against his frame and let out a sigh, his breath coming out in a trail of vapor.

Darshima stepped past the entrance flap of their tent and glimpsed over his shoulder. His eyes lingered upon Khydius, who remained the only one outside.

"Let's get some sleep." Erethalie nudged his shoulder.

"Khydius is still out there. Something is not right with him." Darshima faced her.

"I agree, but give him time. He will make his way back when he is ready." Her lips wrinkled into a worried frown.

"Life here has been a big adjustment for all of us, but especially for the prince." Sydarias looked toward Khydius, his brow furrowed in concern. They moved past Darshima and settled upon their cots for the night.

Darshima stared at Khydius, whose eyes glimmered with a faraway look. As Darshima was about to call out to him, Khydius rose to his feet. He dusted the snow from his trousers and stepped away from the fire. Trudging through the snow, he moved past the tents and toward the shore, his shadow looming amid the moonlight. Khydius reached the water's edge and climbed upon a large, crystalline rock formation that rose at an angle from the surrounding beach. Its glittering form jutted over the rippling waters like an arrow. Khydius carefully walked toward the end of the rock and settled upon its jagged edge. His shoulders hunched over, he stared out over the lake.

His heart thudding, Darshima moved through the entrance of their tent. He closed the flap and stepped back into the cold night air. He couldn't help but wonder why Khydius wanted to be alone. His boots crunched over the powdery snow as he walked toward the shore. Darshima clambered atop the rocky outcropping and walked to its edge. He stood beside Khydius.

"May I join you?" Darshima motioned to the space between them.

"It's not necessary. I'm sure you're exhausted." Khydius looked up toward Darshima, his eyes glinting in the starlight.

"I could use a bit of relaxation before turning in for the night." Darshima sat upon the rock, his shoulder brushing against Khydius. He shivered as the cold dampness seeped through his trousers. A memory of his promontory back on Gordanelle briefly flashed before his eyes. Back then, he sought understanding beneath the starry solitude. Perhaps Khydius was doing the same. Darshima shook his head as the chilly winds brought him back to the present.

"If you insist," mumbled Khydius. He glared forward, his jaw clenched. Darshima looked out over the rippling waters, tracing Khydius' stare toward the dark horizon.

The snow showers had abated, and the clouds parted to reveal the vast night sky. Benai and its vivid rings seemed to float above the horizon. In the western skies, the bright crescents of Ciblaithia, Gordanelle, and Wohiimai hung in an arc amid the countless stars. Darshima's thoughts swirled as he took in the celestial view. His heart sank as he pondered Khydius' growing detachment from him. Khydius was struggling, and Darshima could feel it.

"How are you handling the training so far?" asked Darshima.

"I am doing as well as can be as expected." Khydius pulled his gaze from the sky and stared at Darshima.

A feeling of disbelief seized Darshima as he peered into Khydius' bright eyes, vanishing as suddenly as it had come. Though he was growing to accept the truth, Darshima still couldn't fathom what twist of fate had made them brothers. Darshima was an average young man from Gordanelle, and here he was, seated beside the Prince of The Vilides. Darshima's disbelief had subsided as they grew more acquainted, but at times, it appeared when he least expected it.

"You seem as if something is weighing on your mind." Darshima chased his errant thoughts and moved closer to Khydius.

"I'm fine. You mustn't worry about me." Khydius turned away from Darshima, his eyes glimmering in the starlight.

"Talk to me, Khydius. We're brothers after all," said Darshima.

"So we've been told." Khydius nodded slowly. "I don't want to burden you with my troubles."

"Your troubles are my troubles." Darshima rested his hand upon Khydius' shoulder.

"You wouldn't understand." Khydius pulled away from Darshima.

"I understand more than you think." Darshima's eyes narrowed as he registered Khydius' words. He could understand Khydius' sadness, but his empathy was tempered by the fact that they all had endured a great deal since the invasion. He and Sydarias were enslaved before Tenrai had freed them. He had left his adopted family back in Ardavia. Erethalie's parents died in the calamity, and her elder siblings were being held in servitude somewhere on Navervyne. She had parted with her remaining brother, Shonan, here on this unfamiliar moon. Sydarias had abandoned his life of wealth and security with his family back home in The Vilides.

Despite their own harrowing experiences, Darshima realized that Khydius had perhaps suffered the most drastic change to his life. He had gone from a prince and a future emperor to a slave. Now he was exiled upon a moon once titled to him.

"We may share blood relations, but our lives couldn't be more different." Khydius closed his eyes, and a sigh escaped his lips. "I shouldn't be here. I belong in The Vilides."

"At this moment, our lives are quite similar." Darshima's cheeks flushed at Khydius' harsh tone. "As we all know, The Vilides and all of the moons are occupied territories. We are safest here in Tiriyuud."

"How can you be so sure?" Khydius shook his head in disbelief.

"I believe what Tenrai has told us." Darshima folded his arms across his chest. "He has done everything he can to protect us."

"You are so willing to leave behind the worlds that were once ours." A frown spread upon Khydius' lips.

"What are you talking about?" Darshima shook his head in confusion.

"Tenrai has told us about our Omystikai heritage, but he certainly hasn't told us everything." With a gloved hand, Khydius reached toward Ciblaithia's gilded crescent, then clenched his fist. The dimmed but glittering lights of The Vilides burned like smoldering embers upon the portion veiled in darkness. "I was to be the next emperor."

"Though that is true, the Vilidesian Realm no longer exists." Darshima bowed his head as he felt the weight of his words.

"You do realize that you are my elder brother. In another time and place, the throne would have been your birthright. You would have been the Vilidesian Emperor," said Khydius. Darshima shivered as Khydius' piercing stare went right through him. "The thought must have crossed your mind since we've made each other's acquaintance."

"We don't even know if we are truly of royal birth." Darshima shook his head at Khydius' incredulous pronouncement. Since Tenrai's revelation, Darshima had devoted his energy to surviving in Tiriyuud and training with the guardians. He hadn't allowed himself a moment to think of anything else.

"Tenrai said our mother was a Vilidesian noblewoman." Khydius' eyes narrowed in a studied expression. "Why else would I have been first in line to the throne?"

"None of this matters anymore. Our homeland has been conquered, and we're in exile." Darshima pulled his gaze away from Khydius and glared at the rippling waters. He folded his arms across his chest as a wave of anxiety rose within him.

Though he had accepted his new familial relations with both Tenrai and Khydius, Darshima was loath to contemplate the circumstances of his birth or his separation from them. Had they been raised together, Darshima couldn't fathom how different his life might have been. He shuddered as Khydius' words echoed in his ears, and a fleeting image of the royal palace in The Vilides drifted before his eyes. The idea that he, an adopted boy from Gordanelle, could be of noble birth, let alone the future emperor, seemed as abstract as the stars glittering above them. He couldn't conceive of a reality in which any of this could have been true.

"Our heritage matters to me, and it must matter to you. We cannot simply ignore more than a thousand years of history," said Khydius.

"Perhaps you're unaware, but I was abandoned in the Ciblaithian desert as an infant. My Vilidesian heritage didn't matter then. If it weren't for my adoptive parents, I would've died." Darshima's shoulders slumped as he spoke, the memories of his Ardavian family coming back to him. His eyes grew damp as images of his mother Dalia, brother Sasha, and father Sovani flashed before him. Though his upbringing on Gordanelle was imperfect and incomparable to Khydius' life as a prince, Darshima wouldn't change it for anything.

"I'm sorry, Darshima, I didn't know about your childhood." A contrite frown formed upon Khydius' lips. "It seems that our destinies were chosen before we even knew them."

"You must remember that our uncle, an Omystikai man, risked everything to rescue us from slavery." His pulse thudding, Darshima pulled his gaze from the stars and stared at Khydius. "The Tiriyuusians acknowledge our roots in this kingdom. They are giving us shelter and teaching us their ways. I will always be thankful for what they've done for us."

"I am grateful to Tenrai and his Order, but life here has been hard for me." Khydius bowed his head.

"It's been hard for all of us." Darshima tried to rest his hand upon Khydius' shoulder, but he pulled away.

"I was once the Defender of Iberwight, a title granted to me by the emperor upon my birth." Shivering in the cold, Khydius folded his hands in his lap. "As fate would have it, I find myself exiled in this most hermetic kingdom amid the utter collapse of our realm. An antiquated army that I would've once commanded has relegated me to serve as a mere foot soldier." Khydius lifted his face to the sky, his eyes damp with tears.

Darshima's stomach twisted with regret as he listened to Khydius' lament. He wanted to support his brother, who was grieving all that he had lost, but Darshima didn't know how to comfort him. A memory of their flight from Ardavia after he had brought Sasha back home suddenly came to him. At that moment, Darshima had struggled with leaving everything he had known, and Khydius had comforted him.

"We will make it through this together. We have no choice." Darshima placed his arm around Khydius' shoulder and drew him closer.

"I don't know how..." said Khydius. Darshima raised his other hand, and Khydius felt silent.

"Those are the same words you told me as we fled Gordanelle. I also left behind everyone and everything that I once knew." Darshima looked behind them toward their tent. "We all did." Khydius dashed the tears from his eyes and cleared his throat.

"Indeed, those were my words." Khydius nodded, his voice heavy with sadness.

"We must work with the Tiriyuusians and rebuild our lives," said Darshima.

"How can we move forward amid such devastation?" Khydius shook his head in disbelief.

"From what we have seen here, all is not lost." Darshima peered out over the lake. He tried to glimpse Chryshaihem's skyline beyond the horizon and saw a glimmer of light reflected against the clouds. He thought of the multitudes who carried on with their lives in this hidden corner of their world.

"Somehow, they found a way to escape the worst of Navervyne's invasion," said Khydius.

"Tenrai and Dydan, along with Eikan and the other guardians, will teach us." Darshima gestured back toward the camp.

"I'll learn as much I can while in Tiriyuud, but I must find out the truth about our parents." Khydius nodded slowly.

"In time, Tenrai will tell us everything." Darshima rose to his feet. Khydius stood up and dusted the snow from his uniform. "It's late, and we have a difficult day ahead of us. We should return to our tent."

They walked together atop the rock formation and back onto the beach, the sounds of the water filling the silence between them. They stepped past the fire pit, whose glow had dimmed to a pile of ember and ash. As they stopped before their tent, Khydius turned to Darshima.

"Growing up as a prince, I had more counselors and minders than I could name. There wasn't a material possession that wasn't mine." Khydius stared at Darshima, his eyes glimmering in a sincere expression. "Despite outward appearances, life in the royal court wasn't perfect, and I spent much of my time alone."

"I imagine you felt the weight of responsibility," said Darshima. "Everyone upon the four moons adored you."

"Indeed, they did. I spent my life preparing for the demands of my future role." A pensive frown crossed Khydius' lips.

"I am sorry for the difficulty of your circumstance." Darshima lowered his gaze in a gesture of sympathy. "I'll help you adjust however I can." Khydius looked up at the sky as he processed Darshima's words.

"My emotions must sound selfish at a time like this when there is so much suffering," said Khydius.

"They aren't selfish, and you have to let yourself feel them. You must work through the loss, the pain, and the anger." Darshima rested his hand upon Khydius' shoulder. "We all must." He felt tears forming at the corners of his eyes, the emotions from his own struggles creeping forth.

"I must stop focusing on all that I've lost and learn to appreciate that which I have gained." Khydius faced Darshima. "I'm grateful that you are my brother."

"I am honored to be your brother." His heart rising in his throat, Darshima embraced Khydius, who returned the gesture.

"Tomorrow, I will try anew with the guardians and their training regimen. I can see that you all are truly making an effort. I must do the same," said Khydius.

"We owe it to those who are still enslaved on Navervyne." Darshima's pulse thudded as the memories of their toil flashed before him. A tear fell from his eye, and he shook his head as the images faded.

"Their suffering and ours will not go in vain. I will do whatever I must to succeed." A resolute expression formed upon Khydius' face. They stepped through the entrance of their tent, settled upon their cots, and bid each other goodnight.

Chapter 11

His back to the winds, Darshima struggled as he held onto a jagged cleft in the glittering rock face. His hands ached from both the cold and from holding on for what had felt like hours. He shifted some of his weight to his feet, which were braced against a precarious outcropping, but it did little to relieve his discomfort. Perched beside him, Erethalie, Khydius, and Sydarias appeared equally fatigued from the exercise. They grimaced amid the falling snows, their strained expressions hinting at their determination.

Darshima and the other recruits had been stationed upon the cliff for most of the morning. They had scaled the sheer rock face before dawn amid the whipping winds. They gripped whatever rocky fissure or formation they could find, sheltering themselves from the fierce snow squalls. Darshima tightened his grip and stiffened his shoulders. The gusts grew stronger, cutting through his uniform. He looked behind him and caught faint traces of daylight as the pale orange sun rose over the ripples of the lake.

His pulse thudded with anticipation as he scanned the vast skyline. Further upon the horizon, he saw the studded outline of Chryshaihem's towers and spires traced against the billowing clouds. It was his first clear glimpse of the city since they had left for training nearly two months ago.

His legs aching from bracing against the outcropping, Darshima shifted his stance when suddenly, his foot slipped from the toehold. He winced as his leg skidded downward. His heart thudding in fear, Darshima tightened his grip. The muscles of his back and arms burned as he pulled himself closer to the rock face. He eyed another nearby toehold and regained his footing, his ears ringing with the clatter of tumbling pebbles. His eyes traced the shower of rocks plummeting toward the narrow, snow-covered beach far below.

"Are you okay?" exclaimed a recruit stationed several paces away from him. She instinctively tightened her grip.

"I am exhausted but okay." Darshima nodded toward her.

"You must make subtle adjustments to your form to avoid exhaustion. If your moves are too drastic or you are too fatigued, you will fall and might die." Her sapphire eyes glowed as she appraised his grip.

"I understand," said Darshima. He glanced at the ground below him. His mouth grew dry as he realized how close he had come to falling.

Darshima drew in a breath of cold air and steadied himself, thankful that he no longer had a fear of heights. Memories of his days amid the girders during his construction apprenticeship flashed before his eyes. He would've never imagined that working high above the streets of Ardavia would've prepared him for a moment like this.

As he settled into his new position, Darshima caught a glimpse of the other recruits in their group. They remained still as they hung onto the cliff, their intense gazes seemingly penetrating through the rock face. Many of these Tiriyuusian men and women hailed from the smaller towns and villages throughout the archipelago. Before training with the guardians, several worked in the farming pyramids, ore mines, and factories. During their weeks together, Darshima learned that their recreational activities included hiking mountain trails, scaling glaciers, and abseiling cliffs like these. From their confident bearing, it was clear that these recruits had no fear of heights or inclement weather.

Darshima maintained his balance and carefully looked over to his right. He eyed the sun as it rose above the lake. He felt his hands slipping and held on tighter. He stiffened his shoulders, then turned back around and stared at the rock face. Maintaining his position upon the cliff took a great deal of effort, but the fear of falling motivated him to maintain his grip.

Before they ascended the cliff, Eikan had instructed the recruits to wait until high noon. When the sun reached its zenith, she would sound a bell. The recruits would then leap from their perches and dive into the lake. Once in the water, they needed to retrieve a crystal from the lakebed and swim back to shore. They needed to find the gemstone that called to their spirit. The gem would serve as a reminder of completing this important task. Darshima wasn't sure how a stone could call to him, but he was prepared to open his mind to this unique possibility. He would do whatever he must to succeed.

As Darshima waited for the signal, he closed his eyes and tried to develop a strategy that would allow him to survive the jump and find a gemstone. This perilous exercise marked the halfway point of their training. After today, their instruction would become more technical and spiritual in nature. They all needed to develop the mental strength to invoke the forces that allowed a fully trained guardian to practice eneri-kai.

Darshima looked beneath his feet toward the beach unfurling beneath him. Beyond the line of encampments and their circles of tents, he saw Eikan, Lleidas, and Seibu patrolling the shore, periodically looking up at the recruits. Darshima turned back toward the cliff and closed his eyes. He drew in a breath and reentered his thoughts. He needed to maintain focus if he had any chance of succeeding at this task, but worries about his companions crept into his mind. He looked toward Sydarias and Erethalie, stationed on his right, then over to Khydius perched on his left.

"We are nearly there. Only a little longer, and we will complete this task." Darshima tightened his grip as he spoke, his words muffled by the wind.

"This is one of our more challenging days." Erethalie shifted her weight, her braided locks spilling over her shoulders. She pressed her boots upon the rock and balanced her body against the cliff. After momentarily relaxing her arms, she exhaled. "After today, we'll be ready for anything."

"You're strong, Erethalie." Darshima nodded, impressed at her calm demeanor. Despite the physical strain of her position, she maintained a look of composure. He glanced over toward Sydarias, who gripped an outcropping and shivered with each gust.

"This is difficult," whispered Sydarias, his teeth chattering. The winds swirled around him, blowing his curly, snow-covered locks over his face.

"You can do this." Darshima shifted as close to Sydarias as his precarious position would allow. "I believe in you."

"I am trying my best." Sydarias peered at Darshima, his eyes glittering with tears. He clenched his jaw and stifled his pain. Darshima's heart rose into his throat as he saw Sydarias' distress.

"As we did in times past, we must make it through this challenge together." Darshima stared at Sydarias, his eyes pleading with him. Sydarias drew in a breath and steadied his grip.

"I owe my life to you. I won't let you down." His teeth chattering, Sydarias offered a resolute nod to Darshima.

"You don't owe me anything," said Darshima, his voice catching in his throat.

"It's the truth. I will do whatever I must to stay with you." Sydarias looked upon Darshima, an earnest smile crossing his shivering lips. He stiffened his shoulders and then faced the cliff.

"Thank you, Sydarias." Darshima's pulse bounded as memories of Sydarias being thrown over the edge of the colony on Navervyne flashed before him. A chill much colder than the surrounding air jolted him, and he shuddered. That unknown strength he had wielded to save Sydarias still remained beyond his comprehension. As difficult as this task was, Darshima's heart thudded with a feeling of confidence. He vowed to do whatever he must to summon that same strength. He wouldn't let any harm come to his friends.

Darshima looked over to Khydius as he gripped the rock face, his uniform fluttering in the breeze. They had said very little to each other that morning. Darshima had tried to engage him during their trek to the site, but Khydius had kept to himself. Since their conversation at the lakeshore those weeks ago, Khydius had devoted himself to training and had caught up with the other recruits. He had become more open with Darshima, and when he struggled, he shared his feelings. Darshima felt their kinship grow, but he still sensed a barrier between them.

As Darshima mulled through the next steps of their task, a whisper interrupted his thoughts. He turned to see Khydius glaring at him.

"I don't understand why we must train like this." Khydius' shoulders trembled with fatigue. His face had become ashen, and his eyes were losing their focus. Darshima's pulse thudded as he saw Khydius' distress. As he reached out to Khydius, Darshima caught himself and held back. The recruits were not allowed to offer physical support during this task, but they were expected to encourage each other if they struggled.

"We must train like this to be prepared for our duties as guardians." Darshima leaned toward Khydius, trying to catch his gaze.

"I don't think I am meant for this life." Khydius clenched his jaw as he faced the cliff.

"This is the life we have. We must persevere," said Darshima.

"There has to be some other way." Khydius shook his head.

"We are almost through this task, and then we can rest." A worried frown formed upon Darshima's lips. He sensed Khydius' frustration. The challenges they faced here on Iberwight during their training paled in comparison to the suffering he experienced as a slave on Navervyne. He hoped that Khydius realized that life on Iberwight, though difficult, was incomparably better than the miserable existence they had escaped.

"So I'll complete this task, and then what more must I do?" Khydius drew in a breath and closed his eyes."

"We are all exhausted, but we must push ourselves," said Darshima. "We owe it to everyone who is still enslaved on Navervyne and all who are suffering on the other moons. We must train so that we can fight back." Khydius closed his eyes and nodded at Darshima's words.

"We have lost so much. What right do I have to complain?" whispered Khydius.

"Despite all that has happened, you are still the Prince of the Vilides," said Darshima. "You are still the Defender of Iberwight. That must mean something to you."

"I cannot deny your words." Khydius' eyes glimmered with a look of determination.

"We are brothers, Khydius. I cannot continue this journey without you." His voice growing heavy with emotion, Darshima cleared his throat.

"You have my word. I will press on." Khydius' brow wrinkled in contemplation. He offered Darshima a terse nod, then faced the cliff. Darshima exhaled a sigh of relief as he saw Khydius tighten his grip and steady himself.

The sun reached the highest point in the sky, and the droning winds broke under the thunderous peal of a bell. Darshima snapped out of his cold-induced trance and looked out over the lake. With his remaining strength, he let go of the cliff and jumped from his perch. Erethalie, Sydarias, and then Khydius leaped after him.

Darshima vaulted through the open air with the other recruits, his uniform flapping wildly in the wind. He traced a wide arc over the beach, then plummeted toward the waters. Darshima dove into the lake headfirst in an explosive, icy burst. He held his breath as an acute sense of cold sized every nerve and fiber within him. He tumbled beneath the enveloping waves and forced his eyes open, trying to make sense of his dim, watery surroundings.

Darshima oriented himself toward the shadowy depths and glimpsed the rock-strewn lakebed. As his vision accommodated to the darkness, specks of gleaming light revealed themselves amid the sediment. His pulse thudded as he eyed the vast arrays of gemstones spreading before him. His lungs burning, Darshima swam deeper, trying to maintain his sense of direction. He pumped his arms and legs, the frigid waters sapping his strength. Darshima squinted as his breath escaped his nostrils, the stream of air bubbles brushing against his face. Through the murky light, he could make out the forms of the other recruits swimming toward the lakebed.

Darshima maneuvered past spindly crystal formations and broad rock ledges, their immense forms bathed in dim, spectral rays of sunlight. His lungs burned from exhaustion, but he pushed forward. He calmly fought against the instinct to breathe. His weeks of training had prepared him for this moment. Darshima reached the bottom and lunged for a nearby crystal fragment. The faceted stone slipped from his grasp in a glimmer of yellow light before disappearing into the shadows.

Darshima's hands stirred up plumes of dust as he scoured the lakebed. As he dug through the sediment, an intense flash of fire caught his attention. Darshima reached toward the light and swept away the dirt, revealing a palm-sized, red ruby. His pulse thudded in his temples at the peculiar sight. He recognized the object as his symbolic stone from the ancestral chart that Tenrai had shared with him and Khydius.

Darshima clawed at the gemstone and freed it with a firm tug. He clutched the precious object to his chest and pushed himself back to the surface. Darshima glimpsed over his shoulder, his heart rising with confidence as he saw Erethalie and Sydarias swimming behind him, holding shards of crystals in their hands. He felt a surge of energy propel him as he raced toward the surface. The benthic darkness gave way to the sunlight as he moved upward through the icy volume of water. He swam harder, his sight growing dim as he struggled to hold his breath. In an explosive burst, Darshima breached the surface and inhaled a deep breath of cold air. Darshima shook his damp wavy locks from his face and kept his eye upon the shoreline. He swam along the rippling surface, moving further from the other recruits as he approached the beach. Though he was exhausted, he pushed himself even harder.

Darshima reached the shore and stumbled upon the snow. He felt an arm grip his shoulder and help him to his feet. Shivering in his damp clothes, Darshima looked beside him and realized it was Lleidas helping him along. Despite his solemn expression, his eyes glittered with surprise.

"You did well, Darshima. You must conserve your body heat to ward off illness." Lleidas draped a woolen blanket across Darshima's shoulders.

"Thank you." His teeth chattering, Darshima drew the blanket closer, its welcome, dry warmth seeping into his skin. His nostrils filled with a pleasant, herbal aroma that filled him with a feeling of calmness. He held his crystal tightly against his chest, surprised that he had managed to find such a precious object strewn upon the lakebed. Back on Gordanelle, crystals, let alone gems, were exceedingly rare and only known to come from Iberwight. Here in Tiriyuud, they seemed more than plentiful. Lleidas walked with Darshima toward the tents, periodically looking over his shoulder toward the beach.

"You may return to the camp. I must retrieve the other recruits." He bowed politely, then jogged back to the shore.

Darshima trudged toward the camp, his strength steadily returning. He looked behind him and saw several other recruits walking away from the shore, receiving blankets from Seibu and Lleidas. His ears filled with the chatter of their distant voices and the crackle of the bonfire. As he stepped into the camp, he heard footsteps behind him. Darshima turned around to see Erethalie and Sydarias, damp and shivering, clinging to their blankets with one hand and gleaming gems with the other.

"There you are." Erethalie moved closer, gently nudging Darshima's shoulder with her own.

"You swam so fast," exclaimed Sydarias, looking at Darshima in amazement.

"I didn't even realize." Darshima shook his head in surprise. Several more recruits had arrived at the camp and followed them to the bonfire.

"You were the first one out of the water." A look of incredulity spread upon Erethalie's face. She pointed to the circle of empty spaces before them. Eikan stood beside the fire and offered them all a curt nod.

"Well done, recruits. Gather around and warm yourselves by the fire. Please wait for the rest of your cohort." She gestured to the circle of mats, and the recruits took their seats.

As Darshima sat between Erethalie and Sydarias, his thoughts cleared, and his stomach twisted in a knot of nervousness.

"Did either of you see Khydius?" Darshima looked over his shoulder toward the shore. He could make out the silhouettes of Seibu and Lleidas helping a pair of recruits as they emerged from the lake.

"I saw him swimming but lost sight of him after I grabbed my crystal." Erethalie held a glittering opal in her palms, her brow wrinkled with worry.

"I'm sure he'll be fine." Sydarias drummed his fingers against a gleaming onyx resting in his lap. "He was swimming much deeper than either of us, but he seemed sure of where he was going."

"I'm worried about him," said Darshima. "I hope he completes this task."

"Have faith in him, Darshima. There's a certain strength to the prince that we don't fully appreciate." Erethalie rested her hand upon Darshima's shoulder.

"You're right." Darshima nodded hesitantly.

Lost in his thoughts, Darshima sat beside Erethalie and Sydarias. The heat from the flames dried his uniform and chased away the cold. The day wore on, and the afternoon sun rays penetrated the veil of clouds, casting a muted light over the camp. Eikan settled upon her mat, her gaze drifting periodically between the recruits and the shoreline. Darshima eyed the ruby perched upon his knee. Its facets caught the firelight in a shimmer, and the crystal seemed to glow from within its lattice. Images of the watery lakebed replayed before his eyes. He strained to remember where he had lost Khydius. Darshima wished he would've been able to help him, but he had done all that he was allowed. He shook his head and tried to push aside his worries. Like everyone else, Khydius would have to find a way to succeed.

The thud of footsteps rose over the crackle of the fire, and Darshima glimpsed over his shoulder. He narrowed his eyes against the bright snowdrifts and saw the last recruits leaving the shore, escorted by Seibu and Lleidas. Darshima breathed a sigh of relief as he recognized Khydius' silhouette among the group. Darshima jumped to his feet and ran toward them. Sydarias and Erethalie followed closely behind him.

"You did it, Khydius!" exclaimed Erethalie.

"You all seem surprised." Shivering in his damp clothes, Khydius clung to his blanket. A wry smile crossed his lips, momentarily chasing his exhausted expression.

"I'm glad you succeeded." Darshima nudged Khydius' shoulder.

"You swam so much deeper than the rest of us. I'm curious what you found." Sydarias pointed toward Khydius' right hand, hidden by the blanket.

"I can't explain why I felt drawn to those depths. I've never swum harder in my life." Panting, Khydius shifted the blanket from his shoulders. He opened his hand and produced a brilliant, almost perfectly cut diamond whose facets gleamed in the sunlight. "This is the stone that called out to me."

"A diamond, the same as your chart stone." Darshima's eyes widened in astonishment. He imagined that Khydius experienced the same emotion that he had felt when he found the ruby buried in the sediment.

"I felt a strong urge to take this particular stone." Erethalie showed Khydius her opal.

"What a rare find." Khydius' eyes widened at the glittering object.

"Perhaps this place is influencing us non-Omystikai." A cautious smile spread upon Sydarias' lips as he hefted his onyx.

"I believe it," said Darshima as Tenrai's words echoed in his mind. Tenrai had mentioned that gemstones reflected a person's inner spirit. He imagined Eikan intended for them to find the stone that suited each of them.

"It's getting late. Let's rejoin the others." Erethalie pointed toward the circle of tents and the bonfire, their shadows growing longer against the darkening skies. Darshima, Sydarias, and Khydius followed her back to the camp. As he walked, Darshima tried to focus his swirling thoughts. He felt both thankful and relieved that Erethalie and Sydarias were finding a special connection to this place.

Darshima and his companions entered the camp to the cheers of their fellow recruits. They took their places around the fire and settled upon their mats. A steady shower of snow drifted from the twilight sky. Despite their exhaustion, the recruits enthusiastically held their gemstones, proudly showing them to each other. They warmed themselves amid the flame, and the assistants passed around their dinner trays.

As the recruits ate their dinner, Eikan stood up from her seat and faced them. Seibu and Lleidas joined her.

"Tonight marks the end of your initial training with us. Congratulations to you all." She bowed toward the group. "Tomorrow, you will go on to train at your respective temples with other guardians, but always remember what you've accomplished here." The recruits responded with a round of applause and began to eat. Eikan and her fellow guardians resumed their seats and joined in the meal.

His stomach growling with hunger, Darshima ate a spoonful of the roasted grains and savory, dried roots. As he sipped some tea from his canteen, he felt Khydius tap his shoulder.

"I feel as though something has changed within me. That dive into the lake was unlike anything I've ever done." Khydius bowed his head." Thank you for encouraging me."

"I will always be here for you." Darshima wrapped his arm around Khydius' shoulder. His heart thudded with a pang of empathy mixed with relief at Khydius' revelation.

"You two are finally becoming more like brothers." Erethalie looked toward them, her eyes glittering in the firelight. "I'm glad."

"Indeed we are." Khydius turned toward Darshima, his eyebrows raised in surprise.

"I'm honored to know both of you." A smile crept across Sydarias' lips.

Overcome by their words, Darshima offered a hasty nod. His heart rose into his throat as the emotion of the day finally hit him. He was beginning to see himself as Khydius' older brother and not merely one of his subjects. Darshima's thoughts drifted back to his memories of Gordanelle, and an image of Sasha flashed before his eyes. Darshima had learned many things from his adoptive older brother, who had always been there for him. Now that they were apart, Darshima truly understood why Sasha had done so much for him when they were younger.

Darshima closed his eyes for a moment and drew in a breath, thankful for the bittersweet memory. He finished his meal in silence, listening to

Khydius, Erethalie, and Sydarias as they spoke with the other recruits in their expanding Tiriyuusian vocabulary. The sun dipped below the horizon, its rays glittering upon the waters of the lake. Darshima eyed the ruby in his palm, its gleaming red surface covered in a delicate layer of snow. A smile formed upon his lips as its meaning settled within him. He would always be thankful for this day.

Chapter 12

Darshima huddled beside Khydius, Erethalie, and Sydarias. They stood upon the temple veranda beneath the tiled eaves of a wooden peristyle. His thoughts drifting, he peered over the railing toward the center of the sunken, treelined octagonal courtyard. Yesterday evening, Darshima and his fellow recruits bid farewell to Eikan, Seibu, and Lleidas. Though he had felt a pang of sadness at departing the camp, Darshima knew they all would meet again during the final test of their skill.

Before dawn, Darshima, his companions, and their fellow recruits set out from the beach and went their separate ways. They marched through the forested interior of the island in the direction of their assigned temples. Darshima, Erethalie, Khydius, and Sydarias trekked upon the steep snowy paths and arrived at their temple with the early morning sun. Nestled against a rugged foothill, they found Tenrai and Dydan waiting for them beneath its stately, sloping eaves.

Tenrai and Dydan had given them only a moment to settle into their quarters before bringing them back to the veranda. Darshima looked toward the center of the courtyard, where Tenrai and Dydan faced each other, their gazes hardened beneath the grey skies. Their boots nearly touching, they stood within the confines of a gleaming golden ring inscribed in the smooth black stone. The symbol marked the structural center of the temple, represented its spiritual heart, and served as a sparring ring.

His eyes narrowed, Tenrai glared at Dydan. Standing a handbreadth shorter than Tenrai, Dydan looked at Tenrai with an equally intense stare. A powdery layer of snow coated their black uniforms as they stood poised. A temple priest emerged from the shadows of the courtyard and approached the edge of the circle. Her pale face drawn in a reserved expression, she exchanged gazes with the two men. The priest's stiff black robes, embroidered with gold and blue geometric patterns and wide, structured sleeves, rippled in the gusts. Wielding a carved wooden staff in her left hand, she walked steadily upon the gleaming pavement. A fine coating of falling snow dusted her shiny, grey-streaked black hair, fashioned in a long tail. She held a golden fan in her right hand, and with a flick of the wrist, its filigreed blades clacked open into a gleaming semicircle.

The priest entered the ring and then recited a customary prayer, her clear voice resounding through the courtyard. Then, in a sudden sweeping motion, the priest brought the fan downward, slicing the chilly air between Tenrai and Dydan. She stepped away from them and waited outside the ring. Darshima looked at Tenrai and Dydan, wondering how long it had been since either of them had sparred. As they moved around the ring, he saw their reflexes, cultivated through years of training and experience, instinctively take over.

Dydan made the first move and launched his fists toward Tenrai's chest. Tenrai sidestepped his maneuver, then blocked Dydan with his forearm. Dydan leaped sideways as Tenrai's right fist shot toward his head, then shifted his weight to his back foot. The pair traded forceful jabs, methodically blocking each other's moves. They shadowed each other around the circle, demonstrating a dizzying array of complex punches, blocks, and kicks. As they moved, the priest walked around the edge of the gilded ring and observed their moves. She rhythmically tapped her staff against the pavement, its sharp notes echoing throughout the courtyard.

Darshima watched the pair as they glided through a familiar yet complex range of maneuvers he was still trying to perfect. The accumulating snow sloughed from their uniforms as they completed the opening stances of their match. Though impressed, Darshima realized that it was merely a warm-up routine to loosen their muscles and stave off the cold. The actual match had yet to begin.

Tenrai and Dydan circled each other, and their combinations of moves grew more forceful. The pair landed their punches and kicks with increasing frequency. They took turns falling to the ground, their limbs striking with an audible, exaggerated thud. The match escalated in intensity as the duo moved with a combination of speed, grace, and agility. Darshima drew in an astonished breath when he realized their moves had transitioned from the direct strength of their limbs to the energies of eneri-kai. They stalked each other around the ring, striking their blows from a distance. Though Darshima had seen glimpses of Tenrai's abilities before coming to Iberwight, it was his first time witnessing them in such a full, unrestrained display.

Tenrai deflected Dydan's volley of punches and kicks with a simple flash of his palms. Though Tenrai had the upper hand in the match, Dydan's skills were formidable. Dydan thrust his fists forward, and Tenrai flew violently backward as if knocked over by a powerful gust of wind. They challenged each other, trading forceful blows, falling and rolling back onto their feet. They darted about the ring with such speed that Darshima had difficulty distinguishing their individual forms.

The match culminated when Tenrai seized complete control over Dydan with the unseen strength. Tenrai raised his right palm toward the sky, and Dydan floated high above his head, suspended as if he were a leaf caught in a vortex. With a deft flick of his wrist, Tenrai hurled Dydan out of the ring. Limbs flailing, Dydan soared across the courtyard, then landed onto the ground with a thud. He skidded along the snowy pavement, then came to a stop at the veranda. Darshima and his companions looked on in astonishment.

Tenrai and the priest hurried over to meet Dydan, but he leaped to his feet before they arrived. Dydan and Tenrai stood face to face and offered each other a deep bow.

"It is done. Guardian Nax, Sage Waike, go in peace." The priest offered them a formal bow and spoke in Vilidesian. She clacked the blades of her fan once more and issued a chant in the Tiriyuusian dialect.

"Priest Ikarsu Dawn, we thank you," said Tenrai.

"Thank you for observing us, Priest Dawn," added Dydan. Tenrai and Dydan bowed deeply toward her and then toward each other.

"You both have a significant task before you. You must teach these four well." She stared at Darshima and his companions for a moment, her serious expression softening some. She then stepped away from the circle and crossed the courtyard. Tenrai and Dydan looked on as she merged back into the shadows beneath the eaves.

"Are you okay?" Tenrai turned to Dydan. He reached over and gently dusted the snowflakes from Dydan's shoulders.

"I am fine, Tenrai." Dydan clenched his jaw, his face flushed.

"I didn't intend for you to fall so hard." Tenrai's brow wrinkled in concern.

"I'm sure most guardians would enjoy the chance to throw a sage around from time to time." Dydan shook his head, the flakes of snow falling from the locks of his hair.

"Certainly not." Tenrai reflexively bowed his head in deference. "I respect your rank and your previous service as a guardian."

"You're a talented fighter, but don't forget, I am still a sage." Dydan's serious expression softened some. "If I return bruised and battered to the temple, you will have to answer to the seer." A soft chuckle escaped his lips.

"I see that all of the meditating in the temple has dampened some of your reflexes." Tenrai's eyebrows arched in surprise.

"I can assure you the talents that matter for my purposes as a sage are perfectly intact." Dydan's lips wrinkled in a slight frown.

"I'm sure you could pray circles around me." Tenrai rested his arm upon Dydan's shoulder.

"I always have." Dydan playfully rolled his eyes. They both shared a laugh, then departed the courtyard. Tenrai followed Dydan up the narrow wooden stairway leading to the veranda.

Darshima drew his uniform against his shivering frame as he watched them approach. The snow showers had lessened, but the temperature had fallen.

"Unbelievable." Sydarias' eyes widened in surprise. "How was any of that possible?"

"Sage Waike and I will help you perfect your stances. Someday soon, you will be ready to spar as we did." Tenrai gestured toward the courtyard.

"How would it even be possible for people like us to make someone levitate with the wave of a hand?" Erethalie folded her arms across her chest. She turned to Tenrai, a look of incredulity spreading upon her face. "We're not Omystikai."

"As you witnessed, it is not impossible." Dydan turned toward her, his eyes glimmering with a hint of reassurance. "There is no difference between us." He pointed to her and then to himself. "You will learn that heritage has little to do with our abilities."

"Think of all that you four have accomplished thus far." Tenrai offered them a reassuring nod. "You may not realize it, but each day, your training brings you closer to achieving what you saw in the ring and so much more."

"I want to understand, but your art seems to defy the known laws of physics." Erethalie shook her head in disbelief.

"Much of what guides our world remains unseen." Dydan cast his gaze toward the sky. "There are physical forces beyond our comprehension, more complex than any known laws described by the Vilidesian scholars. These forces influence and interact with all natural phenomena, whether it is the orbit of our moon, the precession of Benai, or the sacred energies that give life to humans and other beings." Dydan turned to Erethalie. "Kai, or the sovereign strength, permeates everything. Sensing, understanding, and interacting with kai is the essence of our art."

As Darshima listened, his mind raced back to the slave colony on Navervyne. An image of Sydarias bound in chains falling, then floating toward him, flashed before his eyes. His throat tightened at the memory, and it dissolved into the falling snowflakes beyond the veranda. He wondered if he had found a way to interact with one of the mysterious forces Dydan described during that harrowing moment.

"I'll do whatever it takes to learn. Please teach me." Sydarias bowed toward Tenrai and Dydan.

"It is our duty to teach you all." Dydan rested his hand upon Sydarias' shoulder.

"When you are done training, you will look back on this day and remember our sparring match as an unremarkable occurrence." An earnest smile formed upon Tenrai's lips.

Tenrai and Dydan guided Darshima and his companions away from the veranda toward an entrance along the peristyle. Tenrai slid open a wooden doorway, and they stepped across the threshold. Darshima drew in a breath as they reentered the warmth of the temple, his nostrils filling with the pungent fragrances of smoke and incense. Tenrai led them through a shadowy corridor and up a staircase. They walked past the doorway marking their living quarters. Much to Darshima's surprise, when they had arrived there earlier that morning, its layout was strikingly similar to their accommodations back in Chryshaihem. They followed Tenrai and Dydan toward the end of the dim, torchlit hallway,

Tenrai slid open another wooden door and ushered them into a square room. Sturdy bookcases lined its walls, and they contained numerous rows of leather-bound tomes. An oval, granite hearth sat at the center of the room, aglow with flame. They removed their boots and overcoats and placed them by the door. Tenrai led them across the dark wooden floorboards toward an array of windows that gave a sweeping view of the courtyard. Darshima gazed out upon the glistening pavers, arranged in a radial, tessellated pattern. The temple roof's wooden eaves and ceramic tiles were coated in a thick layer of snow and had a faded appearance under the falling flakes.

"Please make yourselves comfortable." Dydan gestured to the circle of woven rugs arranged around the flickering hearth. He and Tenrai settled beside each other, their backs facing the window. Darshima, Khydius, Erethalie, and Sydarias sat across from them.

"How are you all finding your accommodations thus far?" asked Dydan.

"Our rooms are comfortable." Sydarias nodded politely.

"It is an improvement over sleeping on the beach," said Khydius.

"I enjoyed camping outdoors with our fellow recruits." Erethalie cast a furtive glance toward Khydius. "It was a good experience."

"This temple is ours to use for the remainder of your training." Tenrai's gaze wandered around the room.

"I like it here." Darshima loosened his collar amid the warmth of the flames, his heartbeat slowing with a sense of peace.

"Guardians and other members of the Order have been studying here for more than fifteen centuries." Tenrai looked around the space. "Sage Waike and I trained here together with many other talented people."

Dydan's eyes narrowed in a wistful expression at Tenrai's words. Darshima looked through the window toward the courtyard, his gaze lingering upon the golden sparring ring. He tried to imagine the unique souls that had passed through this temple over the ages, honing their skills upon that hallowed circle.

Today marked the beginning of the second half of their training as guardians. After what he witnessed in the courtyard, Darshima was eager to learn. He would be happy to demonstrate even a fraction of Tenrai and Dydan's skill.

"We will devote this morning's session to the philosophy of eneri-kai," began Dydan.

"I've never witnessed such a martial art. Will you be teaching us how to call upon the forces you and Tenrai used during your sparring match?" Erethalie pointed toward the courtyard.

"Eneri-kai is more than a martial art. It is a quintessential part of our body of knowledge." Dydan turned toward her.

"So it's both a system of knowledge and a fighting style?" Darshima shook his head in confusion.

"How is it different than the Vilidesian martial arts?" asked Sydarias, idly massaging his knuckles. A smile crossed Darshima's lips as he remembered Sydarias bravely fighting the Navervynish soldiers after their capture. He imagined Sydarias would learn eneri-kai faster than all of them.

"Though the Vilidesians are skilled fighters, eneri-kai is more than simply a fighting style." Tenrai's brow furrowed in a pensive expression. "It is a means of enlightenment and protection. One can use it to guard the body, mind, and the spirit."

"Our ancestors developed this way of life ages ago on Ciblaithia, and we practice it here in Tiriyuud," added Dydan.

"How is it any different from the teachings of the other Omystikai orders?" Khydius folded his arms across his chest, his brow furrowing in a doubtful expression.

"Tiriyuud is the source of all Omystikai heritage here on Iberwight. All other Orders derived the modern interpretation of their faith, culture, and way of life from our ancestors, who were first exiled upon these islands." Dydan turned to Khydius. "Every tradition, every ritual you witnessed your Omystikai counselors perform in the imperial court had their origin here, among the exiles."

"I understand," said Khydius, a contemplative frown forming upon his lips.

As Dydan explained, eneri-kai was an ancient art whose exact origins were shrouded in secrecy. Generations of Tiriyuusian philosophers had contemplated how to characterize Kai and gain influence over it. They were the ones who cultivated eneri-kai over the ages.

"After their exile on Iberwight, our ancestors guarded our most sacred records, which were transcribed and kept in Chryshaihem." Dydan rose to his feet, walked to the shelves behind him, and grabbed a book. He sat down beside Tenrai and rested it upon his knee.

"What is that?" Darshima pointed to the tome, his eyes lingering upon the rows of gleaming, golden symbols embossed upon its leather cover.

"This is what we call the ophon eneri-kai. It is a canonical text and a treatise on the sovereign strength. One day, you all will know its most important passages by memory." Dydan's fingers caressed the symbols. The morning sun grew brighter, and Darshima sat rapt as Dydan introduced the text to them.

Tiriyuusian scripture proclaimed that the first humans arose from the same dust that coalesced to form the sun, its lone planet Benai, and its many moons. The sovereign strength, or kai, that created these celestial bodies had also created sentient beings imbued with judgment, wisdom, power, and language. These were the first Omystikai to have ever lived. Kai moved like a ceaseless, unseen wind throughout all of existence. It had the power to create and to destroy, to bring life and to take it away.

Despite these gifts, the Omystikai were only human. As vulnerable creatures of flesh and bone, they sought a suitable home where they would not only survive but create civilization. These first Omystikai set about exploring the heavens, sojourning amongst Benai and its moons in pursuit of a home. Unsuccessful in their attempt to find a suitable refuge on an existing moon, they decided to create one of their own.

The Omystikai set about using kai to fashion a unique world to suit their needs. With the might of their collective strength, they willed into creation a new moon. It was dry and warm to stave off the cold, damp void from which all of existence had come. Steadily, the remnants of cosmic dust coalesced into an arid golden orb that they named Ciblaithia.

"I've heard a fable similar to this," whispered Erethalie. "It's why Ciblaithia is so sacred to the Omystikai."

"This is what we believe to be true," replied Dydan.

"How could a people fashion a moon with only their collective will?" Darshima shook his head in disbelief.

"I thought our universe arose from some cataclysmic, primordial explosion, from which all matter and energy were derived." Sydarias shrugged.

"You're referencing the Vilidesian explanation for the origin of the universe. It is a sophisticated but incomplete attempt at understanding the truth," replied Tenrai.

"All of the Omystikai orders believe this founding fable." Khydius steepled his fingers.

"Maybe there is something to it," mused Darshima. So many things he had learned as a child had proven to be false. The Navervynish conquest of the realm had demonstrated they were not alone in the universe. The Vilidesians weren't the supreme arbiters of knowledge, wealth, and power, as he had once believed.

"The Vilidesians explained matter, energy, and life in a very eloquent manner. However, their postulates and physical laws can not truly tell you how they relate to one another. This text, among others, will." Dydan drummed his fingers against the volume.

"We want to understand," said Erethalie. Darshima and the others nodded in unison, and Dydan continued.

Though the Omystikai had succeeded in creating a home for themselves, they were unable to create a world with life, as the sovereign strength had done for Benai and its other moons. In its infinite wisdom, kai had changed these worlds, bringing life, seasons, and even other humans that established their own civilizations.

Fearing that their home would remain barren, the Omystikai ceded some of their control and allowed kai to fashion the details of their world. The sovereign strength flooded the valleys of arid golden sand with blue oceans. It populated Ciblaithia with creatures of the air, land, and sea and vegetation to sustain them. It imbued Ciblaithia with natural forces such as weather, which allowed it to renew gradually over the ages.

The Omystikai flourished on Ciblaithia and established several renowned civilizations. However, as the sovereign strength changed Ciblaithia, raising the seas and shifting the dunes, the Omystikai realized they were losing their ability to control it. Their influence over inanimate matter, the much-coveted power their ancestors used to create Ciblaithia, was fading. They were left only with the ability to sense kai. They could deflect and channel its flow, and they could also use it to influence living things. They also could use the sovereign strength to see into the future.

Fearful of this loss of power, the Omystikai focused their studies on mastering the full extent of their remaining abilities. As civilizations rose and fell on Ciblaithia, the Omystikai passed this art from one generation to the next. Over the ages of exile on Iberwight, the Omystikai residing in the realm's dominions beyond Tiriyuud eventually lost their abilities to physically influence living things. They, however, retained the ability to peer into the future. The Tiriyuusians continued to study their art, honing it over the centuries.

Chapter 13

Darshima drew in a halting breath and locked eyes with Tenrai, who returned his stare with a vivid, glowing gaze. His right hand outstretched, Darshima moved around the sparring ring. Tenrai extended his hand in a similar gesture as he shadowed Darshima. The chilly evening winds whipped through their uniforms. A heavy shower of snow fell from the cloudy skies, accumulating upon the eaves of the temple. Pairs of large cast-iron torches spaced around the courtyard's perimeter flickered with a soft, yellow flame, illuminating the darkness. Darshima glimpsed over his shoulder and saw Erethalie, Sydarias, and Khydius perched upon the veranda, watching him intently.

Priest Dawn sat upon a wooden stool perched at the edge of the sparring circle. Darshima caught her stern gaze as she followed his moves. She drummed her wooden staff against the pavement, filling the air with a sharp, staccato sound. Flakes of snow layered upon the creases of her black and gold robes, sloughing off as she kept rhythm. Dydan stood beside her, his blue cape fluttering around him. Darshima shuddered at his intense stare.

As Darshima turned back to Tenrai, he felt an overwhelming force seize his legs. His gaze shot downward, and he saw nothing but his creased trousers. Darshima looked up at Tenrai, who extended both of his hands toward him. Tenrai flashed his palms, then made a subtle pushing motion. Darshima's boots scraped against the pavement as the force pushed him out of the ring. Tenrai lifted his hands above his head, and Darshima felt his feet lose contact with the ground as he floated upward. He drew in a breath, then let out a grunt as he struggled to break free from Tenrai's spectral grip. Darshima's limbs flailed as he tried to reach for the ground. His heart pounding with a mixture of exhaustion and frustration, Darshima let himself go limp. Enveloped by the gusts of wind, he felt as if he were adrift.

Darshima drew in an anxious breath as he floated even higher above the eaves of the temple. His chest tightened when he realized how far above the ground he was. Darshima looked toward the sky, squinting against the flakes of swirling snow. Benai's halo of rings shimmered through a thin veil of clouds.

"You are losing your focus," said Tenrai, his voice echoing in Darshima's ears.

"I don't know what to do." A strained sigh escaped Darshima's lips. Without warning, he felt the force weaken its grip around him. He plummeted down through the snow showers and landed upon his feet with a thud. Darshima faced Tenrai. He bit his lip as he tried to hold back his disappointment.

"I can feel your strength, but you must try harder." Tenrai rested his hands upon Darshima's shoulders.

"What am I doing wrong?" Darshima panted, shaking his head.

"The strength you need dwells within you. You must learn to use it." Tenrai gently tapped Darshima's chest with his index finger.

"You must focus all your attention within the ring." Dydan pointed toward the golden circle.

"Try again, Darshima." Priest Dawn tapped her staff against the pavement.

"You can do it," said Sydarias, his voice echoing across the courtyard. Erethalie and Khydius clapped loudly in support.

"You three must pay attention. Your skills will soon be put to the test." Dydan glanced over his shoulder at them, his frown lessening some.

"Focus on me." Tenrai beckoned with a wave of his hand.

"Begin." Priest Dawn struck the ground with her staff, and Darshima snapped his head toward the center of the ring.

His hands outstretched, Darshima moved around the circle. He narrowed his eyes in concentration as he looked at Tenrai's form, trying to sense a potential opening. Darshima drew in a breath and exhaled slowly. He willed himself to conjure the same energetic burst that Tenrai had used to lift him off the ground.

Without warning, Tenrai leaped toward him. Darshima's heart thudded in surprise, and his fingers tingled with electricity at the sudden motion. As Tenrai was about to tackle him, Darshima swiftly ducked past him. He spun on his heels and faced Tenrai. His hand extended, he felt a surge of energy build within him, then dissipate in a jolt of force that whipped the snowflakes into a fierce gale. Tenrai charged forward as the sovereign strength momentarily seized him.

"Try harder." Tenrai let out a grunt as he sprinted through what seemed like an invisible wall. Tenrai darted across the ring in a burst of speed and then tackled Darshima, who landed upon the ground with a painful thud.

Darshima looked up at the clouds and struggled to catch his breath. Tenrai loomed over him and extended his arm. Darshima gripped his uncle's hand and pulled himself off the ground. His muscles aching, Darshima stood hunched over, with his hands upon his knees.

"I felt your strength coming through, but you must focus even harder." Tenrai gently squeezed Darshima's shoulder.

"This is tough," said Darshima, his chest heaving.

"I'm your uncle, but also your teacher. I must be tough on you." Tenrai's eyes glimmered with concern.

"I don't know what else I can do." Darshima shook his head, his eyes growing damp. He felt mired in his frustration.

"We shall pause for a moment," said Priest Dawn. Darshima looked beyond the ring and saw her and Dydan in the midst of a conversation. She beckoned Tenrai, and he joined them. Darshima listened as they spoke and tried to understand their hushed dialogue. His pulse thudding with a mixture of exhaustion and anxiety, he glared at the sparring ring. The gleaming circle reminded him how drastically his life had changed and how much he still had to learn.

Darshima, Erethalie, Sydarias, and Khydius had been at this stage of their training for more than three weeks. They spent most of their days sparring in the courtyard and building their strength by taking turns with Tenrai and Dydan. Much to their astonishment, they made tangible progress every day, accomplishing feats that would have been unimaginable months ago. As Dydan had predicted, they each demonstrated an innate ability to channel and deflect the sovereign strength.

As the weeks wore on, their sparring matches grew more intense and required more skill. Priest Dawn observed each of them and offered her critique, occasionally stepping into the ring to help them with their form. Sydarias and Erethalie had grown more capable in their technique. They could slow down and even push an opponent out of the ring with a mere hand gesture. Khydius had demonstrated enough strength to make an opponent briefly levitate above him.

Darshima also had accomplished similar feats, but he felt the weight of expectation upon him. During their first meeting, Tenrai had told him about the unique strength that dwelled within him. At times Darshima could feel it, but he didn't how to harness it. His thoughts drifted back to the slave colony on Navervyne, and the factory in Stebbenhour, when it had burst forth in a powerful and uncontrolled fashion. Back then, Tenrai had promised to teach him how to control this energy when they reached Iberwight. Now here he was on this frozen moon, struggling to learn. His chest tightened with despair as he thought of how much progress he had yet to make. As he looked at the snowflakes falling around him, feelings of doubt crept into his mind. Maybe he wouldn't be able to achieve what Tenrai saw in him.

His feelings weighing upon him, Darshima threw up his hands and let out an exasperated sigh. As he stepped out of the circle, Dydan called out to him.

"Please, stay." Dydan pointed toward the ring.

"Why should I?" asked Darshima, his voice trembling. "I don't believe I can do this." As Tenrai opened his mouth to respond, Priest Dawn raised her hand. Tenrai pursed his lips and bowed his head.

"You appear frustrated, Darshima." She turned to him.

"I don't know what else I can do. I'm trying, but I cannot gain control of whatever this strength is." Darshima tapped his foot impatiently.

"You let your doubts get in your way." She rose from her seat and approached Darshima, her staff tapping rhythmically against the ground.

"I don't know how to move past them," said Darshima. His heart thudded as she stood at the edge of the circle. He felt as if there was something more than self-doubt holding him back.

"Kai moves like a raging and unpredictable sea. You must learn to be like the skilled mariner who navigates it." Priest Dawn peered into his eyes, seeking a hint of understanding. Darshima's mind drifted back to his upbringing back on Gordanelle. An image of the uniformed mariners navigating the Eophasian River came back to him.

"How can I navigate currents that I cannot see?" Darshima shook his head in confusion.

"Mere eyesight will not help you. Though you do not realize it, you and your companions are developing a different sort of vision. It is a vision that comes from within." She pointed toward Darshima's chest.

"I feel something, but I don't know how to use it." Darshima clenched his jaw, recalling the sensation of electricity zipping through his fingers.

"Let me show you." She beheld him, her sapphire eyes glowing with stark intensity. She stepped into the ring and held her staff out in front of her. She proceeded to whisper a string of Omystikaiyn phrases. Darshima understood it to be an incantation summoning eneri-kai. Her dialogue then transitioned into Vilidesian.

"May we see, if for a moment, all that flows from within, all that ebbs from without, and all that permeates from beyond." With a swift motion, she struck the golden circle with her staff. The courtyard echoed with a thunderous clap that seemed to shake the ground beneath them. Darshima's entire body vibrated with the deafening sound of an unseen bell. He raised his hands to his ears, and his vision suddenly went dark. It was as if a curtain had fallen before his eyes.

"What's happening?" Darshima blinked frantically, groping the space around him. His sight gradually returned, but everything appeared starkly different. Gossamer veils of shadow shrouded the temple, and he could only make out the silhouette of the courtyard, its peristyle, and the eaves. The surrounding pairs of torches flickered with a ghostly, blue flame.

Darshima looked toward the golden ring surrounding him, which glowed with a brilliance that rivaled the sun. He looked around but no longer saw Tenrai, Dydan, or Priest Dawn. He felt the cold flakes of snow strike his face but could not see them. He looked up and saw no clouds. Instead, Benai and the other moons shone brightly against the vast sky of glittering stars.

"Where am I?" asked Darshima, too frightened to move.

"You are safe, Darshima." Priest Dawn materialized from the darkness and stood at the opposite edge of the sparring ring. The gold embroidery upon her robes glowed with the same iridescence as the ring. She stared at Darshima, an earnest expression spreading upon her face.

"What is this place?" Darshima looked around them, his pulse thudding.

"We are where we have always been, at the temple. I want you to focus your thoughts, so I have temporarily removed all distractions."

"Tenrai did something like this before, but how?" Darshima shook his head in confusion, remembering when Tenrai helped him recall the dream that led him to Khydius and Sasha.

"Look around you, and you will see what we are meant to feel." Priest Dawn gestured toward the sky. Darshima craned his neck upward and peered into the darkness. Amid the stars, he saw what appeared to be infinite showers of silver, gold, and blue sparks. They descended in glowing streaks like comet tails, illuminating the entire sky. The multicolored pinpoints of light flowed in swift currents below the clouds, coming toward him in waves. They washed over him, swirling in eddies, seemingly rising and falling from a place beyond the stars. Darshima looked directly above him, and the points of light merged into a fearsome, glowing cyclone.

"What is happening?" Astonished, Darshima threw his hands over his head. The rotating showers of sparks descended around him in a scintillating, helical veil. They exploded in blinding, silent flashes of light as they dissolved into the golden sparring ring. His skin tingled with the same electricity he had felt on that day when he had saved Sydarias from death. It was the same jolt he felt when he confronted the Navervynish troops during their escape from Stebbenhour.

"I can feel your spirit struggling to make sense of kai," said Priest Dawn. She tapped her staff once again upon the circle. Another shower of sparks fell from the sky and hung about her shoulders like a glowing cloak.

"I don't believe what I'm seeing," murmured Darshima. Out of the corner of his eye, Tenrai and Dydan came into view, and swirls of glittering sparks surrounded them. Darshima looked over his shoulder and saw, Erethalie, Khydius, and Sydarias standing upon the veranda, gazing at him. Waves of the curious light flowed around each of them in a luminous display.

"Kai has been around since the beginning, and it will be with us until the end. It has always been a part of our universe," said Priest Dawn. "As living creatures, we are merely its conduits." The priest extended her staff toward Darshima, lightly tapping his right arm. Darshima drew in a sharp breath as a current of sparks flowed from his fingertips in a myriad of colors before dissolving into thin air.

"Now, set your thoughts on your abilities. Think of how they influence our surroundings." She gestured around them.

"What do you mean?" Darshima shrugged.

"There are two types of kai. Tiriyuusians of the Order of the Gilded Moon are taught the ability to control the kai that flows through living beings." Priest Dawn gestured toward Tenrai and Dydan. Streams of silver and gold sparks flowed through them, subtly deflecting as she moved her hand. "This ability is uniquely heightened in you, Darshima." She turned back toward him. "You have the rare ability to control the type of kai that flows through inanimate matter." She again pointed toward his hand. Darshima noted a preponderance of blue light flowing amidst the sparks of silver and gold. "This ability has not shown itself in a Tiriyuusian for several thousand years. It is the gift of our ancestors, who used it to create Ciblaithia." Darshima looked toward his hand and saw the multicolored sparks swirling around his forearm, coursing through his fingertips and radiating from his markings. He shivered as he felt jolts of electricity travel through his arm and dissipate through his entire body.

Darshima's mind raced back to the factory in Stebbenhour when he miraculously broke the shackles upon Khydius' and Sasha's feet. His heart rose into his throat as he thought of his anguish in those moments and his incredulity when he defied the known physical laws to free them.

"Tap into those memories and those feelings, Darshima," said Priest Dawn.

"The part of your spirit that overcame despair in those seemingly hopeless moments is your gift. It is how you control kai." She briefly rested her fingertips upon his forehead, then stepped away.

"What can I do to control it?" asked Darshima.

"Free your mind, and let it see what is unseen. Unburden your thoughts, and let them guide the actions of the beings and objects around you," replied Priest Dawn. Before Darshima could ask any further questions, she tossed her staff toward him. It hurtled in his direction, a trail of blue sparks cascading from its filigreed edges. As Darshima instinctively reached out to catch it, a stream of glowing blue particles flowed from his fingertips and enveloped the staff. He gasped in astonishment as it floated in mid-air before him.

"Now, use your strength to send it back to me," she said. Darshima narrowed his eyes and willed himself to believe in the seeming impossibility of what he was seeing. He let himself imagine the staff floating back to Priest Dawn. He extended his hand, then made a pushing gesture. The glowing particles emanated from his hand and pushed against the staff. The object forcefully sailed back toward her. She seized the staff and held it out before her.

"Do not forget what your heart is feeling and what your mind is sensing in this moment. Your eyes may not believe what they are seeing, but trust your mind and your heart, for they know the truth." Priest Dawn leaned against her staff, waves of shimmering silver and gold particles enveloping her.

"I won't forget," said Darshima. His pulse thudded in bewilderment as he observed the phenomenon.

"Though this lesson is over, there are many more to learn." She raised her staff in an exaggerated motion, then firmly struck the pavement. The ground shook beneath their feet and hummed with the tone of a distant bell. Darshima blinked as the vibration coursed through him. When he opened his eyes, his vision returned to normal, and the swarms of particles were gone. He looked down at his hands and saw no flowing points of light. Astonished, he rubbed his eyes and looked around him. Everything appeared undisturbed, as it had before. Tenrai and Dydan stood outside of the ring, and Priest Dawn faced Darshima.

"Did you listen to Priest Dawn's advice?" asked Tenrai. "Tiriyuusian priests can see and feel things that most others cannot." He bowed his head toward her in reverence.

"She explained everything," replied Darshima. His heart pounded in his chest as he replayed the incredible experience in his mind.

"I will leave you to it, Darshima." A knowing smile spread upon Priest Dawn's lips, and she stepped outside of the ring. Darshima didn't know what had happened, but he felt something had changed within him.

"Shall we continue?" Tenrai stepped back into the sparring ring.

"I'm ready." His focus renewed, Darshima offered Tenrai a formal bow, then crouched into a defensive stance.

Chapter 14

Darshima looked out over the snow-covered hills, his eyes narrowing against the rays of the afternoon sun. Erethalie, Sydarias, and Khydius stood on either side of him, leaning against the balustrade framing the terrace behind the temple. They gazed out upon the undulating hills, which met the lakeshore in the distance. The clouds steadily dissipated, revealing patches of blue sky. The crisp air held the scent of charred wood and tree resin.

Darshima's eyes darted back and forth between two dark specks racing amid the snowdrifts. They performed an intricate dance upon the carpet of snow, leaving massive plumes of white flakes behind them. They skated back and forth, dashing along the hills, etching a complex pattern of trails as they chased after each other.

The paired specks grew larger as they rushed toward the temple, transforming from mere pinpoints into two human figures. Darshima lifted his hands to his brow, shielding his gaze from the sun. He made out the forms of Tenrai and Dydan, each perched upon a long, gleaming board shaped like a large dagger blade. The pair raced toward the terrace, their features becoming more evident. Tenrai glided past Dydan down a steep embankment in front of the temple. They rushed up a snowy hill before launching into the air in a dramatic flourish. Tenrai and Dydan performed a dizzying array of aerial twists, somersaults, and spins upon their boards. They climbed higher, gaining speed as they reached the top of their trajectory. Seemingly immune to the force of gravity, they vaulted upward into the sky and flew above the temple.

"How are they flying? Their boards have no sort of engines!" exclaimed Sydarias as he pointed toward their vanishing forms.

"I've never seen anything like it." Erethalie shook her head in disbelief.

"This must have something to do with the sovereign strength." Darshima looked on in amazement. He remembered Priest Dawn saying that the Tiriyuusians had lost the ability to influence inanimate matter. However, it seemed as if Tenrai and Dydan were using their boards to defy gravity.

"However they're doing it, it's a sort of technology that the Vilidesian aerial corps never had." A studied frown crossed Khydius' lips as he observed the spectacle. Darshima stood spellbound as he watched Tenrai and Dydan soar higher into the sky. They pierced through a thin layer of clouds, their forms again shrinking into two specks as they disappeared.

Tenrai and Dydan were demonstrating uniquely Tiriyuusian art of aizuuren or cloud-walking. It was an ancient practice that the Omystikai of Gilded Moon had developed not long after the separation of the Orders and the creation of the dominions on Iberwight. Aizuuren was practiced and had been perfected solely by the guardians who lived upon the Tiriyuusian archipelago.

Tenrai and Dydan sailed over the temple as if carried by a strong gust of wind. They flew over the terrace, the bottoms of their boards glistening with droplets of melting snow as they carved invisible, intertwining paths through the sky. Balancing precariously upon their boards, they raced each other, speeding toward the horizon, until they diminished into two tiny specs. Moments later, they turned back around in a wide arc and flew toward the temple.

They landed in front of the terrace, their boards kicking up showers of snow and ice as they glided to an effortless stop. Astounded by the display, Darshima and his companions burst into a round of applause. Tenrai and Dydan lifted the tinted glass visors from their black metal helmets and strapped their boards to their backs. They trekked over the snow, climbed the stairs up to the terrace, and rejoined the group.

"Do you have any questions?" asked Dydan as he dusted the snow from the shoulders of his uniform.

"I've never seen anything like it before," exclaimed Erethalie.

"Will we be able to fly like that?" asked Darshima, imagining himself perched upon a board, soaring through the skies.

"With enough strength and patience, you all will be able to navigate the kai fields that trained guardians use to fly upon their saigura." Tenrai pointed toward the hills.

"Don't forget the occasional sage who still remembers how to use a cloudboard." Dydan shook his head at Tenrai's remark and suppressed an annoyed grimace.

"Despite all your time in the Sages' Temple, you're still formidable, Dydan. I'm impressed." A genuine smile crossed Tenrai's lips.

"I remember more than you assume." Dydan's frown faded, and he chuckled to himself.

Tenrai ushered everyone from the terrace back into the temple. He closed the doors behind them, and the winds tempered into a soft drone. They followed Tenrai into a utility room toward a wooden cabinet. Darshima's eyes adjusted to the dim sunlight filtering through a frosted row of windows.

Tenrai slid open the cabinet doors and revealed a set of four cloudboards identical to their own. Standing shoulder high, the finely crafted, blade-like boards glinted a deep, metallic blue. A tapered edge of etched gold wrapped around each board's perimeter, glittering in the rays of light. Each center featured an engraved gold disk bearing an intricate cutout of an interlocking halo of eight crescents surrounding an eight-pointed, crystal blue star.

"What does that symbol mean?" Darshima pointed to the boards.

"It is both the emblem of Tiriyuud and the Order of the Gilded Moon," murmured Khydius.

Tenrai and Dydan reached into the cabinet and handed over the saigura. Darshima accepted his board from Tenrai and turned it over in his hands, astonished by its uncanny lightness and exquisite craftsmanship. He looked closely at the seal, and below it, noted a line of Tiriyuusian script that drew his attention. Since their arrival to the temple, Priest Dawn had taught them basic Omystikaiyn script and Tiriyuusian grammar. His heart skipped a beat when he recognized his name etched upon the board.

"These are our personal boards?" asked Darshima, his eyes widening in surprise.

"You have made this far in your training, and these boards belong to you now," said Tenrai. Darshima looked over at Erethalie, Sydarias, and Khydius, who examined their new cloudboards. Dydan opened an adjacent cabinet and fitted them each with a helmet.

"This will protect you against the sun and the snow." Dydan fastened the leather strap under Khydius' chin. Darshima and the others did the same and adjusted their helmets. As he slid the visor over his eyes, the blue crystal automatically brightened, and he was able to peer through the shadows of the room. A smile briefly crossed his lips, as he remembered wearing a similar visor those many months ago, when he and Sydarias explored the Omystikai ruins in the village of Pardesp, beyond the city limits of The Vilides.

With their boards tucked under their arms, Tenrai and Dydan ushered Darshima and his companions through the utility room, back onto the terrace. Darshima bounded down the stairs and onto the powdery snow.

"We will start with a simple exercise." Tenrai pointed to a nearby hill. They hiked up the incline, their boots crunching in the snow. Darshima looked at the surrounding hills and the nearby temple, his visor dimming against the sunlight. Tenrai and Dydan stood in front of them and placed their boards at their feet.

"Now, step carefully upon your cloudboards. We will review the basic maneuvers," said Tenrai. He and Dydan stepped upon their boards with one foot in front of the other, then lowered into a crouching stance. Darshima and his companions put their boards upon the snow and assumed a similar posture.

"It is important to sense the kai fields flowing around us. It's how we navigate the terrain and take to the skies," said Dydan.

Darshima gingerly stepped upon his board, half expecting it to slip from under his feet, but to his surprise, it held firm.

"Why isn't it sliding against the snow?" Darshima stared at the board in disbelief.

"Cloudboards are made of a rare metal that interacts with kai," explained Dydan.

"The sovereign force has a topography, not unlike these surrounding hills, and a direction, like the wind." Tenrai gestured around them. "You must learn to feel its strengths and variations."

Tenrai faced away from the temple. "Follow me, and I will guide you." He called out over his shoulder. Dydan positioned himself beside Tenrai, and they glided down the gentle slope. Darshima, Erethalie, Khydius, and Sydarias followed behind them, trying to remain upright upon their cloudboards.

Darshima held his arms out to his sides as he descended the slope. He stiffened his legs and back and tried to maintain his posture upon his board. The scenery moving swiftly beside him, Darshima focused on Tenrai and Dydan as they moved ahead of him. He shook his head in surprise as they skated effortlessly through the valley. He couldn't fully describe it, but the feeling of electricity he had grown accustomed to felt amplified as he moved upon the board. He sensed its pulsations more strongly in some parts of the terrain than others.

"Watch out!" shouted Erethalie. Sydarias let out a yelp, followed by a thud and the crunch of snow. Darshima looked behind him to see both of them upon the ground, peals of laughter escaping their lips. Darshima carefully angled sideways and drifted to a stop. Khydius slowed down beside him.

"This is harder than it looks," exclaimed Erethalie. She leaped to her feet, dusted the snow from her uniform, and stepped back upon her board. "I feel myself gliding upon the snow, but there's definitely something else propelling me along."

Sydarias shook his head as he stood up with his board, leaning against it momentarily. "I feel a strange tingling sensation, and it changes as we move." He turned toward Darshima and Khydius.

"It's the same feeling I have when we spar with Tenrai and Dydan," added Erethalie. "I can almost see it." She pointed toward the sky with an index finger.

"So you all sense the kai fields too?" exclaimed Darshima. He looked toward Khydius, Erethalie, and Sydarias, and they all nodded in agreement. He thought he was the only one who felt it. A memory of Priest Dawn's incredible vision during his sparring match with Tenrai flashed before his eyes. The sovereign strength flowed through all of them, and they each were developing the ability to interact with it. During their time in Tiriyuud, they were learning the skills that other people had lost long ago.

"Why couldn't we ever feel the effects of these kai fields back home in The Vilides?" asked Erethalie.

"Kai fields exist everywhere in our universe, but you have to learn to feel and interpret them," said Dydan.

"Of all of the unseen energies and particles that continually pass through our world, kai is the most consequential of all." Tenrai nodded. "Tiriyuusians are the best at sensing it, but as Vilidesians, you all are progressing very well."

"Let us continue." Against the force of gravity, Tenrai floated upon his board and glided toward Darshima and the others before gently settling himself down upon the snow. Darshima rubbed his eyes at the seemingly miraculous sight.

"There isn't much daylight left." Dydan positioned himself upon his board and hovered a handbreadth above the snow. He adjusted his visor and looked over the hills. The shadows grew longer as the sun neared the horizon.

"We're ready." Darshima steadied himself upon his board.

They glided down the hills behind Tenrai and Dydan, getting used to the feeling of gravity propelling them along the terrain. Despite several falls and scrapes upon the snow, they were learning to feel not only the sensation of gravity but the vagaries of the sovereign strength. Beneath the cold flashes of wind brushing against his skin, Darshima felt subtle yet strangely familiar pulsations deep within him as he moved. The same waves of ethereal light that Priest Dawn had shown him in the sparring ring seemed to tease the corners of his eyes. When he turned in their direction, he saw nothing.

As Darshima followed Tenrai's path, he felt his board move in ways for which neither gravity nor momentum could fully account. He smiled to himself, imagining Tenrai and Dydan using a much more developed intuition to guide them. Darshima glimpsed over his shoulder and saw Erethalie, Khydius, and Sydarias following him, working to maintain their balance as they tackled the gentle slopes.

Their first day of cloudboard training progressed, and by dusk, the four had grown more comfortable navigating the hills surrounding the temple. As the sun sank below the horizon, they journeyed back to the terrace, fatigued from the day's exercises but happy with what they had learned thus far.

Chapter 15

Darshima followed Priest Dawn along the walkway of the peristyle. Her staff tapped rhythmically against the pavers. Snowflakes gathered at the hems of her robe as she led the way. Pale beams of moonlight spilled over the eaves of the temple, illuminating the pathway. The courtyard echoed with the footsteps of Erethalie, Sydarias, and Khydius, who shuffled beside him.

The sun had set some time ago, and they had not long finished their evening meal with Tenrai and Dydan. As they were preparing for the night's rest, Priest Dawn invited them to join her for an evening session.

"It is only a little further," she called over her shoulder.

"Are you sure Tenrai and Dydan won't mind?" asked Darshima. Priest Dawn came to a stop, then turned around.

"Guardian Nax and Sage Waike are responsible for much of your training. However, there are things that I must do to prepare you to become guardians. They know you are here with me." Her eyes gleamed a vivid sapphire in the shadows.

"If I may ask, are you a guardian as well as a priest?" Erethalie nodded in a sign of respect.

"I was called to the priesthood after serving as a knight. I spent most of my youth rising through the ranks. I am now a guardian emerita. Assisting with the training of recruits is one of my most important duties." She looked toward the sky, appearing as if she were reliving a memory.

"I imagine that you must've experienced so much," replied Darshima.

"I have both learned and given my fair share of lessons in this life. Whom do you think taught Guardian Nax and Sage Waike when they were in training?" A subtle smile crossed her lips.

"You instructed them?" asked Sydarias, his voice rising in surprise.

"I instructed both of them, along with several other remarkable recruits," replied Priest Dawn, her voice bearing a hint of melancholy.

Though she appeared older than Tenrai and Dydan, it hadn't occurred to Darshima that she had been their teacher. Darshima's mind flashed with images of her expert guidance during their sparring sessions. Her close rapport with Tenrai and Dydan now made sense to him.

"I taught them here in this very temple, where you find yourselves training." She peered around them, her lips pursed in contemplation. "Shall we continue?" Priest Dawn motioned toward a stairway at the end of the walkway.

Priest Dawn led them up the worn wooden treads and through a doorway. Darshima and his companions walked with her down a narrow corridor lit by crystal lanterns. She stopped before a doorway with a golden seal at its center. She pressed the symbol, and the doors slid apart. She ushered them past a threshold as the panels closed behind them.

Darshima looked around the room toward a wall of windows looking out over the rolling, snow-covered hills. The hills ended in a series of cliffs that abutted the moonlit lake. On the horizon, Darshima saw a glimpse of Chryshaihem's glowing skyline, shimmering upon the waters.

Priest Dawn made her way across the wooden floorboards and stood beside a circular stone hearth in the center of the room, glowing with subdued flame.

"You are more than halfway complete with your training." She looked at each of them.

"It's hard to believe," said Darshima, memories of their experiences thus far flashing before him.

"We've all learned so much," added Erethalie.

"Though you all have come far, you have more to learn if you are to succeed." Priest Dawn pursed her lips in a pensive expression.

"What do you mean?" Khydius shook his head in confusion.

"There are skills beyond eneri-kai that you must master in order to become competent guardians." She walked toward another set of doors that parted as she approached. "A guardian always seeks peace first. When neither peace nor eneri-kai work, we rely upon other methods. Please, join me."

Darshima and his companions walked through the doorway into a large, torchlit square room. Wooden cabinets lined the walls, each marked with elaborate, polygonal symbols that he did not recognize. A set of low granite tables in the shape of a divided torus sat at the center of the room.

The paired tables surrounded a glowing, blue crystal ring inscribed into the polished black stone floor. A small transparent crystal in the shape of an icosahedron sat at the center of the ring. Glittering like a diamond, it rotated upon one of its vertices as if impelled by an unseen force.

Beams of moonlight streamed through a pyramidal glass canopy, casting the space in soft light and shadow. Priest Dawn gestured toward the tables, and Darshima and his companions sat beside each other upon a row of stiff, woolen rugs.

"You have learned the basic tenets of eneri-kai, but there will be times when your skill alone is not enough to defeat your opponent." She folded her arms across her chest.

"We saw Tenrai do astounding things with the sovereign strength," said Darshima, memories of their escape from Navervyne replaying in his mind. "When wouldn't it be enough?"

"Eneri-Kai is the guardians' most important skill in combat, but it is not our sole means of defense."

Priest Dawn walked toward one of the wooden cabinets. She opened a drawer, removed a lacquered wooden box, and set it upon the table before Darshima and his companions. She lifted the cover, retrieved four palm-sized spheres, and carefully rested them in individual impressions carved into the honed surface. Darshima's eyes swept over the spheres as they shimmered in the torchlight. The sphere on his left appeared a translucent white. The adjacent objects glittered bluish grey and verdant green. The rightmost orb seemed to be made of a yellow, lustrous metal like gold.

"What are they made from?" asked Darshima.

"They look valuable," added Erethalie.

"They're made of quartz, opal, jade, and gold." Sydarias casually pointed at the spheres.

"They aren't what they appear to be." Khydius drummed his fingers upon the table. "My advisors told me about rare classes of substances here on Iberwight, found nowhere else."

"Is that so?" Erethalie looked toward Khydius.

"The Tiriyuusians are known for mining obscure materials with physical properties that seem to defy the known laws of physics." Khydius' eyes narrowed as he examined the spheres resting motionlessly upon the table.

"Over the ages, Vilidesian scholars have tried to obtain and study some of these materials, but the Tiriyuusians were incredibly secretive. They revealed nothing."

"You are correct, Khydius," said Priest Dawn. "These spheres are made of materials that are abundant in Tiriyuud. They do not exist elsewhere among the four moons."

"What can they do?" Darshima moved closer and inspected them. Their gleaming surfaces interacted with the light in a subtle yet peculiar haziness, appearing as if they were vibrating at a high frequency.

"As you've learned during your cloudboard exercises, different Tiriyuusian materials interact with kai in unique ways." She gathered the spheres in her hands and then approached the glowing ring, which pulsated as she stepped across its threshold.

"This ring is different from the golden ones you've sparred in thus far. It is made of a rare crystal that can focus and amplify the surrounding kai fields." Priest Dawn stepped further into the ring, and the spheres in her hands scintillated with light. She peered at the objects, her face illuminated by the varied colors.

"Each of these spheres contains a mineral that interacts with the sovereign strength in a unique way." She paced back and forth, her robes sweeping against the crystal ring. "You all may approach, but please stay outside of the circle." She placed the orbs in pockets nestled the folds of her robe. Darshima and his companions rose from their mats, then spaced themselves around the edge of the circle.

"How do they interact with kai?" asked Darshima.

"Cover your ears." She gestured toward them.

"I don't understand." Khydius eyebrows furrowed in confusion.

"I will repeat myself only once more." She retrieved the emerald-colored orb from her robe, along with a pair of glowing orange pebbles.

As instructed, Darshima and his companions raised their hands to their ears.

"These crystals deaden sound, and I won't be able to hear you." She slipped the small objects into her ears.

Priest Dawn held the orb out in front of her, then threw it in an exaggerated arcing motion. The object flew from her hand toward the opposite end of the circle. As it hurtled toward Darshima, it deflected in an arc that traced the crystal ring inscribed upon the floor. Darshima looked on in amazement as the sphere defied gravity. The orb accelerated around the circle until it appeared as a vibrating band of green light levitating in mid-air. As the sphere careened around the perimeter, the air in the room vibrated with a deep rumble that steadily increased in volume.

Darshima pressed his hands against his ears as successive sound waves crash against him. He looked over to his companions. They pressed their hands against their ears, and their eyes grew wide in fear. Darshima held his breath as he felt a particularly forceful compression, then rarefaction jolt through him. His chest tightened with a crushing sensation that felt as if his heart were bursting. When he thought he could withstand no more, the light extinguished itself, and the orb fell to the ground with a sharp thud. It rolled beyond the perimeter and bumped against Erethalie's boot.

"What happened?" Erethalie stooped down to pick up the object and hefted it in her hand.

"This orb contains a small amount of idorifym. This mineral issues a sonic pulse when subjected to a strong kai field. A handful would be enough to stun an entire division of soldiers." Priest Dawn removed the sound-deadening pebbles from her ears and stowed them in her pocket.

"How were you able to withstand that force?" Sydarias shook his head in disbelief.

"I am standing in the center, where multiple fields are balancing each other. The crystal ring focuses the kai fields, but the rotating gem acts as a void and negates the energy. I am unaffected," said Priest Dawn. She gestured toward the icosahedron at her feet, which rotated even faster.

Before Darshima or anyone else could ask any further questions, Priest Dawn withdrew the white crystalline orb from the folds of her robe and held it out before her.

"Please avert your gazes." She hefted the sphere in her hand, then hurled it toward the opposite end of the circle. As with the green orb, it vaulted in a circular pattern, accelerating until it became a blinding flash of white light. Darshima closed his eyes as the light intensified. It was so bright that he could see the veins on the inside of his eyelids. He put his hands to his face and felt an intense flash of heat dissipate from the orb. The room went dark, followed by the clatter of the orb hitting the ground.

"Incredible," murmured Sydarias as he grabbed the rolling sphere.

"We call this mineral ikarifym. This sphere contains a minuscule quantity. When activated by a kai field, a small amount can generate enough electromagnetic energy to disable a foreign vessel."

"It seems like it could blind your enemies as well," added Sydarias.

"When used in combat, a large enough quantity would vaporize an aircraft." Priest Dawn frowned as she watched Sydarias handle the orb. Sydarias' eyebrows arched in astonishment at her words. He moved toward the table and gingerly rested it back upon the surface.

Priest Dawn withdrew the opal orb from her robe, then threw it to the opposite end of the circle. As with the others, it raced around the perimeter in a glowing streak of dazzling blue. The orb let out a high-pitched whine, then exploded in a shower of glittering, crystalline mist. Priest dawn stepped into the haze and, without warning, disappeared.

"Where did she go?" asked Darshima, his pulse thudding in surprise. He walked in a circle around the perimeter, but she was nowhere to be found.

"What type of magic is this?" Khydius stood opposite Darshima and shrugged in disbelief.

"I still stand before you," said Priest Dawn, her voice echoing throughout the room. She reemerged from thin air, and eight identical images of her appeared in the ring. Darshima's chest grew tight as he witnessed the unbelievable sight. He couldn't understand how his eyes could so dramatically deceive him. Priest Dawn and her eight spectral images walked around the perimeter, staring at Darshima and his companions.

"None of this makes sense. How could there possibly be more than one of you?" Erethalie shook her head in disbelief.

"There is only one me. It is a mere illusion." The mist dissipated, along with the ghostly images, and a solitary Priest Dawn stood before them.

"We call this mineral kagamifym. A small quantity can interact with kai fields and distort both visible light and electromagnetic waves. We occasionally use it as a cloaking mechanism for our vessels.

"That's unbelievable." Darshima shook his head in wonderment. "Do guardians use it to cloak themselves?"

"Occasionally, a group may cloak themselves or scare off an enemy with this method," said Priest Dawn.

"I imagine seeing advancing multitudes of guardians would scare anyone," murmured Sydarias.

"Some guardians develop unique psychic abilities and can influence the thoughts and perceptions of others. They can move about with ease, undetected by most. They don't require this mineral." Priest Dawn paced around the circle. Darshima remembered his first meeting with Tenrai in the slave colony and witnessing his ability to disguise them in plain sight. He had been amazed then, but now he was even more astonished at his talent.

"What does the golden orb do?" Darshima pointed to the remaining sphere hidden in her robe.

"That will be my last demonstration. Why don't you all sit for a moment." She gestured toward the tables, and Darshima and his companions resumed their seats.

"I've only shown you a small amount of what our crystallographers have refined and put to use over the ages." She walked around the circle, her hands folded behind her back. "There is more that I must teach you."

Not long after their exile, the ancient Tiriyuusians came to realize that their new homeland was more than a desolate mountainous archipelago amid the ocean. They discovered that their islands contained an abundance of unique physical materials found nowhere else. Over the ages, Tiriyuusians devoted themselves to studying and characterizing the myriad substances they encountered. Among their discoveries, scholars found minerals that could store and dissipate vast quantities of energy. They also found metals that could defy gravity.

As their civilization expanded upon the islands, the Tiriyuusians discovered a unique metal that interacted strongly with kai fields. This precious blue ore was located beneath some of the tallest mountains in the archipelago. Metallurgists named this metal aozuura, or blue spirit. Lightweight and virtually indestructible, it only succumbed to intense heat. Most remarkably of all, kai fields influenced this metal much stronger than electromagnetism or gravity. Though their ancestors had lost the ability to use eneri-kai to manipulate inanimate objects, they felt kai fields with their senses, much like a mariner develops a keen sense for the direction and speed of the wind.

The Order sent its surveyors to quantify the amount of this precious ore throughout the archipelago. They kept the stores of aozuura a closely guarded secret. This metal was the only physical matter propelled over long distances by kai fields, and Tiriyuud was the only known place with any significant deposits. Over the ages, aozuura gained an essential use within the kingdom. The guardians crafted fine boards, which they used as personal transportation. Light enough to wear on one's back and strong enough to use as a shield, the guardians' saigura or cloudboard was among their most important tools. The guardians used the kai fields to propel their boards over the snowy mountain valleys and through the skies of the kingdom at speeds equivalent to most of the Order's ships.

Tiriyuusians had discovered other metals with gravity-defying properties, which they used to fabricate much larger vessels. Virtually all of Tiriyuud's defense craft, passenger ships, and trade vessels were made with these materials. They were lighter, faster, and used small quantities of a crystalline fuel unique to Tiriyuud. As such, the kingdom's fleets of trade vessels plied the routes between the moons, calling at distant ports of the realm, using only a fraction of the energy as Vilidesian ships of comparable size.

"So Tiriyuud manufactures its own vessels and maintains a trading network?" Erethalie shook her head in confusion. "Why have I never heard of this?"

"Though we are an isolated kingdom, we engaged in abundant trade with the wider realm," answered Priest Dawn.

"If Tiriyuud is self-sufficient, what benefit did you derive from trade?" asked Darshima.

"We purchased gold from Ciblaithia, silver from Wohiimai, and medicines from Gordanelle," said Priest Dawn. "Tiriyuud has many things, but it does not have those precious metals or Gordanelle's unique botanical resources. As you've seen, gold and silver are important symbols and ornaments in our culture. Our metallurgists use them in industry. We also use them for currency."

Aware of the rarity of many of Tiriyuud's resources, Chryshaihem strictly regulated the export of much of its raw materials. Though the Order forbid the sale of precious minerals, Tiriyuud exported large quantities of diamonds, rubies, sapphires, among other gems and manufactured goods. Prized commodities in other parts of the realm, Tiriyuud and its industries grew wealthy from trade.

"Speaking of gold, what does the remaining sphere do?" asked Khydius.

"It is one of our rarest materials." Priest Dawn walked toward the opposite edge of the circle. "Please remain seated. Whatever happens, you must hold onto the table." Darshima exchanged perplexed glances with Erethalie and Sydarias, then gripped the edge of the table in anticipation.

Priest Dawn pulled the gleaming orb from the folds of her robe. She drew her arm back, then pelted the object toward the other side of the ring. Like the other spheres, it accelerated around the perimeter in a flash of light.

"Make sure to hold on tightly." Priest Dawn hurriedly moved toward the center of the circle.

The glowing ring of light cast the room in a shimmering burst of gold. As the orb accelerated around the circuit, Darshima felt a primal and unrestrained force pull him toward the center of the room. He looked toward the torchlights, whose flames bent acutely in the direction of the circuiting sphere.

His heart pounding in surprise, Darshima gripped the desk as the atmosphere grew heavy. For a moment, he felt as if he were submerged in water and being dragged into a whirlpool. Darshima's stomach sank in fear at the aggressive force pulling him toward the center of the room. He pressed his feet upon the floor and tightened his grip, but the orb pulled harder.

The room filled with the sounds of the rumbling cabinet doors and groan of the desks as the unseen force pulled them inward toward the circle.

"What's happening?" Khydius shook his head in bewilderment.

"Please, stay where you are." Priest Dawn stood calmly in the center, her hands at her sides.

"I cannot withstand this." Khydius closed his eyes and instinctively let go of the desk. As he stood up to walk away, the force seized him and dragged him toward the circle. He staggered back as the racing orb pulled him inward.

"Khydius, wait!" shouted Darshima. His face contorted in terror, Khydius threw his arms up to protect himself. Just as the force yanked him to the edge of the ring, Darshima instinctively stretched his right hand toward the circuiting object. A familiar tingle of electricity surged through his fingertips. His eyes widened in disbelief as the orb suddenly froze in mid-air. It hung for a moment above the crystal perimeter, then clattered to the ground. The pulling sensation ceased, and Khydius fell to his knees.

"What happened?" shouted Erethalie.

"Are you okay, Khydius?" Darshima jumped from his seat and gripped Khydius' arm.

"I'm fine." Slightly dazed, Khydius shook his head. Darshima helped Khydius back to his feet and led him back to the table. They resumed their seats beside Erethalie and Sydarias.

"That is one of our most unique minerals, juurofym." Priest Dawn walked toward them. "It interacts with kai and increases gravitational fields. A minute quantity is strong enough to pulverize a fleet of ships."

"Incredible," murmured Sydarias.

"Excellent work, Darshima." Priest Dawn nodded toward him. "You have the strength that our ancestors lost, and it is growing." Darshima looked toward his hands. Though he was growing accustomed to his abilities, at times, he found them unsetting.

"Why didn't you stop it sooner?" Khydius' eyes widened in disbelief. "I could have been killed."

"It was a minute quantity. It would have given you a few bruises, but it wouldn't have killed you." A practical expression formed upon her face.

"What kind of demonstration is this?" murmured Khydius as he straightened the wrinkles in his uniform.

"This was a simple demonstration. There are far greater threats that you will face as a guardian." A frown formed upon her lips. "Khydius, you must learn to heed instruction. I cannot allow you to injure yourself."

"I understand." Khydius let out a sigh, then offered a contrite nod.

"You all have come such a long way and are approaching the final test." Her frown faded, and a wistful smile took its place. "You remind me of four special guardians that I had the privilege of instructing many years ago. Over time, they each achieved remarkable things."

"You mentioned that you taught Tenrai and Dydan." Darshima leaned closer as he recalled her words.

"Indeed, they belonged to a group that I once taught." She nodded.

"Whom else did you train?" asked Erethalie.

"Sage Rion Nax and the most exalted, Oracle of Tiriyuud belonged to one of my first groups of recruits." Priest Dawn bowed her head in deference.

"You knew our father?" Khydius' jaw dropped in astonishment.

"Our father was a Sage of Tiriyuud?" Darshima's chest tightened as he registered her words.

"He was so much more." Priest Dawn's eyes glittered with tears amid the torchlight. "Perhaps I've said too much." She cleared her throat, arranged her robes, and regained her composure. Darshima's mind raced at her revelation. Since learning the truth of his origins, Darshima had longed to understand more about his parents. Now he sat face to face with the woman who was instrumental in his father's training. There was so much he needed to know.

"What was he like?" Darshima's heart rose into his throat as he spoke. His eyes grew damp as his mind attempted to sketch a portrait of the unfamiliar man who was their father. Before she could answer, the door slid open with a creak. Darshima looked over his shoulder and saw Tenrai waiting patiently.

"Pardon my intrusion, Priest Dawn, but the hour is late." Tenrai looked around the room. "Our recruits need their rest for tomorrow's lessons."

"But Priest Dawn was telling us about our father..." stammered Darshima. Tenrai raised his hand, and Darshima fell silent.

"We will discuss it another time. There is much yet to accomplish." Tenrai waved toward Darshima and his companions. They rose from their seats and joined him at the door.

"Guardian Nax, you mustn't keep avoiding this discussion with your nephews. You have carried this burden for far too long." Priest Dawn stood in the middle of the circle, her arms folded across her chest.

"I appreciate your concern, Priest Dawn. In time, I will tell them every-thing," said Tenrai, his voice restrained as he held back his emotions. He offered her a deep bow and then exited the room. Erethalie, Sydarias, and Khydius followed him. As Darshima walked behind them, he looked over his shoulder and caught Priest Dawn's concerned gaze. He hurried past the threshold before he could say anything further.

Chapter 16

Darshima tipped his visor against the bright rays of sunlight and crouched lower upon his cloudboard. His stomach sank as he raced down the steep slope toward the bottom of the valley. The winds whipped around him as he careened upon the glistening expanse of snow spreading before him. In the distance, he eyed the approaching shore and the jagged range of mountains hemming in the opposite edge of the lake. Dydan and Tenrai raced ahead of him, leaving arcs of shimmering, crystalline powder in their wake.

"On your right," called out Erethalie, her voice muffled by her visor. Darshima looked beside him, and she glided past in a rush of wind and snow. She raced ahead, catching up with Dydan.

"Wait for me!" shouted Sydarias as he sped past Darshima's left flank. As Darshima repositioned himself upon his board, Khydius glided past him.

"Let's keep moving." He waved at Darshima, then dashed ahead. Darshima bent his knees and braced himself as he drifted down the slope. He careened over the uneven mounds of snow, his cloudboard vibrating beneath his feet. He held his hands out to his sides and tried to stabilize himself.

Darshima slid further into the valley and tried to close the distance between himself, Khydius, and the others, but it only seemed to grow. His pulse thudded as he fell further behind them. His teeth chattering in the cold, Darshima clenched his jaw and tried to suppress his frustration. He glared down at his cloudboard, then ahead at the imposing, serpentine course.

Since learning how to cloudboard, Darshima had undoubtedly improved. He had learned to use gravity to his advantage and could speed across the snow. Nonetheless, he felt as if he were falling behind his companions. Erethalie, Sydarias, and Khydius were starting to sense the sovereign strength and using the surrounding kai fields to propel themselves faster than with gravity alone. They hadn't taken to the skies yet, but they had achieved long jumps and astounding flips. Darshima attributed their performance to a Vilidesian sensibility with operating different types of high-speed vehicles, both terrestrial and airborne. Back home on Gordanelle, Darshima walked everywhere. He had taken an aerial coach only a few times and had never piloted anything in his life.

Darshima looked on as Khydius caught up with Sydarias. Khydius had mentioned that members of the royal family received basic military training and knew how to pilot aircraft. Darshima moved behind them, carving through the snowdrifts. He watched their silhouettes shrink against the glistening snow as the distance grew even more between them.

Darshima knew their prowess couldn't solely be their familiarity with piloting aircraft. He stared at his board as he drifted further downhill.

"Why can't I do this?" Darshima shook his head in frustration. There had to be some other reason why he was struggling.

Amid the quietness of the valley, the rising sound of the wind filled his ears. Darshima lifted his gaze to see Dydan carving a path uphill, racing toward him. Before Darshima had time to react, Dydan slowed to a stop in a wide semicircle, fanning an arc of snow around them.

"You must try harder, Darshima." Dydan approached him, his board gliding upon the frozen ground. Darshima slowed his pace, and they skated forward together.

"What am I doing wrong?" Darshima looked over to Dydan, who drifted effortlessly alongside him.

"Allow yourself to feel the sovereign strength. It cannot be forced." Dydan looked toward the sky.

"Everyone else seems to be making more progress than I am." Darshima peered into the distance and saw his companions racing toward the lakeshore.

"You are capable of the same and much more." Dydan gently pressed his index finger against Darshima's chest.

"I can only feel the wind and nothing else." A frown spread upon Darshima's lips.

"Kai flows between the moons and stars. It shifts beneath the winds and dwells between each wave in the sea." Dydan extended his hand, deftly probing the surrounding air as if it were a stream.

"I don't understand." Darshima shrugged.

"I trust you've been reading the texts from the ophon eneri-kai I assigned you." Dydan's sapphire eyes narrowed in an inquisitive stare.

"I've read some, but it is difficult to understand." Darshima lowered his gaze. With the help of Khydius, Darshima, Erethalie, and Sydarias had reviewed the volume, but its instructions were abstract and hard to understand. He looked toward Dydan and tried to think of a passage that might help him.

"As the first line reads, set your mind upon the space between space. Let your spirit dwell where hidden planes intersect." Dydan gestured around them and pointed toward his forehead, then his chest.

"The space between what?" asked Darshima, shaking his head in bewilderment at the cryptic phrase.

"You must read more." Dydan tapped his fingers against Darshima's temple. "Kai has always existed in the interstices. It flows between space, time, and within the substance of life itself. We are all meant to feel it, some more strongly than others." Dydan nodded toward Darshima.

"Breathe, focus your thoughts, and allow yourself to feel the kai fields around you."

Dydan looked toward the shore. "May it always protect you in times of vulnerability, lift you when you fall, and deliver you in your weakest moments." Dydan gently pressed his hands against Darshima's forehead. Darshima drew in a breath of the frigid air. He felt his frustration dissipate, and his heart rate slowed down under Dydan's touch. Dydan released his hands and offered Darshima a bow.

"Thank you," said Darshima, grateful for the unexpected moment of calm.

"I will see you on the other side," said Dydan. He crouched upon his board, then launched himself upward in a spray of snow. He climbed into the sky, and Darshima saw his silhouette vanish into the clouds overhead. Darshima craned his neck forward and watched Dydan soar above the valley, toward the lakeshore. He slowed his approach, made a steep descent, and landed upon the snowdrifts near Tenrai.

"I must somehow do the same." Darshima's pulse pounded in astonishment as he observed Dydan's skillful flight.

Darshima leaned forward upon his board and drifted down the slope, the scenery moving swiftly around him. Dydan's words echoed in his mind as he raced toward the shore under gravity's pull. His mind went back to the moment in Navervyne when he had taken that death-defying leap onto the departing aerial ship. He had felt something guide his path then. He now knew that it had been the sovereign strength all along. He needed to find a way to feel it here, in this moment.

Like times before, Darshima felt the surging kai fields rise through his legs and dissipate through his fingertips. Throughout the day, Darshima had felt it stronger in some parts of the valley than others.

"I must walk among the clouds as they do," said Darshima, his voice rising with determination. He carved a serpentine route downhill, sensing the strengths and weaknesses of the fields around him and taking mental notes. Darshima raced faster down the hill, his eyes narrowing as he viewed the glistening waters of the lake.

As he vaulted forward, Darshima instinctively closed his eyes. He felt the wind rush against his face and through his uniform. Below the gusts, he felt the familiar pulses of electricity sweeping through him. The sound of rushing snow rumbling in his ears grew softer until it faded to silence.

The gusts of wind settled, and he no longer felt the breeze upon his face. The brightness of the sun filtered through his closed eyes, growing so bright that he could see the veins in his eyelids. Though he felt his body in motion, the buffeting sensation against his board dissipated. His anxiety disappeared, and his pulse slowed with a sense of calmness.

"This is where I am meant to be," whispered Darshima in astonishment, his heart thudding as he contemplated Dydan's instructions. He had felt the edges of this subliminal space during his dive from the cliff and their sparring matches at the temple, but he had never fully entered it until today.

Darshima's eyes fluttered open, and he saw the shore at the bottom of the hill. He approached the others as he carved his way down the steep path. Erethalie, Sydarias, and Khydius raced upon a trio of hills leading to the water's edge. They leaped over the first small hill, one after another. They lingered in the skies as they floated over the middle hill, seeming immune to the effects of gravity. Erethalie, followed by Khydius and Sydarias, descended upon the snow, landing atop the peak of the last hill.

Darshima aimed his board toward the shore, the sense of electricity growing stronger as he eyed the crystalline pebbles of the beach. His entire body pulsed with a charge so intense that he felt as if he would leap out of his skin. He drew in a breath and tried to acclimate to the sensation.

"I must allow myself to feel this," he whispered through clenched teeth. His muscles seized as the charges coursed through him. The winds whipping past him, he willed himself to stay upright.

Darshima aimed his board away from the hills, racing past Tenrai, Dydan, and his companions in a spray of snow. Darshima bent his knees in an instinctive move, then leaped, and his cloudboard pressed firmly upward against his feet. Darshima's stomach sank as he climbed into the sky. The ground shrank beneath him, and he crouched lower, maintaining his balance. The winds tore at his uniform, and the valley below disappeared beneath a thin veil of clouds. He looked over his shoulder to see Tenrai and Dydan soaring behind him, joined by Erethalie, Khydius, and Sydarias. They followed Darshima higher into the sky and ventured over the lake.

His chest fluttered with a feeling of weightlessness as he approached the mountains. He felt a rush of wind, then saw Tenrai, then Dydan gliding beside him.

"Remember this moment, Darshima," said Tenrai. "This is how it feels when you are ready to take to the skies."

"I will!" shouted Darshima. He looked around him in disbelief as he vaulted above the lake. Tenrai saluted Darshima, then flew further ahead.

"Excellent work," said Dydan, his words taken by the wind. He offered Darshima a nod, then raced to catch up with Tenrai.

Darshima looked toward the mountains rising at the edge of the lake in a nearly vertical wall of jagged stone. His ears filled with joyous shouts as his companions approached him from behind. He looked to his sides to see Erethalie, Sydarias, and Khydius soar alongside him.

"This is unbelievable!" shouted Erethalie, her hands extended outward as she maintained her balance.

"Flight with no engines!" yelled Sydarias. He expertly tucked into the wind and folded his hands behind his back.

"The Vilidesians never even conceived of such a thing!" Khydius shook his head in astonishment. He flew beside Darshima as they climbed higher into the clouds.

"We will fly over the mountain range and then turn back." Tenrai glanced over his shoulder and pointed ahead, his voice barely audible amid the whipping winds.

They approached the snow-capped peaks, their boards buffeted by a series of powerful downdrafts. Darshima drew in a breath and focused on his balance. His head felt as if it were floating amid the thin oxygen.

As they soared over the mountains, he eyed a sinuous river that seemingly cleaved the mountains in half. The river led toward the ocean beyond the sheltered lake in a series of fortified weirs and locks. A pair of curving, arched stone bridges ran along the banks of the river. Darshima squinted and made out the individual cars of a lengthy train racing upon one of the gleaming tracks on its way through the mountains, toward the ocean.

"Where is that train going?" Darshima pointed in the direction of the river.

"That train goes to the Outer District," called out Dydan.

"What's that?" asked Darshima.

"The Outer District is the only part of Tiriyuud where foreigners are welcome. It is an offshore island used for diplomacy, education, and trade." Khydius turned toward Darshima, his voice barely audible above the winds. They vaulted above the mountains and soared over the open ocean. Darshima's eyes followed the paired bridges spanning the waters, fading into the mists as they traveled toward the horizon. He squinted but saw no trace of the island.

Darshima followed Tenrai as he led them further over the ocean. He looked over his shoulder and glimpsed how far they had traveled. He drew in a surprised breath as he saw the mountainous island rising behind them. Its majestic peak remained hidden by a thick layer of clouds.

"What a sight!" yelled Khydius, pointing behind them. "Tiriyuud's northernmost island is remarkable."

"Indeed it is!" shouted Darshima. Tenrai guided them on a course heading south, parallel to the rugged coastline. Beneath the shroud of mist, Darshima eyed a dozen immense aerial ships forming a line above the coast.

Their elongated, black angular hulls were embellished with golden polygons and featured sets of stout wings at the bow and the stern. The aft doors were open, revealing multiple decks housing smaller winged aircraft.

"What are those?" Erethalie pointed excitedly ahead of them.

"Those are some of the larger ships in the Tiriyuusian fleet," said Tenrai. Darshima stared at the craft in awe. The ships were as large as any Vilidesian craft he had ever seen.

Months ago, when he first arrived in Tiriyuud, Darshima assumed they had come to an antiquated and hermetic kingdom. His time thus far showed him that Tiriyuud was quite the opposite. He shook his head in disbelief as he observed the gigantic ships cruising in formation along the coast. This kingdom was far more sophisticated than he had imagined.

"Tiriyuud has long maintained a military force separate from the Vilidesians," called out Dydan.

"Impressive," said Sydarias.

"You all will learn more about the Order's fleets in due time." Tenrai pointed toward the ships as they receded in the distance.

"We should head back," called out Dydan. Tenrai nodded in agreement. They raced ahead and banked right in a steep arc, expertly balancing upon their cloudboards. Darshima followed them, doubling back as they aimed toward the island.

They approached the tall mountain range rising from the ocean, forming a protective barrier around the immense oval lake. Chryshaihem's islands and its vast skyline gleamed upon the opposite shore. Darshima raced ahead with his companions, and the mountains filled their entire field of view.

Out of the corner of his eye, Darshima noticed Khydius veering off course.

"Where are you going?" asked Darshima, as Khydius flew further south along the coast. Darshima swerved upon his board and raced toward him.

"I sense something in the kai fields, and I want to go further south." Khydius pointed toward the open ocean.

"What are you doing?" shouted Erethalie, catching up to Darshima and Khydius. Sydarias followed closely behind her. Before Khydius could respond, Tenrai and Dydan approached them.

"You are much too far from the planned course. We must return at once." Tenrai's eyes narrowed beneath his visor.

"I'm sorry, but something is compelling me here." Khydius shrugged, anxiously scanning the waters below them.

"Let us head back to the temple." Dydan angled back north.

Darshima and his companions followed Tenrai toward the mountains. The sun hung low over the horizon, and the late afternoon rays glimmered upon the waters. As they sped over the ocean, something in the water caught Darshima's eye. He looked down and saw what appeared to be pair of immense, dark objects lying beneath the rippling surface.

"What is that?" he muttered, unsure of what he was seeing. Darshima broke away from the others and floated down toward the water's surface to get a better look.

"Where are you going?" asked Khydius as he drifted alongside Darshima. Erethalie and Sydarias hovered nearby.

"There's something unusual in the water." Darshima pointed toward the silhouettes. As they neared the surface, the shapes grew clearer. Large and oblong, the objects glinted beneath the waves.

"They look like vessels of some sort," said Erethalie.

"They are huge." Sydarias shook his head. "Why would there be sunken vessels off the coast?"

Darshima's eyes swept over the wreckage, and he glimpsed a series of faded symbols marking the angular fuselages. He could make out what appeared to be a series of four crescents beneath a golden shield. His heart froze as he realized what they were.

"Those are Vilidesian aerial ships!" yelled Erethalie. She descended closer to the waves. Darshima, Sydarias, and Khydius joined her.

"That doesn't make any sense." Darshima shook his head in confusion.

"Why would there be a pair of sunken imperial ships upon Tiriyuud's shore?" asked Khydius, his voice trembling. "It cannot be."

"We barely know anything about this kingdom, let alone a past conflict between The Vilides and Tiriyuud." Erethalie looked toward Darshima. "Is that even possible?"

"There is clearly something that we don't know. We must ask Tenrai." Darshima looked toward his companions, his heart racing as the image of the wreckage seared itself into his mind.

In a gust of wind, Tenrai and Dydan floated down and joined them.

"We are due at the temple for evening meditation." Tenrai pointed toward the mountains. "We must continue."

"What happened here, Tenrai? Why are there sunken vessels?" Darshima floated above the waves. Tenrai glared at the wreckage, then turned to Darshima and his companions. He opened his mouth to speak, but no words came forth. Visibly uncomfortable, Tenrai drew in a heavy breath and stared down at the water.

"We have much to tell you, and in time you will learn what occurred here," said Dydan.

"There was a battle in this location. Why do we know nothing of it?" asked Sydarias, a look of incredulity spreading upon his features.

"Let us first return to the temple." Dydan pointed toward the mountains then floated upward. A somber expression crossed Tenrai's features. Darshima's chest tightened as Tenrai looked at him with a sorrowful stare.

"What's wrong, Tenrai?" asked Darshima, taken aback by his uncle's change in demeanor. Before he could say anything more, Tenrai and Dydan soared higher. Darshima and his companions flew silently behind them.

Darshima's pulse bounded as they vaulted over the mountains and back over the lake. The sun sank below the horizon as they returned to the training island. They descended into the valley amid the twilight and glided toward their temple. As they made their approach, Darshima tried to focus on the kai fields surrounding him. He navigated as best as he could, but his mind was elsewhere. He couldn't believe what he saw beneath the waves, nor could he understand Tenrai's unexpected reaction. He needed to find out what happened to those vessels.

Chapter 17

Darshima lay upon his bed in a state of half slumber. It had been another long day of sparring in the courtyard, flying exercises with the cloudboard, and studying from the texts Dydan had assigned them. The low drone of the wind and the faint tap of snowflakes against the window filtered through his thoughts. Darshima drew his covers over his shoulders and buried his face into the stiff fabric of his pillow.

As he felt himself drift off into another bout of sleep, an image of the sunken pair of aerial ships off the shore floated before his eyes. It had only been yesterday since they had encountered the wreckage, and it was still fresh in his mind. He closed his eyes tighter. Darshima mulled over the details of the submerged vessels and their gleaming imperial seals, rippling beneath the waves. They appeared as if they were suspended in time. He imagined the hundreds of souls that might be trapped down there, entombed in a watery grave.

Darshima shook his head at the haunting images and forced his eyes open. He peered through the frosted windowpanes and saw the swirling snowflakes mingling with the beams of moonlight. Darshima tore his gaze from the window and glared at the coffered ceiling above him. A shiver coursed through him, and he pulled the bedsheets up to his chin. He couldn't understand why Tenrai wouldn't say anything about those vessels.

Darshima racked his mind, trying to think of some explanation he might have learned when he was younger. He couldn't remember ever learning of a battle or a war between The Vilides and Tiriyuud. A sigh escaped his lips as the mystery tugged at him. He needed to get Tenrai to tell him what he knew.

His eyelids heavy, Darshima felt himself slipping into another restless bout of sleep. A soft knock at the door interrupted his slowing thoughts. His eyes fluttered open, and the knocking resumed in a more insistent rhythm.

"Darshima, it's me," whispered Khydius, his voice muffled behind the door. Darshima scooted out of bed and shuffled across the floor. He pulled his nightshirt over his shoulders, then gripped the handle. He paused for a moment as the fog of sleep cleared, then slid open the door.

"Why aren't you in bed?" Darshima looked at Khydius, still dressed in his full training uniform.

"We must talk about what happened yesterday." Khydius stepped forward and closed the door behind him. "I cannot think of anything else." Their footsteps thudded softly against the floor as they crossed the room. They sat beneath the window and faced each other. A beam of moonlight illuminated Khydius, and the folds of his uniform seemed to meld into the surrounding shadows.

"What could've happened to those vessels?" Darshima searched Khydius' eyes for any hint but found none.

"I don't know, but the sinking of two Vilidesian warships would have been an unprecedented act of aggression." Khydius shook his head. An expression of disbelief spread upon his face.

"None of it makes sense." Darshima shrugged.

"A major battle happened here in Tiriyuud, and there is no mention of it anywhere in our records." Khydius clenched his jaw. "None of my counselors ever recounted such an event. The Order must know something."

"Tenrai will tell us everything when the time is right," replied Darshima.

"He has had several opportunities, but he has remained silent." Khydius' brow wrinkled in frustration. "I am tired of waiting. Tenrai knows more than he is willing to share."

"We have to focus on our training. Tenrai only wants what is best for us." Darshima looked down at his hands and avoided Khydius' piercing stare.

Darshima was equally frustrated at not knowing more about their past, but he tried to keep everything in perspective. Tenrai had rescued them, protected them, and was doing everything he could to train them. Darshima knew there would come a time when Tenrai would tell them about their past, and he was willing to wait.

"I can no longer be patient with him. I am going to find out for myself." Khydius drummed his fingers against his knees.

"How will you do it?" Darshima straightened his back, his pulse thudding as he anticipated Khydius' reply.

"As we did yesterday, I will fly beyond the lake, past the mountains, and over the ocean. I must explore the wreckage for myself." Khydius steepled his fingers in contemplation.

"It's the middle of the night, and the location is remote. The tides will be treacherous at this hour, and you may not even find anything in the darkness." Darshima's stomach sank as he pondered Khydius' risky proposal. "Let's discuss it tomorrow with Tenrai."

"How much longer must we wait for the truth?" A look of incredulity spread upon Khydius' face.

"Tenrai is a man of his word, and we won't have to wait much longer." Darshima turned his gaze away from Khydius and glared through the window. "We have more to do to prepare for the final test."

"There is an unaccounted Vilidesian shipwreck on the shores of this isolationist kingdom." Khydius gripped Darshima's shoulder. "Something of great consequence happened here, and I believe that we are somehow connected to it."

"How can you be sure?" Darshima shook his head in disbelief.

"We are estranged brothers who are half Vilidesian, with an Omystikai man who has claimed us as his nephews. There have been too many unknowns since our arrival here." A sigh escaped Khydius' lips. "This incredible finding only adds to the mystery."

"I believe you," said Darshima. Though he had tried to ignore it, he sensed something profound in Tenrai's silence yesterday as they floated above the ocean.

"Will you stay here, or will you join me?" Khydius rose to his feet.

"No matter what I say, you're clearly determined to return to that wreck. I am only going to protect you." Darshima stood up, his stomach twisting in an anxious knot as he pondered Khydius' plan. "We must speak with Tenrai in the morning."

"If we must," said Khydius. Darshima walked over to his wardrobe, hastily changed out of his nightclothes and into his uniform.

He followed Khydius out of his room and carefully closed the door behind him. They laced their boots in the common area of their suite, the low, flickering flames of the hearth casting their shadows against the walls.

"We'll grab our cloudboards, then venture to the site," whispered Khydius. As they approached the entryway, the sound of an opening door broke the silence.

"Where are you going?" asked Erethalie, her silhouette appearing in the parted doorway to her room.

"Why is everyone awake?" Sydarias gently slid open his door.

"Khydius wants to investigate the shipwreck we saw yesterday." Darshima peered at both of them, his voice bearing a hint of nervousness.

"I have no choice but to find out what happened." Khydius impatiently tapped his foot.

"We won't let you go by yourselves," said Erethalie.

"I will be fine. Darshima is coming with me. It's much too late, and I don't want to disturb either of you." Khydius shook his head.

"We will travel together. It's safer that way," said Sydarias.

"Well, get changed then." A sigh escaped Khydius' lips, and he glared at them.

Erethalie and Sydarias closed their doors and moments later emerged in their uniforms. They put on their boots, then joined Darshima and Sydarias at the entrance. They quietly exited their suite and walked through the corridor. They followed Khydius down the stairs and along the torchlit hallway.

Darshima walked with them through a passageway leading to the terrace at the back of the temple. They stopped in the nearby utility room, collected their cloudboards, and continued in the darkness. Khydius slid open the doors at the end of the corridor, and they stepped into the chilly night. Darshima's heart froze as he glimpsed a trio of silhouettes standing along the balustrade, staring out at the snow. He drew in a surprised breath when he realized Tenrai, Dydan, and Priest Dawn were outside together. Darshima and his companions stood still as Priest Dawn turned around and faced them.

"Everything you require at this moment exists right here in this temple. Set your cloudboards aside. You need not travel to find the answers you seek." Her eyes glittered in the moonlight.

"How much longer must we wait?" asked Khydius. His anxious voice came out in puffs of steam. Tenrai turned around and faced Khydius, then Darshima.

"The past several days have brought forth many difficult memories for me, but they are not mine alone. You both have a right to know everything." His damp eyes narrowed in a melancholy expression. Darshima's heart sank as he registered Tenrai's anguish.

"We will return to our quarters." Erethalie exchanged a solemn glance with Sydarias, and they turned toward the door.

"Please, stay." Darshima turned to them, his pulse thudding in anticipation.

"We will stay if that's what you want," said Sydarias. He and Erethalie moved beside Darshima and Khydius.

"Let us return inside and warm ourselves around the hearth." Priest Dawn pointed toward the entrance with her staff. Dydan rested a hand upon Tenrai's shoulder and guided him away from the balustrade.

Darshima and his companions stepped through the entrance and walked down the corridor. They returned their cloudboards, then followed Priest Dawn into a room facing the courtyard. Darshima settled in front of the hearth beside Khydius. His chest tightened with worry as he stared at Tenrai, Dydan, and Priest Dawn, who sat opposite them.

"Where should I begin?" Tenrai stared at Khydius and Darshima. He hesitantly rubbed his hands together.

"You must tell them everything." Priest Dawn turned to Tenrai, an earnest frown forming upon her lips.

"Why are there sunken Vilidesian ships at Tiriyuud's shore?" asked Darshima.

"What battle occurred here?" Khydius shook his head in confusion.

"There was indeed a conflict not so long ago on our shores," said Tenrai.

"Who could've possibly sunk those ships?" Khydius clenched his jaw as he tried to suppress a look of disbelief. "They were among the most advanced aerial carriers of their era. It would've been impossible for a Tiriyuusian aircraft to sink those vessels." Tenrai stared at his nephews, and a pensive frown formed upon his lips.

"What happened, Tenrai?" pressed Darshima, his heart thudding as he waited for a response.

"Your father sank those vessels." Tenrai bowed his head.

Chapter 18

Darshima stared numbly at Tenrai as he recounted the story of their father, Rion Nax. He wasn't sure how much time had passed, but from the corner of his eye, he saw the starry night sky had faded into subtle shades of blue. Since learning about his origins, Darshima had yearned to hear more about the man who was their father, yet Tenrai had asked them to focus on their training. Darshima and Khydius had dutifully done as requested, but as events unfolded, Tenrai could no longer withhold the truth from them.

Darshima tried to sift through the improbable details, but he could barely grasp them.

"Why was I never told about this?" Khydius dashed away a tear as it rolled down his cheek. Erethalie and Sydarias looked concernedly upon him.

"Nothing like your father's story has ever happened in our kingdom's history. It was easier to let the truth stay hidden and carry on with our lives," said Dydan.

"What happened then was difficult, but the Order holds dear Rion Nax's sacrifice. His legacy is an example to us all." Priest Dawn looked upon Darshima and Khydius, an expression of sadness crossing her features.

According to Tenrai's account, their father, Rion Nax, was born two years before him. Rion was Tenrai's only sibling, and they were close as children. Many believed that Rion was among the most gifted members of the Order to have ever lived. From an early age, Rion showed a remarkable ability to control kai.

Long before he received formal training, Rion demonstrated the ability to read minds and influence the will of those around him. He showed an impressive ability to channel the sovereign strength and could physically overwhelm people. It was said that even as a small child, his parents had found it difficult to control him.

Word of his talents spread from their village of Foseidem to the leaders in Chryshaihem. In his early teenage years, Rion's parents were persuaded to let him train as a guardian. He became the youngest recruit the Order had ever accepted. Rion excelled in every discipline, and he outperformed the other recruits in his class in every measure.

"He accomplished astounding feats in the sparring ring, and upon his cloudboard," added Priest Dawn.

"When I was in training, he was one of my teachers. I remember him sparing against three of us at one time. It goes without saying, but he defeated all of us." A smirk crossed Dydan's lips. Tenrai nodded, his eyes narrowing fondly at Dydan's recollection.

Under the tutelage of Priest Dawn and other guardians, Rion's skills became formidable. Even before completing his training, he could mentally and physically overwhelm even the most capable challengers. He passed the ultimate test at the end of guardian training and won every single accolade and merit. At the age of fifteen, he was inducted as the youngest ever Tiriyuusian guardian.

"He didn't stay with us for long." Priest Dawn shook her head and chuckled.

"He had plans bigger than any of us would've imagined," said Dydan.

He steadily moved up the ranks in the guardianship, and his abilities became even more renowned. In the span of two years, he demonstrated enough wisdom and skill to become a knight, an achievement that often took an entire career. Despite his youth, he demonstrated insight and humility far beyond his years.

Intrigued by his profound abilities at such a young age, the Sages of Tiriyuud invited him to train with them. Rion enjoyed being a guardian and was reluctant to leave his position. Despite his desire to remain a guardian, a request issued by the Council of Sages could not be easily refused. He felt a great deal of pressure from his family and friends to accept the council's invitation. To be chosen by the sages was a rare honor. The council's acknowledgment bestowed much status and respect upon an individual and their family. Only the most talented guardians were awarded the opportunity to train with the council. Rion humbly accepted the invitation and began his journey toward becoming a sage.

"He was my age when he trained to become sage," mused Darshima. He closed his eyes for a moment, trying to imagine his father and the strengths he wielded.

"I had only completed my training when Rion left the guardianship," said Tenrai. "I remember his sadness when he left the shrine for the last time."

Despite his best efforts, Rion disliked training with the council. He was by far the youngest person ever to train with them, and his fellow apprentices were years older than him. Mainly invited from the Order's leagues of prelates and clerics, they seemed out of touch with the kingdom beyond the temple walls.

Despite his reservations, Rion studied hard and excelled. He advanced through the curriculum, and his instructors helped him hone his growing abilities. Within three years, Rion had mastered the arts of cognition and divination, exceeding the other sage apprentices. He had become more skillful than those who instructed him.

Never having trained anyone as capable as him, the Council of Sages realized how important he was to the kingdom. There were murmurings among its members that kai had destined Rion to become the next Oracle of Tiriyuud and lead the kingdom. Amid much celebration and anticipation, The council conferred upon him the status of sage at age twenty-one. Rion began an intense phase of study with a select group of talented sages, one of whom would someday assume the role of oracle.

Though Rion dedicated himself, the demands of the council and his rigorous preparation for leadership were taking their toll. The lifestyle of a sage was much more austere than the life he had enjoyed as a guardian. He became isolated from his family and friends. He was not allowed to leave the temple complex except for official business and only had limited contact with his family. Perhaps most difficult of all, sages were discouraged from seeking romantic companionship, and never married.

"The solitary life of a sage must be difficult," said Sydarias.

"It poses a challenge for some sages. Each of us finds our own way to cope with the demands of the sagehood." Dydan's voice trailed off as he stared intently at the flames.

Rion pursued his studies with all his effort, and his abilities became stronger. Despite his progress, he longed to return to his days as a guardian. He was resigned to the fact that he was fulfilling what those around him believed was his destiny.

Though he excelled in his first year as a sage, Rion began to struggle. He had grown unhappy with his decision, and his fellow sages could sense it. Fearing that his discontent may slow his preparations for becoming the oracle, Rion's instructors encouraged a leave of absence. Rion did not contest their decision and returned home.

"So, he didn't want to be a sage?" Khydius shook his head in confusion.

"Your father was a man of immense talent who wanted to serve his Order and his kingdom," said Dydan.

"In some respects, his talents were a burden," added Priest Dawn.

"The weight of expectation was difficult for him. I wanted to help, but I didn't know how." Tenrai closed his eyes, and a pained sigh escaped his lips.

"You did the best you could." Dydan rested his hand upon Tenrai's shoulder.

Though Rion was happy to return to Foseidem and be among family and friends, he found that things had changed. Villagers were aware of his abilities and his rising stature within the Order. Everyone treated him with a reverence that made him uncomfortable. To his relief, Tenrai and their parents regarded him no differently. To them, he was simply Rion.

Though concerned about his wellbeing, The Nax family was anxious for him to resume his training. Rion was the first sage to ever come from their family. His rank within the Order and his likelihood of being the next oracle had brought their family much distinction. They wanted nothing to impede his progress.

"He had so many expectations placed upon his shoulders." Darshima bit his lip as he pondered his father's immense burden. His thoughts drifted to Gordanelle, and an image of his adoptive brother, Sasha, flashed before his eyes. The expectations placed upon Sasha by Sovani had been significant. His heart thudded with a pang of regret as he thought of the envy he had once felt toward Sasha. When Darshima was younger, he had never even considered the pressure Sasha might have felt as they grew up under Sovani's dutiful gaze.

"He hid his struggle from all of us until it was too late." A shadow of sadness crossed Tenrai's features.

Tenrai had shown sympathy toward Rion. Like his older brother, Tenrai's abilities in the ways of kai were remarkable. He had served with the guardians and had received the rank of knight at a young age. Tenrai had also been invited to train as a sage and felt the pressure of expectation. Much to their family's consternation, Tenrai had declined the invitation. He saw how unhappy Rion had become and sought to avoid a similar fate.

Rion spent three days at home with his family and took a much-needed rest. His mood had improved, and he was ready to return to Chryshaihem. He bade his family goodbye and left Foseidem one morning amid a severe snowstorm. Much to the dismay of the sages and the anguish of the Nax family, Rion never made it to Chryshaihem.

"He disappeared?" Khydius shook his head in disbelief.

"He never returned to the Sages' Temple. One year after Tenrai and I were inducted into the guardianship, I left to join the sages. I followed Rion into the council. He was my mentor as I trained to become a sage." Dydan closed his eyes and let out a pained sigh. "His absence hurt deeply."

Fearing the worst, the Order dispatched a contingent of guardians to locate him. They scoured the entire archipelago, but there was no sign of Rion. His abrupt disappearance wounded Tenrai. They had shared a close bond and had been inseparable since childhood. Amid his anguish, Tenrai had a lingering sense that Rion had disappeared for a reason.

As the months passed, Rion's absence became a great source of shame for the Nax family. So they might redeem their name, Tenrai sought to look for Rion and bring him back to Chryshaihem.

"So you were solely responsible for finding him?" Darshima's eyebrows arched in surprise. He tried to comprehend the internal struggle that compelled his father to abandon everyone and everything he knew.

"I didn't know his fate, but I needed to find closure for the Order and our family." Tenrai's eyes lingered beyond the window. The skies had momentarily cleared, and the triple crescents of Gordanelle, Wohiimai, and Ciblaithia glowed softly against the sky.

Based upon their divination, the sages had advised Tenrai where to search for his brother. They felt he was somewhere near Chryshaihem, but Tenrai wasn't convinced. Something deep inside told him that Rion had ventured much further away. Tenrai followed his intuition and traveled to each of Tiriyuud's eight main islands in search of Rion. The first weeks of the journey were difficult. Though a Tiriyuusian knight, he was at heart a young man from the hinterlands. Before joining the Order, he had occasionally traveled beyond the borders of his village for ritual pilgrimages to Chryshaihem.

Tenrai left Tiriyuud after finding no sign of Rion. He spent months traveling through the Omystikai Dominions. He voyaged to Gordanelle, searching cities and villages for some trace of his brother. Realizing that finding Rion was his most important mission, he suppressed his emotions about being so far away from his fellow guardians.

Though he never admitted it aloud, Tenrai felt a lingering sense of anger at Rion for abandoning their family without so much as a word. As time stretched on, his search felt more and more in vain. At many points during his sojourn, Tenrai contemplated returning home to Tiriyuud, but the weight of his family's disappointment pushed him onward.

"How much time did you spend searching for him?" asked Darshima.

"More than a year," replied Tenrai.

"How did you find the strength to press onward?" Erethalie's eyes widened in surprise.

"Neither distance nor time deters me when I must find those whom I hold dear." Tenrai turned to Darshima and then Khydius, his eyes narrowing in an earnest stare.

After searching throughout the realm, Tenrai had made it to Wohiimai and still found no sign of Rion. One night, he found himself alone in a grassy field beyond the glowing lights of the capital, Renefydis. Both physically and emotionally exhausted, Tenrai was on the verge of giving up his search. The Renefydans had been hostile toward him, and he feared for his safety in the city.

Tenrai had grown up hearing that Omystikai were both a rare sight and unwelcome throughout most of the realm. He felt like an outsider everywhere beyond Tiriyuud, but he had never felt it more strongly than on Wohiimai.

"I'm sorry you had that experience in Renefydis." A contrite frown crossed Erethalie's lips. "I assure you, we are much more hospitable in Pelethedral."

"I would never blame anyone," said Tenrai. "The peoples of the realm are taught to treat us with scorn and disdain. It took seeing the world outside of Tiriyuud for me to understand."

Unable to find food, lodging that would accept him, or any information about his brother, Tenrai felt that he had no choice but to return to Tiriyuud. As he plotted his journey back to Iberwight, a powerful vision of Rion came to him.

"I saw a clear image of his smiling face, somewhere amid the skyscrapers of The Vilides. He seemed happy." A smile crept across Tenrai's lips as he recounted the memory.

Tenrai left Renefydis and set out for Ciblaithia, arriving in The Vilides after a three-day voyage. Tenrai spent days scouring the neighborhoods, streets, and alleys but found no trace of Rion. Despite his struggle, he found the Vilidesians to be more hospitable than the Renefydans. After a week in the capital with no sign of Rion, Tenrai abruptly decided to end his search. He had done everything in his power to find his brother, but he felt that he could no longer continue.

As fate would have it, on his final day, Rion ended up finding Tenrai. To his surprise, Rion called out to him as he was walking back to the port. Rion appeared different from Tenrai's last memory. He had adopted the style and mannerisms of The Vilidesian Omystikai, who belonged to the Order of the Crystal Moon, based in the Dominion of Fauridise.

"So, he changed Orders? Is that something one can do?" asked Khydius.

"We had no prior knowledge of it ever happening." Dydan shook his head.

Tenrai's disbelief at his brother's transformation was palpable. He had spent more than a year traveling to the ends of the realm, trying to learn his fate. Rion had abandoned his kingdom and his future as oracle. Tenrai seethed at his brother for forsaking their heritage. Rion understood Tenrai's disappointment and sought to explain everything to him.

Tenrai only spent a day with Rion before returning to Tiriyuud. Over the years, he returned to The Vilides several times to visit Rion and reestablish their relationship. Each time he departed, Rion swore Tenrai to secrecy and asked that he remain silent of his whereabouts. Each return back to

Tiriyuud was especially difficult for Tenrai. He had to deny finding his brother to their parents, the Order, and those who missed him.

Tenrai was left distraught at his brother's decision to leave their homeland. He felt a deep sense of shame at hiding the truth. Tenrai had one day planned to tell their parents about Rion's new life in the capital, but unexpected illness and their grief at his absence had taken them both before their time. Their deaths left Tenrai with profound feelings of guilt. As the years passed, he continued to visit Rion and grudgingly came to understand his brother's decision.

"He left everything behind. How could you forgive him?" asked Khydius.

"He felt that he had no other choice," said Tenrai. He deferred his gaze toward the floor. "He was my brother. I could do no less than forgive him."

The expectations of the council had ultimately been too great for Rion. Though he had managed to persevere early on, his return home to Foseidem had put everything in perspective. Rion didn't want to spend the rest of his life meditating amid the austerity of the temples in Chryshaihem. He dreamed of venturing out into the world beyond Tiriyuud. He saw his future as oracle, with its irrevocable path and rigid protocols, and was desperate to avoid it. With this in mind, Rion decided to flee Tiriyuud and journey as far away as possible.

Rion spent several months wandering the moons, but he found it difficult to live among the other peoples of the realm. Like Tenrai, his appearance and heritage attracted unwanted, sometimes hostile attention. After many months, Rion made his way to The Vilides, where he felt a degree of anonymity amid the cosmopolitan atmosphere. His presence drew the attention of the influential population of Vilidesian Omystikai, and they formed relationships with him. He learned that some had even integrated into the fabric of Vilidesian society, forsaking traditional dress and their customs.

Rion marveled at how the Vilidesian Omystikai managed to reestablish a presence in the capital despite their ancestors' exile from Ciblaithia. They enjoyed a longstanding relationship with The House of Fyrenos, offering religious and political counsel to the emperor and the dynasty. They used their reading of kai to divine future events, having lost the ability to use it for combat.

The Vilidesian Omystikai sensed Rion's abilities and beseeched him to join them. Alone in a society vastly different than his own, Rion saw it as his only option if he were to survive in The Vilides. They inducted him into the Order of the Crystal Moon, and not surprisingly, he swiftly moved up their ranks. Rion was granted the status of counselor and worked directly with the members of the dynasty. He assisted with ceremonial tasks, performed divinations, and offered religious counsel. His kind manner, keen insight, and perennial wisdom made him a natural advisor. Despite his newness, the members of the royal family sought his guidance in times of trouble.

"It was hard not to like Rion." A content smile crossed Priest Dawn's lips.

"He had a disarming nature that could stir anyone's heart," added Dydan.

Though it had been a difficult decision to leave Tiriyuud, Rion had found happiness in The Vilides. His profile among the Vilidesian Omystikai increased. To his surprise, Rion had managed to find love in a most unexpected place. Her name was Mona. She was the Princess of The Vilides and the Defender of Wohiimai. As the eldest child of the widowed Emperor Oluduin, she was first in line for the throne. What began as a strictly professional encounter developed into something more profound. As a counselor, Rion was forbidden to pursue a relationship with anyone from the dynasty. A young man named Aximes Ithrena, the scion of a prominent industrial family, had already been chosen for her, and she was to marry him within the year. Mona felt nothing for her suitor and desperately wanted to prevent the marriage from happening.

As he came to know her, Rion's feelings toward Mona grew stronger. Their increasing closeness attracted the attention of both Emperor Oluduin and his counselors. The princess was assigned other counselors, and Rion was given other duties away from the palace. Despite attempts to separate them, they met each other in locations throughout the city, away from the prying eyes of the imperial court.

Rion and Mona's courtship continued, and they fell deeper in love. They grew frustrated by the circumstances in which they found themselves.

They wanted nothing more than to spend their lives together and resented the forces keeping them apart. Days before she was to marry, they contemplated fleeing The Vilides but decided against it. As heir to the throne, Mona was recognized wherever she traveled. Rion considered fleeing to Iberwight and seeking refuge for them, but he wasn't sure if he would ever be welcomed again in Tiriyuud. Furthermore, he would have great difficulty bringing Mona. Though she was the Vilidesian Princess, she was still viewed as a foreigner and would not be granted entry into the kingdom.

To complicate matters further, Mona discovered she was pregnant. They realized that it wouldn't be long before their secret became known, so they spoke candidly with the emperor and expressed their feelings for one another. As she was his eldest child and heir, she found much favor with him. The emperor was upset at her decision to be with Rion but tried to understand their plight.

Emperor Oluduin realized that forcing his daughter, the future Vilidesian Empress, into an undesired marriage would have profound consequences. Despite his desire to fulfill the previously brokered union, he knew that Mona needed to choose her husband. Emperor Oluduin valued her happiness more than anything. Despite Rion's unique Tiriyuusian origin, the emperor took comfort in the fact that he was a good and wise man who made his daughter happy.

Much to the court's astonishment, the emperor gave his blessing to the couple. Shortly thereafter, they were married with a full imperial ceremony, in an event broadcast to the entire realm. There were celebrations upon all of the moons. With their union official, Rion was no longer an Omystikai counselor but a Prince of The Vilides and a full member of the dynasty.

Despite the auspices of the emperor, the Vilidesian Omystikai were displeased. In short order, Rion, an outsider, and newcomer had broken the principles that guided their relationship with the dynasty. He had managed to gain more favor and influence than any other Omystikai had ever achieved. Furthermore, the Order of the Crystal Moon had brokered Mona's marriage into the Ithrena clan and stood to gain financially from it. Had circumstances been different, the union would have solidified a bond between the dynasty and one of the most influential industrial families in the realm.

"So our mother was a princess and heir to the Vilidesian throne." Khydius shook his head in disbelief. "She was the future empress."

"This is true," said Tenrai.

"And our father was destined to be the Tiriyuusian Oracle." Darshima looked to Tenrai, his pulse thudding.

"Rion was the one whom kai ordained." Priest Dawn bowed her head. Darshima turned to Khydius, his mind racing as he tried to conceive an image of the two individuals that were their parents.

Rion and Mona led a charmed life as members of the dynasty. She gave birth to their first child, a son whom they named Darshima. Soon after, they again became pregnant. Nine months later, they gave birth to their second son, whom they named Khydius. They devoted much of their time and energy to raising their two sons and enjoying their newfound family life. The couple became well known throughout the realm for their good nature, kindness, and charity. They garnered much respect and admiration for the dynasty, which had been embroiled in a series of scandals.

"Prince Rion and Princess Mona had immense potential." Dydan's eyes grew misty.

"Their union and their sons represented a watershed." A hesitant smile crossed Tenrai's lips.

"The marriage between a future empress and a future oracle." Khydius brow wrinkled in contemplation.

"Though unexpected, their marriage was heralded as an everlasting bond through kinship. You both embodied a truce in living, breathing flesh between our peoples." Priest Dawn stared at Darshima and Khydius, her eyes glowing softly.

"An enduring union between The Vilidesian Realm and the Kingdom of Tiriyuud." Darshima's chest tightened as he said the words, the seemingly impossible concept settling within him.

Though Darshima and Khydius were to be raised in The Vilides, Princess Mona embraced their Omystikai ancestry. Rion intended to teach them everything about their Tiriyuusian heritage. Tenrai continued his regular visits to see his brother and his young family. He was delighted by his two young nephews and knew they were full of potential. Both Rion and Tenrai had divined what markings to place upon them. Rion placed the markings on Darshima's forearm, and Tenrai placed the markings on Khydius' chest.

Markings were a tradition unique to Tiriyuud, and they figured greatly into the mysticism of the Order of the Gilded Moon. Though they were Vilidesians and members of the dynasty, Rion was thrilled that his sons would bear an essential reminder of their heritage. They continued their lives and raised their family, unaware that forces beyond their control gathered against them.

Rion's marriage to Princess Mona and his newfound status was without precedent. There had never been a marriage between an Omystikai and a member of the dynasty. Emotions seethed among the Vilidesian Omystikai at Rion's decision. He had stepped beyond the role of his position. Ax5mes, the spurned bridegroom, was humiliated by the dissolution of his marriage agreement to Mona. As the eldest son of the House of Ithrena, he was heir to a vast Vilidesian industrial conglomerate, with a presence on all of the moons. His clan had ancient familial ties to members of the House of Fyrenos, and over the centuries, there had been several marriages between the two families.

Axnmes observed the royal couple's happiness, growing family, and increasing stature from afar, and became consumed by his rage. Axnmes reasoned that the only way he could get past his shame was through revenge. He devised ways to reclaim what he believed was his rightful acceptance into the imperial court. He vowed to take his vengeance even further by overthrowing the emperor, whom he viewed as culpable for the termination of the marriage agreement. He would not be satisfied until Emperor Oluduin was deposed.

Axnmes secretly met with the Vilidesian Omystikai to air his grievances. They too, were upset with the turn of events and were sympathetic to his frustrations. The Vilidesian Omystikai watched in dismay as Rion's influence increased while theirs diminished. They refused to allow their centuries-old influence over the dynasty and affairs in The Vilides to disappear on account of an Omystikai sage from a long-forgotten kingdom. It was in this spirit of reprisal that Axnmes and the elders of the Order of the Crystal Moon conspired to take over the throne and be rid of Mona and Rion.

Chapter 19

Darshima and his companions sat around the hearth in silence. Morning light streamed through the windows, and a light dusting of snow fell upon the courtyard. The air felt heavy with the astounding truths that Tenrai, Dydan, and Priest Dawn had revealed to them, yet there was more to hear. Darshima bowed his head and drew in a breath. He had longed to know the truth, but it was difficult to bear.

"Aximes, the man whom I thought was my father was not the rightful heir to the throne," said Khydius, his voice trailing off.

"Sadly, this is the truth." Tenrai turned to Khydius, his eyes glowing with concern.

"I remember hearing of a coup that happened when we were children. I had no idea how much had changed in the realm because of it." Erethalie shook her head in disbelief.

"The coup caused much suffering throughout the realm," said Dydan.

"The Vilidesians suppressed information about that calamity. They wanted to forget its horrors," added Priest Dawn, her gaze solemnly deferred. "The rupture in their dynastic lineage led to much instability."

"We were never told any of this growing up," murmured Sydarias, his brow knit in frustration.

At sunset on a sweltering Ciblaithian evening, the Omystikai whom Rion had once considered friends and colleagues kidnapped him, Princess Mona, and their two children. They separated him from his family and held him in isolation. The Omystikai counselors used their abilities with kai to mentally overpower the legions of soldiers guarding the palace. They led Aximes and his personal army of mercenaries to the palace's innermost chambers, directly to the emperor. Aximes gave the defenseless monarch an ultimatum: he must abdicate his throne, or his soldiers would execute the entire court.

The counselors escorting Aximes claimed that their divination had forecast this event and that for the dynasty to continue, Emperor Oluduin must renounce the throne. Believing his counselors, Oluduin brokered a deal that resulted in him abdicating the throne to spare his life and the members of the dynasty. That very night, the counselors and the court stood witness as Aximes crowned himself the new Emperor of The Vilides and head of the House of Fyrenos.

Emperor Aximes forced most of the court into exile and replaced them with his allies. Not content with having attained the throne in the span of an evening, he sent the Omystikai counselors to bring forth Princes Mona. He issued a decree, voiding her marriage to Prince Rion, and planned to wed her that very night.

His mercenaries separated Princess Mona from her two sons and brought her to him. He demanded her hand in marriage, but she refused. Furious, he directed his soldiers to execute her, but they refused out of lingering loyalty to the dynasty. Before they could change their minds, Mona fled the palace and was never found again. Furious at her rebuke, Emperor Aximes ordered the Omystikai to kill Rion and their two children.

Emperor Aximes knew that despite seizing the throne, he would never be seen as a legitimate ruler if he did not marry a member of the House of Fyrenos. The deposed emperor only had two daughters, Mona, the heir to the throne, and Keleyra, her younger sister. There had been Vilidesian Empresses in the past, but tradition stipulated that it could only be the firstborn daughter. Aximes knew this and ordered the court to bring forward Keleyra. Though she had not been in the line of succession to the throne, he would bolster his title as emperor upon marrying her and assuming her dynastic name. His ascension to the throne represented the first time that the direct lineage had been broken.

"So, Empress Keleyra was truly my aunt." A sigh escaped Khydius' lips as he processed Tenrai's words. "Everything I grew up believing was a complete lie." He folded his arms across his chest, his eyes growing damp with tears. Darshima looked toward his brother, his heart pounding as he processed his own disbelief.

Though Darshima was equally stunned by Tenrai's account, he could not identify in the same way. Life and culture in the imperial court seemed as foreign to him as the vagaries of Tiriyuusian custom. Though he didn't fully understand, Darshima empathized with Khydius, remembering his own shock when he learned the truth about his adoptive family back on Gordanelle.

The Omystikai counselors brought Princess Keleyra to Emperor Aximes. He demanded that she marry him and guaranteed the members of the dynasty safe exile if she agreed. The Omystikai counselors and the deposed emperor pressured her to proceed with the marriage to the new emperor. They saw it as the only way that the House of Fyrenos could endure this calamitous circumstance. With the immense weight of this obligation upon her, she agreed to the terms and married Emperor Aximes that very night.

Young Darshima and Khydius were held in a palace nursery, away from the commotion and violence. Under Emperor Aximes' orders, they were to be killed. He wanted to destroy every trace of the union between Rion and Mona. As they were highly protective of their two children, neither the Omystikai counselors nor the Vilidesian public had ever laid eyes upon them.

When they encountered Darshima and Khydius later that evening, Emperor Aximes' counselors sensed very strong and unfamiliar flows of the sovereign strength within them. They felt a keen sense of foreboding about what bringing harm to them would cause for everyone involved.

"This is too much to bear." Khydius began to stand up, and Darshima grabbed his hand.

"We must hear it. We cannot move on unless we know the whole truth." Darshima looked up at him. Khydius wiped away his tears, then sat back down.

The Omystikai counselors convinced Emperor Aximes to keep Khydius. They sensed that as he matured, his strengths would be useful to them. They felt that he would bring a long and prosperous reign to the new emperor's rule. Much to his chagrin, Aximes acquiesced to their counsel. He grudgingly claimed Khydius as his son and heir. Under threat of death, he swore the entire court to secrecy of Khydius' true parentage.

The Omystikai counselors felt something unfamiliar and frightening, yet fascinating, within Darshima. Fearful of what this child would one day be capable of, Emperor Aximes decided that he must die. Aximes went against his counselors and instructed his mercenaries to kill him. They separated the brothers and took Darshima away from the palace grounds.

Beneath the void of night, they placed Darshima amid the dunes be-yond The Vilides. They lit a ring of fire around him and performed an an-cient Omystikai ritual intended to render him powerless before he died. They then left him for the beasts of the desert to devour. It was from these flames that Dalia and Sovani had rescued Darshima as they fled to Ardavia.

"How could he have been so cruel?" Khydius glared numbly into the subdued flames of the hearth. "I remember him as magnanimous toward his subjects."

"In many ways, Aximes wasn't the man that most Vilidesians believed he was," said Tenrai.

"His cruelty abated as he assumed his role, but the tumult of his early years endured in the lives and hearts of many." Priest Dawn narrowed her eyes in contemplation.

Rion remained in anguished isolation amid the chaos. Not content with his mere execution, Emperor Aximes wanted to send a strong message to his people in Tiriyuud. He ordered Rion aboard a Vilidesian aerial squadron, where he was held captive. The pair of ships voyaged to Iber-wight and approached the skies over Tiriyuud. The emperor's soldiers tor-tured him, demanding that he reveal the way around the perpetual storms surrounding the archipelago. They intended to unleash incendiary bombs over Chryshaihem as a warning against ever interfering with Vilidesian af-fairs.

In one last desperate attempt, Rion mustered what strength he had left and fought back. He succeeded in slaying his captors and downing their ships before they even glimpsed Tiriyuud's shore. He died as the damaged craft fell from the sky, crashed into the waters, and slipped beneath the waves.

"How did he manage to take down the ships?" asked Sydarias.

"He did as I taught him," said Priest Dawn. "I believe he used a ju-urofym orb that he always kept with him. The gravitational waves would have been strong enough to destroy those Vilidesian vessels." Darshima's jaw dropped in astonishment. He remembered Priest Dawn's demonstra-tion and how it had nearly injured Khydius.

"Though Rion was no longer a part of this kingdom, he gave his life to save it," said Dydan.

"He prevented the Vilidesians from laying siege to Chryshaihem, and we will forever be thankful for his bravery." Priest Dawn bowed her head.

"Is he still down there?" Darshima's chest grew heavy as he recalled the haunting image of the vessels beneath the waves.

"After the ships fell from the sky, I dove into the ocean and tried to save him." Tenrai closed his eyes, briefly overcome with emotion. "I found the wreckage and recovered his body."

"The Order of the Gilded Moon gave him proper last rites," said Dydan, his voice wavering with sadness. "He was buried as a Tiriyuusian Sage."

A heavy silence filled the room as the sunbeams filtered through the frosted windowpanes. Darshima's thoughts were clouded with a mixture of fatigue, and his heart ached with feelings of uncovered grief.

"We will take the remainder of this day to rest and reflect." Priest Dawn looked at all of them, a somber expression forming upon her face.

"The truth is painful, but it is the only path toward healing." She rose to her feet, along with Tenrai and Dydan. Darshima and his companions stood up and joined them. They filed out of the room and into the corridor. As they were about to part ways, Tenrai stood before Darshima and Khydius.

"I didn't have the courage to tell you about your father when I first met you." Tenrai bowed his head. "Please forgive me."

"You don't have to ask us for forgiveness," said Darshima. His heart rose into his throat as he ruminated over the incredible story of Rion's life. "Thank you for telling us about him."

"I wish we could have met him and our mother." A sorrowful expression formed upon Khydius' face.

"Rion was a remarkable man." A melancholy sigh escaped Tenrai's lips. "After his death, I sought a way to rescue you both. I wanted to bring you back to Tiriyuud and raise you as he would have wanted." Tenrai's voice grew heavy as he spoke. "I could not find a way to get to you. Khydius was a Vilidesian Prince and heir to the throne, and Darshima had been left to die in the desert." Tenrai dashed a tear from the corner of his eye. "Your fate was unknown to me."

"You found us, and we are together now. That is what matters the most." Darshima hugged both Tenrai and Khydius, and they returned the gesture with a heartfelt embrace.

"Despite these difficult truths, you are more prepared for the upcoming test of your skills than you know. You both have exceeded my expectations during your training." An earnest smile formed upon Tenrai's lips. "Your father would be proud."

"We won't let you down, uncle," said Darshima. Khydius nodded in agreement. Tenrai bid them farewell, and they retired to their quarters.

Chapter 20

Darshima looked out over the lake as the ship's bow carved through the misty surface. He drew his overcoat around him and tried to stave off the cold, steady wind. The sun hovered above the horizon, streaking the blue sky in hues of orange and red. Dydan navigated at the helm, peering through his crystal as he gazed upon the changing scenery. Priest Dawn sat beside him, her robes fluttering in the wind. She gripped her staff, steadying herself as the craft glided over the ripples. Tenrai sat at the vessel's rear, his hand gripping the steering lever as he made subtle corrections to their course.

Erethalie, Sydarias, and Khydius sat silently, occasionally peering over the sides of the craft. Darshima saw their anxious expressions, and he felt the same. Today marked the beginning of the final test of their skills. During the next three days, their performance would determine whether the Order would induct them as guardians or send them away from Tiriyuud.

Though Tenrai and Dydan reassured them, Darshima still worried about meeting their expectations. He mulled over his early struggles with sparring and cloudboarding. His heart thudded with a feeling of confidence as he took stock of what they all had accomplished so far. Darshima and his companions managed to overcome their initial obstacles since arriving in Tiriyuud, and now they were thriving. Like they had done before, they would meet and surmount whatever trials came their way.

Darshima glimpsed over his shoulder and saw the trio of rugged training islands shrinking in the distance. Amid the snowy stands of trees, he saw the curved temple roofs gleaming in the sunlight. A lump formed in his throat as they sped further away. It was hard for him to believe that their training was complete. Soon, they wouldn't be merely recruits but fully-fledged guardians.

His nostalgia getting the better of him, Darshima tore his gaze from the islands. In the surrounding waters, he saw dozens of identical craft crossing the lake. Groups of guardians and their recruits raced by, their tails of spray fanning behind them.

"We have only a little further to travel." Dydan pointed toward a large island rising from the waters. A series of rolling hills spread out before them, covered in dense stands of snowy trees.

"This is where all recruits perform the first stage of the final test," said Tenrai, his words mingling with the wind. Darshima heard a note of wistfulness in his voice.

"We're ready." Erethalie confidently tapped her foot against her cloudboard.

"These months of training have prepared us," said Sydarias.

"You must rely on all that you've learned from your exercises." Dydan glimpsed over his shoulder at them.

"They are capable, and they are ready." Priest Dawn gently tapped Dydan's foot with her staff. "I believe they will surprise us all." She looked over her shoulder toward Darshima and his companions, offering a reassuring nod.

"We will make you all proud." Darshima bowed toward them.

Despite his nervousness, Darshima was in good spirits. He and his companions had trained as hard for this day as their fellow Omystikai recruits. They had more than earned the privilege to submit to the final test. Darshima's thoughts were interrupted by the sound of coughing. He looked over to Khydius on his left, who brought his hands to his mouth. His chest heaving, he glared blankly ahead.

"How are you feeling?" Darshima turned to his brother, his eyes widening in concern.

"I feel exhausted." Khydius' teeth chattered as he spoke. His cheeks appeared flushed, and he drew his coat over his shivering shoulders.

"Will you be able to go through with the test?" whispered Darshima.

"I have no other choice." Khydius shrugged.

"I know you can succeed." Darshima stared at Khydius for a moment, then faced forward, his heart fluttering with a sense of anticipation. He also felt slightly different today. He thought it might be his anxieties surrounding the test, but the feeling was seated much deeper within him.

Darshima gripped the side of the ship as it jostled over the waters. He drew in a breath as subtle jolts of electricity coursed through him. Though he had gotten used to the feeling, the surrounding kai fields upon the lake felt much stronger than usual. He briefly closed his eyes as the feeling passed.

Darshima felt his chest tighten with an unexpected pang of anxiety. He drew in a breath as Tenrai's revelation echoed in his head. Whenever Darshima found himself in a quiet moment, the shocking truths rushed back into his mind. It had been a week since Tenrai shared the story of their mother and father. The gravity of his revelation made it difficult for him to focus upon anything else. Darshima felt his former sense of self unraveling and the stirrings of a new and unfamiliar one emerging.

Darshima looked down at his forearm. The intricate markings gleamed upon his bronze skin, peeking out from beneath his fabric sleeve. Rion Nax had sensed his strengths as an infant and placed those markings upon him. Darshima wondered what else Rion had seen in him. Tenrai was his connection to Rion, and he needed to know more.

By midmorning, they approached the island's narrow bay. Darshima felt the craft sway as Tenrai guided them along a wooden pier with several other boats. Dydan and Priest Dawn disembarked and walked along the bleached planks. Darshima and his companions grabbed their cloudboards and stepped off the vessel. Tenrai followed them and secured the boat to a stone pier with a length of rope.

Darshima walked with his companions along a paved path tracing the shoreline, hemmed in by the dense forest. A few paces ahead, he saw the other groups of recruits arranging themselves along the pebble-strewn beach. Dydan and Priest Dawn led them toward the shore, where they stood together. The rhythmic sound of water crashing against the rocks filled the air.

As they waited, a trio of guardians approached them, with their recruits in tow. Darshima's heart rose into his throat as he recognized Eikan, Seibu, and Lleidas standing before them.

"You four have made it this far. Show us all that you have learned, and you will become guardians." Eikan offered them a curt bow. Seibu and Lleidas followed her gesture.

"We won't let you down." Darshima returned with a deep bow. Erethalie, Khydius, and Sydarias echoed Darshima's thanks and bowed toward them. Eikan and her fellow guardians bid them farewell and continued along the beach with their recruits.

Tenrai stood with his back to the lake while Dydan arranged Darshima, Khydius, Erethalie, and Sydarias into a line. Priest Dawn gazed at each of them, and her eyes narrowed in an appraising expression.

"We will start with a few light exercises to prepare you for your first sparring matches." Tenrai stepped back and looked toward Darshima.

As he stood in position, Darshima brought his hand to his brow and stared at the mountains separating the lake from the ocean. The sunlight reflected off the snowy peaks in a shimmering flash of light that caught his attention. Before he could look any further, the crunch of footsteps filled his ears.

Tenrai and Dydan paced in front of them, reviewing their posture and adjusting their uniforms. Tenrai reached out and straightened the seam of Khydius' overcoat. Darshima drew in an anxious breath as he saw Khydius' worsening appearance. His skin appeared flushed, and he shivered uncontrollably.

"What is wrong, Khydius?" Tenrai pulled him aside.

"I don't know, but something doesn't feel right." He put a hand to his chest and drew in a halting breath.

"You must try and settle yourself. After this morning's sparring session, you will have a chance to rest." Tenrai's brow wrinkled in worry.

"I will do my best. May I rejoin the others?" Khydius stared at Tenrai. He dug his boots into the soil as if trying to steady himself.

"If your condition worsens, please tell me." Tenrai's gaze lingered upon him. Khydius stepped back into line beside Sydarias.

Darshima waited patiently, his pulse racing. He tried to remember everything he had learned since arriving in Tiriyuud. Tenrai and Dydan had shared the essentials of the test, but they had been sparse with the details. In a few moments, they would march to the island's interior, where they would engage in the first of several sparring trials to assess their skill. Subsequent sessions would be devoted to demonstrating their abilities on the saigura and their mastery of the Orders armaments. In between these exercises, the guardians would test the recruits on their knowledge of passages from the canonical texts they studied.

Darshima looked out over the glistening waters, his ears prickling against the chilly air. Amid the calm, he pointed an ear toward the forest. A series of bells would sound, signaling the recruits to enter the forest and begin the first sessions. He drew in steady breaths and centered his thoughts, recalling the methods that Priest Dawn had taught them to keep calm during the most intense sparring sessions.

As Darshima waited with his companions, he shivered as the winds rose over the lake. The ripples grew stronger, turning into choppy waves. Walls of foamy surf crashed ashore, soaking his uniform in their icy mists. Darshima stared at the unexpected scene, unable to recall a time when the conditions upon the lake had changed so suddenly. A low, pervasive drone rose over the crash of the waves.

Darshima eyed the guardians and the other recruits, who looked around them in confusion. The sound grew into a deep roar, and the air around them vibrated in a sonorous tone that rattled in his chest. Darshima's heart sank as the ominous sound burrowed into the deep recesses of his memory. It was a sound he recognized. His mouth grew dry as fiery images of the invasion flashed before him. His chest tightened with the same weight of fear that he had felt back then.

Darshima's eyes narrowed as hundreds of enormous ships flew over the mountains and descended over the lake. Their enormous, greenish airframes broke through the shroud of mist, casting their reflection upon the water's rippled surface.

"What is happening?" Sydarias sank to his knees and stared fearfully at the skies.

"Tiriyuud is under siege." Erethalie pointed to the aircraft, shaking her head in disbelief. Darshima glared at the aerial fleet, his heart pounding with a sickening familiarity.

"Those are Navervynish ships." Khydius clenched his fists as he glared at the horizon. "They have finally breached the last free corner of our world."

"We must summon our fleets. Chryshaihem is under threat." Tenrai turned to Dydan.

"This is a surprise attack. We have little time and must tell the others." Dydan turned toward a pair of guardians beside them. He flashed a series of hand signals, and they ran from the beach and into the forest. Sydarias rose to his feet and stood beside Darshima.

"Can we use kai to stop them?" shouted Darshima over the growing mechanical drone, his face contorted in a look of fear.

"We can use kai on their soldiers, but it is difficult." Priest Dawn closed her eyes and gripped her staff. "I will communicate with the guardians stationed in Chryshaihem." She walked toward the lake, the surf soaking the hems of her robes. Priest Dawn paced solemnly along the shore with her eyes closed, murmuring a series of Omystikaiyn phrases.

"We must try and do what we can." Tenrai turned to Dydan, whose jaw parted in a look of subdued horror. Several other guardians stood in a line beside them. They instinctively grasped each other's hands and looked out upon the advancing fleet of ships.

His heart pounding in terror, Darshima dug his boots into the ground and steadied himself. He glared at the Navervynish fleet as they drew closer. The skies beyond the mountains burst into glowing spheres of red as fiery rockets vaulted toward the sky.

"Their ships are traveling swiftly. Our projectiles will not reach them in time," uttered Tenrai, his voice rising in disbelief. The fusiform rockets raced toward the vessels in streaking trails of light. The projectiles exploded in flashes of fire and thunderous echos, seemingly deflected before they struck the rapidly advancing fleet.

Darshima's pulse thudded with a mixture of incredulity and anger as he witnessed the unfolding calamity. Owing to its secluded location, perpetual storms, and the protective kai fields surrounding the archipelago, Tiriyuud had remained in isolation, unscathed in the turmoil that had seen empires rise and fall upon the moons over the ages. He felt helpless as he stood there, bearing witness to an invasion that threatened its very existence.

"We must do something," murmured Darshima, looking on in stunned disbelief. He turned to Tenrai, Dydan, and the other guardians, who stood together as they faced the fleet.

Darshima's heart rose into his throat as he waited for their impending destruction. His eyes grew damp as he remembered fleeing with Sydarias as fire from those very same ships rained terror upon The Vilides. Tiriyuud's fighting forces and weapons, though formidable, were no match for an adversary that singlehandedly conquered an entire realm. Navervyne had the element of surprise on its side, and Tiriyuud did not.

Eyes narrowed, Darshima cast a steely gaze upon the approaching ships, spanning the sky in a wide, threatening arc of metal. His pulse thudded in his temples as a rising sense of anger overwhelmed his fear. Like countless others, he had suffered through the invasion, slavery, and its lasting consequences. Darshima's stomach twisted into a knot as he imagined the Tiriyuusians confronting the same devastating fate.

The ships descended through the shrouds of mist and hurtled toward the beach.

"Take cover!" Tenrai looked over his shoulder and called out to the gathered recruits. The other guardians broke ranks from the line and guided their recruits into the forest. Tenrai, Dydan, Priest Dawn stood firm. Darshima remained still, his ears filling with the sounds of pounding footsteps and the deafening roar of aircraft. He heard voices frantically shouting his name, but they sounded distant and muted. His mind was in another place, and he focused on the vast fleet careening toward them.

A familiar rush of power and emotion surged within him. He trained his eyes upon the advancing fleet, the sensation growing so strong that he felt faint. He stood firm and dug his heels into the ground. A seething rage roiled within him as the aerial ships flew brazenly in their path, the waters below stirring in their wake. The winds whipped around Darshima as the vessels drew closer to the shore, his uniform flapping in the stiff gusts.

Darshima felt the surge of electricity jolt through seemingly every sinew and synapse, but it did not overwhelm him. His heart slowed, and his mind grew calm with a sense of control that felt familiar and foreign all at once. He instinctively outstretched his right hand toward the speeding fleet. His jaw clenched, Darshima glared upon the vessels and held his hand out in front of him. He drew in a stunned breath as an overwhelming force slammed into his body, pushing him backward. The innate surge of electricity flowed stronger within him. He stood firm, and with all his might, Darshima pushed back harder. He clenched his teeth and struggled against the incredible force, his lungs burning as he strained.

To his utter disbelief, the massive fleet slowed in their approach. The airframes issued an ear-piercing shudder of creaking metal and ground to a halt in mid-air. Buffeted by a tremendous, unseen force, their engines groaned as they struggled forward, trying to break free from Darshima's astral grip. Darshima's eyes widened in unalloyed awe when he realized that it was his hand alone restraining the mighty fleet.

Darshima's anger overpowered his remaining calmness as he stared down the craft in their wanton path toward destruction. His eyes grew damp with feelings of grief and rage at the heinous act that Navervyne was about to commit.

"I won't let them do this." Darshima stifled a sob and drew his fingers together in a tight, unwavering fist.

Before Darshima's very eyes and those of the guardians and recruits, the vast fleet buckled under the awakened, stupendous force of his grip. The massive aerial ships lost control of their course, their fuselages violently crashing into each other in a shower of dazzling sparks and gashed metal. Darshima clenched his fist even tighter, and their airframes deformed into grotesque and crooked shapes. The ships groaned loudly, and within moments, the fleet collapsed, bursting into a searing line of fire and a shower of sparks beneath the clouds.

The earsplitting shriek of twisting metal and shattering glass filled the air. Acrid plumes of smoke and debris wafted down from the sky. The burning wreckage hung motionlessly under Darshima's grasp. The remnants of the airframes glowed white-hot as the fires from their fuel tanks burned brightly against the sky. Glowing rivulets of liquid metal poured from the melting ships as they imploded. Clouds of hissing steam rose from the lake surface as the metal splashed into the waters.

Darshima deftly waved his hand upward, and the ruined fleet suddenly vaulted into the sky like a swirl of burning ash. Moments later, the flaming wreckage plummeted downward and crashed into the lake, sending a torrent of waves racing toward the shore. The waters grew still as the charred, smoking wreckage bobbed amid the ripples, then slipped below the surface.

Darshima stood still as the waves washed ashore. Water flecked with ash, oil, and debris, lapped over his boots. An uneasy calm settled over the beach.

"Darshima!" Tenrai rushed to Darshima's side and grabbed his shoulders. "Please come with me. We must flee to Chryshaihem." Tenrai's eyes widened in an expression of incredulity.

"What happened?" His heart racing, Darshima stared down at his trembling hands. His head spun as the surging energy dissipated from his body.

"You have saved Tiriyuud," said Tenrai, his voice catching in his throat. His eyes filled with tears as he stared at Darshima. Tenrai grabbed Darshima's hand and led him from the shore. Priest Dawn and Dydan called out to Khydius, Erethalie, and Sydarias. Their faces were contorted in expressions of terror, and they had taken cover behind a stand of trees.

They all followed Tenrai back to the pier, boarded their vessel, and departed the island with the other guardians and recruits.

Darshima braced himself against the side of the craft as it carved its way across the lake, his aching muscles feeling every wave. A fog hung before his mind, and his stomach twisted in a queasy knot. He squinted against the sunlight, its rays glaring harshly upon the rippling waters. Priest Dawn and Dydan sat at the head of the craft and kept an eye out for obstacles in their path. Darshima glimpsed over his shoulder and saw Tenrai steer the craft, carefully weaving between the other vessels crossing the lake.

Darshima closed his eyes for a moment and tried to clear the haze that clouded his thoughts. The blackness behind his eyelids dissolved into flashes of searing light and images of the exploding Navervynish fleet.

"Did that really happen?" Darshima drew in a deep breath. He shook his head in disbelief.

"You destroyed that entire fleet, Darshima," said Khydius.

"It can't be." Tears filled Darshima's eyes. "How is any of this possible?" He vigorously shook his head and tried to rid himself of the terrifying images, but they stayed with him, no matter how much he blinked.

"You saved us." Sydarias wrapped his arm around Darshima's shoulder, and Darshima shuddered in his embrace.

"You did something incredible!" exclaimed Erethalie. She rested her hand upon his knee and tried to console him. Darshima allowed the tears to fall from his eyes, the rhythmic motion of the ship offering some comfort. He didn't want to believe that he had wielded enough power to down an entire fleet, but he knew there was no other explanation.

"Your actions saved all of us." Khydius turned to him, his eyes glimmering with a hint of awe.

"They all died because of what I did," whispered Darshima, his voice trailing off.

"Navervyne nearly invaded Tiriyuud, as they did the realm." Erethalie looked directly at him, her brows wrinkled in a steely expression. "It was either them or us. You have no reason to feel guilty." Darshima offered her a hesitant nod and glared ahead. He knew she was right, but the scale of the destruction he caused left him speechless.

"I can see the capital, and from here, it looks unscathed," said Dydan, his voice tense with worry.

Darshima eyed the dense skyline of Chryshaihem. Its stone spires and tiled roofs unfolded upon the horizon in shimmering hues of blue, gold, and black. Darshima breathed a sigh of relief as he saw no apparent signs of destruction.

"I pray that the other islands have remained secure." Tenrai adjusted the rudder as they approached a wide harbor, silently moving amongst dozens of other watercraft.

"I believe they have, but only time knows for how long." Priest Dawn glared at the city rising before them.

"How did the Council of Sages fail to predict this unexpected siege?" Dydan wondered aloud, his voice wavering with emotion.

"We have long prepared as guardians for an invasion from The Vilides," murmured Tenrai. "This attack was unlike anything we expected."

"This is no time to cast judgment on our Order." Priest Dawn firmly tapped her staff against the floor of the ship. "Darshima's hand has bought us precious time that we cannot afford to waste." Darshima's heart thudded at her words. His gaze lingered upon the markings upon his arm.

"What about the final test? Mustn't we complete it?" Darshima looked toward Tenrai.

"There is no time." Tenrai's eyes narrowed as he looked at Darshima and his companions. "Your class of guardians will be tested and judged upon the only true proving ground - the battlefield." He gripped the lever and guided their craft ashore.

Chapter 21

Darshima's gaze lingered upon the snows as they fell from the skies. The flakes landed upon the black stone courtyard of the Guardians' Shrine, glistening as they melted. As his fatigue lessened, a sense of familiarity came over him. A hesitant smile crossed his lips as he remembered following Tenrai across this very courtyard when they had first arrived in Chryshaihem nearly four months ago. Back then, he would've never fathomed how much circumstances would have changed when he returned.

Darshima looked to his sides and saw Erethalie, Khydius, and Sydarias standing beside him amid the crowds. Hundreds of young men and women stood silently at attention, their icy breaths mingling with the snowflakes. They all wore new uniforms consisting of black trousers, vests, and split-toed boots. Their long black overcoats were trimmed in leather ribbons and tessellated golden octagons, signifying their rank as new guardians.

Darshima adjusted the decorated, diagonal leather straps securing his cloudboard upon his back. Despite the cold temperature, he felt comfortable in his new uniform. They had recently arrived at the shrine from their journey and were issued new guardian uniforms. This meeting in the courtyard was their first official duty.

At the opposite end of the space stood a large wooden stage, sheltered under the tiled eaves of the peristyle. Several dozen guardians stood in rows and looked out at the crowd. A guardian knight, distinguished by a golden sash upon his right shoulder, stood at a wooden lectern, his words echoing through large amplifying crystals hanging from the eaves of the courtyard. Darshima eyed Tenrai and Priest Dawn, who stood with the other guardians upon the stage. Shortly after returning to Chryshaihem, Dydan bid them farewell and returned to the Sages' Temple, where the council convened an emergency meeting.

Darshima glimpsed past the stage through the ornate stone arcade enclosing the octagonal space. The lofty spires and buildings of the capital spread out majestically below them in a dense, vivid tapestry of carved stone, wrought iron, and stained glass. The guardians took turns speaking at the podium. They spoke in the Tiriyuusian dialect, and though Darshima understood much of what they were saying, his thoughts lingered elsewhere. This ceremony would mark their entrance into the Order of the Gilded Moon and their new status as guardians. Today was anything but a cause for celebration, and their induction was happening under the most unimaginable circumstances.

The threat of invasion meant that Darshima and his recruits could not complete the final test. From what Priest Dawn had told them on their journey back to the capital, no class of recruits had ever been inducted into the guardianship before passing the final test. Theirs would be the first and only class of untested recruits brought back to Chryshaihem. They were also the first new class of recruits to face a threat of such magnitude.

Though they had not long returned to the city, Darshima sensed the worry among his fellow recruits. Their solemn expressions and sober frowns belied the anxiety they were feeling. They faced a fight unlike any other in the history of the kingdom. Darshima pondered the incredible fact that Tiriyuud remained the only sovereign and unoccupied territory among the four moons. From what he witnessed this morning, he believed it was only a matter of time before Navervyne would attempt another invasion.

The unimaginable circumstance in which Tiriyuud found itself meant that Darshima and his fellow recruits would be initiated as guardians that very morning and prepare for battle over the coming days. Tenrai's words echoed in Darshima's mind as he looked around him. There would be no time for them to submit to the final test of their skill. The recruits would be endorsed by the guardians who had trained them. Their strength and bravery would be ultimately be proven in battle.

It had only been a few hours since they returned to Chryshaihem, but the morning's unfathomable events were already sinking into his memory. Though he tried to ignore them, Darshima felt the furtive stares of his fellow recruits as he stood among them. Everyone had witnessed the strength he had wielded on the shore. He had demonstrated power far beyond what he knew that he was capable of, but he no longer was surprised.

Darshima thought of how he had spared Sydarias from death during that fateful night in the slave colony on Navervyne. He also thought of that moment when he destroyed the group of soldiers during their flight from

Stebbenhour. During those harrowing moments, he had felt the same anger and emotion as he had experienced that morning, but the months of training gave him a sense of control that he never felt before.

An anxious knot formed in his stomach as he tried to focus on the proceedings. Again, with a wave of his hand, he had wrought death and destruction. He obliterated an entire armada of invading ships with a mere gesture. He had saved Chryshaihem and spared Tiriyuud from what would have been, without question, a brutal invasion. Again, he had saved innocent lives by extinguishing those that had threatened them. His pulse thudded with a growing sense of unease.

Darshima's mind swirled with the events of that morning and what it all meant. As he listened to the guardians speaking at the podium, he felt a tap upon his shoulder. He looked over to Sydarias, whose face was drawn in a solemn expression.

"What will this attempted invasion mean for us, for Tiriyuud?" Sydarias looked toward Erethalie and Khydius.

"This is now a kingdom at war. We all must fight until the end, whatever that may be," said Darshima.

"As of now, we are members of the Order of the Gilded Moon. We are duty-bound to defend this kingdom." A pensive frown formed upon Erethalie's lips. Khydius stood silently, his eyes narrowed in thought. He then turned to Darshima.

"As with The Vilides and the rest of the realm, Tiriyuud stood virtually no chance of repelling an advance from Navervyne." Khydius pointed to Darshima, and his eyes widened in awe. "Your hand has changed the fate of this kingdom and potentially much more."

"I don't know what that means," said Darshima, his voice trailing off. He knew that he had saved Tiriyuud, but he had yet to contemplate the stakes Khydius clearly saw.

"Your strength will give Tiriyuud an edge against our enemy." Khydius grasped Darshima's hand and stared at him intently.

Those many months ago, when Tenrai had rescued them and shared his plans, Darshima envisioned the five of them as a small group waging a covert campaign against Navervyne to liberate those still enslaved. The events of that morning, however, had changed everything.

Their time in Tiriyuud had lulled him into a false sense of security. The events of that morning had shattered any lingering peace that he felt. The thwarted invasion by Navervyne was an act of war, and he knew the Order had no choice but to respond in kind. Instead of the small group he had imagined, it would now be the Kingdom of Tiriyuud fighting against the full force and fury of the Navervyne Republic and its newfound empire.

Darshima's gaze wandered past the innumerable rows of recruits surrounding them, beyond the temple walls to the city below. He pondered their chances of victory against such an enormous threat. The Vilides ruled over the four moons for more than a millennium and had been brought to its knees by Navervyne in a matter of weeks. Its entire realm had fallen to the invading forces in mere months. He wondered how this small island nation, with its strong but small army and finite resources, could prevail against such a powerful enemy.

The knight finished speaking, and the guardians marched down the steps and into the courtyard. They fanned out among their newly minted colleagues for the conclusion of the ceremony.

"Congratulations, fellow guardians." Priest Dawn approached them, her stern expression softening as she stood before them.

"You four have exceeded my expectations. I am proud of all that you've accomplished." Tenrai looked at each of them. "I know you will serve both Tiriyuud and the Order with distinction in our hour of need."

"Thank you, Tenrai. We won't let you down." Humbled by Tenrai's recognition, Darshima felt his voice grow heavy with emotion. Erethalie, Khydius, and Sydarias bowed their heads at Tenrai's words.

"The leader of our kingdom will be addressing us." Priest Dawn bowed her head in deference. "We must show our respect."

As the crowd settled, the sound of chanting broke through the din of conversation. Darshima and the other guardians clicked their heels and stood at attention, their unified movements echoing throughout the shrine. The deep, harmonious voices grew louder, and moments later, the Sages of Tiriyuud emerged. Dressed in pleated robes of black and gold, they emerged from the shrine and marched in a stiff line. The Seer of Chryshaihem led them across the stage, her vivid red and gold costume contrasting with the flakes of glistening snow. Wearing his sages robes, Dydan walked a few paces behind her, his face bearing a stoic expression.

The sages carried black pennants bearing an eight-pointed blue star surrounded by a halo of interlocking golden crescents.

The procession made its way toward the front of the stage, and the guardians stepped aside, forming lines at the platform's edges. The sages ceased their chanting.

"Behold, the Oracle of Tiriyuud!" they shouted. In one swift and sudden motion, the guardians and sages dropped onto their hands and knees in unison. Unfamiliar with the tradition, Darshima, Erethalie, Sydarias, and Khydius did the same. They lay prostrate on the ground amid the silence and the snowfall. Darshima's heart thudded in surprise at the dramatic gesture. Prior to Priest Dawn's words, he didn't know that the oracle would be making an appearance. He hadn't realized the deference the Tiriyuusians showed to their leader.

Darshima and his fellow guardians lay still until they heard a lone voice summoning them to rise. The sages, knights, and the hundreds of guardians rose to their feet in a thunderous beat, shaking the very ground beneath them.

With anxious eyes, Darshima stood at attention and waited in silence. The sages stepped beneath the eaves of the peristyle. Only the slivers of their robes were visible in the shadows. The oracle moved toward the center of the stage and faced the vast army of guardians. Crisp black robes adorned with golden rays, and crystal polygons draped her slender frame. An octagonal crown of gold and crystal sat atop her long black locks, shining like a halo against the grey skies. Her porcelain skin blended with the falling flakes of snow.

Her smooth oval face bore the radiance of youth, but her sapphire eyes belied a fierce wisdom. The oracle's fine features held a somber expression as she cast a cursory glance over the guardians standing attention.

"Seer of Chryshaihem, sages, knights, and guardians of Tiriyuud, we convene at this hallowed place in our most perilous hour." She raised her hands and spoke in a clear voice that echoed through the shrine.

Darshima stood rapt as she spoke in clear Tiriyuusian. His mind flashed with a feeling of momentary surprise as he understood words that once had been foreign to him. His pulse thudded as he saw the assembled crowd looking toward her with their undivided attention. Overcome by the moment, many of them clasped their hands together, their glowing sapphire eyes glittering with tears as they beheld her.

In poignant words, the oracle recognized the recruits' accomplishments. She endorsed their newfound status as guardians and full members of the Order of the Gilded Moon.

"The calamity that Tiriyuud nearly suffered is without precedent. Our defenses have been severely tested, but we are not defenseless." She clenched her gloved hands as she spoke.

The oracle emphasized the urgency of the circumstance they faced. She exhorted the guardians, both new and veteran, to use their strength and wisdom to defend the kingdom and the Order.

"Brave Guardians of the Order of the Gilded Moon, who have trained these brilliant young men and women, do you affirm their strength and dedication?" She cast her hand out toward them.

"Without any doubt or reservation." Speaking in unison, Tenrai and Priest Dawn turned toward Darshima and his companions and bowed deeply. His heart rising into his throat, Darshima returned the gesture, and Erethalie, Khydius, and Sydarias did the same. A rousing cheer erupted from the assembled guardians.

"Valiant protectors of Tiriyuud, do you affirm the knowledge, wisdom, and faith of this new generation of guardians?" asked the oracle.

"By our honor, we affirm them," said the guardians in unison.

"Guardians, these young people in your midst. Whom have they become in our eyes?" The oracle raised hands in exhortation.

"They are guardians as we are," they responded in a deafening chant.

After their cheers calmed down, the oracle continued. "Young men and women, you are now Guardians of the Order of the Gilded Moon, the sworn protectors of Tiriyuud. Go forth!" She extended her open hands toward the crowd. At her pronouncement, Darshima and his companions cheered with their fellow guardians in a deafening roar.

The oracle waited as they issued joyous shouts and then raised her hand. The guardians fell silent and looked upon her. In a low voice, she chanted the words of an ancient blessing, meant to guard their strength and protect them in battle. She finished the incantation, lowered her hand, and the sages escorted her back into the shrine.

The staccato sound of commands echoed around the courtyard. Darshima and his fellow guardians stood attention, clicked their heels, and saluted their senior guardians. Darshima moved forward as the lines of men and women marched, their footsteps shaking the very foundations of the shrine. They walked under the falling snows and across the pavement.

Darshima and his companions stepped under the encircling arcades and the soaring gates marking the shrine's entrance. They spilled out onto the main axis of the city, marching in neat lines upon the pavement. The sharp click of their boots echoed against the wrought stone and wood canyons. He looked up at temples, shrines, and buildings rising at the city center, obscured in a flurry of snow. Giant banners of black gold and blue, bearing the emblem of Tiriyuud, fluttered from the balconies flanking the avenue.

Darshima marched in lockstep with the other guardians along the avenue. A lump formed in his throat when he saw the enormous crowds lining the street. Uniformed sentries surveyed the throngs and maintained order. The people let out a deafening cheer that resounded in the streets, their many hands waving Tiriyuusian flags in frenzied bursts of color.

"Can you believe this?" Sydarias looked around them. Moved by the display, his eyes grew damp with tears.

"I would have never imagined anything like it." Darshima nudged Sydarias with his elbow.

"This is similar to my experience with the imperial parades held in Gavipristine when I paid my annual visit to see the Sovereign," mused Khydius.

"This is a different time and place, Prince Khydius." Erethalie turned to him. "The Tiriyuusians are cheering for us all."

Darshima, Khydius, Sydarias, and Erethalie marched among their fellow guardians, the frenzied crowds waving at them. Despite their exuberance, Darshima read a tangible sense of worry upon their faces. He imagined that word of the attempted invasion had spread throughout the kingdom. Nevertheless, Darshima felt hope in their cheers and shouts of gratitude. He, like his companions, had gone through their own personal struggles to reach this moment. His heart fluttered with a mixture of accomplishment and fear, relief, and anxiety.

Little more than a year ago, Darshima knew very little about the Omystikai or anything about this isolated corner of the fallen realm. Now he and his companions were Guardians of the Order of the Gilded Moon and citizens of Tiriyuud. In the months before this morning, he would've never imagined that the challenges they would face as new guardians would have become so urgent or so significant.

Darshima was aware of the vast strength of their enemy. He had seen it firsthand. But he had faith that their training would guide them through the most challenging circumstances. Though he felt apprehension about not submitting to the final test, he would find a way to move past it. The invasion that he miraculously thwarted that morning made him realize that much greater trials awaited them all. As guardians and as Tiriyuusians, they would fight with everything they had, and they would prevail.

Chapter 22

With his head bowed and his hands resting upon his knees, Darshima sat quietly upon a stone platform in the center of the enclosed sanctuary. A crystal ring surrounded the space, emitting a pale blue curtain of light. Darshima looked over to his right and saw Tenrai maintaining the same pose without even a hint of motion. He glimpsed to his left and saw Sydarias, Erethalie, and Khydius, seated in a similar position with their eyes closed, holding their concentration.

Darshima looked around the space as his companions meditated. He drew in a breath of the incense-filled air and tried to regain his focus. The sanctuary was one of dozens lining the octagonal inner sanctum of the Guardians' Shrine. A large curtain of clear glass spanned from the floor to the ceiling and enclosed the room in a semicircle.

Night had fallen, and Darshima glimpsed through the panes behind him. His eyes swept over the glittering Chryshaihemese cityscape surrounding the shrine. Flickering lights from lines of aerial convoys glided above the city like glowing sinewy threads against the dark skies. Benai occupied the eastern skies, its dimmed glow casting a soft light over the lake.

Tendrils of fragrant smoke billowed from a pale crystal censor suspended above their heads. The rafters terminated in a glass pyramid with an unobstructed view of the starry skies. Amid the silence, Darshima closed his eyes and pondered the next moments. They were due to attend a meeting with the guardians, knights, and commanders to discuss the Order's next steps in preparing Tiriyuud for its fight against Navervyne. During his training, he had seen hints of Tiriyuud's capabilities. He wondered how the kingdom would hold up against such a powerful adversary.

His chest grew heavy with worry as he pondered the strength of Navervyne. Its armies had brought The Vilidesians and its realm to their knees. Its soldiers had killed and enslaved so many. Navervyne had ruthlessly imposed its rule upon the moons of Benai, and every man, woman, and child had become its unwilling subjects. They ruled everyone except for the citizens of Tiriyuud. Darshima pondered the astounding fact that this small collection of islands remained the only unconquered territory among the four moons.

His thoughts weighing him down, Darshima opened his eyes. He looked at the glowing ring surrounding them and tried to recenter himself. His gaze swept over the intricate lines of golden script etched in the dark stone beneath him. His pulse thudded in recognition as he saw the words from an Omystikaiyn prayer, asking for strength and enlightenment.

As Darshima closed his eyes, the soft peal of a bell interrupted the silence.

"It is time." Tenrai rose to his feet and beckoned them.

"What will they ask of us?" Erethalie turned to Tenrai.

"They will not ask anything that you cannot answer. You all must listen and learn from this evening's meeting." Tenrai nodded earnestly.

Darshima and his companions stood up and followed Tenrai off the platform. As was the custom, they had removed their boots before entering the shrine. They shuffled out of the sanctuary in their black woolen stockings and back into the cavernous space. Dozens of other men and women emerged from identical sanctuaries lining the inner sanctum.

Darshima followed the crowds toward a circular, quartz platform that lay in the center of the shrine. The members of the Order wore uniforms bearing various gold and leather stripes, polygons, and tessellated patterns that denoted their rank within the guardianship. They organized into lines as they moved toward the dais.

Large stone pillars rose from the smooth floor, forming an elaborate arcade surrounding the platform. They supported a radial web of large, wooden beams in the roof high above. The slanted ceiling gave way to a glazed, pyramidal canopy that sheltered the center of the shrine. Light from Benai and the moons streamed through the transparent panes, casting the platform in pale beams of light.

Dozens of black woven rugs surrounded the platform in concentric circles. Darshima remembered from their training that the Guardians' Shrine was built many centuries ago. The complex sat upon one of the highest hills in Chryshaihem and stood beside the Sages' Temple. Perched atop Chryshaihem's tallest hill, the Oracle's Palace towered over the Guardians'

Shrine and the Sages' Temple. The palace served as the personal residence and administrative center for Tiriyuud's oracle.

Darshima peered around, awestruck by the subdued but elegant atmosphere of the shrine's inner sanctum. His pulse thudded as he walked with his companions. They were now guardians. As Tenrai emphasized when they had returned from the morning's procession, this place was now officially their home.

"You four will sit together." Tenrai gestured toward a group of rugs at the edge of the platform. Darshima and his companions took their seats, and Tenrai stepped onto the pale, gleaming dais. Darshima watched as the guardians arranged themselves into two concentric circles. Tenrai took his seat with the knights and commanders in the inner circle, and the senior guardians settled together in the outer ring.

Darshima looked on as they recited a chant. Their voices rose and fell in unison as they affirmed the enduring strength of the guardianship, the Order of the Gilded Moon, and the Kingdom of Tiriyuud. The shrine echoed with their prayers, seeking the guidance and wisdom of the generations of guardians who preceded them.

After a moment of reflection, the man seated beside Tenrai rose to his feet. He approached the center of the circle, the gold embroidery in his overcoat glistening in the moonbeams. His long black hair, greying at the temples, was fashioned in a braided tail that hung down his back. His chiseled face and square jaw bore a stern frown.

"Welcome, General Akaike Heede." The surrounding guardians bowed their heads and clapped their hands as he took his place. Darshima recognized him from the speeches in the courtyard.

"Today, we witnessed a most unfathomable event. Tiriyuud was nearly invaded under our watch." He clenched his jaw as he uttered the words.

Darshima listened as General Heede shared what the Order had learned thus far about Navervyne's surprise attack. Unbeknownst to Tiriyuusian forces, Navervyne had stationed much of their fleet on Iberwight, in the Omystikai dominions of Nyzhaiheb, Keverese, and Fauridise. Though Iberwight had not experienced the devastation of Navervyne's conquest like the other moons, the dominions still suffered greatly.

To avoid destruction, Keverese and Nyzhaiheb had declared themselves open shortly after the invasion, and Navervyne subsequently assumed control. Gavipristine, the capital of Fauridise, served as the administrative capital and hosted the majority of Navervyne's forces.

"How was Navervyne able to breach our defenses when The Vilides could not?" asked one of the seated guardians.

"Their ships are far more advanced, with a much greater range than Vilidesian craft." General Heede solemnly bowed his head. The guardians mulled over the fact that the attack had been the most severe threat the kingdom had ever faced. Even the mighty ships of the Vilidesian fleet had never made it beyond the wall of rugged mountains sheltering Chryshaihem and its vast lake from the open sea. Navervyne's ships had flown clear over those mountains and the waters of the lake. They would have reached the city had it not been for the events of that morning.

As the meeting wore on, several senior commanders concluded that the sage's reading of kai must have been misinterpreted. They had never failed in predicting the major events to befall the kingdom, and some of them openly wondered why it had been different this time. Others secretly feared it was a sign that they were losing their ability to read kai.

The debate raged about why Chryshaihem had come under attack. All manner of speculation surfaced. Some felt that the Tiriyuusians were being punished for their lack of devotion. Others openly denied the fall of the realm and even speculated that the attempted invasion was a covert Vilidesian action to gain control of the kingdom through a foreign power.

"There is too much foreign influence these days," voiced one of the older guardians. "For centuries, Tiriyuud stayed out of the realm's affairs, and we had peace and control over kai. Now things are different." Several other guardians seated beside him murmured in approval. He lamented the Vilidesian influence in the Outer District and its effect on Tiriyuud's culture. When he finished speaking, the guardian glared at Darshima and his companions. Darshima drew in a surprised breath at the man's harsh words. He looked over to Erethalie, Khydius, and Sydarias, whose expressions grew somber as they made sense of the man's statement.

Darshima felt a bitter taste at the back of his throat as he tried to quell his disappointment. Though they were guardians, some clearly saw them as foreigners. Others possibly feared them. He wondered if the members of the Order would ever truly accept him and his companions.

The discussion grew heated, and other guardians conjured even more tangential reasons for the attack. Tenrai raised his hand, and the assembled group fell silent. He stood up and moved beside General Heede.

"Is this how most of my fellow guardians feel?" Tenrai gazed around the circle, his eyes glowing intently. "Who among you questions my decision to bring Rion's son's, my nephews, and their Vilidesian companions here to Chryshaihem?" Anxious whispers rose from the guardians.

"We do not question your judgment, but Tiriyuud finds itself at a crossroads. What are we to make of this?" asked one of the commanders.

"While we welcome these Vilidesian subjects seated before us, it is hard not to draw a correlation between their arrival and the attempted attack." The older guardian stared pointedly at Tenrai.

"If it eases your fears and soothes your temper, I will take the blame for the threat that now faces our kingdom," said Tenrai. An audible gasp rose from the circle, and the commanders exchanged puzzled stares at his unexpected words. Tenrai continued amid their evident confusion. "We all bear responsibility. This near-disaster happened on our guard."

Reluctant voices of support rose among the guardians, and Tenrai looked around the circle.

"For those of you who worry about foreign influence on Tiriyuud, we nearly faced our demise at the hands of a foreign power." Tenrai gestured to the starlit sky above them. "We cannot deny that it was also my nephew Darshima, a foreign-born man, now a guardian, who saved our kingdom from its doom."

Before anyone could respond, Tenrai continued, his measured tones barely concealing his frustration. "Many months ago, I came to this shrine and stood on this very spot to warn of the threat that we faced. Oemiri's scriptures told us that this day would come." The room fell silent. Tenrai looked around for a hint of understanding their eyes, then continued. "I shared my vision with you, the sages, and anyone who would listen. Many of you openly doubted me, thinking that only the sages were able to see into the future." Several guardians nodded in support. "I warned you that an invasion was impending, and if Tiriyuud were to be spared, we would have to find Rion's sons." Tenrai pointed toward Darshima and Khydius.

Tenrai paused for a moment, gaining strength from the silence. "Everyone in this circle stood upon the beach this morning when the invading ships descended from the sky. You all witnessed with your very own eyes what happened. With the strength of his ordained hand, Darshima spared Chryshaihem and this kingdom from certain destruction."

The guardians nodded in unison as Tenrai's voice echoed throughout the shrine.

"Darshima showed mastery of the sovereign strength that had been lost by the guardians and the sages for eras." As the voices rose again, Tenrai raised his hands, and the group fell silent. "All of these events were forecast and written by Oemiri, long before today. If you believe that my nephews or their companions have brought misfortune upon us, you are wrong. Your failure to recognize the truth is the real threat to this kingdom."

Darshima's jaw parted in surprise as Tenrai's incisive words settled over the room. The same story Tenrai shared upon rescuing him was no less poignant. Many months ago, before his sojourn, Tenrai had been the only one in the entire kingdom to presage the impending invasion by Navervyne. No one had ever heard the name of this alien nation. Most people openly doubted the existence of other worlds beyond Benai and its four moons. Tenrai had been ridiculed and scorned by many of his fellow guardians. The Sages of Tiriyuud had discredited his vision as mere fantasy and considered Oemiri's script no more than an ancient parable.

"Since my vision, I have largely borne the responsibility of carrying out Oemiri's orders on my own." Tenrai bowed his head.

Tenrai described his repeated warnings to the commanders and the sages and his calls to action. Tenrai had been the only one to divine the existence of Oemiri's lost tablets in the sands of Ciblaithia, buried amid Omystikai ruins. It was Tenrai who found the treasured writings and brought them back to Tiriyuud. At his behest, the Order's scholars deciphered their script and elucidated what was necessary to ensure the kingdom's survival. With the support of Dydan, Tenrai decided to search for Rion's sons. He had been the only guardian willing to travel beyond Tiriyuud's shore to find them.

"While we dither and debate, a storm is gathering beyond our shores." The group looked at Tenrai intently as he spoke. "The Vilides, Ardavia, Renefydis, the territories of their respective moons, and the Omystikai Dominions here on Iberwight, have all fallen to the same threat that we now face. The Navervyne Republic is regrouping as we argue trivialities amongst ourselves. Now is not the time to sow doubt or fear. As an Order, we must act. We must rise together in defense of Tiriyuud." The commanders nodded in unison at his words.

The sound of a staff tapping against the floor rose above the chatter. Darshima's heart rose into his throat as he saw Priest Dawn stand up and approach the dais.

"I trained these four guardians along with Guardian Nax and Sage Waike." She tipped her head toward Darshima and his companions. "I have also trained many of you seated upon that dais." Her eyes swept over the assembled group in a stern gaze. "Guardian Nax's nephews and their companions are among the most talented people I've ever trained. They will serve Tiriyuud and the Order with distinction." She offered a pointed stare toward the older guardians seated upon the platform. "A bit of humility would serve the guardians well, given the circumstances we face." She resumed her seat beside the dais. Darshima drew in a relieved breath as he listened to her words of support.

"Thank you for your testimony, Priest Dawn." General Heede bowed toward her. He cast a withering gaze at the guardians assembled before him.

"Tenrai speaks the truth. His judgment has never failed the Order or his fellow guardians. He had the talent to become sage but has dedicated himself as a knight. He has borne the burden of his vision and Oemiri's prophecy. His tireless journey on behalf of the kingdom has proven invaluable. Not all of us have doubted Guardian Nax." General Heede then gestured toward Darshima, Erethalie, Sydarias, and Khydius. "This is not the time nor place to blame anyone within this kingdom for such a tragedy. Tenrai's nephews and their companions have learned our ways. We must make no distinction. They are Omystikai, and they are Tiriyuusian. We do not have the luxury of fighting amongst ourselves when we face such an immense threat."

General Heede paced around the circle and looked at the guardians surrounding him.

"If it weren't for Rion's son Darshima, Tiriyuud would have met the same cruel fate as the territories of The Vilidesian Realm." The commanders signaled their agreement with a rousing chant, and General Heede continued. "We must be unified if we are to beat back this enemy and prevent incursion into our homeland."

General Heede continued the meeting, and Tenrai resumed his seat. Darshima breathed a sigh of relief as he thought of Tenrai, Priest Dawn, and General Heede's words of support. The most senior guardians saw him and his companions as full members of the Order. Darshima pushed aside the older guardian's misgivings and focused on the rest of the meeting. No matter what others thought, he and his friends belonged here, and they would do everything they must to defend Tiriyuud.

Chapter 23

Dydan Waike

His arms folded tightly against his chest, Dydan braced against the frigid night air. A thick blanket of clouds drifted over the dark sky. Puffs of steam trailed from his nostrils as he walked. The blustery winds howled through the steep canyon of buildings, and he drew the folds of his black overcoat closer against his frame. He strode faster down the damp street, the thud of his boots echoing softly against the carved stone facades. The clouds above broke in a shower of snow, and the flakes swirled around him.

It was well past midnight, and sunrise was still several hours away. Dydan walked through the street amid his thoughts. He stared at a four-wheeled transport vehicle that passed him in a hushed whir. Snowflakes swirled past its angular chassis and through its rear toroidal crystal engine in a frenzied cloud, its circular blue light pulsating as it drove down the desolate street. Large wet snowflakes evaporated as soon as they hit the heated cobblestones, forming puddles and shrouding everything in a thin veil of mist. Subdued white light from crystalline lanterns lining the street burned in glowing halos through the shadows and vapor.

Dydan walked upon the cobblestones, and his hands burrowed into his coat pockets for warmth. His fingers methodically ran over a stiff paper card in his right pocket, and his thoughts raced as he pondered the message written upon it. Though his eyes had read the note several times, he could barely believe its instructions. Dydan shook his head, focused upon the path ahead, and kept walking.

It had not been long since Dydan had left the Sages' Temple that evening. He had completed lengthy rounds of divination and prayer with his fellow sages. As a sage, it was his responsibility to divine the future of the kingdom. In times before, it had been a routine exercise, but today he felt a heightened sense of urgency due to the attempted invasion.

Dydan had given his whole energy to divination that evening, but to his frustration, he had come up with no new hints about Tiriyuud's fate. Though they carried out their duties, Dydan and his fellow sages were despondent. They had failed to predict the attempted invasion. Dydan and the other sages had been unable to fulfill their chief responsibility, and it left them in a state of distress.

Every class of sages that preceded them had channeled the sovereign energy and predicted the future. They protected Tiriyuud in centuries past and had forecast the most significant threats of their eras – famines, floods, storms, seismic events, among other perils. Dydan's class of sages had not foreseen the invasion of The Vilides nor the attempted siege of Chryshaihem. Their collective failure had thrown the legitimacy of the council into question.

As he walked along the road, Dydan tried to center his thoughts and find peace. Though no sages predicted the invasion, the one Tiriyuusian who had foreseen this calamity had been Tenrai. Dydan had been the only sage on the council to believe Tenrai and heed his warning. Dydan had convinced the other sages to lend the support and resources of the Order for Tenrai's journey.

Though Dydan had persuaded the council, they ridiculed him for heeding the mere dreams of a guardian. Their scorn did not bother him. Dydan had always known Tenrai to be truthful. Dydan listened to Tenrai's divination with his whole heart and offered assistance to help him undertake the voyage that led him to Darshima and Khydius. As the events of Tenrai's vision had unfolded, the other sages acknowledged Dydan's astuteness in believing and supporting Tenrai.

Dydan had known Tenrai since they were children growing up together in Foseidem. He was a year younger than Tenrai, and their families had known each other for generations. They both demonstrated keen abilities with the sovereign strength at an early age and were chosen to train as guardians during adolescence. Among the youngest in their class, their experience together had brought them closer.

As thoughts of Tenrai filled Dydan's mind, his heart thudded. He pressed a hand to his chest and drew in a nervous breath. Dydan was hesitant to admit it, even to himself, but he held a deep fondness for Tenrai. He tried to bury his sentiments over the years, dedicating himself wholly to the Order, but it was difficult. Dydan's unexpected feelings toward Tenrai had pushed him to leave the guardianship and join the sages. Though he tried to forget them, distance had only made his feelings stronger.

Though uncommon, companionship between people of the same gender was accepted in Tiriyuud. Even so, Dydan didn't know how to reconcile his own feelings. As romantic partnerships were forbidden for sages, Dydan neglected his emotions and sought fulfillment in his duties. His recent stint with Tenrai, training his nephews and their companions, conjured feelings he wasn't ready to confront. It also brought back cherished memories of their time together.

Dydan walked faster and tried to purge his errant thoughts. A sense of guilt filled him as he made his way. The kingdom was under threat, and he was wasting time pondering his own emotions. As in times before, Dydan focused his thoughts upon the Order and the kingdom. A shiver coursed through him as he recalled what he had witnessed only the day before. He pondered the ancient force that Darshima had summoned to protect Chryshaihem. He had studied accounts of the Omystikai ancestors wielding astounding strength as they molded Ciblaithia into being, but he never imagined witnessing such a feat in his lifetime.

Dydan continued down the lonely street, doing his best to avoid being seen. As a sage, he was discouraged from leaving the temple complex for anything other than conducting the council's business. When sages took trips away from the temple, it required elaborate rituals for both entry and exit of the compound. Moreover, they were required to travel in a convoy of vehicles, escorted by a retinue of sentries, prelates, and servants.

Fearing for a moment that his absence would be noticed, Dydan looked over his shoulder. The soaring, tiered silhouette of the Sages' Temple loomed above the surrounding tiled rooftops, glowing softly amid the snowfall. He wasn't too far away and could return at once if needed. He had left quietly after his fellow sages had retired for the evening. He was confident that no one would notice his absence.

Dydan walked down another desolate street amid the falling snows, gripping the card in his pocket even more tightly. His mind replayed the unexpected events of the evening. As he was preparing to leave the inner sanctum of the temple to rest for the evening, a servant had brushed past him, pressing the square of gilt paper into his palm, vanishing as briefly as he had appeared. The note contained Dydan's name, a time, a place, and instructions to come alone. Never in his life had he received such a mysterious summons.

Dydan walked faster beneath the dark skies. He had missed the latenight incantation, and a feeling of guilt tugged at his heart. In another time, avoiding his duties would have upset him, but tonight he felt different. During his years as a sage, he fulfilled every one of his responsibilities, attending every ceremony and carrying out every meditation.

Despite his guilt, he was thankful for a moment beyond the walls of the temple. At times, its atmosphere was suffocating. The gravity of the situation facing Tiriyuud made it feel strange to be cloistered in such a rarified space. He hated the idea of being separate from his fellow Tiriyuusians when their homeland was preparing to fight for its very existence.

Like the falling snows, feelings of confusion stirred within him. Though he tried to suppress them, the nighttime solitude brought them forth. He had spent so much time meditating and divining, yet his efforts had not been enough to predict the disaster that befallen them. He wondered if his incantations and prayers over the years had served any use.

Dydan's heart thudded with a sense of doubt so powerful that he paused in the middle of the desolate street. He stared at the cloudy sky and let out a sigh as he searched for an answer, his breath mingling with the tendrils of mist swirling around him. He shook his head and continued down the road, the solitude and the sense of independence he felt as he walked reminding him of his former life as a guardian.

Unlike the other sages, he was still relatively young, and his tenure as a guardian hadn't been so long ago. He had not yet found comfort in spending his days meditating like the other sages. He often reminisced of his days traveling with Tenrai throughout the kingdom, conducting affairs for the Order. The routine and instincts of his days back then were still strong within him. His months with Tenrai and Priest Dawn at the training grounds made him miss those days even more. A hesitant smile crossed Dydan's lips as he thought of sparring with Tenrai back upon the training islands.

Dydan descended a wrought iron staircase and walked down another narrow street, snaking through the hilly, urban landscape. As he approached the address upon the card, he pondered who would've summoned him and what might be awaiting him. The address was in an industrial area with workshops and small factories, a neighborhood unfamiliar to him.

At the end of the path, he spied a door with numbers matching the message. Etched below the elegant script, he eyed the eight crescent seal of the Order and shrugged in surprise. He hadn't realized that the Order maintained an address so far from the complex of temples at the city center.

Dydan slowed his pace as he neared the doorway. He peered at the embellished, wrought gold entrance and its dark wooden door. It stood apart from the understated wood and stone edifices surrounding it. Dydan stepped through a billowing cloud of steam and climbed the stone steps. He cast a furtive gaze around, then withdrew the card from his pocket, confirming the address.

Dydan raised his fist and knocked upon the door, the sound of his rapping knuckles echoing loudly in the street. He waited in the cold air, brushing the falling snowflakes from his overcoat. The sound of a disengaging lock and the screech of metal broke the silence. A narrow slat opened in the door, and a pair of glowing azure eyes stared out into the street.

"Please, introduce yourself," said a low voice.

"I am Sage Dydan Waike, and I received this note." Dydan held up the card. The pair of striking eyes narrowed as they read the message, and the slat closed with a thud. After a moment, the door slid open with a groan. Dydan stepped into the darkness, and a pair of unseen hands gently ushered him into a dimly lit hallway.

An inviting blast of warm air greeted him, and he moved forward as the door shut behind him. The hands guided him toward an awaiting elevator at the end of the corridor. The stranger accompanied him inside the wrought-iron carriage and pressed several buttons as the door closed. In the dim crystal torchlight, he saw that the voice, and the hands belonged to a young man wearing the distinct black and gold robes and folded blue polygonal headdress of a temple priest.

The carriage lurched upward, clicking as it made its rapid ascent. Moments later, the elevator slowed to a stop, and the doors slid open. The priest ushered Dydan into a long, cavernous room. They walked toward several figures seated upon rugs around a glowing hearth at the far end. The light from its dancing flames cast a subdued glow amid the room's ornate interior.

Dim light from the cloudy night sky filtered through the large stained glass windows in the vaulted ceiling, revealing hints of its gilded splendor. Though most of the details remained obscured by darkness, Dydan felt his heartbeat slow amid the staid ambiance of the temple. He and the priest approached the group, who rose to their feet upon recognizing his presence. Dydan stepped into the light of the hearth. His heart skipped a beat, and a flicker of recognition crossed his face as he saw the subdued expressions of Seer Aodren Ryte and General Akaike Heede. Tenrai stood between them.

"I present Dydan Waike, Sage of Tiriyuud." The priest offered a deferential bow, then dissolved back into the shadows.

"Please join us, Sage Waike." Seer Ryte gestured toward the hearth.

Dydan settled beside Tenrai and looked toward the seer and the general, his pulse thudding as Tenrai gently nudged his shoulder. Out of the corner of Dydan's eye, he noticed Tenrai gripping a card between his fingers, much like the one he had been given.

"We apologize for the clandestine nature of this meeting." General Heede straightened the gold sash crisscrossing his guardian's uniform.

"What is this place?" Dydan looked around him, trying to gather the details of what appeared to be a long-forgotten temple.

"We are in an old shrine. It was once used for routine meetings between the guardians and the sages." Seer Ryte gestured around them. She adjusted the folds of her red robe, the gold embroidery glittering amid the flames.

"As our current circumstance has shown us, the guardians and sages must reestablish a deeper level of communication if our kingdom is to survive." The general nodded, his voice striking a somber tone.

"Sage Waike, Guardian Nax, we have requested your presence this evening to share information that we have recently obtained," began Seer Ryte. "In the hours since the attack, we have received messages from beyond our shores, and it appears that the danger we face is far greater than we feared." A look of worry crossed her face.

"The Order has been in contact with the Dominions of Keverese and Nyzhaiheb. They have shared details about the current situation on Iberwight and beyond," said General Heede.

From what the Order had learned thus far, the Navervyne Republic had assumed complete control of Iberwight. Like the other moons, the dominions had been overrun by Navervyne's armies. They established a significant presence in Gavipristine, basing most of their military operation and civil administration in the city. During its conquest of Iberwight, Navervyne's aerial fleets had visited both Keverese and Nyzhaiheb, who chose to surrender instead of facing utter ruin as had the other moons. Without so much as a shot fired, the dominions capitulated to Navervyne's forces.

Though they had been spared destruction, the Omystikai dominions were forced to accept Navervyne's troops and citizens in their territory. They disbanded the remaining Vilidesian armed forces and destroyed their equipment. Though they didn't face the same degree of hardship as other people, life had become difficult.

The Navervyne Republic halted trade between the dominions and the other moons, which impoverished many citizens. The Omystikai had little choice but to either toil in Navervynish factories established on Iberwight or work in mines and quarries in the frozen hinterlands. The Omystikai were forced to extract vast quantities of jewels, crystals, and rare metals to fulfill Navervyne's insatiable desire for raw materials.

"And what about Fauridise? You mentioned that they've served as a base for the invaders. Why is this?" asked Dydan.

"The administration in Gavipristine has not responded to our entreaties. They are not allied with us, like Keverese and Nyzhaiheb." A somber frown spread upon General Heede's face. He paused for a moment to gather his thoughts. "Sadly, I now believe the rumors about Fauridise and its relationship with Navervyne."

"What do you mean by relationship?" Dydan's brow wrinkled in confusion. The seer and the general exchanged a knowing glance.

"I have heard murmurings, but it cannot be true." Tenrai stared into the flames, his voice growing heavy.

"Evidently, I am the only one who is unaware of a relationship between Fauridise and the invaders?" Confused, Dydan's gaze darted between the seer, Tenrai, and the general.

"Based on information from Keverese, we believe that Fauridise may have been in contact with Navervyne years before the invasion," said Seer

Ryte. "The true nature of their relationship is unknown." A look of disbelief formed upon Dydan's face as he listened to the revelation.

As Seer Ryte described, Navervyne's superior technology had allowed its emissaries to travel to the realm undetected. Their first mission took them to Iberwight, the furthest moon from Benai. Navervyne's envoys first encountered the Fauridisians in their dominion and sought to learn everything they could about the Vilidesian Realm.

They came to understand the tragic history of the Omystikai and the centuries of mistreatment inflicted upon their ancestors. Though precise details of the arrangement were unknown, the Keveresians believed that the Navervyne Republic and Fauridise formed an alliance. The Vilides was then subsequently invaded.

"This cannot be true. What would Fauridise have to gain from the fall of the realm?" Dydan hunched over, shaking his head in disbelief.

"Perhaps the Order of the Crystal Moon sought influence beyond what the Vilidesians would grant them," mused General Heede.

"I believe they sought to gain from the chaos of invasion and usher in a new order. Gavipristine was not invaded, but it is struggling no less than the other dominions," added Seer Ryte.

"How could our kin in Fauridise be complicit in such an evil act?" Dydan looked up at the seer and the general, his eyes wide with disbelief.

"Our contacts in Nyzhaiheb have confirmed that Navervyne's forces on Iberwight are organized in Gavipristine. They send their troops to maintain control throughout Iberwight and suppress dissent." Seer Ryte steepled her fingers as she spoke.

Dydan drew in a pained breath, briefly closing his eyes amid his raging thoughts. He couldn't fathom how an Omystikai order could have been complicit in the act that had wrought untold devastation upon their world.

"We are certain that Navervyne's attempted invasion of Tiriyuud was planned and launched from within Fauridise." General Heede clenched his jaw in subtle frustration.

"This is likely why the administration in Gavipristine has refused to respond to our requests for information," added Seer Ryte.

"What they have done is unconscionable." A hardened frown spread upon Tenrai's face.

"Tiriyuud cannot let this stand." Dydan slammed his fist against the floor, the sound echoing through the room. It was difficult enough to accept that the Order of the Crystal Moon had abetted the fall of the Vilidesian Realm. However, the fact that they had allowed Navervyne to stage an attack on Tiriyuud from within its territory was unbelievable.

"This is Tiriyuud's loneliest hour. We will have to summon all of our strength if we are to survive." General Heede stared at Dydan and Tenrai.

"The seer and I summoned you both here to discuss the way forward."

"The sages were unable to predict this invasion, but Tenrai, your vision foretold of this day." Seer Ryte looked upon Tenrai, her eyes glowing intently.

"Dydan, you were the only one among the sages who believed Tenrai when he shared his vision. You were the one who insisted that the Order support him in his search for his nephews. Furthermore, you stepped aside from your duties with the council to assist Tenrai with their training." The general nodded firmly toward Dydan. "You did not forget your training as a guardian."

"You both have shown valor and intelligence. You have served Tiriyuud honorably in this most difficult time. The general and I are looking to you both to help us lead the battle to save Tiriyuud." A frown formed upon Seer Ryte's lips as she spoke.

"With all due respect, I am a sage, and my responsibility is to the council." Dydan's eyebrows arched in surprise.

"General Heede and I have discussed this. You and Tenrai must continue to work together. We expect you to serve directly in the war effort," said Seer Ryte, her words were weighted with a finality that did not invite further questions.

"I am ultimately in service to Tiriyuud and will do whatever is asked of me." Dydan bowed deeply toward Seer Ryte and General Heede.

"Given our grave circumstances, the Order requires your service and must expand your responsibilities. Therefore, I am appointing you to the position of chancellor." A look of incredulity spread upon Dydan's face. In the history of the council, there had only been a few sages elevated to the rank of chancellor, and it had only occurred in a time of great upheaval. In addition to diplomatic responsibilities, a chancellor had duties similar to a guardian commander. He would also be expected to lead a squadron into battle. Chancellors were also given the privilege of having a direct audience with the oracle.

"I am not worthy of this position, but I will serve our Order in whatever capacity is needed," said Dydan. The seer nodded, a hint of satisfaction glimmering in her eyes.

"As Seer Ryte stated, Tenrai, you were the only one to presage the threat we now face. You had the courage and the perseverance to find a way to protect us." General Heede stared at Tenrai. "The Order is fortunate to have you as a guardian. I hereby appoint you to the position of commander."

"I gratefully accept." Tenrai bowed deeply and thanked the general. As commander, Tenrai would also plan the war and lead a squadron into battle.

"Tenrai, you had the foresight to prepare for this disaster. Dydan, you had the wisdom to believe him and arrange support. Tiriyuud is in its greatest hour of need. The fate of our nation rests with you both," said General Heede. A shiver coursed through Dydan as the general's stern words echoed throughout the temple.

"We are sworn to protect the Kingdom of Tiriyuud and the Order of the Gilded Moon. We will not flinch nor fail in our duty." Tenrai lifted his right hand to his brow and offered a firm salute.

"We will seek out those who brought this attack upon us. We will seek justice, and we will prevail in Tiriyuud's name." Dydan bowed his head.

"We pray that this moment of danger soon passes, and we might afford you a celebration worthy of your new statures within the Order," added Seer Ryte."

"We understand," replied Dydan. Their dire circumstances allowed precious little time for celebration or revelry. Honor and recognition would come from serving Tiriyuud, and for Dydan, that was more than enough.

Seer Ryte and General Heede dismissed Dydan and Tenrai. The two men offered their gratitude, departed the shrine, and stepped back into the snowy streets. Dydan walked beside Tenrai, the silence of the evening filling the space between them. The snow fell upon their shoulders as they made their way through the empty district. Faint streaks of light glimmered through the clouds as the sun made its ascent above the horizon.

They passed through a narrow alleyway lined with closed shops and food stalls, the square panes on their wooden doors covered in a fresh layer of snow. Hanging lanterns swayed above their heads as they approached the main axis. Dydan's mind raced as he mulled over the meeting with General Heede and Seer Ryte. He willed himself to accept the truth about Fauridise and Navervyne. He desperately wished their words had been a lie, but he could conceive of no other explanation.

Dydan understood that Crystal Moon and the other orders had diverged from much of the old Omystikai customs and traditions. In their headlong rush to modernity and embrace of Vilidesian hegemony, the other orders appeared unrecognizable to most Tiriyuusians. Dydan never believed that he would have seen the day when the actions of an Omystikai order would cause so much strife and suffering in their world. What Crystal Moon was accused of doing was unforgivable. He couldn't fathom what sort of greed or lust could have compelled them to conspire with a foreign power in the defeat of The Vilides and its once-mighty realm.

Dydan clenched his jaw as he ruminated upon the dangers his people now faced. The Tiriyuusians had always sought peace and only fought in defense of their territory. Fauridise's collusion had wrought incalculable devastation and despair among the four moons. The dominion's alliance with Navervyne now posed a direct threat to Tiriyuud.

He had not left Chryshaihem since becoming a sage, but like most Tiriyuusians, Dydan cared about the wellbeing and safety of others. Tenrai's harrowing accounts of foreign soldiers, raining fire, and ruined cities sank into the depths of his soul. Tenrai's reports of starving children, impoverished masses, and people in chains toiling in a distant world had shaken him to his core. Overwhelmed by his thoughts, Dydan tried to brush them aside and focus on the monumental task ahead of them.

"What are we to make of these events?" Dydan turned to Tenrai.

"It is hard to believe, but there is no other explanation." Tenrai pursed his lips and let out a sigh. "Though I saw this day coming, living through these times is no less difficult."

"We must work together to unify our Order. Our unhealed divisions will doom our efforts, and this kingdom will fall." Dydan glared at Tenrai amid the snowfall.

"We need more sages like you, who will work with and listen to the guardians." Tenrai clasped Dydan's hand. "We cannot let Tiriyuud fall."

As they approached the Sages' Temple, Dydan rested his hand upon Tenrai's muscular shoulder. Tenrai stopped and faced him.

"If I may ask, how did you manage to survive out there amid so much tumult and chaos?" Dydan beheld Tenrai, shaking his head in astonishment.

"I relied on the presence of kai and the lessons we learned during our training as guardians. Most of all, I relied upon my faith in Oemiri's prophecy," said Tenrai. He looked up at the sky and drew in a breath, appearing as if he were trying to suppress his emotions.

"I missed you and prayed for your safety while you were gone," said Dydan, his voice catching in his throat. "I am glad that you are safe."

"I will always thank you for your prayers." Tenrai patted Dydan's shoulder. "They gave me strength."

"I pray that I can demonstrate even a quantum of the strength and bravery you've shown." Dydan felt his heart flutter under Tenrai's hand. He offered Tenrai a curt bow.

"You will serve Tiriyuud well. You have a distinct type of courage that will astound us all. I can feel it." Tenrai rested his hands upon his chest. "You've already shown your mettle in training my nephews and their companions."

"I was glad to help you train them," said Dydan. "It brought back many fond memories."

"Same here." Tenrai nodded toward Dydan, his eyes glittering in an earnest expression.

The pair reached the temple complexes near the center of the city. Dydan's pulse thudded as he walked next to Tenrai. He felt a mixture of anticipation for the moments to come and the time they would spend together. He felt a smile cross his lips at the thought, then suppressed it.

Together, he and Tenrai would bear significant responsibility for planning the strategy to defend Tiriyuud. He took solace in the fact that they would have each other. Dydan bid Tenrai farewell beneath the early dawn sky and headed toward the Sage's Temple. He looked over his shoulder and watched Tenrai as he walked toward the Guardians' Shrine, his silhouette fading under the snowfall.

Chapter 24

Darshima sat against the upholstered bench and peered through the rectangular window at the rapidly changing scenery. His body jostled rhythmically as the train car sped through the wintry landscape. The imposing chain of mountains in the distance stood against the brightening skies, obscuring the sun. Wispy clouds rolled down from the peaks to the snow-covered foothills, clinging to them in a thin veil of fog. The hills gradually met the rippling waters of the lake, its rocky beaches covered in delicate layers of ice.

Darshima glimpsed behind him and saw Chryshaihem's dense skyline appearing through the mists. Its jagged lines rivaled the majestic mountain peaks encircling the opposite shore of the lake. The glittering, snow-covered roofs and spires of the capital gleamed in the sunlight, their fractured reflections shimmering upon the lake. The train moved swiftly, tracing an arc along the coast, the city shrinking rapidly from view. The striking countryside unfolded before his eyes as they raced by, lakeside villages both small and large appearing and vanishing past the window in a matter of moments.

They sped through the frozen landscape between villages, and Darshima eyed clusters of the immense glass and stone pyramids used for farming. The humidity and warmth inside clouded their slanted, transparent glass walls. They approached the glowing structures, and Darshima saw the minuscule silhouettes of farmers through the trapezoidal panes, hard at work upon dozens of cantilevered terraces arranged within them.

The train sped past, and the giant pyramids flashed by in a rush of wind and a frosted blur. Entranced, Darshima kept an eye toward the window, taking in every detail as they glided through a snow-swept valley. Billowy wisps of scorching steam rose from the tracks as they moved along, momentarily fogging up the windows before the icy morning air chased it away.

It was the first time Darshima had ever traveled aboard a train. Virtually all passenger travel throughout the realm occurred by air, road, and sea to a lesser extent. Throughout the moons, trains were used for hauling freight. Darshima remembered once reading about Vilidesian enterprises and their extensive rail networks. They routinely transported vast quantities of Ciblaithian gold and Iberwightian minerals across immense continents. Vilidesian trains moved perishable Wohiimaian crops and valuable Gordanellan timber from the hinterlands to the cities for export to the wider realm.

A lump formed in Darshima's throat as he reminisced upon life as it once was. Though circumstances were far from perfect, they had freedom of movement and expression. They had relative stability and economic opportunity as Vilidesian subjects. He never realized what they truly had under Vilidesian rule, but now it was gone.

Darshima brushed aside his melancholy thoughts and pulled his gaze from the window. He saw Tenrai and Dydan seated opposite him. Dydan's eyes were closed, and he rested his head upon Tenrai's shoulder. Tenrai relaxed against his seat, his eyes occasionally peering through the window beside him.

Darshima looked beside him and saw Khydius sitting quietly, his hands folded in his lap. Despite Darshima's eagerness at the experience, his pulse thudded with worry. They were currently on their way to the Outer District for an urgent and unexpected meeting with the Sages of Fauridise. Earlier that morning, they boarded one of the Order's private trains at a station deep beneath the Guardians' Shrine.

As Dydan had explained during their departure, Tiriyuud had built a complex and expansive network of high-speed trains many generations ago. The kingdom's territory was modest in size, and aerial travel was only practical for the most distant outlying islands. The train network spread out from Chryshaihem in all directions. Countless bridges and undersea tunnels served as vital links to all of the cities and villages of the eight main islands and dozens of smaller islands comprising the Tiriyuusian archipelago.

The Tiriyuusians had developed a unique system of gravity-shielding crystals and magnetic tracks that propelled the trains at high velocity. They used pressurized steam to keep the tracks clear of snow and ice. The trains were efficient and swift, traveling at speeds that rivaled both Tiriyuusian and Vilidesian aerial vessels. The system permitted rapid, uncomplicated, and inexpensive travel throughout the kingdom for ordinary Tiriyuusians both near and far.

Darshima peeled his gaze away from the window. He leaned against the back of the seat and closed his eyes for a moment. He had woken up early that morning and was still fighting off the last vestiges of sleep. This journey had been unexpected.

Earlier that morning, Khydius had awoken Darshima out of his sleep and shared a vivid dream he experienced. Khydius had no longer remembered the details, but for some reason, thoughts of Dydan had weighed heavily upon his mind. To their surprise, the Council of Sages had received an urgent meeting request from the Order of the Crystal Moon. Dydan had been summoned to the Outer District to meet with the Sages of Fauridise.

Dydan had approached Tenrai that morning with the unexpected turn of events. Given the nature of the meeting, Tenrai insisted they join Dydan for support. Erethalie and Sydarias had wanted to accompany them, but Tenrai had assigned them other duties that morning to help prepare Tiriyuud for battle.

The unusual request had put the entire Order on alert. Relations between Tiriyuud and Fauridise had been frigid at best, ever since the ancient split of the exiled Omystikai tribes on Iberwight. They had grown further apart, when Tiriyuud thwarted the Vilidesian conquest of its territory at the outset of its millenary, hegemonic rise. Fauridise had long severed its ties with Tiriyuud, and the two peoples maintained no formal diplomatic relations.

"The Sages of Fauridise finally responded to the seer?" Tenrai turned to Dydan, who was now awake.

"After ignoring us, they demanded this meeting." Dydan shrugged. "I don't know what to make of their sudden change of heart."

"We now know that Fauridise's alliance with Navervyne resulted in the invasion of The Vilides and the attempted attack on Chryshaihem. We must be measured in our interaction with them." Tenrai steepled his fingers.

"Though we had our suspicions, it is still hard to believe." Khydius shook his head in disgust. "I spent a great deal of time in Fauridise, cultivating relationships and reaffirming Vilidesian rule. Gavipristine's actions are nothing short of a complete betrayal."

Darshima couldn't imagine the intent of the meeting, but he was certain that it was grave. He had heard whisperings of the poor relations between the Orders of the Crystal and Gilded Moons, but as he heard of Fauridise's link between Navervyne, his fears about their complicity in the invasion only grew.

Darshima's chest tightened with anxiety as he thought about facing them. The truth about his father Rion and his violent end at the hands of those whom he viewed as friends was difficult to accept. It was the same Order that had killed Rion and orchestrated the coup that brought Emperor Aximes to power. They had left him to die as a helpless infant in the desert sands.

His pulse thudded as he mulled over the grief that Crystal Moon had brought to the realm and his family. It would be all he could do to maintain his composure when he faced the Sages of Fauridise. Darshima exhaled and tried to release his feelings of anger. He realized that this meeting was not about his personal grievances. Far more was at stake.

"The Sages of Fauridise wanted this to be a meeting between sages alone. However, I could not compel anyone else from the council to leave the temple." Dydan let out an exasperated sigh.

"That's understandable. These are unusual circumstances. The guardians are with you, and we lend our support." Tenrai rested his hand upon Dydan's forearm.

"Thank you." Dydan politely bowed his head, his cheeks flushing slightly.

Darshima peered at the surrounding rows occupied by uniformed guardians, their cloudboards resting at their feet. Jostling forward with the movement of the train car, they stared ahead with unflinching expressions. Darshima was glad they were there. The guardians had planned on attending the meeting in the Outer District with Dydan, despite Crystal Moon's insistence. The Sages of Fauridise were meeting on Tiriyuusian soil and could not dictate the terms.

Darshima turned to the window, his mind searching for some sort of distraction, a temporary respite from the sense of dread weighing upon him. The countryside flashed by in an arresting tapestry of green forests, ancient temples, and quaint villages amid the snowy valleys. Darshima's cloudboard thudded against his feet, in time with the movement of the train.

He briefly turned to Khydius, who stared ahead with a contemplative gaze. Darshima's thoughts raced with the surreal events that happened in only the span of a single day. He had witnessed Tiriyuud face down a fierce and powerful enemy. He had used his own strength to thwart an invasion. He was now part of an untested group of guardians joining the Order under the most unimaginable circumstances.

The train approached the arc of mountains hemming in the opposite shore of the lake. White cascades spilled from wide fissures in the mountain, crashing into the waters below and sending up violent clouds of mist. The train glided away from the shore and onto an arched stone bridge that crossed the rippling surface. Sheets of clear water poured down the windows as the train passed through the cascades, the torrent thrumming against the metallic cars. They traveled through a narrow inlet between the mountain peaks, moving swiftly through a steep river gorge.

Darshima eyed the water flowing between the enormous pylons of the bridge. Heavily fortified weirs jutted from the river like teeth, the currents swirling around them in brisk eddies. Fleets of angular, waterborne vessels plied the river below in either direction. Some floated gently upon the water, and others hovered high above the surface, navigating the weirs before splashing back down in a spray of mist.

Darshima jostled back and forth as the train vaulted through the serpentine gorge, leaning into each curve with a mechanical whisper. The surrounding rock faces raced by the windows, casting intermittent shadows throughout the train car. In a flash of light, the train sped through the mountains and raced over the ocean. Darshima peered behind him to see the mountains of Tiriyuud's northern island diminishing in size. He looked out over the expansive waters and tried to catch a glimpse of the pair of sunken Vilidesian ships.

"Do you see the wreck?" Khydius leaned toward the window.

"I'm looking, but I don't see it." Darshima shrugged.

"Our father managed to take down a pair of vessels with his skill and with Tiriyuusian weaponry. You succeeded in destroying an entire fleet with a wave of your hand." Khydius stared at Darshima, his eyes narrowed in contemplation.

Darshima's blood ran cold at Khydius' statement. Yesterday's extraordinary events on the beach still hadn't settled within him. He was loath to learn what others might think of him.

"What are you trying to say?" Darshima tore his gaze from the window and glared at Khydius, an image of the burning fleet of ships flashing before his eyes.

"The Nax family is apparently known for its talents. Tenrai can read minds and alter perceptions. Rion was known for his strength and wisdom. You have, without a doubt, demonstrated your abilities." Khydius traced his index finger along the markings inked upon Darshima's right arm. Darshima's skin tingled at his brother's touch.

"I did what I needed to do to protect us all," said Darshima, his voice trailing off. He pulled away from Khydius and folded his arms across his chest. His heart rose into his throat as the images of the destruction faded.

"I wonder if I have any talent that might measure up to the Nax family." Khydius' brow furrowed in an uncharacteristically worried expression. Darshima stared at Khydius, his apprehension diminishing some.

"You have a unique strength within you, but I sense that you restrain it." Darshima rested his palm upon Khydius' chest, feeling his heartbeat through the fabric of his uniform. Darshima's mind traced through the memory of the markings upon Khydius' smooth skin. To his surprise, Darshima's fingers tingled with a subtle jolt of electricity, the same type he learned to feel during their training.

"I will try harder." Khydius bowed his head as he listened to Darshima's words.

As the train raced forward, Darshima eyed a rocky, diamond-shaped island rising from the waters. Densely crowded with multi-tiered temples, gilded domes, and elegant stone towers, the Outer District looked much like the rest of Chryshaihem.

"The Tiriyuusians appear to have adapted some of our architectural styles." Khydius pointed out of the window, a smile spreading upon his lips. Darshima looked through the window as they vaulted over the bridge. Between the distinctly Tiriyuusian buildings, Darshima spotted clusters of soaring glass and metal towers that bore a striking resemblance to those found in The Vilides. Though not as large as the Vilidesian buildings, they were still impressive.

The train rushed onto the island and made an arcing path toward the center of the Outer District. They sped above the sparsely crowded streets, slipping between the edifices, their facades gliding past the train windows. The train descended from the sloping stone trestle, and the track entered a tunnel beneath the streets. Darshima's eyes acclimated to the rhythmic shadows moving through the cabin as they vaulted through the darkness. Darshima lurched forward, grabbing the armrests of his seat as the train decelerated.

"What an interesting way to travel," he murmured.

"We are nearly there." Dydan stood up from his seat and walked toward the end of the train car.

"We will follow your lead," said Tenrai as he rose to his feet. Darshima, Khydius, and the rest of the guardians grabbed their cloudboards, disembarked through a pair of sliding doors, and walked onto a stone quay.

The thud of their footsteps echoed as they moved through the vast, octagonal station. Dydan led the group toward the entrance. His shimmering black cloak, embroidered in a complex golden pattern of interlocking polygons, trailed behind him as he moved forward. The group crossed the immense station, its interior cast in a myriad of bright rays from the stained-glass panels in its vaulted, pyramidal canopy.

The air echoed with the low drone of magnetic engines and the hiss of steam. Darshima eyed a train as it pulled into the station, its black and gold prismatic cars covered in a thick layer of snow and ice. Another train departed the station, accelerating along the tracks. A pulsating white glow emanated from arrays of crystal panels positioned beneath its hovering cars.

Passengers dressed in Tiriyuusian attire, mostly in hues of blue, grey, and black, with flashes of gold and silver embroidery milled about the concourse. The presence of Dydan, Tenrai, and the group of guardians attracted curious stares from the passengers.

Darshima and Khydius walked with the group through a grand, arched exit and emerged out onto the cobbled streets, spreading out before them in a radial pattern. A steady shower of snow fell from the cloudy skies, covering everything in a fine powder.

"The Outer District is usually much busier." Tenrai looked around them as they walked down the central axis, past rows of stately stone and wood edifices.

"It looks quite empty," said Darshima. He reached out and dusted a layer of snow from a closed wrought iron gate,

"After the attempted invasion, the seer issued an edict ordering the evacuation of the district." Dydan pointed to the train station behind them.

Dydan led them toward an imposing structure located at the end of the road. The building struck a staid presence with its square stone base and paired towers with tiered, sloping roofs.

"Welcome to the Temple of Peace." Dydan pointed ahead of them.

"May it bring us such a thing," murmured Tenrai as he gazed upon the structure.

The Temple of Peace was where Tiriyuud handled diplomatic affairs with the Vilidesians, the Omystikai Dominions, and officials from the other moons. Darshima looked upon the spires of the temple and saw the fluttering black and gold banners of Tiriyuud, their bold crescents gleaming against the grey clouds. Waving beside the Tiriyuusian flag, he eyed the red and silver crossed banners of the Order of the Crystal Moon, signaling the arrival of The Sages of Fauridise.

Darshima and Khydius followed Dydan and Tenrai toward a broad staircase leading to the entrance.

"All of the guardians shall enter the palace to assist Chancellor Waike," said Tenrai. The guardians nodded at Tenrai's orders. Darshima's heart thudded in anticipation as they ascended the snowy staircase.

"Please, follow my lead." Dydan led them through an arched gateway and into the courtyard.

Chapter 25

Erethalie Danthe

Erethalie stared through the clear glass canopy surrounding the cockpit and adjusted the blue crystal visor of her helmet. She narrowed her eyes amid the darkness, focusing upon a bright pinpoint of light in the far distance. She looked below the windows toward an array of large, glowing screens and instrument panels flashing messages in Tiriyuusian script. Erethalie settled into the upholstered pilot's chair and gripped the semi-circular steering controls in front of her. Her gloved fingers left indentations in the fine-grain leather.

She drew in a breath and relaxed her hands, trying to calm her nerves. Apart from the distant sound of hissing steam and the pulsating drone of the accelerators lining the tunnel, the cabin was silent.

"Are you ready, Erethalie?" Seated in the chair to her right, Guardian Eikan Faite glimpsed over toward her, speaking in Tiriyuusian.

"I am as ready as I'll ever be," said Erethalie, replying in Tiriyuusian. She snapped out of her thoughts and looked toward Eikan.

"You and your companions have learned our language quite well." Eikan's eyebrows arched in surprise.

"I'm learning new words every day," replied Erethalie. A small smile spread upon her lips as she accepted the compliment.

Erethalie was thankful that Guardian Faite was seated beside her. She had learned so much from Eikan during the first phase of their training. Erethalie turned back to the instrument panel and looked over the various polygons and characters moving upon the screens. Satisfied, she lifted her gaze and peered through the windshield, focusing on the pinpoint of light.

Erethalie stared into the darkness toward a series of pale blue crystal halos lining the tunnel, extending toward the entrance in the distance. Though the sun had risen several hours ago, that distant patch of sky at the end of the tunnel was her first glimpse of daylight. Earlier that morning, after she had parted ways with Sydarias, Darshima, and Khydius, Eikan had met her at the shrine. She introduced Erethalie to the other members of Gilded Wing, the Order's distinguished aerial corps. After a brief orientation, they boarded a train that carried them through a network of underground tunnels away from the capital. They were now in an aircraft hangar beyond Chryshaihem's city limits, buried deep beneath the mountains.

Since Navervyne's thwarted attack, Gilded Wing arranged for immediate training of new guardians with prior flight experience to take part in practice sorties.

"Though our introduction to the flight systems was brief, do you understand them?" Eikan reached over and toggled a row of switches.

"They appear similar to some of the Vilidesian craft I used to fly with my father." Erethalie tugged at the control wheel, adjusting its position. She eyed levers for the throttle, thrusters, and an array of switches that controlled the wings. Her pulse thudded with anticipation as she peered around the cabin. When she had arrived on Tiriyuud those months ago, she never imagined piloting an aircraft such as this. Despite the newness of the equipment surrounding her, the feel of the cockpit was a comforting and familiar experience.

"Our aircraft may seem old compared to what you're used to, but they are quite agile." Eikan pressed a gleaming button next to Erethalie's right hand. The craft's paired, trapezoidal wings issued a mechanical whir as they adjusted their angle outward.

"I've only read about winged aircraft in old manuals," mused Erethalie.

"Our fixed-wing craft perform well." Eikan gestured beyond the windshield. "Nevertheless, we use gravity shielding alloys for our larger craft, aerial carriers, and attack vessels. Learn as much as you can from this sortie. You'll be issued your own aircraft in the coming days."

"I can't wait to fly it." Erethalie secured her safety harness.

"With the attempted invasion, flight instruction for your cohort will be abbreviated. We must get as many of you in the air as soon as possible," said Eikan.

"I am ready," replied Erethalie. Her heart thudded at the mention of the previous day's near-cataclysm. She had barely given herself time to process what happened, but the image of Darshima destroying a fleet of vessels with a flash of his palm seared itself into her mind. From the day she had first met him in The Vilides, Erethalie knew that Darshima was someone special. Though she had grown accustomed to his abilities, she never imagined seeing him wield such an inconceivable power that defied known physical laws.

"From what Commander Nax told me, you are already an accomplished pilot. You have experience with Navervyne's aerial tactics." Eikan offered Erethalie a respectful bow. "Gilded Wing is lucky to have you."

"I am honored to serve." Erethalie pulled herself from her thoughts and returned the gesture. A memory of her harrowing flight through the misty skies of Stebbenhour flashed before her. Erethalie closed her eyes for a moment, drew in a breath, and looked over the instrument panel once more.

Despite her eagerness to fly, her heart thudded with a sense of sadness. She missed her brother Shonan and thought of him constantly. In her previous life, she and Shonan often flew together. His absence weighed heavily upon her. She shook her head and tried to get past the feeling. Shonan was safe and being cared for by a loving family. It was the best circumstance she could have imagined. When they met again, she would share her experiences with him.

Erethalie adjusted the controls around her, pleased she was able to read the flashing script and moving symbols. When she had arrived on Iberwight those months ago, Erethalie wondered how she would survive. Now she sat at the helm of a Tiriyuusian aircraft as a trained guardian and a member of Gilded Wing.

She readjusted her visor and readied herself in the seat. As she sat amid the silence, anxious thoughts stalked her mind. It would be her first sortie flown as a guardian. Her pulse thudded with feelings of worry, but they faded with a sense of calm. Eikan was accompanying her and would make sure she was ready and able to pilot this aircraft. Nonetheless, this flight would be different. No longer a recruit, she was flying on behalf of the Order in preparation for an impending battle.

"I can sense your worries, Erethalie." Eikan tapped her shoulder. "You are ready for this."

"I am ready," repeated Erethalie, trying to reassure herself. She thought of the extensive flying she had done since childhood with her father over the skies of Ciblaithia and Wohiimai. She was a capable pilot and learned her first aerial maneuvers over the bustling, gridlocked conurbations of The Vilides and Renefydis. She had flown everyone from The Vilides to Gordanelle and then Navervyne under seemingly impossible circumstances. She was the only guardian beside Tenrai to have piloted a craft over the skies of Stebbenhour.

As she settled in her seat, the ringing echo of a bell broke the silence. The crystal halos pulsated in complex visual patterns as the sound of the bell reverberated throughout the tunnel.

"It is time." Eikan brought her visor down over her eyes. Erethalie checked her harness, tightened her belt, and gripped the steering controls. As the tone faded, the bell pealed again, its low polyphonic sound echoing throughout the cavernous space. Erethalie narrowed her eyes as the halos pulsed brighter. She sat poised, bracing herself for the sound of the third bell. Seconds later, the bell sounded again, and the crystal halos aligned before her flashed in a rapid, forward sequence.

Erethalie reached out and pushed a glowing button to the right of her steering controls. The craft's engines roared to life, and their exhaust plumes cast the cavernous space in a pale white glow. Erethalie looked around her and marveled at the sight. The Tiriyuusian aircraft used a lightweight, energy-dense, crystalline fuel, unlike anything she had seen back home. The pulsating drone of the magnetic catapult increased in frequency, drowning out the roar of the engines. A cloud of steam rose in front of the craft as she waited for the next moments.

Suddenly, the craft vaulted forward. Erethalie drew in a strained breath as she sank into her seat. They tore through the darkness and raced through the glowing rings. The point of white light rapidly increased in size as they rushed through the tunnel. She fought against the crushing acceleration pressing against her chest. Erethalie glimpsed over to her right, and Eikan sat still, her eyes trained forward in a calm expression. Erethalie steadied her grip upon the controls as the aircraft tore along, the veil of darkness fading as they rocketed toward the entrance.

They emerged into the daylight in a burst of white vapor. Erethalie pulled the steering controls toward her, and the craft's nose angled skyward. Rays of sunlight flooded the cabin, and she looked around as they hurtled into the sky. Erethalie glimpsed behind her and saw the jagged peaks of the vast mountain complex through the curved glass panes of the canopy.

She briefly squinted at the shrinking outline of stacked rows of tunnel entrances, glinting through the snow squalls.

As Eikan described before their launch, Tiriyuud's mountainous landscape prevented the building of traditional air bases, which required flat land for runways. Over the centuries, the Order hollowed out several mountain ranges throughout the archipelago, turning them into operational airbases. The mountains shielded them from the near-constant snows and possible enemy attack. Owing to the challenge of digging through igneous rock, the Order's engineers designed shorter runways for their craft. They heated the cavernous spaces with steam and outfitted them with magnetic, gravity-shielded catapults that launched the aircraft into the skies over a much shorter distance.

Erethalie guided her craft higher into the sky, away from the mountains and toward the ocean. She peered at the expansive skies, her heart thudding with a feeling of exhilaration. She never grew tired of the joy she felt when she took control of an aircraft and tested its limits. A dozen identical aircraft pulled alongside her. The sunlight streamed into their cockpits, and she glimpsed the silhouettes of the other guardians piloting their aircraft. They had all launched simultaneously and were participating in sorties throughout the northern island of the archipelago. Erethalie lifted her right hand to her visor in a salute, then flew past the accompanying aircraft, traveling further away from the shore.

Erethalie pulled further against the controls and climbed higher. Her eyes darting between the rapidly changing displays and the windshield, she glimpsed through the side of the cockpit. The aircraft's gleaming black and gold wings carved through the air, leaving a trail of vapor at their angled wingtips. Their flaps automatically responded as Erethalie pitched the craft upward. An instinctive smiled crossed her lips as she observed the action, its novelty amusing her. Winged craft had not existed in The Vilides for many centuries, as more advanced flight technology had rendered them obsolete.

"Excellent work so far, Erethalie." Eikan pulled her gaze from the horizon and nodded at Erethalie.

"The flight systems feel rather similar," exclaimed Erethalie. "It's no less capable than the Vilidesian aircraft." She acclimated to the feel of the craft beneath her hands. It was smaller yet faster and more agile than the aircraft she had grown accustomed to flying.

"Indeed they are." Eikan let out a soft chuckle. "These aircraft can out-maneuver even the best Vilidesian ships."

"How will they compete against the Navervynish craft?" Erethalie shook her head.

"We will soon find out." A contemplative frown formed upon Eikan's lips.

Erethalie looked toward the horizon as they climbed higher over the ocean. She guided the aircraft through a thin layer of clouds and saw a line of a dozen gleaming black aerial carriers. Their enormous fuselages featured pairs of golden, trapezoidal wings at the stern and the bow. They were similar to those she had seen during their training exercise upon the cloud-boards.

"Those ships belong to one of the Order's carrier strike groups." Eikan pointed through the windshield.

"They're enormous," said Erethalie, clearly impressed.

"They are one of many offensive squadrons patrolling our islands," continued Eikan.

Despite the modest size of the Tiriyuusian archipelago, the Order maintained a vast fleet of aerial carriers. A veritable self-contained village, each carrier could travel great distances. They routinely circumnavigated the skies of Iberwight beyond the capabilities of Vilidesian detection. These vessels could also travel through the void of space and voyage to Ciblaithia and back without refueling.

"You will fly closer, then bank away." Eikan pointed toward the row of carriers. Erethalie did as instructed and pressed upon the steering controls. She sank into her seat as the craft accelerated beneath her. The members of her sortie group pulled past her, their aircraft gleaming in the sunlight.

As she approached the rear of the ships, Erethalie counted at least a dozen cantilevered platforms within each carrier, each housing multiple fleets of craft similar to the one she piloted.

"These ships are even larger than the Vilidesian carriers." Erethalie shook her head in astonishment. "Tiriyuud is more heavily armed than I imagined."

"The Order used Tiriyuud's centuries of isolation to prepare for a Vilidesian invasion," said Eikan, her eyes narrowing in a somber expression. "We never imagined witnessing a total collapse of their realm."

"No one thought it was possible," whispered Erethalie, her voice catching in her throat. She banked her craft to the right, moving past the enormous fuselages glinting in the sunlight. Growing up in Pelethedral and The Vilides, Erethalie had rarely heard mention of Tiriyuud beyond its isolated and antiquated culture. She was a Vilidesian subject and never questioned anything she had learned. Now, as she piloted one of Tiriyuud's agile aircraft and eyed a fleet of their advanced carriers, she realized how little she had known.

Erethalie flew her craft at a sharp angle upward, soaring higher above the clouds. She steered left in a wide arc, then aimed toward the coast. Tiriyuud's mountainous shore appeared as a jagged tracing upon the horizon. Erethalie depressed a lever on the control panel, and the thrusters at the craft's rear issued a low grown. She raced ahead and caught up with the aircraft in her sortie group, pulling into a line with them as they approached the shore. Their objective was to patrol Tiriyuud's northernmost island and guard the airspace over Chryshaihem from another surprise attack.

"Our mission is for training and reconnaissance purposes, but you must learn how to deploy your defenses if needed." Eikan pointed to a glowing screen between their seats.

"I understand." Erethalie pulled her gaze from the windshield and eyed the moving icons indicating the weapons at her disposal.

"If all else fails, and you cannot escape your enemy, you can use the guided juurofym missiles. They can interact with the most subtle kai fields. Their gravitational waves are inescapable and will implode anything with mass in the near vicinity." Eikan pointed toward the rotating symbol.

"You will have to fly swiftly to avoid getting drawn in its field. One missile will be enough to end any hostilities."

"I hope I don't need to use them," said Erethalie, memories of Priest Dawn's harrowing demonstration with the unusual minerals coming back to her. A chill ran through her as she remembered Darshima stopping the dangerous charge with a mere wave of his hand.

They charged through the skies, and Erethalie glanced out upon the horizon, its curving arc meeting with the hazy blue atmosphere. She lifted her gaze and peered through the canopy, the black veil of space seemingly within her grasp. Erethalie stayed in formation with the craft in her group, flying virtually wing to wing. She tapped a row of icons on the screen, indicating her intent to change position. She then guided her craft ahead and led them in a delta configuration.

"Excellent maneuver. You are a natural pilot." Eikan's eyebrows arched in surprise.

"As you know, I'm skilled with Vilidesian vessels. The Tiriyuusian aircraft are surprisingly easier to operate," replied Erethalie. The hushed sound of wind rushing over the cabin broke under the crackle of a speaker overhead.

"Please stand by for our return to Chryshaihem." A glowing circular crystal panel pulsated with the transmitted voice of their fleet's leader.

Erethalie pushed her steering controls forward, and for a brief moment, felt weightless as they descended. The accompanying craft flew in unison with her, and the rugged, frozen features of the Iberwightian surface came back into view. The air around the cockpit briefly flashed white as they pierced through a layer of clouds.

As they swept over the shore, Erethalie took in every detail. She led the fleet through mountain passes, over hills, and through valleys. The roar of their engines shattered the tranquil morning, sending gigantic plumes of snow in their wake. She guided the fleet further inland and spied an immense line of rocky plateaus where the Order kept the northernmost island's largest vessels.

Erethalie and the rest of her group flew over the dense forests surrounding Chryshaihem's lake. The capital stood perched upon its walled islands, arranged in the shape of an arrow. Its clusters of towers and stately temples glittered in the sunlight. She soared high above the city, banking sharply left, then right as her group maintained their formation.

"It's beautiful." Erethalie drew in a breath as she beheld the city from the air, its snow-covered edifices glistening through the tendrils of fog. She reveled in the unique sight, realizing that she was one of the few outsiders with the privilege of viewing Chryshaihem from above.

"We must do everything to protect our kingdom." Eikan solemnly bowed her head, the rays of sun glinting against her visor.

"I will do everything I must," replied Erethalie. Though a Pelethedran at heart, Chryshaihem was one of the most striking cities Erethalie had ever seen. She was now a Tiriyuusian, and her duty called her to protect the city gliding below her.

She slowed her craft as another member assumed the lead of their fleet. She gripped her steering controls, maintaining her position as they performed another precise loop around Chryshaihem, then over the vast blue waters of its lake. Erethalie followed the group toward the mountain range separating the lake from the open ocean.

As Erethalie hurtled forward, her heart thudded in her chest as she felt an unexpected sense of freedom. As a child, she had longed to make a career of flying. Thoughts of her late father floated into her mind, and a lump formed in her throat. She missed him dearly. As a pilot, he struggled with being away from their family and had discouraged her from flying. Now she was a pilot at the helm of her own craft, readying herself to carry out a crucial mission. She felt a pang of sadness as she realized that, like her father, flying was also separating her from her family. She shook her head and refocused her thoughts. Becoming a pilot was her dream and now was essential to her survival. She hoped that her family would be proud.

Erethalie gently pulled on the steering controls as they approached the middle of the lake, and the speaker crackled to life.

"We are changing course. There is a fleet of foreign craft stationed beyond the Outer District. Prepare to engage." The voice echoed throughout the cockpit.

"Commander Nax and Chancellor Waike are attending a meeting there." Eikan reached over and tapped a row of moving symbols upon the control panel.

"I hope they're okay." Erethalie's chest tightened as she thought of them. Darshima and Khydius had joined Tenrai and Dydan that morning, and she wondered what might be happening there. Erethalie's grip on the controls instinctively tightened. She followed her fleet over the opposite shore of the lake, toward the mountains. Though Darshima and Khydius had informed her and Sydarias about the meeting, she learned the true purpose only moments before she boarded her craft.

"Whatever happens, Gilded Wing will protect them." Eikan nodded firmly. "What little trust Tiriyuud had in Fauridise has been lost." Her voice grew heavy as she spoke.

Like her fellow guardians, Erethalie was wary of this meeting. After the invasion of The Vilides, she heard rumors of Fauridise and its alliance with Navervyne. The sudden nature of the request, combined with Navervyne's attempted siege of Chryshaihem, had put the entire Order on edge.

"I will engage if necessary." Erethalie nodded toward Eikan, then focused upon the horizon. She steadied her aircraft against the buffeting winds as they flew over the mountains.

Erethalie maintained formation with the other craft as they again ventured over the open ocean. She eyed the arched stone spans linking the island, appearing as paired, floating ribbons upon the water. Erethalie and her fleet aligned their course, the Outer District rising before them. She was ready and prepared to fight.

Chapter 26

Darshima gazed across the vast octagonal courtyard encircled by a granite arcade. The pair of tiered towers loomed above them, their swooping eaves casting shadows upon the black stone pavement. His heart thudded as he saw the approaching group of men and women. They were the Sages of Fauridise.

He narrowed his eyes amid the swirling snowflakes, trying to make out their features. Khydius stood beside him. Tenrai and Dydan waited ahead of them, their hands folded in front of them. The contingent of guardians accompanying them stood at attention at the perimeter of the courtyard. The sages approached, their red and white robes fluttering in the squalls of snow.

"I can't believe we're here," murmured Khydius, as he glared ahead.

"I hope they come in peace," replied Darshima.

"After learning what they've done, peace is clearly not their mission." Khydius narrowed his eyes in a somber stare.

Darshima clenched his jaw and tried to suppress his anger as he watched the approaching sages. His heart rose into his throat as he sifted through the tragic details of his parents' story. The revelation that the Vilidesian sect of Crystal Moon had played a role in their murder, his estrangement from Khydius, and his abandonment as an infant, left him with an aching bitterness. Darshima was unsure how he would react when he faced them.

Darshima straightened his stance and stared at the group as they drew nearer, their silver heeled boots clicking sharply upon the pavement. Darshima's heart thudded in time with their footsteps. The blood pulsed in his temples, and he drew in a measured breath to calm himself. He didn't know what to expect from this unanticipated encounter, but his chest felt heavy with a sense of foreboding.

The Sages of Fauridise arrived in a group of twelve. Accompanying them were dozens of their order's own soldiers. The Fauridisian sages wore long red coats trimmed in white, emblazoned the symbol of their order, a triplet of silver crosses. They stood as tall as Dydan and looked similar to

216

the Tiriyuusians. They were also pale-skinned, but their wavy black hair was shorn at ear length. Their eyes, a light shade of auburn, lacked the unique blue iridescence common to all Tiriyuusians. The two groups stood facing each other, their gazes locked in stern silence.

Their leader stepped forward and met Dydan within the confines of the golden ring at the center of the courtyard. Dydan's cloak billowed around him as he faced the sage. Tenrai stood beyond the perimeter, his eyes narrowing in a wary gaze.

"Dydan Waike, Sage of Tiriyuud," said the man, speaking in clear Vilidesian. He extended a black leather envelope toward Dydan. Appearing older than his counterparts, he looked at Dydan with an appraising stare. The sage clenched his square jaw and cast a disdainful gaze around the courtyard. Falling snowflakes speckled his wavy locks.

"Osaien Harke, Sage of Fauridise." A veiled look of anger crossed Dydan's features as he accepted the envelope.

"The Dominion of Fauridise and the Navervyne Republic are officially declaring war upon the Kingdom of Tiriyuud. The envelope contains the articles of surrender, written on behalf of our sovereign. We urge Tiriyuud to comply with Navervyne's request and allow for a peaceful transfer of power." Sage Harke pointed to the document in Dydan's hand.

Dydan grew pale as he registered the words. He glared at the envelope in his hand, then back at Sage Harke. Darshima's heart thudded as the sage's words settled within him. It was now chillingly clear why he had felt a sense of disquiet about this meeting. Fauridise effectively gave Tiriyuud a choice to either submit to foreign rule or fight a bloody war whose outcome was all but inevitable.

"Tiriyuud will never relinquish its sovereignty." Dydan's eyes glowed as he articulated each word.

"Your people have a clear choice. Either acquiesce to Navervyne's rule over Iberwight and the moons of Benai or face the onslaught of a war, which ultimately will destroy your homeland. I urge you to accept the former," said Sage Harke, his voice echoing throughout the courtyard.

"This war began when Navervyne sent its fleet of ships into our territory and attempted a siege upon Chryshaihem. As you very well know, their ships did not return. Do not underestimate Tiriyuud's strength." Dydan glared at Sage Harke.

"You're mistaken if you think Navervyne's war against your isolated kingdom began yesterday. It was Tiriyuud that launched the first salvo those many months ago when one of your guardians ventured to Navervyne." Sage Harke turned to Tenrai.

"You are wrong." Dydan shook his head in confusion.

"Guardian Tenrai Nax journeyed to the Navervyne Republic where he seized four slaves and escaped with them. Though details remain unclear, an entire division of troops was massacred during their flight from Stebbenhour." Sage Harke pointed toward Tenrai's chest. "Let it be known that it was your kingdom's aggressive act that brought on this attack."

Darshima's blood ran cold at the sage's pronouncement. He contemplated the possibility that Navervyne justified its coordinated assault on Tiriyuud due to Tenrai's selfless rescue and his lethal attack upon that group of soldiers. His eyes grew damp as Sage Harke's accusation echoed in his head. Perhaps Tiriyuud would have remained at peace if Tenrai had never found him and his companions.

His boots thudding against the pavement, Tenrai stepped into the circle beside Dydan and faced the sage.

"Your accusation is false and treacherous. I journeyed to Navervyne and rescued my nephews and their companions. They were brutally captured against their will and enslaved by your ally's armies. Navervyne launched this war, and its invasion of the realm was complete when I rescued them." Tenrai's eyes narrowed in disgust as he spoke to Sage Harke. "We did what we needed to survive, which resulted in their soldiers' death. Unlike Fauridise, we harbor no illusions. Navervyne issued the first threats."

"Your Order must take Tiriyuusians for fools. Navervyne would have continued its bloody conquest at Tiriyuud's shore, whether or not we rescued them." An angry frown formed upon Dydan's lips.

"The accusation stands, and Navervyne seeks retribution for the aggressive act perpetrated by your kingdom." Sage Harke clenched his fists as he spoke.

"To enslave another human is a grievous crime that the Tiriyuusians will not tolerate. The Omystikai must fight this scourge whenever and wherever we encounter it," said Tenrai.

"The Omystikai of Fauridise have forgotten the burden and suffering of our ancestors. You have willfully stood by as Navervyne has systematically destroyed a stable and prosperous civilization." Dydan's fists shook as he spoke. "Your dominion's odious alliance with the invaders has resulted in death, ruination, and enslavement."

Sage Harke interjected, "Tiriyuud forgets that the Vilidesian's forebears came to Ciblaithia from Benai. They nor their ancestors were no better than the Navervynish. They dispossessed us of our ancestral moon and exiled us here."

"Though inheriting a legacy of invasion, cruelty, and cultural assimilation, the Vilidesians never enslaved anyone. They were far from ideal, but they sought to unite the four moons," said Dydan.

"They failed." Sage Harke narrowed his eyes in disgust. "For thousands of years, they have reaped incalculable benefit from Ciblaithia and our exile." He gestured to the snow falling around them.

"An empire of death and destruction has replaced their rule, and Fauridise is complicit." Dydan shook his head. Sage Harke raised his hand to speak, but Dydan continued. "It is evident that Fauridise holds a long-held grudge against Tiriyuud. We have fought to remain a sovereign people, unlike others. Your enmity was worsened by your Order's relationship with Sage Rion Nax of The Vilides."

"You dare speak his name in our presence?" Sage Harke's lips wrinkled in a look of suppressed rage. He looked over Dydan and Tenrai's shoulders toward Darshima and Khydius, his eyes glinting with a spark of recognition.

"Those brown-skinned men standing behind you are Rion Nax's sons." Sage Harke shook his head in disbelief. The sages accompanying him glared at Darshima and Khydius.

"Yes, it was them and their companions who were enslaved and subjugated by your ally," said Tenrai, who glimpsed over his shoulder toward Darshima.

"Never mind them," spat Sage Harke. "Tiriyuud is but an antiquated kingdom whose time has long passed. Either surrender or face your demise, like the Vilidesians."

"Tiriyuud is among the oldest civilizations upon the four moons. We measure time in Ciblaithia's axial precession, the moon of our ancestors, whom you have disrespected with your evil complicity." Dydan briefly looked toward the snowy skies. "Our people have witnessed empires rise and fall on Benai and all of its moons. We outlasted the Vilidesians, and we will certainly outlast the Navervynish."

"Don't let nostalgia and astrological predictions cloud your judgment," growled Sage Harke. "If you think the fleet of ships that flew over Chryshaihem's lake was large, you're mistaken. Navervyne has more ships, armaments, and soldiers than you can fathom. Tiriyuud does not stand a chance."

"You speak like a defeated subject, deluded by the power of your new master. Fauridise is but a mere vassal in Navervyne's vile empire," said Dydan, his voice rising with anger. "Fauridise's greed for power has brought the world to its knees. Tiriyuud will not be bound by the same fate. We will wage war in kind."

"Your kingdom's isolation has left it woefully deluded and unaware of the circumstances beyond your barren, windswept shores. Your ancient traditions and alleged powers cannot save you from the destruction that awaits you." Sage Harke briefly flashed his teeth. "Navervyne will devour these islands, and even the memory of your nation will be wiped clean from the face of Iberwight."

Tenrai glared at Sage Harke. "Beneath the hardened armor of every power lies its ultimate weakness. It is only a matter of time before your hubris leads to your destruction."

Sage Harke shook his head in disdain as he beheld Tenrai and Dydan.

"Take them all into custody." Sage Harke and his council stepped aside, and the soldiers behind them marched toward them.

"They cannot capture us in Tiriyuusian territory." Darshima turned toward Khydius, his stomach sinking in fear.

"I don't believe this." Khydius looked at Darshima, his eyes widening in disbelief.

The Fauridisian soldiers drew pistols from their belts and aimed squarely at Tenrai and Dydan. As they faced Sage Harke, the sounds of pounding footsteps echoed through the courtyard. Before long, the space filled with Fauridisian troops.

"Either you comply and surrender to our soldiers, or you will all be killed. It is your choice," said Sage Harke.

"When we offered to meet you, we did not agree to be threatened in our own territory." Dydan drew closer to Tenrai and clenched his fists.

"Navervyne acts with dishonor, and so does Fauridise," said Tenrai.

Darshima looked around at the guardians of Gilded Moon. They stood in fighting stances with their hands extended, poised to react. He wondered what they would do to see off this threat. If Tenrai and Dydan summoned them, it would result in a bloody firefight that may end with severe casualties and the potential loss of the Outer District.

Darshima's pulse thudded amid his rising anger. He glared at his right hand, the sensation of electricity surging through his fingertips. A shiver coursed through him, and his arm grew tense. He pondered the potential outcomes if he channeled the surrounding kai fields.

He broke into an anxious sweat, fearing that he might harm his fellow guardians. An image of those burning soldiers in Stebbenhour flashed before his eyes. He blinked as he tried to forget the searing images. He stood frozen, unsure what to do.

"Either surrender or perish," said Sage Harke.

Before Dydan or Tenrai could react, Khydius stepped into the ring, ahead of Tenrai and Dydan. He faced Sage Harke.

"Tiriyuud chooses neither," said Khydius, his voice echoing loudly. Darshima's heart thudded in surprise as he watched his brother confront the sage.

"What are you doing?" whispered Dydan, his eyes widening in disbelief.

"This kingdom will fight Navervyne and Fauridise until the very end." Khydius stood firmly, his fist clenched at his sides.

"Mere empty words from a fallen prince." Sage Harke scowled at Khydius' pronouncement. After a tense moment, Sage Harke stepped away from him.

"Seize them all." He waved dismissively.

The Fauridisian soldiers advanced toward Khydius, Tenrai, and Dydan. The Guardians of Gilded Moon assumed a martial stance, readying themselves to summon kai for a counter-attack.

To Darshima's surprise, Khydius darted toward the soldiers, who trained their weapons squarely upon him.

"Khydius, wait!" shouted Tenrai. Darshima watched in astonishment as Khydius rushed headlong toward the soldiers. As he was about to collide with them, Khydius came to a standstill. He shut his eyes, placed a hand upon his chest, and everything fell silent.

Chapter 27

Sydarias Idawa

Sydarias trained his gaze upon the narrow forest trail as he glided through the swirling snowflakes. His feet planted firmly upon his cloudboard, and he flew forward at a torrid pace. The snowy tree boughs lining the path were a mere blur of white and green, teasing the corners of his eyes. A dozen other guardians flew beside him and maintained their formation amid the frigid gusts. The sound of wind rushing by filled his ears as he maneuvered upon his board.

As he soared above the trail, Sydarias felt the muscles in his limbs tingle with electricity. Though he was getting used to the sensation of the kai fields, it still amazed him. He corrected his course, aiming his cloudboard where he felt it flow the strongest. Heavy snowflakes clung to the pale blue crystal of his visor, and he brushed them off with his gloved hand. Seibu Reede and Lleidas Vowe, the guardians who trained him, soared beside him. He raised his hand in salute, and they both waved back. Sydarias crouched upon his board and sped into the howling winds.

Sydarias and his group of guardians were sent out earlier to assess the security of the coastal village of Inaido, which was located on a neighboring island south of Chryshaihem. They were now returning home to the capital. Dozens of groups like theirs had been given missions to protect the cities and villages throughout the kingdom. Sydarias and his group of guardians spoke with stationed soldiers and ordinary citizens and assessed preparations for another potential invasion.

Like his fellow guardians, the surprise attack on the capital had shaken Sydarias to his core. A shiver coursed through him as memories of Navervyne's destruction of The Vilides flashed before his eyes. His pulse thudded, and he drew in a measured breath as the haunting images of fire and death dissolved into the surrounding snowflakes. Though time had passed since the invasion, the painful memories still stalked him.

His uniform flapping in the stiff breeze, Sydarias flew with the other guardians along the curving forest path, gliding through the chilly morning air. The group had intended on flying over the dense woods upon their return to Chryshaihem. However, given the thwarted attack, they took an alternate path to surveil the forests surrounding the city. As Sydarias flew above the dense canopy, he eyed uniformed soldiers and sentries positioned along the snowy forest trails, solemnly guarding their posts. Sydarias let his mind tune into the rapid flows of kai, guiding his board higher through the invisible eddies and currents.

Though he was the newest guardian among the group, Sydarias was assigned to lead the mission. During the later stages of training, he had distinguished himself with the cloudboard, having developed one of the keenest senses of kai fields among all of the recruits. He was among the fastest, most agile of the Gilded Moon's new guardians upon the saigura and even flew faster than Darshima.

Like many Vilidesians, Sydarias had learned from very early on how to operate aerial vehicles. These experiences had helped him develop a strong sense of balance and direction that prepared him well. Even so, flying with the cloudboard was a different and thrilling experience. It was a departure from anything he knew.

As Sydarias mastered its use, he grew to love the saigura more than any other craft he had ever piloted. Its lightness, speed, and agility were unrivaled. In one moment, he could skim the ground at the slow, steady clip of those walking around him. In another, he could propel himself rapidly above the clouds at a speed that surpassed more sophisticated Vilidesian craft. He smiled to himself as he flew higher above the forest. If someone told his younger self that a craft like the saigura existed, he would've thought it was simply Omystikai lore.

Sydarias eyed the approaching lakeshore and glimpsed Chryshaihem's skyline, visible above the treetops. The snow showers lessened, and he soared over the forests surrounding the lake. As he reached the water's edge, Sydarias climbed skyward, the ground falling away from him. He banked sharply to the right and flew above the long filamentous span connecting the wooded lakeshore to the main island.

Sydarias and his fellow guardians flew over the massive stone ramparts encircling the capital. He led them through the steep, snowy canyons of towers, past stone buttresses, and tiered roofs. He veered sharply left, then right, in a show of his agility. He raced around the soaring spires of shrines and temples, seemingly within arms reach.

Sydarias looked past the geometric web of streets spreading beneath him, toward the central hill. The Guardians' Shrine, the Oracle's Palace, and the Sages' Temple stood prominently amid the cluster of edifices. They were due to check in with the senior guardian in charge of their mission and report their findings. In the distance, Sydarias eyed the range of mountains flanking the opposite shore of the lake.

He drew closer to the Guardians' Shrine and tilted his board down toward the central courtyard. With the others following closely behind him, Sydarias drifted nearer to the complex, the icy wind howling behind his visor and into his ears. He trained his eyes upon the golden circle at the center of the vast space. Sydarias leaned forward, narrowing the angle between his body and his cloudboard.

As they descended below the eaves of the roof, the air around them filled with a deep, sonorous rumble. Sydarias' heart thudded in surprise as the sound reverberated through the entire shrine. He instinctively aimed his board toward the sky, and the other guardians followed him. In a matter of seconds, they floated high above the courtyard, halfway between the ground and the clouds.

Sydarias and his fellow guardians hovered above the bustling city, anxiously staring around them. His stomach twisted in a knot of fear as he contemplated the source of the disturbance. He wondered if there had been a tremor or perhaps another attack upon Chryshaihem. Before Sydarias could say anything, the surrounding air crackled with a current of electricity.

Without warning, enormous bolts of jagged lightning streaked from all directions across the grey skies, illuminating everything in an iridescent shade of white. The bolts zipped through the clouds, the hair on the nape of Sydarias' neck standing up as they passed directly over him. With stupefied eyes, he traced the swiftly moving bolts as they arced above the city's main island and across the lake.

The electricity raced beyond the mountain ranges, over the open ocean, and toward the horizon. Sydarias visor automatically tinted as the light dissipated in a blinding flash. The sky darkened, and moments later, a series of ear-splitting, thunderous claps punctuated the silence.

"What was that?" exclaimed Sydarias, his eardrums throbbing. Stunned, he floated above the shrine.

"It must be another attack," said Lleidas, his eyes widening in disbelief.

As the noise subsided, Sydarias and his fellow guardians drifted down toward the courtyard. The receivers in his visor crackled to life, and the voice of their commander filled his ears.

"There has been a grave incident in the Outer District. Prepare to assess for casualties."

Sydarias' heart sank as he listened to the transmission. A lump formed in his throat as he looked toward the mountains in the distance, trying to imagine what catastrophe might have happened beyond them. His thoughts went to Darshima and Khydius, who had joined Tenrai and Dydan to meet with the Sages of Fauridise.

"We must hurry." Sydarias waved toward his fellow guardians. They took to the skies, flew over the city, and raced toward the Outer District.

Chapter 28

Darshima stood behind Dydan and looked on in disbelief as Khydius confronted the soldiers. The air in the courtyard crackled with an energy that felt much different than his own. An ear-splitting clap of thunder shook the skies overhead, and bolts of blue and white lightning arced beneath the clouds. Darshima's eyes traced them in incredulity as the columns of light struck Khydius in a blinding flash, flowing from the top of his head, through his torso, and down to his feet.

The very foundations of the palace shook beneath them as the energy surged through Khydius, who stood unperturbed. Sage Osaien's eyes widened in shock, then rolled into the back of his head. His mouth hung open as if to speak, and then he collapsed into a motionless heap upon the pavement. Along with their soldiers, the other sages lost consciousness before tumbling to the ground. The air rang with a metallic click as their weapons scattered upon the pavement.

The air fell silent and filled with the pungent odor of electricity.

"What happened?" exclaimed Dydan, turning to Khydius.

"Khydius has saved us all." Tenrai grasped his nephew's shoulders, and his eyes widened in unalloyed disbelief. His pulse thudding, Darshima looked on as Khydius stood with Tenrai at the center of the courtyard, the Sages of Fauridise and their troops lying at their feet in a stunned heap. Moments later, the guardians rushed over to the fallen sages and soldiers and assessed their condition.

"We must take command of their ship," said Dydan, looking toward the group surrounding them.

"As you command, Chancellor Waike," said one of the senior guardians, offering him a salute. She gestured to the guardians behind her. They mounted their cloudboards and took to the skies.

"They must do everything to secure the ship that brought them here," said Dydan, as he watched the guardians' silhouettes fade into the clouds.

Dydan, Tenrai, Darshima, and Khydius walked away from the ring as the other guardians secured the area.

"Are they still alive?" asked Khydius. His voice wavered as he looked at the stricken members of Crystal Moon. Darshima approached one of the stunned soldiers and knelt beside him. His eyes were closed, and his ashen face was contorted in a painful grimace. Darshima eyed the motionless soldiers surrounding him, their chests rising and falling rhythmically. Darshima placed his hand upon the soldier's neck and felt his pulse bounding strongly.

"He is still alive, but they all are incapacitated." Darshima looked up at Khydius, his heart thudding in awe at what he had witnessed. A group of guardians restrained the sages and the soldiers with woven metal threads and sat them against the stone pillars of the peristyle.

Darshima rose to his feet and stood beside Khydius as he took in the evolving scene. His ears still rang from the thunderous clap that shook the skies. His mind replayed the harrowing images of Sage Osaien and his soldiers threatening Tenrai and Dydan, then Khydius channeling the sovereign energy to stop them all.

"You saved us." Darshima turned to Khydius, his eyebrows raised in astonishment. He had felt something unique in Khydius that morning on their journey here, and now he understood what it was. His mind raced with feelings of amazement and fear at what he had witnessed.

"I remember feeling anger, then dread as their troops advanced, and then an overwhelming sense of serenity before the fogginess." Khydius put a hand to his chest and closed his eyes.

"You saved all of our lives," exclaimed Dydan. "You accompanied us this morning for a reason, and I thank you."

"I can't escape the feeling that Tenrai's rescue of us from Stebbenhour provoked these attacks." Khydius bowed his head, a somber frown forming upon his lips.

"These attacks were unprovoked, and no one in this kingdom is to blame," said Tenrai.

"It was the will of kai, through your father Rion Nax that brought you and your brother into this world. Kai protected you both during your most vulnerable moments. It was kai, through the strength and wisdom of your uncle which guided you to Tiriyuud." Dydan cast his gaze around the courtyard as the guardians restrained the remaining sages and soldiers.

"It was kai that Darshima channeled to defend Chryshaihem yesterday and that you used to save our lives moments ago."

"Though we rarely understand it, the will of the kai is righteous and will always protect the Omystikai of Tiriyuud. It works through each and every one of us in mysterious and profound ways," added Tenrai. He bowed solemnly at Dydan's pronouncement.

As Darshima stood with them, a fleet of Gilded Wing craft thundered overhead in formation, the wake from their exhaust shaking the ground beneath his feet. He lifted his head to see their shiny black silhouettes and golden wings flashing against the sky as they patrolled the palace and its surroundings. His heart rose into his throat as he imagined Erethalie soaring above, protecting them from another incursion.

"What will happen to them?" Khydius cast an eye toward the sages and soldiers as the guardians loaded them upon wooden stretchers and carried them from the courtyard.

"They will be given food and shelter, and we will tend to their wounds." A pensive frown crossed Tenrai's features. "They are now prisoners of the Order. We must learn everything they know about Navervyne and these attacks."

As he surveyed the scene, Darshima felt the air stir around them. He gazed upward to see a formation of guardians upon their saigura descending from the sky. Within moments, Sydarias, Seibu, Lleidas, and the rest of their group landed in the courtyard. They slung their cloudboards over their backs and approached them.

"What happened?" exclaimed Sydarias as he lifted his visor. He looked around the scene, barely able to conceal his astonishment as the guardians carried the members of Crystal Moon out of the courtyard.

"Chryshaihem was threatened again," said Darshima, his voice rising in anger. "Khydius saved us." Darshima rested a hand upon his brother's shoulder.

"I still can't believe it." Khydius shook his head in amazement.

"What will happen now?" Darshima turned Tenrai and Dydan.

"We must consult the oracle," said Dydan, his eyes glowing. "Our battle has truly begun."

Chapter 29

Darshima stood with his hands at his sides. He listened attentively to the harmonious chants of a choir echoing through the enormous, gilded doors closed firmly before him. Tenrai and Khydius stood beside him, with their faces drawn in contemplative expressions. They all wore fine Tiriyuusian costumes consisting of polished black boots heeled in gold, grey pleated trousers, white shirts, and embroidered black sashes fastened around their waists. Over their garments, they wore loose black wool coats with long tails, trimmed in complex patterns of gold thread. With their gleaming blue and gold saigura fastened to their backs, the trio made a striking impression amid the group of prelates and priests accompanying them in the anteroom.

Darshima looked past the cuff of his overcoat toward his new golden gauntlet, glinting in the sunlight. Extending from the back of his right hand, all the way up to his forearm, the heavy piece bore an intricate, filigreed design. His eyes swept over the details, which were identical to the markings that Rion had placed on his forearm as an infant.

It was customary for the Omystikai of Tiriyuud to wear gold jewelry that bore their ceremonial markings on important festivals and ceremonies. Darshima shook his head in disbelief as he eyed the exquisite object. He had never owned a piece of jewelry and was deeply grateful to his uncle. Darshima glimpsed over to Khydius, whose engraved golden breastplate gleamed beneath the folds of his jacket. Tenrai wore golden epaulets upon his shoulders, linked in an elegant cross brace that spanned his upper back. The ornament bore engravings like those inked upon his shoulders.

As Tenrai had explained when he presented the objects to them that morning, he had the gauntlet and breastplate fashioned many years ago by a goldsmith known to the Nax family. Despite their separation, Tenrai knew that he would meet his nephews again one day. He wanted them to have these important objects to honor their Tiriyuusian heritage.

Darshima waited patiently as the chorus concluded their chant. He furtively stared at the group of palace priests standing ahead of them.

Dressed in stiff black and gold robes with wide sleeves, they waited in silence. Darshima's thoughts raced as he stood amid the group.

After they had returned from the attempted attack on the Outer District, Tenrai informed him and Khydius of the oracle's request to meet them. Darshima was unsure what to say to the oracle or how to conduct himself during such an important meeting. Tenrai assured him that they would not be asked anything they couldn't answer. Darshima glimpsed over to Khydius, who appeared calm and unhesitant. He imagined that as a prince, Khydius felt comfortable in the company of dignitaries and leaders.

An image of the oracle floated in Darshima's mind as he waited before the doors. He only caught a glimpse of her during her speech at the induction ceremony, but her presence and her words moved him. As he drifted deeper into his thoughts, the chanting faded. The sharp click of bolts disengaging, followed by the groan of the two enormous golden doors filled the air. A flood of brilliant light spilled through the entrance as the doors opened, washing over them.

"Do as I do, and show your respect to the oracle. It is all I ask," whispered Tenrai as he gestured toward the parted doors.

Darshima narrowed his eyes against the rays and peered into the space. The group of robed priests beckoned them, and Tenrai ushered them forward. The doors issued a low groan as they closed behind them. Awestruck, Darshima followed Tenrai and Khydius further into the room, furtively peering all around him.

Immense and lavishly decorated, an arcade of massive stone arches encircled the octagonal room. Pairs of sentries dressed in black and gold uniforms stood at attention at the foot of each supporting pillar. The arches vaulted high above them, supporting a vast domed canopy of jewel and crystal panes. Sunlight filtered through them in a spectrum of colors, casting the room in a rainbow of dazzling light. Long chains of gold and crystal hung in catenaries from the dome high above, showering the room in stippled rays of reflected light.

Encased within the arches, clear panes of glass gave unparalleled views of the Chryshaihemese cityscape, the surrounding lake, and the mountain ranges in the distance. Darshima took in the scenery as they moved toward the center of the room. In all his life, he had never been amid such opulence. Darshima walked with Tenrai and Khydius, their boots clicking against the shimmering black stone floor. Inlaid with radiating lines of gold and crystal, the floor hosted a large design of eight interlocking gilded crescents.

Darshima looked toward a sunken, octagonal stone reflecting pool set in the center of the room. A crystal blue dais in the shape of an eight-pointed star rested in the middle of the tranquil waters. Appearing as if cut from a single stone, the platform cast a gentle blue light amid the ripples.

A large golden throne in the shape of an octagonal frustum sat atop the glowing platform. Various polygons and geometric motifs embellished its matte surface. Darshima lifted his gaze to see the oracle perched upon its blue velvet cushions, dressed in a voluminous, structured robe of black and gold. Her sapphire eyes lingered upon Tenrai, Darshima, and Khydius as they approached. An engraved golden crown with a halo of eight crescents sat atop her silky black hair. Long chains of crystal ornaments in the shape of bird feathers hung from the crown, draping over her shoulders and down her back.

Seer Ryte sat upon a small platform made of sapphire, positioned on the left of the oracle's throne. The Sages of Tiriyuud sat upon the dais in a semicircle to her left. Darshima caught a glimpse of Dydan seated among them. General Heede rested upon a platform made of onyx. Several of the guardian commanders sat in a semicircle to his right. Dozens of priests, clerics, and prelates sat upon black velvet cushions arranged in a wide semicircle upon the floor facing the throne, at the edge of the reflecting pool. They trained their gazes upon Darshima, Khydius, and Tenrai as they moved past them.

Darshima took in the richness of the scene as they approached the oracle. He stole a gaze at Tenrai, who glared forward. A somber frown formed upon his lips, reflecting the gravity of the moment. Not wanting to attract attention with his obvious stares, Darshima trained his eyes upon the throne.

The trio approached the oracle, and when they arrived at the edge of the reflecting pool, Tenrai fell to his hands and knees. Darshima, then Khydius did the same, hitting the ground with a thud.

"All bow before the most exalted, Anaidys Rexe, the Oracle of Tiriyu-ud." The sages and guardians lowered themselves upon their hands and knees as they chanted in the Tiriyuusian dialect. Darshima lay prostrate upon the ground, his forehead touching the cool stone floor.

"You may approach," said the oracle, her clear voice cutting through the silence. Tenrai, Darshima, and Khydius rose to their feet and crossed a series of crystal steppingstones leading onto the dais. The oracle summoned them with a wave of her hand, and they followed Tenrai to the edge of the throne.

"Speak, Commander Nax," said the oracle, in clear Vilidesian. She cast her eyes toward Darshima and Khydius.

"Most exalted one, we thank you for the rare honor of being in your presence." Tenrai briefly knelt in deference and replied to her in Vilidesian.

"I would like to present to you my nephews, Guardians Nax-Foseidem Darshima and Nax-Foseidem, Khydius." Darshima and Khydius bowed deeply at the waist as Tenrai introduced them. Darshima's pulse thudded as the room fell silent.

"I have come to learn much about you both during these past few hours." The oracle nodded in their direction, the ornaments adorning her crown clinking softly. "The guardians have relayed the astounding accounts of your bravery and skill in defending the kingdom against the invaders."

She rose from her throne, descended the steps, and made her way toward them. Tenrai gently nudged Darshima and Khydius in front of him. The train of the oracle's robes trailed behind her as she approached them. She stopped an arm's length from Darshima and Khydius. Equal in height, the oracle gazed intently at Darshima. Her grace gave him pause. Her flawless skin was the hue of fine porcelain, and her silky black hair draped over her shoulders. Her eyes were an intriguing shade of sapphire that seemed as deep as the lake surrounding Chryshaihem. Her glowing gaze seemed to stare right into him. She then turned to Khydius, then rested her hands upon their shoulders. The oracle briefly closed her eyes and sighed.

"Your nephews are the ones that kai has chosen to save Tiriyuud in its most desperate hour, I can sense it," she said, her words transitioning into Tiriyuusian. The oracle opened her eyes and turned toward Tenrai, her features drawn in a somber expression.

"I did all that was necessary to rescue them." Tenrai bowed his head at her pronouncement.

"Oemiri's scriptures predicted this day long ago. Yesterday Darshima ably demonstrated with the power of his ordained hand that he is the Omystikai chosen to protect our nation," said the oracle. Darshima's heart pounded as she spoke his name.

She turned to Khydius, her eyes narrowing in tacit acknowledgment.

"Today, Khydius showed a rare strength that defended the Outer District. Chryshaihem, Tiriyuud, and the entire Order of the Gilded Moon owe its continued existence to you both." Darshima, then Khydius bowed deeply at her words.

The oracle then faced Tenrai. "Commander Nax, you were the only one in all of Tiriyuud to presage this threat. You had the wisdom to seek the answer to our salvation and the strength and shrewdness to bring Rion's sons home to safety. The Order and the Kingdom are indebted to you." Tenrai bowed at the oracle's words.

The oracle stepped away from Tenrai and walked toward her throne. Darshima, Khydius, and Tenrai took the places of honor and sat upon the dais before her. As the oracle resumed her seat, her gaze swept over the assembled group.

"This is a perilous time for Tiriyuud. For centuries we maintained a stable detente with the Vilidesians. With the fall of their realm, our very existence is under threat." The oracle looked around, her voice echoing throughout the room. "Yesterday's attack by Navervyne showed us how vulnerable we truly are in the face of this enemy." After a moment, she continued. "Chryshaihem was mercilessly threatened, and we cannot allow this to stand." Murmurs rose from both the sages and guardians seated beside her.

The oracle turned toward the guardians. "Describe the plans you have prepared for Tiriyuud's next actions."

General Heede rose from his seat and approached the foot of the throne.

"I have been in contact with the remaining commanders in Keverese and Nyzhaiheb. They were equally stunned by the surprise attack that we suffered. They seek an alliance with us against Fauridise and Navervyne." A studied frown crossed General Heede's lips.

The oracle narrowed her eyes as she pondered his statement. "That is encouraging information. However, they, like the other Omystikai dominions, are conquered lands. Their defenses have been destroyed, and their citizens are either starving or destitute. Their offer is commendable, but what can they do to aid Tiriyuud?"

General Heede nervously cleared his throat. "These dominions have maintained diplomatic relations with both Gavipristine and The Vilides. They have shared critical information with us."

"Describe the information of which you speak," interjected the oracle, her eyes narrowing in a look of impatience.

"We have learned that Darshima Nax's actions yesterday have dealt a severe blow to much of Navervyne's aerial fleet on Iberwight. Their capacity to launch another attack upon us at the moment is greatly diminished," answered General Heede.

"So, for the moment, Tiriyuud is safe." The oracle's eyebrows arched in a hint of surprise at the general's statement.

"The sages whom we captured yesterday in the Outer District revealed that Navervyne is directing its remaining ships stationed on Iberwight to our shores," said General Heede. Audible gasps rose from the assembled group as he continued. "They have called in additional battalions of soldiers and aerial reinforcements from Gordanelle and Wohiimai."

"It is clear that Tiriyuud still faces a significant threat." The oracle glared at the general, her fingers steepled in contemplation.

"As our kingdom is distant from Fauridise in comparison to Nyzhaiheb and Keverese, these dominions have granted Tiriyuud unrestricted rights to use their skies, waters, and territories to stage counterattacks against Navervyne's main base in Fauridise."

"This is a difficult situation." The oracle deferred her gaze in contemplation as the general spoke.

"There is one more request, issued by both dominions, if they are to continue aiding us with information," added General Heede.

"What else are they requesting?" asked the oracle, her voice rising in incredulity.

"These dominions offered their unconditional surrender to the Navervyne Republic. Though they avoided the destruction of war, they have experienced much suffering and destitution under foreign occupation," said General Heede.

"Their circumstance is most unfortunate," said the oracle.

"The Sages of Nyzhaiheb and Keverese have offered our forces unconditional access to all of their territories if Tiriyuud agrees to liberate them from Navervyne's rule." General Heede bowed his head.

Hushed murmurs rose from the sages and the guardians as they exchanged expressions of disbelief. Amid the murmurs, Darshima remained silent. He lived through the cruelty of Navervyne's rule during his enslavement and witnessed the pervasive suffering throughout the fallen realm. His heart sank as he imagined the plight of the already disadvantaged Omystikai, struggling to live in the occupied dominions.

"They expect our forces to liberate their territories?" The oracle cast an incredulous gaze at General Heede. "Never in Tiriyuud's history has the Order of the Gilded Moon been asked to rescue an Omystikai dominion. Our kingdom has never waged a battle to defend territory beyond our own shore." The oracle glared forward, her eyes narrowing in contemplation.

The entire room waited as she sat in silence. Darshima turned to the assembled dignitaries as he sat upon the dais. The audience deferred their gazes from the throne, avoiding the oracle's glare. There was no easy answer to this predicament. Throughout its long history, Tiriyuud had only waged war to defend the islands of its kingdom. Virtually all of the battles and skirmishes it faced had been with the Vilidesians. The era of fighting between Tiriyuud and The Vilides had ended many centuries ago. The kingdom and the realm had maintained a state of relative peace.

The oracle lifted her head, her expression growing somber. She looked beside her to the assembled sages and the guardians. "I am disinclined to accept their offers. The dominions' requests entail risks that Tiriyuud cannot afford at this moment." The sages nodded in agreement, and the guardians sat motionlessly.

Darshima listened to the oracle's words, but he couldn't understand her hesitation. He was surprised that no one else was willing to consider the dominions' pleas for help. Images of the Omystikai of Keverese and Nyzhaiheb, suffering under the overwhelming force of the Navervynish, floated through his mind. A shiver coursed through him as harsh memories of his own toil and suffering in the humid fields came back to him.

The silence persisted, and to Darshima, it felt deafening. His heart thudded against his chest as a sense of frustration rose within him. The oracle's words echoed through his mind, and he pondered them with a growing sense of incredulity. He, Khydius, Sydarias, Erethalie, and many others had trained for battle. They were ready to defend Tiriyuud with their lives.

Darshima realized that the kingdom faced an extraordinary set of circumstances and needed to protect its own territory above all. To him, this objective felt short-sighted. He was prepared to fight against Navervyne wherever they posed a threat. His desire to fight back had pushed him through the most difficult moments of his enslavement. It had convinced him to leave behind everything he had known back on Gordanelle. His urge to right the wrongs of the invasion had driven him to persevere through the grueling months of training with his fellow guardians.

Darshima clenched his jaw as his mind flooded with the painful images of the suffering and destruction he witnessed in the occupied Vilides and on Navervyne. He looked around the silent room, deeply troubled that neither the sages nor guardians had the will to discuss the matter further. Apart from Darshima, his companions, and Tenrai, none of the assembled guardians and sages truly understood the degree of devastation beyond Tiriyuud's shore. A sigh escaped Darshima's lips as he pondered their predicament. There must be a way for Tiriyuud to help those suffering under Navervyne's rule.

Before he even realized it, Darshima rose from his position upon the dais. He could feel both Tenrai and Khydius' hands deftly trying to hold him back, but their grasp slipped. To everyone's astonishment, Darshima approached the throne, his heart thudding with each step. Surprised gasps rose from both the guardians and sages.

"Guardian Darshima Nax, you do not have permission to approach the oracle." Seer Ryte leaped to her feet and approached him. Her hands outstretched, she tried to direct him away from the throne. Before she could reach Darshima, the oracle spoke. "Let him approach."

Seer Ryte froze in mid-step. She turned to the oracle, and an expression of disbelief spread upon her face. She walked back to her seat and glared at him.

Darshima stood before the throne, then fell upon his knees and gazed up at the oracle.

"This is most unusual. What has compelled you to approach my throne unrequested?" The oracle folded her hands in her lap, her piercing gaze staring right into him.

"With all due respect, most exalted one, I beseech you to reconsider the requests for help issued by the other dominions." Darshima remained upon his knees as he held her gaze.

A tide of angry shouts rose from both sides of the throne. Seer Ryte stared at Darshima, and her lips parted in disbelief. "A guardian must never question the oracle's judgment," she murmured, shaking her head.

"There will be no displays of anger or hostility in my presence." The oracle glared at the crowd, and their voices fell silent.

The oracle turned to Darshima. "I have already made my decision. No one has ever dared question me. I am intrigued by the temerity and naiveté that brought you unrequested to the foot of the throne."

"I mean no disrespect." Darshima bowed his head.

"Tell me, young guardian, why must I reconsider my decision?" She stared at him with an unflinching expression. The room filled with an anxious silence as the audience awaited his response. Darshima looked back at the oracle. His heart thudded in his chest, and his mind raced as he pondered her question.

"Tiriyuud will not survive the onslaught of Navervyne's armies for much longer if we only defend these islands," answered Darshima.

"In times of both peace and conflict, Tiriyuud has avoided involvement in external affairs. We have survived and prospered while other peoples have perished." A terse frown spread upon the oracle's lips.

"I understand that this course of action has protected Tiriyuud in past eras, but it will not work this time." Darshima shook his head. The oracle steepled her fingers with growing impatience as he continued. "This enemy is much more vast, far more brutal than anything Tiriyuud has ever faced.

Even the mighty Vilides and its entire realm fell to its forces. If the Order only defends these shores, we too shall be overwhelmed."

"We Tiriyuusians are a peaceful people and do not seek war or bloodshed. As we defend our islands, we must remain hopeful that we can arrive at a suitable resolution to this calamity," said the oracle.

"I understand that Tiriyuud embraces peace, but the invaders seek otherwise. As we witnessed both yesterday and this morning, the Navervyne Republic intends to establish its hegemony upon these islands. If they cannot accomplish it through our surrender, they will surely seek our destruction."

Murmurs rose from the guardians and sages as they contemplated Darshima's words. He continued unperturbed. "There shall be no peace for Tiriyuud on Iberwight so long as Navervyne rules this moon. Our forces can beat them back from these shores for a while, but they will continue their relentless assault until we are too battered and exhausted to fight."

"Tiriyuud's defenses are more than capable," countered the oracle.

"Navervyne has control of an entire realm from which they can draw strength and resources. Tiriyuud is but a small kingdom of eight distant islands amid a vast ocean. We must use every advantage we have if we are to vanquish Navervyne," said Darshima.

"You propose that Tiriyuud vanquish Navervyne? How do you suggest we accomplish this?" A look of incredulity crossed the oracle's features, and Darshima fell silent. He hadn't yet thought of a way that Tiriyuud could effectively wage war against Navervyne. He realized that his and Khydius' abilities, along with the skills of the guardians, would be vital in saving Tiriyuud. Even so, he realized that Tiriyuud would have to fight with everything it had in order to survive.

"We will vanquish them by liberating Keverese and Nyzhaiheb, then by finally waging war against Fauridise. Tiriyuud must use its forces to chase Navervyne from every ocean, every continent, and every island of this moon." Darshima looked around the room to see the eyes of the oracle, the guardians and sages trained squarely upon him. He continued, "Tiriyuud will only survive if we defeat Navervyne. Tiriyuud must gain unquestioned control over Iberwight." The oracle briefly cast her eyes downward as she mulled Darshima's words.

Darshima waited amid the tense silence, his pulse thudding in his temples. "Tiriyuud has a responsibility that it can and must fulfill." The sages and guardians shifted in their seats, listening as Darshima spoke.

"My sole and sacred responsibility is to Tiriyuud and Tiriyuud alone," said the oracle. Darshima looked up at her, his eyes glistening with tears.

"Khydius and I survived both the invasion of The Vilides and our enslavement upon Navervyne. We have experienced the destruction and desolation that awaits Tiriyuud." Darshima cleared his throat, his voice thick with emotion. "Though these islands remain the only sovereign territory among the four moons, we are not truly free." Several guardians nodded in agreement.

"I grieve at the suffering you experienced. You have found sanctuary here and will defend it with the rest of the Order," said the oracle, her voice growing somber.

"I am truly grateful for refuge here, in the land of my father." Darshima clasped his hands together in a sign of thanks. "Though I count my own good fortune, I have no right to think of myself alone when the world around us has been driven to the edge of destruction," said Darshima. The oracle's expression softened as he continued. "The Tiriyuusians are in a unique position to fight back. We must do what we can to right the wrongs that have been committed against us. We can begin by answering the pleas of Keverese and Nyzhaiheb." The sages' and guardians' voices rose in surprise at Darshima's admonishment, but he continued. "The Kingdom of Tiriyuud must liberate this moon."

Chapter 30

His legs folded beneath him, Darshima sat beside Khydius upon the circular stone platform of the dimly lit sanctuary. His downcast eyes traced the shimmering blue glow of the crystal ring surrounding him. Darshima nervously adjusted the folds of his ceremonial garments. Tenrai sat across from him, and he tried to avoid his uncle's stern gaze.

They had returned to the Guardians' Shrine moments ago. The guardians were holding sessions and taking a recess from their meeting with the oracle. The sages gathered in conclave with the seer. All would reconvene with the oracle later that evening.

Darshima sat under the withering stare of his uncle, who was barely able to conceal his displeasure.

"I have failed you." Tenrai shook his head.

"I am sorry." Darshima's heart rose into his throat as he reacted to Tenrai's disappointment.

"Your conduct was without precedent." Tenrai leaned forward and tried to catch Darshima's gaze.

"I didn't mean to be disrespectful." Darshima glared at the floor.

"You approached the oracle's throne and openly challenged her wisdom," said Tenrai, his voice rising in frustration. Khydius remained silent and stared at Darshima, his eyes narrowing in a sympathetic expression.

"I understand the error of my ways," whispered Darshima. As his mind replayed the events in the oracle's chambers, he realized that his emphatic speech might have upset the assembled dignitaries. Though he was a guardian, he was still an outsider and among the lowest in the Order's hierarchy.

"You are intelligent and have astounding abilities, but your understanding of our ways in Tiriyuud is woeful," said Tenrai. An uneasy silence settled between them.

Unable to bear Tenrai's displeasure, Darshima lifted his gaze toward him.

"Don't you understand the gravity of what you have done?" Tenrai narrowed his eyes. His voice had an edge that Darshima did not recognize.

"Again, I'm sorry," whispered Darshima. He fell silent, unsure what else to say.

"I'm sure Darshima intended no disrespect." Khydius cleared his throat, his eyes darting between Tenrai and Darshima.

"Though the oracle overlooked your breach of etiquette, your actions were shocking to the Council of Sages and the assembled guardians." Tenrai glared at Darshima. "You are no longer an Ardavian. You are an Omystikai, and you must adhere to our rules and traditions. As a guardian, you must never approach a superior in an unsolicited manner." Tenrai vigorously shook his head. "You must never approach someone with such direct questions without express consent unless there is urgent cause."

"Isn't the plight of Keverese and Nyzhaiheb urgent cause?" asked Darshima.

"What the oracle says is final. We must follow her orders as dictated." Tenrai's displeased look gave way to an expression of veiled hesitance. Darshima glared at the ground, his brow wrinkling in frustration. He respected Tiriyuusian tradition, but the kingdom was facing such dire circumstances. He couldn't understand why the Order's customs prevented an honest and open debate.

"What about your plight, Tenrai?" asked Darshima.

"What do you mean?" Tenrai shook his head in confusion.

"If you had adhered to the rules and prevailing customs of the Order, you would have ignored your own vision. You would've never searched for Khydius or me," said Darshima, his heart thudding as he challenged Tenrai. "Your leap of faith against all odds and entrenched custom saved our lives."

"Darshima makes an important point," added Khydius. "Your act of subversion spared us from our unending torture and what would have been a miserable death in chains." Overcome with emotion, Khydius briefly closed his eyes.

Tenrai's stern glare softened as he contemplated his nephews' poignant words.

"You both are my only family. I would have crossed the starry voids to rescue you, even without a prophecy." Tenrai bowed toward them.

"Thank you, Tenrai," said Darshima, returning with an even more profound bow, and Khydius did the same.

"In time, you will come to understand our ways. Tiriyuusian culture is by no means perfect, but we have learned to survive and prosper where other nations have failed." Tenrai looked through the window at the gleaming city surrounding them.

The trio sat in contemplation until an unexpected knock at the sanctuary door caught their attention. Darshima rose from his seat and stepped off the stone platform. He slid open the door to find a palace priest standing on the other side. Her elaborate black and gold robes and folded headdress signified her position in the oracle's personal retinue.

"The oracle has requested that the sages and guardians return to her palace at once." She bowed solemnly, her face bearing a grave expression. Tenrai and Dydan stood up, stepped off the platform, and joined Darshima at the doorway.

"This is highly unusual," mused Tenrai.

"I am delivering the oracle's message. Her word is my command." The priest bowed, her sapphire eyes betraying a flicker of worry. She offered her apologies for the disturbance, stepped away from the door, and walked to the other sanctuaries lining the perimeter of the shrine, alerting the other guardians.

"We must leave." Tenrai turned to Khydius and Darshima, his expression softening some. "We will finish this discussion later." They walked into the shrine, joining the other guardians as they prepared to return to the palace.

Chapter 31

Kneeling beside each other before the throne, Dydan and Khydius looked upon the oracle. Tenrai knelt with them, his head bowed. The Council of Sages and the senior guardians had resumed their seats on either side of the throne. Darshima eyed Sydarias and Erethalie, seated amid the rows of guardians at the edge of the reflecting pool. Hundreds of Tiriyuusian prelates and high priests sat behind them, their eyes intently fixed upon the oracle.

They reconvened in the palace's great chamber, where the oracle had addressed them earlier that day. The late afternoon sun hung low in the clearing sky, its golden rays bathing everything in a smoldering glow. The vast, frozen cityscape lay beyond the ornate windows, scintillating in bursts of glittering light. Beyond the thin covering of clouds, the pale, bleached forms of Benai and its moons hung against the blue sky.

Leaning forward upon her throne, the oracle peered around the opulent space. Her gaze fell squarely upon the assembled group. She gripped the black envelope that Dydan received from the Sages of Fauridise.

"Fauridise and the Navervyne Republic have officially declared war upon our kingdom." Her voice echoed sternly throughout the room. "We have been attacked twice in as many days." She looked at Darshima and then Khydius, "If it weren't for the sons of Rion Nax, this nation would have already met its doom."

Her features drawn up into an expression of concern, the oracle summoned General Heede to the throne. He rose to his feet and made his way toward her.

"Our enemies have demonstrated their determination. I have given both the sages and the guardians enough time to devise a solution to this growing crisis. How do you plan on defending our kingdom against these invaders?" She waved the envelope, her eyes narrowing in concern.

"We have sent several battalions of guardians and their soldiers on missions throughout the kingdom to ensure the security of our shore. Squadrons from Gilded Wing are patrolling the skies over Chryshaihem and the islands of the archipelago," answered General Heede.

"Is that truly enough to ensure our security?" The oracle's eyebrows furrowed in an expression of doubt.

"The attacks that we experienced were unexpected and highly unusual. As of this morning, the Outer District has been evacuated and sealed from any foreign entry." General Heede squared his shoulders as he spoke. "Those who carried out this attack are in confinement and being interrogated as we speak."

"Tell me your plans for preparing our defenses." The oracle leaned forward, glaring at the general.

"Before these attacks, the guardians had maintained a modest standing army. We have called upon our reserves and are currently training as many troops as possible, given the dire circumstance," said General Heede.

"How do our forces measure up against the invaders?" asked the oracle.

The general drew in an anxious breath and looked up at her. "We are outnumbered." She clenched her jaw as she heard the blunt remark. General Heede continued amid the hushed murmurs of the audience. "We have an army that counts ten thousand guardians and five hundred thousand troops among its ranks. The Order has several fleets of seaborne craft, and Gilded Wing maintains several hundred aerial craft, both large and small. We estimate that Navervyne has more soldiers and craft."

"How many more?" she asked.

"At least a magnitude of order," said General Heede.

"This is a most unfavorable circumstance. What options do we have to maintain our sovereignty?" The oracle lowered her gaze, a look of worry briefly crossing her features.

"The Order is working to maintaining the security of Tiriyuud's islands, skies, and waters. Though our defenses are strong, it is only a matter of time before Tiriyuud is overwhelmed." General Heede looked up at the oracle, his eyes bearing a look of contrition.

The room fell into a stunned silence at General Heede's candid admission. The assembled group lowered their eyes in a moment of uneasy reflection. Amid the silence, the oracle looked at the audience before her.

"The will of kai has protected us through the ages, up until this moment. We Tiriyuusians have no other choice but to take up arms against the threats we now face." The audience surrounding the throne lifted their faces as she spoke. "We have been severely tested in these past several days. Three of our guardians have risen to this unprecedented challenge. They have defended this kingdom in ways that none of us would have ever believed possible." The oracle nodded toward Tenrai, Darshima, and Khydius. "Now is time for all of us to rise together in Tiriyuud's defense."

"As you wish, most exalted one." General Heede bowed at the oracle's words.

"Earlier this morning, one guardian found the courage to approach my throne unrequested. He expressed his sincere opinion about the threats facing us and our way forward as a nation." The oracle turned to Darshima. "With these series of attacks, I now concur with Guardian Darshima Nax's assessment about the scale of our challenge."

Uneasy murmurs filled the room as the oracle acknowledged Darshima's unsolicited words. Darshima's pulse thudded in disbelief as he processed the oracle's unexpected statement of support. Feeling the eyes of the guardians and sages upon him, Darshima bowed toward her.

"This morning's attack has proven that in the presence of such an overwhelming and aggressive threat, our kingdom's shores are not defensible in their current state. The Navervyne Republic and Fauridise have now declared war upon Tiriyuud. As our enemies have cruelly proven twice, they are not afraid to challenge our sovereignty. They will not surrender at our shores, and thus our defense can no longer be limited to them." She paused for a moment, collecting her thoughts, and then continued. "Tiriyuud will accept the offers put forward by the Dominions of Nyzhaiheb and Keverese."

Worried voices rose from the crowd as the oracle's words resounded through the room. Seer Ryte rose from her seat and approached the throne.

"Speak, Seer Ryte." The oracle gestured toward her.

"With all due respect, Tiriyuud has never fought a war of offense. It is strictly against our tradition." A fearful expression spread upon Seer Ryte's face.

"This threat is like no other. Our enemies have left us no other choice. If we limit our defense to our own territory, we shall face certain destruction, as amply demonstrated." The oracle raised a hand to the seer.

"The ebb of time has proven that Tiriyuud has but only enemies beyond the shores of these islands. How can we be sure to trust Keverese and Nyzhaiheb?" asked the seer.

"We have maintained limited but good relations with these two dominions over the centuries. I have no reason to believe that they would deceive us," replied the oracle.

"It is my duty as the leader of Chryshaihem to carry out your orders as requested. I will make the necessary preparations." Seer Ryte bowed and resumed her seat. General Heede moved closer to the throne.

"If we intend to aid these dominions, we must act swiftly. Much of Navervyne's aerial fleet on Iberwight has been destroyed by Darshima Nax's earlier counterattack." He looked upon the oracle. "Reinforcements from Ciblaithia and the other moons have yet to arrive." The oracle looked upon the large gathering before her, pensively gripping the armrests of her throne.

"Tiriyuud will come to the defense of both dominions in exchange for control of their territories," said the oracle.

"Your will be done, most exalted one." General Heede offered a deferential bow.

"Tiriyuud will dispatch its ships to Keverese and Nyzhaiheb and liberate these two dominions. Once Tiriyuud achieves these aims, we will continue onto Fauridise. Tiriyuud's battle for survival shall begin at dawn."

Chapter 32

The late afternoon sun hung low in the clearing skies over Chryshaihem. The clouds dissipated after issuing another shower of heavy snow. Darshima walked with Khydius, Erethalie, and Sydarias along the cobbled streets, their boots crunching upon the fresh layer of snow. Dressed in their full regalia, they had left the Oracle's Palace and were returning to the Guardians' Shrine. Tenrai and Dydan had stayed behind to attend senior-level meetings.

Though the hour was growing late, the streets teemed with both soldiers and citizens, moving at a hurried pace, their overcoats and garments covered in powdery flakes of snow.

"There are so many people in the streets," said Darshima as they moved amid the pedestrians. Despite the crowds, Darshima was struck with how quiet and subdued they were as they carried out their affairs.

"They know about the impending war. People are preparing for the hardships to come." Erethalie looked upon the crowds, a pensive frown forming upon her lips.

"At least they have time to ready themselves. We had no chance in The Vilides," said Sydarias. Word about Tiriyuud's offensive had spread throughout the city, and seemingly every street was filled with frenetic activity. From what Darshima understood, Tiriyuud had never faced such a dire challenge.

Darshima walked with his companions toward the shrine, past shop windows, banks, and temples, each with harried crowds and lines extending from their entrances.

"Tiriyuud had never engaged in a battle like this. I'm sure the Chryshaihemese are worried," said Khydius. "We are used to conflict and strife. The Vilidesians waged wars that engulfed entire moons." Darshima frowned as he listened to Khydius' words, remembering the turmoil that regularly occurred on Ciblaithia and Gordanelle, even before the invasion.

They walked through a bustling outdoor market as they neared the shrine. Darshima watched as people bought and sold items and bartered for provisions. Darshima's heart rose into his throat as he saw mothers holding their infants, bundled in swaddling cloth, protecting them against the cold. He saw fathers grasping their children's hands and older siblings guiding their young charges. Despite the cold and the falling snow, he couldn't help but compare the similarities to his old life back in Ardavia. An invasion by Navervyne would bring untold suffering to them, as it had done to everyone else.

"We have to protect them," said Darshima, his voice growing heavy with sadness. "We can't let them suffer as we did."

"We will do our best." Khydius rested his hand upon Darshima's shoulder as they walked through the crowds.

Darshima and his companions walked past Chryshaihem's main rail terminal, located near the Guardians' Shrine. The entrance to the stately, pyramidal building burgeoned with people, their arms laden with luggage and leather cases. Frightened by the attempted attacks, he imagined many citizens were seeking refuge in villages and hamlets both near and distant.

As they moved past the edifice's arched gates, Darshima witnessed a crowd of people standing and kneeling at the entrance of an adjacent temple. Huddled beneath its curved eaves, he listened as a priest lead them in chants, a layer of snowflakes stippling her robes and accumulating upon the folds of her headdress. The crowd offered up their worries and fears in prayer and asked for kai to protect them. Though the other regions of the kingdom had not faced the threat of attack, Darshima imagined similar scenes of preparation and prayer, anxiety and anticipation playing out in cities and villages across the archipelago.

As they approached the shrine, Darshima lifted his gaze toward the sky. Since the attempted attacks, the ordinarily peaceful temple complex had transformed into a veritable hive. Swarms of aerial and terrestrial vehicles shuttled between the Oracle's Palace, Guardians' Shrine, and the Sages' Temple, ferrying members of the Order to various meetings throughout the day.

Darshima and his companions came to a stop in front of the gates amid the frenzied activity.

"What are the kingdom's chances of victory?" Erethalie faced the shrine.

"Keverese and Nyzhaiheb are dominions that span entire continents. Tiriyuud is but a small and distant island nation." A worried frown formed upon Sydarias' lips.

"I wouldn't count them out," said Khydius. "They are far better equipped than I ever imagined. They have hidden their strengths from us all." Darshima nodded in agreement. From what they had seen during training, Tiriyuud would bring its unique capabilities to battle. Whether it would be enough to defeat Navervyne remained unclear.

"If the oracle is willing to fight against Navervyne, I am determined to give my life to this cause," said Darshima, his heart thudding. Erethalie, Khydius, and Sydarias bowed their heads in agreement. His mind still raced with the improbable fact that the oracle agreed with him and saw the need to wage war.

As they walked through the gates and toward the shrine, Darshima ruminated on the Order's preparations thus far.

"Tiriyuud is prepared for battle, but from what the Order has shared thus far, they are planning for the long term when the fighting abates," said Khydius.

"The Order's dossier is comprehensive," added Erethalie. "It's clear they have prepared Tiriyuud for a wide-ranging offensive."

Darshima and his companions had received their first written briefings earlier that afternoon. The document contained information about Tiriyuud's plans for war. Tenrai had emphasized the importance of these dossiers, and they read them together as they shuttled between meetings. As Tenrai told them, all guardians needed to be aware of the Order's broad objective and goals, no matter their rank.

Within moments of the oracle's pronouncement of war, the Order of the Gilded Moon prepared its plans for the liberation of Keverese and Nyzhaiheb and the war against Fauridise and Navervyne. Housing the majority of the meetings, The Guardians' Shrine would serve as the base of operations for the war, as it had done since ancient times. Sages and guardians, priests, and prelates convened throughout the day to formulate the Order's strategy.

As the leader of the kingdom, the oracle was directly involved in many of these meetings and authorized the Order's final strategy. Though

Navervyne's forces outnumbered them, the Order believed that Tiriyuud's strength would lie in its agility. Despite their centuries of isolation, the Tiriyuusians had come to know Iberwight's terrain intimately. Theirs was the oldest civilization upon the moon, and they had been among its first explorers.

The ancient Phidaxians of Benai had neglected Iberwight. They had claimed the frozen moon as their own but never established any colonies. It had subsequently had been left to the first waves of exiled Omystikai to chart the first maps of its inhospitable and complex topography. Over the ages, The Guardians of Tiriyuud became master cartographers, documenting every intricacy and vagary of Iberwight's terrain. The Tiriyuusians cultivated their knowledge of the moon. They sought to protect themselves from potential conflict and improve their trade routes to the dominions.

Faced with the daunting prospect of war, the Order would use their armaments and their knowledge of Iberwight's geography to their advantage. Their first action would be to liberate both allied dominions simultaneously. They estimated that their forces would have less than a fortnight to carry out their missions before Navervyne's reinforcements would be ready to strike back. Tiriyuud would devote significant resources to free Keverese and Nyzhaiheb and guarantee a successful outcome.

"I'm impressed with what we've seen thus far. Despite Tiriyuud's plans, I wonder how long these islands can withstand Navervyne's onslaught." Sydarias bit his lip in contemplation.

"Don't let the size of their territory fool you," said Khydius. "The Tiriyuusians are more formidable than they appear."

"They held off the Vilidesians for more than ten centuries. I wouldn't discount them against the Navervynish," added Darshima.

Per the Order's dossier, Tiriyuud's engineers had previously organized strategies to cope with the material demands in the scenario of a long war with the Vilidesians. Tiriyuud maintained ample amounts of artillery to supply the guardians and their troops. The Order's munitions and aircraft factories had long operated at full capacity, maintaining vast stocks for what they believed would be an inevitable war with The Vilides.

The Order had issued requests to the kingdom's most prominent manufacturers to retool their factories to produce vital materiel and goods.

Plans to increase the output from mines and quarries were being organized throughout the Tiriyuusian islands. In preparation for the demands upon Tiriyuud's resources, new mines would be tunneled both underground and undersea to access its vast, untapped wealth of resources.

The Order's engineers estimated that Tiriyuud could ably launch and sustain an initial war effort with its current resources. However, they expected increasing demand upon their soldiers and materials as their presence expanded on Iberwight. Shortly after the first attack, The Order issued a decree throughout the kingdom, soliciting men and women to work in the factories to support the effort.

"So, if Tiriyuud somehow wins this war, how will they maintain peace on Iberwight?" asked Erethalie.

"They will have to do as the Vilidesians did and build consensus," said Khydius.

"Easier said than done." Darshima shook his head. He remembered the cultural clashes that roiled beneath the veneer of civil relations between the four moons.

"At least they are all Omystikai. Perhaps they have more in common than we did," added Erethalie.

"Well, an Omystikai order and its ally attempted an invasion of Tiriyuud." Sydarias' lips wrinkled in a frown. "The Omystikai are more like us Vilidesians than they admit."

Throughout the meetings, the oracle, guardians, and sages finalized the steps that Gilded Moon would take once Keverese and Nyzhaiheb came under the control of Tiriyuud. Both dominions were more populous than Tiriyuud, and it would take a great deal of effort to maintain stability. The Order would station squadrons throughout the skies of each dominion and soldiers on the ground to establish order. Auxiliary vessels bearing provisions and relief supplies would accompany them.

Despite Tiriyuud's challenging climate and rocky terrain, its farmers displayed an ingenuity that had made them among the most successful anywhere. Over the centuries, they were the only people that had mastered agriculture on Iberwight, and the kingdom was more than able to supply its own needs. As fully integrated members of the fallen realm, Keverese, Fauridise, and Nyzhaiheb imported virtually all of their foodstuffs from Wohi-imai and maintained no agricultural practices.

With thousands of greenhouse pyramids throughout the archipelago, the farmers raised crops and livestock year-round, utilizing the heat and humidity of the underground steam and crystals that amplified the sunlight. Along with unique food preservation methods, the kingdom had accrued a vast and stable store of grain and provisions. They would be able to provide foodstuffs to feed themselves as well as the people of the dominions. Nonetheless, the farmers of Tiriyuud were warned that the war effort would strain their supplies. The Order issued directives for the farmers to increase their output.

If Tiriyuud succeeded in defeating Navervyne, the Order would establish its presence in the dominions. Tiriyuud would seek lasting peace with the citizens by helping them refashion their destroyed infrastructure and rebuild their institutions. They would work to reestablish trade and alleviate the crushing poverty that the invasion had created. The Tiriyuusians knew that the economies of both dominions would require a great deal of assistance. They were prepared to offer help.

As Keverese and Nyzhaiheb counted many more citizens than Tiriyuud, the Order would recruit young men and women from the dominions to train as soldiers to support Tiriyuud's effort. Tiriyuud's only chance of restoring peace would happen if they united the Omystikai Dominions and fought against Navervyne as one force.

Darshima and his companions approached the entrance to the Guardians' Shrine. His thoughts were weighted by the immense challenge confronting them. As they stepped through the arcade leading to the courtyard, he turned to them.

"Though our chance at victory may be fleeting, I will stand with the Tiriyuusians until the very end," said Darshima, his voice growing heavy.

"Whether in The Vilides or Navervyne or here in Tiriyuud, we will always stand with you." Sydarias rested his hand upon Darshima's shoulder.

"We are with you," said Erethalie, nodding toward Darshima.

"We will defend Tiriyuud's sovereignty with everything we have," added Khydius. Darshima looked at his companions, and his heart rose into his throat. Whatever happened, he was thankful that they would fight together.

Chapter 33

Darshima, Khydius, Erethalie, and Sydarias took their seats at the front of the large, circular auditorium with the other guardians. He drew in an anxious breath as the lights dimmed around them. A conical machine recessed within the ceiling issued a soft whir, mingling with the audience's whispers. Darshima watched as its array of cylindrical crystals rotated, focusing a myriad of colored beams in the center of the room.

The beams converged into a white point of light. In a silent explosion, the light rapidly expanded into a giant, white orb. Darshima's eyes acclimated to the diaphanous sphere floating above the dais at the center of the auditorium. The details of the orb came into focus, and he realized that it was a three-dimensional rendering of Iberwight. Never having seen such a phenomenon, he peered into the depths of the holographic image, astounded at the Tiriyuusian machine that created it.

Tenrai and Dydan stood upon the dais at either side of the rotating orb, the bright flickering light illuminating their faces.

"Fellow guardians, the hour of battle is upon us." Tenrai gestured toward the image.

"The sages and guardians have consulted with the oracle, and the missions have been finalized," said Dydan. "We will share the overall aims. However, each of you has predetermined roles, which will be discussed at the adjournment of this meeting."

Darshima leaned forward in his seat as he anxiously awaited their words.

"As General Heede stated earlier, Tiriyuud has but only a small window of opportunity to act before Navervyne's reinforcements arrive on Iberwight." Dydan pointed toward the rotating orb, which came to a pause over the Tiriyuusian archipelago. The image magnified on Chryshaihem, rendering the cityscape in vivid detail. Dydan continued, "Our first missions will require much effort and skill."

Dydan turned to Tenrai, who shared further details. "Eight carrier squadrons from Gilded Wing will lead the Order into battle. Four squadrons will be directed to Keverese, and the other four will travel to

Nyzhaiheb." Dydan then turned his attention to the orb as its topography shifted. The image of Chryshaihem shrank, and the archipelago came back into view. Darshima followed the miniature images of aircraft as they moved away from Tiriyuud's islands and over the ocean. The orb made half a turn as the craft charted their way to the Omystikai Dominions.

Never having seen such a precise rendering of Iberwight, Darshima now understood how isolated the Tiriyuusian archipelago truly was. Located on the opposite side of Iberwight, near the moon's northern pole, the kingdom was surrounded by the vast ocean and immense glaciers. The orb showed images of the three dominions, each located upon separate continents near Iberwight's equator.

"The squadrons will depart this evening from Tiriyuud, with a planned arrival in Keverese and Nyzhaiheb at dawn. Our forces will neutralize any hostile craft and military installations in the city and surrounding territories." Tenrai gestured to the allied dominions.

"Tiriyuud will formally claim each capital city and annex the surrounding territories. Once deemed safe, support craft will arrive with additional soldiers, crew, and provisions for their struggling citizens," added Dydan. The aircraft formations fanned in separate directions about the orb and came to a stop at different locations in the territories of Keverese and Nyzhaiheb.

Dydan continued, "Gilded Moon must work swiftly to establish peace in the allied dominions. These squadrons will remain in Keverese and Nyzhaiheb. They will maintain order and support our soldiers on the ground." The orb made another rotation then stopped again over Tiriyuud.

"We will destroy remaining enemy elements. We aim for both dominions to come under Tiriyuud's complete control within days." Tenrai gestured to the map as he spoke.

"After the initial phase is complete, the Order will send six additional Gilded Wing squadrons to Gavipristine. They will be joined by the lead squadrons from the initial phase of the battle."

Dydan looked toward the image of Tiriyuud, his eyes narrowing as he studied the graphic. "The Order will keep three carrier squadrons in Keverese and Nyzhaiheb to guard against future attacks. We expect to face a fierce battle in Gavipristine and may call upon additional resources."

An image of eight squadrons of craft moved along the orb's surface, then landed in Fauridise.

"Given the complex geography of Gavipristine, the Order will be sending naval fleets for support." Tenrai pointed toward the glowing image as it magnified into a complex map. Appearing as a vast city of soaring crystal skyscrapers, canals, and bridges, Gavipristine sat upon the snowy islands of a large river delta. Both its scale and architecture bore a striking resemblance to parts of The Vilides.

"Why does it look so similar to The Vilides?" whispered Erethalie, surprised at its plan.

"The Vilidesians built the realm's capital on the ruins of an Omystikai city and copied most of the ancient plan." Khydius turned to Erethalie. "The Gavipristinians tried to resurrect what their ancestors had originally built upon the frozen lands."

Darshima turned back to the image and scoured the details, his pulse thudding in surprise at Khydius' observation. Growing up, he remembered the Vilidesians portraying the realm as eternal and their capital as the center of their world. The map of Gavipristine floating before his eyes reminded him that The Vilides, like all civilizations, were but ephemeral. Darshima looked on as realistic images of angular black and gold ships clad in heavy plated armor plied the waterways of the detailed map.

His pulse thudded as he absorbed Tenrai and Dydan's words. As the images depicting Tiriyuud's next steps played out before his eyes, his chest felt heavy with a growing sense of responsibility. The Order would be committing much of its precious resources to liberate these dominions and engage Fauridise. It was Darshima who had dared suggest that Tiriyuud save Keverese and Nyzhaiheb and wage an offensive war with Navervyne and Fauridise. It was clear to him that both the oracle and the Order understood his words and accepted the threat that Tiriyuud faced.

Darshima drew in an anxious breath as he contemplated the dangers the guardians would face as they acted to carry out Tiriyuud's objectives. As he mulled over the perils that lay ahead, the turn of events over the past several hours stalked his mind like a shadow. Fauridise and Navervyne had tried yet again to attack Chryshaihem, and if it hadn't been for Khydius, the city would have surely been invaded.

His heartbeat slowed with relief when he remembered that he was one among many with the ability to use kai. He had witnessed other guardians demonstrate feats of strength and astounding skill during their training. Even so, Darshima realized that his abilities to channel kai were rare. He didn't believe any other member of the Order could match him until now.

Darshima had witnessed Khydius' abilities during their training, and his feat in the Outer District demonstrated a unique mastery of the sovereign strength. Darshima couldn't help but be impressed. Deep down, he knew Tiriyuud's forces, though prepared, would feel the strain of this war. Darshima anticipated that he and Khydius would be called upon to lend their strength to support the Order.

Darshima stared at the rotating image floating before him, its moving figures and intricate maps plotting out the kingdom's future steps. The situation had evolved so swiftly. Though the first attack had only happened days ago, it had already begun to feel like a faded memory. Despite his lingering worries, Darshima knew that Tiriyuud had no other choice. Both attacks demonstrated their enemies' unmistakable intent to defeat and destroy the kingdom. If the Order of the Gilded Moon and the Kingdom of Tiriyuud were to survive, it too would have to engage in war and conquest. It was their only hope.

Darshima sat with his fellow guardians and listened as Tenrai and Dydan shared more details about the plans for the capture of Gavipristine. From what he gathered, it would be the most difficult challenge they would face. Victory would require a coordinated effort from Tiriyuud, the entire Order, and its allies in Keverese and Nyzhaiheb. Having lost much of their fleet on Iberwight, Navervyne and Fauridise were regrouping and readying themselves to confront Tiriyuud.

The Order of the Gilded Moon anticipated that the occupation and reconstruction of the Dominions of Keverese and Nyzhaiheb would be a difficult but surmountable challenge. The Order would face an intense struggle in gaining control over Fauridise. There were only a limited number of ways to succeed and a myriad of ways in which they could fail. The briefing ended, and Tenrai and Dydan issued the guardians instructions for additional meetings before their deployment. Darshima and his companions rose from their seats and filed solemnly out of the auditorium.

Chapter 34

Darshima and his companions sat in a circle upon the floor of their suite. Late afternoon sunlight streamed through the large window, casting the orderly space in a subtle glow. They had finished their meetings, eaten a brief supper, and returned to their quarters for the first time since morning. Eyes cast downward, they remained silent, their anxious thoughts filling the void. They had received their missions and would report to the shrine's courtyard at midnight for deployment.

Darshima and Sydarias would join the carrier group heading to Keverese, led by Tenrai. Khydius and Erethalie would join the group heading to Nyzhaiheb, led by Dydan. When these dominions were liberated, Darshima and his companions would regroup for the battle against Fauridise. The thought of Tiriyuud going to war had seemed like a distant concept, but the moment was swiftly approaching.

Despite his confidence, Darshima felt a pang of nervousness. Though officially inducted as guardians, they remained untested. He knew the training they had received as recruits would be challenged in myriad ways. Even so, Darshima believed they would overcome the trials that war would surely bring their way.

Darshima sat in silence, enjoying the moment of peace. The past several months and the most recent days of turmoil had strained them all. The missions ahead would mean that they would see less each other, which would be difficult for him. Moments such as these, when they were all together, would be far and few. Darshima mulled the dangers they would face in combat. Some would threaten their lives, and others would change them forever.

As he looked upon his friends, Darshima knew that the days and weeks ahead would harden them and teach them. His eyes narrowed in a wistful expression as he contemplated the coming hours.

"What's on your mind, Darshima?" A concerned look formed upon Erethalie's face.

"We have faced some very difficult times together, and the path ahead is uncertain." Darshima turned to her. "Your friendship has meant everything to me. You all have kept me alive. You gave me hope when I thought all was lost."

"We're all in this together," said Erethalie, a warm smile spreading upon her lips.

"I owe you my life, Darshima," added Sydarias, his eyes growing damp with tears.

"If it weren't for you, Sasha and I would have died long ago in that factory in Stebbenhour. I will never forget what you did to save us." Khydius pulled Darshima into an embrace.

Darshima drew in a breath and looked at his friends. His heart rose into his throat as he contemplated the extent of their sacrifice. They left behind their former lives and their families. They had devoted themselves to training in Tiriyuud and to the struggle that lay ahead.

"There is no place else I'd rather be than here fighting beside you." Sydarias rested his hand upon Darshima's shoulder.

"Despite everything we've lost, we are lucky to be here. We have no choice but to fight." Sydarias peered through the window at the surrounding city. Darshima and the others nodded in agreement.

Despite their uncertain future, Darshima was grateful to Tiriyuud. When the realm had fallen, and there was nowhere else to turn, Tiriyuud had sheltered them and accepted them as their own. The kingdom had allowed them a moment of peace amid the turmoil. As a Tiriyuusian and as a new guardian, Darshima was prepared to defend his new homeland with his life.

"Well, at least we shared some happy memories before the world came undone," said Erethalie. A wry chuckle escaped her lips.

"What are you talking about?" asked Darshima, genuinely curious.

"The night you came to my cafeteria, in the middle of the sandstorm." Erethalie smiled as she recounted the memory.

"I'll always remember our evening together at the Omystikai ruins, during the eclipse," added Sydarias.

"I'll never forget either of those experiences," exclaimed Darshima, chuckling as the cherished moments came back to him.

"I'll never forget when I saw you at the palace with your Ardavian family," said Khydius. "I remembered feeling an inexplicable connection to you when our eyes met. I would've never guessed that you were truly my brother." Khydius eyes widened as he relived the memory.

"I also felt it. Who would have imagined the truth?" mused Darshima. Tears formed in his eyes as he thought of the memories he shared with his friends. They cared about him as much as he cared about them.

"You all mean everything to me. I know we will meet again," said Darshima. He embraced Sydarias, Erethalie, and Khydius. They laughed and shared more memories, and the somber mood thawed. For a moment amid the fading sunlight, they escaped the gravity of the challenges awaiting them.

Chapter 35

Tenrai Nax

Tenrai and Dydan sat in a semicircle upon a stone platform within the elaborate sanctuary, along with several senior guardians and commanders. Their silhouettes reflected upon the polished black surface in a muted tableau. These men and women would be leading soldiers, squadrons, and carrier groups into battle at dawn.

Tenrai looked toward the oracle, seated before them upon a crystal dais, its soft white glow illuminating the ground around her. Seer Ryte and General Heede sat on either side of her. She wore a fine black and gold uniform, nearly identical to the attire of the commanders. A halo of gold and crystal sat upon her locks, cascading over her shoulders. Smoldering beams from the waning sun filtered in through the tall windows encircling the octagonal room. Lights throughout the city flickered to life, burning against the encroaching night.

A heavy mood pervaded the room as they listened to her assessment. She had summoned them to her private quarters after the final meeting in the palace. Though Tenrai and those seated around her remained straight-faced, he was surprised to see the oracle in such an informal setting. Apart from official meetings in the throne room, he hadn't been in her presence since she left the guardianship and trained as a sage. Tenrai realized their presence among the oracle highlighted the extraordinary circumstances facing Tiriyuud.

"What else can the Order provide to ensure the success of your missions in Keverese and Nyzhaiheb?" asked the oracle, her gaze sweeping over the group.

"We believe that we are ready, most exalted one," said General Heede, turning to Tenrai and Dydan.

"As our plans have laid forth, we will direct the lead carrier squadrons. Chancellor Waike and I will carry out these missions in your name." Tenrai and Dydan bowed in deference toward the oracle.

As the evening progressed, the oracle questioned every guardian, knight, and commander about their plan, altering the specifics of each mission as she saw fit. Though it was the purview of the guardians to devise a strategy and wage war on behalf of the kingdom, Tiriyuud's armed forces were under her control, and the decision to deploy them had ultimately been her own. Those attending the meeting appreciated her insight and vowed to carry out her plans.

General Heede discussed the specifics of the craft being deployed, the air routes to the foreign dominions, and the artillery they would use. The oracle listened intently, questioning every detail. Before her time as a sage, she had served as a commander and developed a deep understanding of the Order's military capabilities. Tenrai and those seated around her were keenly aware of the unique situation she faced as Tiriyuud's oracle. Under her guidance, they would be embarking on a strategy that had never occurred in Tiriyuud's history. Whatever the outcome, she would bear the ultimate responsibility.

As the meeting concluded, the oracle rose from her seat.

"May the flows of kai protect and sustain you all as you travel to distant shores." She extended her hands over them as she spoke in the Tiriyuusian dialect. They bowed before her and issued a chant affirming her leadership. The oracle dismissed them, and the palace priests ushered the group away.

"Commander Nax, Chancellor Waike, I request more of your time," said the oracle as the remaining guardians left the sanctuary.

"Certainly, most exalted one," said Dydan. Tenrai and Dydan bowed toward her and returned to the dais.

"Please, join me on the terrace." She motioned toward an open doorway at the opposite end of the sanctuary, leading outdoors.

"Without question, most exalted one," said Dydan.

The oracle led them past the threshold onto the black pavement of the balcony. A light dusting of snow covered its surface, crunching underfoot as Tenrai shifted his weight. The three stood in silence as they looked out over the balustrade at the glittering lights of the city surrounding them. The steam of their breath trailed toward the skies as they took in the scene. The sun rays slipped beneath the horizon. Tenrai looked on as the sky ceded its final rays to the night's enveloping void.

"It is a most trying circumstance that reunites the three of us again," said the oracle.

"Indeed, most exalted one." Tenrai exchanged a familiar gaze with her, recollections of their shared past flickering in his eyes.

"It has been far too long." Dydan bowed his head. For a moment, the rigid barriers of tradition and ancient protocol dissolved between them, giving way to memories of a youth spent together both as children and as guardians.

They came from the village of Foseidem and grew up together amid the snowy hills and mountain valleys. Their families had been close for generations, and several marriages between the clans had bound them together through the centuries. Before her ascension to the throne, they knew her as Anaidys Rexe.

Her physical strength and her psychic abilities were clear from childhood. As Anaidys matured, there was no doubt among those in Chryshaihem that she would become someone of immense talent. She had progressed through guardianship training in the same cohort as Rion, where she honed her skills. Before she followed Rion into the sagehood, she had served as a mentor to Tenrai and Dydan when they joined the guardianship. As time went on, they went their separate ways. She had served as Tenrai's commander for several years before becoming a sage and then the youngest oracle to had ever ruled Tiriyuud.

Despite her youth, her abilities made her among the most powerful Omystikai in her generation. Her only peer had been Rion, who renounced his position as a sage. As such, she had rightfully ascended the throne. Though they had followed different paths, the three still felt the strong bonds of their upbringing.

The oracle looked upon Tenrai and Dydan, an expression of concern crossing her features.

"How are you both handling these developments?" she asked.

"We are preparing as best as we can," replied Dydan.

"We will do our utmost to defend Tiriyuud," added Tenrai. She nodded as she listened to their responses.

"It is in times like these that your strength reminds me of Rion." The oracle looked at Tenrai. "After all of these years, his loss still weighs upon my heart."

"No matter the time that passes, we remain bereft," said Dydan, his voice thick with emotion.

"Rion would have wanted us to fight for Tiriyuud. Despite the unexpected trajectory of his life, he defended our nation with his last breath. His sons, Darshima and Khydius, have defended Tiriyuud once again. We must do the same," said Tenrai.

"You both have displayed more courage in these past few months than most sages and guardians have during their entire lives. At dawn, you shall lead the first carrier groups into battle. You must show that same courage and determination if we are to defend Tiriyuud. Our way of life, our very survival depends upon it." She looked at them, and her eyes narrowed in a solemn gaze.

"Without question, we will sacrifice everything for Tiriyuud," replied Dydan.

"Tenrai, your nephews have demonstrated a rare power over kai that will be of utmost importance to our nation's survival. You both must do everything in your power to protect these men."

"You have my word," answered Tenrai.

"Commander Nax, Chancellor Wake, go forth. Lead the Order of the Gilded Moon into battle. Defend the sovereignty of these islands." She raised her hand and offered a blessing to secure their health and strength.

Tenrai stood in silence and looked out over the city. He observed the capital and the lake beyond their high perch, its smooth ripples glistening in the moonlight. Night had fallen, and the stars shone brightly, casting the city in a pale glow. The distant drone of aerial vessels filled the air, their lights twinkling as they made their way across the expanse of sky. Tenrai cast an eye toward the east and stared at the ghostly form of Benai. Its halo of red and white rings blotted out the stars in its path.

The glowing discs of Gordanelle and Wohiimai hung in the skies to the west, arranged in a close pair. His eyes lingered upon Ciblaithia's gilded crescent. Tenrai beheld the conquered orbs ensconced amid the stars. His heart thudded with a sense of sadness as he remembered the toil and suffering he witnessed during his travels.

Tenrai's eyes lingered upon the horizon, and his sadness only deepened. He strained to see beyond the stars, into the darkness of space, his eyes sifting through the blackness from whence the Navervynish had come. The distant invaders had seized the moons above in their odious grip. They controlled every speck of land, sea, and sky beyond the Tiriyuusian islands.

Tenrai watched as the oracle surveyed the city around her. Her eyes glowed in incandescent flashes of blue, and then she closed them. She gripped the balustrade and stood still. Tenrai held his breath as he witnessed her in the midst of a divinatory state. He remembered learning that the oracle could hear the voices of the okainym - sages, guardians, and oracles from ages past, whose energies had long since rejoined the kai fields. Like every oracle who preceded her, the ability to hear the okainym made her strengths vital to the kingdom.

Tenrai sifted through his memories of her hearing those voices during their childhood. Her listening abilities increased during her training as a sage and had guided her ever since. As Tenrai learned a long time ago, only those destined to become the oracle could hear the okainym. The only other sage in recent memory with this ability had been Rion Nax.

The oracle opened her eyes and gazed at Tenrai and Dydan.

"How are you, most exalted one?" asked Dydan, his eyebrows raised in concern.

"I sense difficult times ahead, but our ancestors want us to persist. They expect us to persevere as they did." The oracle nodded as she spoke, her eyes attenuating to a soft glow.

"We understand, most exalted one." Tenrai bowed in her direction.

As Tenrai turned back to the city, he mulled over the past several days, whose events had shaken him to his core. For centuries, Tiriyuud had only known the hegemony of the Vilidesian Realm. They had found a way to live in independence under Vilidesian rule of the four moons. In the wake of the realm's fall, Tiriyuud now faced the most severe threat to its existence in its history.

"We must not falter in our mission," said the oracle. "Oemiri has predicted this day, and we must find a way to prevail." Her robes stirred with the rising winds. "In a few hours, you both will be leading our nation into an unprecedented battle. We have no history upon which to consult or to learn. It is being written as we live and breath."

"We understand and will not fail you." Dydan bowed deeply. Tenrai offered a bow to the oracle and reflected upon her candid words. It would be the first time that Tiriyuud would advance beyond its own shores for the sake of its survival, and their oracle was leading the charge.

Despite two attempted invasions, she remained their unquestioned leader, and Tiriyuud was still sovereign. Tiriyuud had never needed a stronger oracle more than it did now. Tenrai looked up to the stars, his heart beating with a silent vow to defend the Order and the kingdom with everything he had. Together, he and Dydan would marshal their forces to vanquish Navervyne and liberate Iberwight. Tiriyuud had been shaken, but it would not fall.

Chapter 36

Erethalie Danthe

Her eyes trained forward, Erethalie sailed through the night sky. Her cloudboard pressing upward against her feet, she leaned into the wind as it howled past her ears. She wiped the snowflakes from her visor and made out the lines of the desolate streets below, winding their way through the dense city blocks. Their radiating webs glowed softly through the falling powdery flakes of snow.

"It's this way, isn't it?" shouted Sydarias as he flew beside her.

"It's not much further," she replied, her voice torn away by the wind.

They flew further from the temple complex, carving a path through the blustery skies. The gusts buffed them, and they crouched lower upon their cloudboards. They soared over the lake toward Chryshaihem's forested outer islands and their residential neighborhoods.

Erethalie eyed the cityscape moving below her as it changed from clusters of spires and temples to homes, apartments, and large stands of snow-covered trees.

They descended from the clouds, reflexively bending their knees to absorb the shock as their boards made contact with the snowy ground. They skated upon the slick surface, leaving a gentle wake of powder behind them. Erethalie came to a stop and stepped onto the ground beside Sydarias. They secured their boards upon their backs and trudged through the snowdrifts. Night had fallen, and they only had a few hours before they reported for deployment.

"Are you ready to see him?" Sydarias gently tapped Erethalie's shoulder.

"I am," she responded. A lump formed in her throat as she recalled her last memory of Shonan. So much time had passed since they parted ways. She had worried about him every single day, wondering how he was faring with his new family.

Erethalie and the other guardians in their squadron were given a few hours of personal time before reporting to the shrine later that evening. Many chose to rest. However, Erethalie needed to see her brother before leaving Tiriyuud. Not wanting her to travel by herself, Sydarias insisted that he join her. Erethalie had intended on going alone, but she was glad for the company. Sydarias had no family nearby, and she imagined that he sometimes longed for them.

Erethalie's pulse thudded as she made the familiar trek down the torchlit path of the neighborhood. It had been several months since she had seen Shonan, and she wondered how much he had changed since their goodbye. Images of that day flooded her mind, and she drew in a breath of cold air to suppress her sadness. Shonan had been so brave when they parted ways. She wondered how he was getting along with the Byx family and finding his way in their new homeland.

As Erethalie grew familiar with the Tiriyuusian language and customs, she found herself developing an unexpected fondness for the kingdom. She knew that Shonan was strong enough to adapt to anything but worried that he might have become so different that she wouldn't recognize him. Erethalie shook her head and rid herself of the errant thought. Shonan would be different after their months apart, and it would be selfish to expect any less. His survival in this place depended on it. Tiriyuud would change him, as it had changed her.

She and Sydarias walked past the wooden gate and trudged up the steps to the Byx home. As they neared the top of the staircase, the softly lit interior shone through the open door, reflecting upon the surrounding snowdrifts. Erethalie narrowed her eyes against the light and made out a silhouette waiting for them. She and Sydarias hurried their pace up to the terrace.

"Welcome, Guardian Danthe, Guardian Idawa." Hezion Byx peered at them, drawing his overcoat against his shoulders. A smile of recognition formed upon his lips. He ushered them inside and closed the door. The warmth of the home melted the caked layers of snow from their uniforms. Erethalie and Sydarias gently laid their cloudboards at the entrance, removed their visors, and peered about the welcoming space. Sera Byx made her way to the door to meet them, her robes trailing behind her.

"Welcome young guardians." She clasped their hands.

As Sera guided them toward the hearth, the thud of soft footsteps filled the tranquil silence. Out of the corner of her eye, Erethalie spotted a flash rushing down the staircase. Her eyes instinctively snapped toward the moving figure.

"You're here!" Wearing simple blue trousers and a shirt with wide sleeves, Shonan stood directly in front of her, his warm gaze greeting her.

"It's been far too long, Shonan," said Erethalie. Her heart leaped into her throat as she saw how much he had changed.

Though it had only been a few months since she left him, Shonan had grown in stature. Erethalie looked at him in disbelief as he stood almost as tall as she did. Like her, Shonan's deep bronze skin had become a shade paler due to Iberwight's distance from both Benai and the sun. His voice was a little deeper, and his bearing exuded a distinct air of confidence. His facial features were taking on the angular look of adolescence.

Shonan's emerald green eyes bore a look of growing wisdom and self-awareness but also a hint of sadness. His sandy blond hair had grown and was pulled back in a tight queue that fell past his neck. A bright, toothy grin crossed his features as he gazed at his sister. Though he had clearly grown since their last visit, he was still the younger brother she had always known, and she instinctively read it in his smile.

Shonan ran to her and threw his arms around her. They embraced for a moment, hastily dashing away the tears pent up from their months of separation.

"You came, Sydarias!" exclaimed Shonan as he hugged Sydarias.

"You both look well," said Sera. She and Hezion watched the poignant reunion, their eyes misty with tears. Hezion ushered them into the central room, where they sat upon stiff rugs arranged around the hearth, flickering with subdued flame.

"We understand your time is limited this evening," said Sera.

"Thank you for welcoming us, and thank you for taking care of Shonan." Erethalie turned to her brother, her voice catching in her throat.

"Shonan has been a wonderful addition to our family. We love him." Sera wrapped her arms around Shonan's shoulders and drew him closer.

Sera and Hezion praised Shonan and emphasized how he had become like a son to them. He was getting along well with his brother and sister and even helping in the workshop. Slowly but surely, he was finding his way in their culture. He had become fluent in the Tiriyuusian dialect and was excelling in all of his lessons at school.

Their conversation ebbed, and Hezion turned to Erethalie and Sydarias.

"We understand the attacks that have happened and the battles that you both will face." Hezion's eyes burned bright with concern.

"You are our guardians and our protectors. Your duty calls upon you to shoulder a great burden for our kingdom. We are forever grateful." Sera clasped her hands together, her eyes growing damp. "We know how important this time is for you and Shonan," said Sera. She Hezion rose from their seats.

"Go safely, young guardians, and may kai protect you," said Hezion, his voice heavy with sadness. He and Sera embraced Erethalie and Sydarias, wishing them strength and health for the struggles ahead of them. They hugged Shonan, bade him goodnight, and politely excused themselves. Hezion followed Sera from the hearth, and they climbed the stairs to the upper level.

The three sat in silence amid the soft crackling of the flames. Erethalie marveled as she saw Shonan seated comfortably beside her. When she had left him a few months ago, he had seemed so nervous. Now he appeared at ease here in this home, and she was thankful. Before long, their conversation filled the warm space, and Shonan recounted all that he had done since they had separated.

Shonan's eyes lit up as he told them everything that he was learning and about the friends he was making. A smile crossed Erethalie's lips as she sat back and listened. It had been so long since she had seen each other, and she simply enjoyed hearing the sound of his voice again. His mere presence brought back memories of their hectic but pleasant life in The Vilides. Shonan shared his experiences living in Chryshaihem, and Erethalie couldn't help but celebrate his triumphs and empathize with his tribulations. It reminded her in some ways of her own experiences as she trained with the guardians.

Before long, Shonan began to ask questions about the recent events that had befallen the kingdom. She was surprised that he knew so much about the attempted invasion. He understood that the same enemies that had defeated The Vilides and invaded the realm had attempted two attacks upon Chryshaihem. He knew that the Order had managed to defend the kingdom.

"What if they come back?" asked Shonan, his brow wrinkling in worry.

"Tiriyuud will be safe." Erethalie reached over and squeezed his hand, but he didn't seem convinced.

"There are many people like us who will protect this place." Sydarias tried to catch his gaze, but Shonan stared blankly into the flames.

"So you have to go to war?" Shonan glared at Erethalie.

"Yes, we must go. Our squadrons leave tonight," said Erethalie. Her heart froze as she saw Shonan close his eyes and let out a pained sigh. Despite her absence from his daily life, it was important to Erethalie that Shonan was near her. The invasion had taken their entire family, and her brother was all that she had left. Now she would be fighting Navervyne anew and facing untold risk.

Erethalie watched Shonan's expression change as the realization of her departure settled within him. The happiness with which he had greeted her disappeared, and a solemn shadow crept across his features. Erethalie's eyes grew damp as she saw the change in his countenance. It was the same melancholy frown he wore as they eked out an existence in the occupied, war-torn Vilides. Somewhere in the back of her mind, Erethalie had feared that this visit would do Shonan more harm than good. He seemed to be thriving in his new life with the Byx family. Her imminent departure reconjured the specter of war and brought back painful memories for them both.

More than four months had passed since they had arrived on Iberwight. She held tightly onto the memories of their old life in The Vilides, but Shonan had been a younger boy back then. They had endured such hardship after the invasion, and she didn't know how much longer they would've survived there. Life in Chryshaihem had given Shonan a needed sense of normalcy and a chance to enjoy a childhood of abundance, free from violence, want, and fear.

So much had changed for him, and she marveled at his ability not only to adapt but to thrive. She felt a lingering fear that he might hold on less tightly to the memories of their old life as he tried to build a new one here in Tiriyuud. She briefly closed her eyes and dashed the selfish thought from her mind. Shonan's happiness and safety here in this household were the only things that truly mattered to her.

Erethalie placed her hands upon his cheeks and stared at him. "You must stay strong, Shonan. Sydarias and I will return soon."

"I understand," he whispered, avoiding her gaze. Erethalie could feel the hot tears forming behind her eyes.

Erethalie sat with him amid the warmth of the fire, and he rested his head upon her shoulder. Her pulse thudded as she sensed his worry. She wanted to assure him that they would be safe, but deep down, she, like the other guardians, could only speculate what truly awaited them beyond Tiriyuud's shore.

"We must go back to the shrine for deployment." Sydarias scooted closer to them. Erethalie rested her hand upon Shonan's shoulder, and he looked up at her.

"Please be careful out there." His lips quivered as he tried to hold back his emotions.

"We will be careful. I promise to come back as soon as we return." She drew him closer. Together, they rose from the floor, and Shonan led them to the front door. Sydarias collected his cloudboard and moved toward the entrance.

"I will wait outside. Take care of yourself, Shonan." Sydarias embraced him, slid open the door, and stepped past the threshold.

"Please be good to your family here." Erethalie reached over and embraced Shonan again. He looked at her, his eyes growing damp.

"They are very kind to me, but I miss our family," said Shonan, his tears falling. "Please don't forget about our brother and sister when you're out there. If you find them, let them know that I am okay."

"Of course, I will." Erethalie dashed away a tear as it rolled down her cheek.

Her heart thudded as she stared at him. Their last departure had been difficult, but this one was much harder than she had ever imagined. She yearned for a day when they could be together, but at present, it was impossible. Her stomach sank with a sense of loss as she beheld his somber face. The invasion had spared no one. The fall of the realm had cut such a deep wound in everyone. The devastation had resulted in the death of their parents and the enslavement of their siblings. As she prepared to leave her brother, a feeling of bitterness gnawed at her. Navervyne's unrelenting conquest was again the reason for more suffering in their lives.

She never imagined being deprived of the chance to watch her brother grow up, but their present circumstance prevented it. She was grateful that Tiriyuud welcomed them and gave them refuge. Erethalie had done her best to run from war. Though she fled and escaped the devastation for a time, Navervyne had finally arrived upon these shores. She had no other choice but to fight again for survival.

She embraced Shonan once more, and as she let him go, he gripped her hand.

"I want to give you something." He reached into his trouser pocket, retrieved a small rectangular piece of metal, and pressed it into her palm. She turned the object over in her hand and lifted it into the light. It was a framed photograph of Shonan. He wore a Tiriyuusian uniform consisting of a white shirt and black overcoat with a diagonal collar, trimmed in gold polygons. His image stared at her through the frame's clear crystal pane.

She eyed the serious expression gracing his handsome features. A young Omystikai man sat beside him in a formal posture. He wore a similar uniform with a blue sash hanging from his right shoulder. The name of his school was etched in Tiriyuusian script along the edges of the frame. Shonan read his sister's expression,

"It is a school photograph, and he is my professor." He spoke timidly.

Erethalie smiled at the image. It reminded her of their old photographs back when they were students in The Vilides.

"Thank you, Shonan. I will always cherish this." She gently placed the photograph in her pocket. "Until we meet again, you have my love." She kissed his forehead and then grabbed her cloudboard. She slid open the door and joined Sydarias, who waited outside in the darkness.

As they crossed the snowy path, she looked over her shoulder. Bright light flooded through the open doorway, illuminating the night in its golden glow. She saw Shonan's slender silhouette standing at the threshold. She turned around and waved to him. He waved back, and she waved even harder.

"This is so hard," she said, her voice trailing off. Tears streaming down her face, she turned to the path ahead of them. She tried to brush her tears away, but they fell fast.

"It's hard for all of us, but especially you," whispered Sydarias. He wrapped his arm around her shoulder drew her closer as they made their way through the snowdrifts. Her heartbeat slowed at his words, and her grief lessened some. She was glad that Sydarias had joined her. Through misty eyes, she looked at him, and he returned her stare with an empathetic gaze. They stood still for a moment beneath the bright moonlight, taking in a final moment of tranquility before returning to the shrine.

Chapter 37

Darshima and Khydius walked beside Tenrai along the narrow road, beneath the clearing night sky. A light shower of snow fell from above, covering their black coats in cold, crystalline dust. The trio remained silent as they passed through the desolate streets beyond the temple complex. In a few hours, they would report to the shrine for deployment.

Darshima and Khydius had planned to rest along with the other guardians, but Tenrai had invited them to join him for an evening stroll. Darshima sensed that Tenrai's invitation meant something more. When he asked about their destination, Tenrai had remained guarded. Tenrai's somber countenance dissuaded him from pressing the matter further.

They moved through the sparse crowds, past stately edifices and imposing shrines with squared wooden arches. The structures reminded him of the immense arch he saw floating upon the lake, marking the entrance of the training grounds. Though he had been in Tiriyuud for months, Chryshaihem remained new to him. Its ornate buildings and meticulously planned streets exuded a sense of mystery amid its staid elegance.

Darshima and Khydius followed Tenrai to the end of the road, which terminated abruptly at the shore of the lake. Darshima stood for a moment and looked around them. He had never been to this district. From his vantage, he saw that they were at one of the highest points in the city. Behind them, dense clusters of buildings loomed high above, glittering brightly against the night sky in a striking scene. He turned back around to see the snowy ground ending in a steep, rocky cliff that plunged toward the waters of the lake.

The clouds parted, and the starlight gleamed upon the waters. Benai and its bright rings dominated the eastern sky, and its moons hung in a nearly perfect line, glowing brightly against the sky. They stood in silence, taking in the peaceful scene before them.

Tenrai turned to Khydius, then Darshima, and then looked back over the waters.

"Our destination lays over there." Tenrai pointed toward a jagged outcropping of rock. It jutted up from the lake like a spear plunging through its surface. An ornate building sat upon its flattened summit, and subdued white light emanated from its large windows. Its octagonal shape and sloping, multitiered roofs gave it the appearance of a typical Tiriyuusian temple, but it had an inexplicable presence about it that drew Darshima's attention.

Tenrai walked into the field, and his nephews followed him. Moments later, they came to a stop at the edge of the cliff.

"There is something important that I must show you," said Tenrai. Darshima and Khydius exchanged puzzled glances. Tenrai unfastened his cloudboard, placed it at his feet, then stepped aboard. Darshima and Khydius did the same. His feet planted upon his board, Darshima sensed unusually strong flows of kai.

He glided toward the cliff's edge, accelerating as the sovereign strength lifted him above the snowdrifts and into the skies. Tenrai and Khydius followed closely behind him. They raced onward, the fierce gusts of wind whipping past their uniforms. Darshima crouched lower upon his board, skillfully maintaining his balance as the strong fields propelled him directly toward the island. He soared over the waters, and in one big rush, landed upon its icy bluffs. Tenrai and Khydius landed behind him, their boards skidding to a stop.

"Incredible," exclaimed Darshima. "Why are the kai fields so strong here?" Darshima stepped off his board and secured it upon his back.

"That was terrifying," said Khydius as he picked up his board.

"It will make sense to you soon. We do not have much time, so please come with me." Tenrai refastened his cloudboard. He beckoned them onto a tree-lined, cobbled path that wound up the side of the jagged plateau. Darshima peered through the snowy boughs as they walked up the steep trail, catching a glimpse of the moonlight waters of the lake.

The clouds reemerged, and a steady shower of snow fell upon them. They followed Tenrai to the end of the path and stood at the edge of the flat summit. The octagonal shrine sat upon a stone pedestal at the center of a clearing. Chains of crystal hung from its curved eaves, reflecting the starlight in a myriad of colors. Darshima looked toward the arched windows, which cast their golden glow onto the surrounding snowdrifts.

Darshima and Khydius followed Tenrai across the clearing and up the steps leading to the entrance. Before they continued, Tenrai turned and faced his nephews.

"This place holds great significance for the Nax family, Chryshaihem, and all of Tiriyuud." A solemn expression crossed his features as he spoke.

"How come?" asked Darshima.

"This shrine is dedicated to your father, Rion Nax. This sacred place is where he rests." Tenrai bowed his head. Darshima's chest tightened as he registered Tenrai's words. Ever since that painful moment in Ardavia, when Dalia and Sovani told him that he was not an Eweryn, Darshima had yearned to know more about his true past. Now he stood in front of the shrine that held his father's remains. He felt his pulse thud in his temples as he prepared himself for this moment.

Tenrai had been guarded about their father since he revealed the truth of their origins. Darshima understood their difficult circumstances as exiles in a foreign land and didn't press the matter. He knew there would be a time and place when Tenrai would share more with them, but he hadn't expected that it would be this evening.

"My nephews, since your arrival here in Tiriyuud, you have accomplished more than I could have ever hoped. You have learned our ways and have become Omystikai. Your father would have been so very proud," said Tenrai, his voice uncharacteristically heavy with emotion.

"We will do our best to uphold his legacy." A lump forming in his throat, Darshima stared at the paired doors of the shrine and bowed his head.

"At dawn, Tiriyuud goes to war to defend our homeland. The Order has put forth an extensive plan. We shall fight for victory, but as you understand, the outcome of war is never certain. It is your right to know your father's final resting place before we embark upon this mission." Tenrai rested his hands upon their shoulders. He regained his composure and looked toward the entrance.

They ascended the steps, and with a great big heave, Tenrai pushed open the heavy doors. They stepped inside from the chilly night, and a welcoming gust of warm, fragrant air greeted them. Darshima peered around, his eyes growing accustomed to the softly light interior of the somber space.

Faint beams of moonlight shone through a giant, crystal oculus at the apex of the pyramidal roof, casting the center of the shrine in an ethereal light.

Darshima stood for a moment, absorbing the unique atmosphere. Tenrai closed the doors behind them, and they crossed the black stone floor. Pairs of crystal torches hung from a circular, buttressed arcade at the shrine's center. They illuminated the somber space in a pulsating glow. Darshima eyed their three silhouettes moving rhythmically against its granite walls.

As they approached the center, Darshima's pulse slowed. He couldn't fully describe it, but he felt an inexplicable and profound connection to this place. It exuded an unmistakable, almost overpowering sense of familiarity. Darshima's mind raced as he tried to recall a similar experience. He remembered feeling something almost identical during his first encounter with Tenrai on Navervyne during their rescue. He also recalled the same sensation when he first exchanged stares with Khydius in The Vilides at the royal palace those many months ago.

Like a bolt of lightning, the realization struck him. He realized that those intense feelings meant that he was in the presence of his Tiriyuusian kin. His eyes grew damp as he realized the meaning of those feelings.

"I feel it too," said Khydius, his voice rising with emotion. He rested his hand upon Darshima's shoulder.

"Now, you both understand." A nostalgic smile formed upon Tenrai's lips.

They walked beneath the arcade and neared the shaft of moonlight. Darshima saw a dark rectangular slab set into the ground. The statue of a man stood at the head of the stone marker. Darshima's heart sank as he realized he was standing at the foot of his father's tomb. Tenrai genuflected before the monument. Darshima and Khydius fell to their knees in the same gesture.

Darshima's eyes swept over the large obsidian slab. Its polished surface bore lines of Omystikaiyn script and symbols, their gilt dashes and strokes shimmering in the light.

Darshima read the script, realizing that it was a narrative eulogizing Rion Nax. He lifted his gaze and took in the rich details of the monument.

"May your spirit be at rest in kai, be at peace with kai, and find harmony through kai." Tenrai bowed his head as he recited the first verse of the familiar invocation. Darshima's heart thudded in recognition of the words. It was a special prayer for the departed, asking that they remain at peace and imploring them to impart their wisdom and blessings.

They sat in silence, and Darshima reflected upon the trying weeks ahead.

"This place will be a source of courage as we embark upon our mission," said Tenrai, his voice echoing against the walls of the shrine.

"Thank you for bringing us here, Tenrai." Khydius looked around, his eyes glistening with tears amid the torchlight.

"Long ago, when Tiriyuud faced the threat of invasion, it was your father alone who had the courage and the strength to face down Tiriyuud's enemies." Tenrai gazed at both of them. "Your brave deeds have spared Chryshaihem from devastation. You have proven that you are the rightful heirs to Rion's legacy." Darshima lowered his gaze at Tenrai's pronouncement.

Tenrai rose from the floor and approached the statue at the head of the tomb. Darshima and Khydius stood up and walked behind him. The figure, carved from gleaming white marble, stood as tall as Tenrai. Clutching a scepter in one hand and a scroll in the other, the statue portrayed Rion in the ceremonial garments and hood of a Tiriyuusian Sage.

His pulse thudding, Darshima looked up at the statue of his father. Its resemblance to Tenrai was unmistakable. Though hewn in stone, its features appeared as if they were cast from living flesh. Darshima studied the frozen expression of solemnity carved upon the face, trying to memorize the details. Piercing through the darkness, two glowing blue crystals set in the honed eyes peered softly at them. It was a youthful face whose striking features had vitality and a hint of mystery to them.

As he examined the face, Darshima's pulse quickened, and his eyes narrowed in disbelief. He realized that the statue staring back at him was not, as he had anticipated, the face of a stranger. He gazed upon the visage set in stone, its expression calling to the deep recesses of his memory. It was a face that he had seen before. He feverishly racked his mind for a potentially lost memory from his childhood when the answer suddenly came to him.

The statue shared the appearance of the lone, mysterious Omystikai he saw in The Vilides, walking along the bluffs moments before the invasion. Though Tenrai denied it, Darshima still somehow felt that it had been his uncle after learning of his voyage to Ciblaithia before the invasion. As he faced the statue, he now believed otherwise. A shiver coursed along Darshima's spine as he realized that he had, in fact, seen his father.

"It was indeed Rion's spirit who appeared to you on the day of the invasion." Darshima felt Tenrai's arm upon his shoulder. Khydius' eyes widened as he heard Tenrai's pronouncement.

"You also saw him?" exclaimed Khydius.

"He appeared moments before the ships arrived in the skies," said Darshima, his voice trembling as he recounted the details.

Darshima listened in astonishment as Khydius shared his vision of their father. Khydius had initially dismissed Rion's apparition as an Omystikai reveler awaiting the start of the procession at the palace gates. Nevertheless, Khydius felt drawn to the man, noticing his garments were unlike anything worn by the Omystikai counselors of the imperial court. He remembered shivering at the sight of Rion's piercing gaze. Alarmed by his directness, Khydius turned away, and when he looked back, the man evaporated into thin air. Not long after, the drone of foreign craft shattered the revelry, and the invasion had begun.

"I'll never forget those radiant eyes," said Khydius as he stared at the statue.

"As you have seen, only Tiriyuusians have that feature," replied Tenrai, his eyes glowing softly.

Darshima remembered being taken aback by Khydius' intense cerulean stare and Rion's intensely sapphire gaze. Apart from his own cobalt eyes, Khydius was the only person Darshima had ever seen with the distinguishing feature. He wondered why he hadn't made the connection sooner.

Darshima looked on as Khydius stood up and reached toward the face of the statue. He briefly closed his eyes and caressed its cheek.

"It is truly him," said Khydius, his voice catching in his throat. Darshima stared at the statue and recognized his features in its sculpted lines.

"Why did he appear to us before the invasion?" Khydius turned to Tenrai.

"He knew that you both were about to face the most difficult ordeal of your lives. He wanted you to know that he would be there with you," said Tenrai. They stood at the foot of the statue and listened as Tenrai spoke about their father. A rare smile crossed Tenrai's lips as he recounted the memories.

"It is time for us to go," said Tenrai. He looked around the temple and let out a pained sigh.

"I will never forget this experience. Thank you, Tenrai." Darshima offered his uncle a polite bow.

"I am grateful to know where our father rests," said Khydius, his voice wavering.

They lingered for a moment, and then Tenrai led them toward the entrance. As they walked beneath the arcade, Darshima looked over his shoulder toward the tomb. He glimpsed their three shadows flickering against the shrine's wall. Darshima drew in a surprised breath as he saw the shadow from his father's statue mingle with theirs in a subtle trick of the light. A lump formed in his throat as their four silhouettes stood together. Rion was indeed with them.

Darshima and Khydius followed Tenrai down the stairs, back into the cold night. The steady snowfall covered their footsteps as they walked out of the clearing. They made their way down the winding trail toward the bluff. As they reached for their cloudboards, they stood for a moment and beheld the cityscape looming across the channel of water. Darshima took in its glowing details, his heart thudding with a sense of duty. The missions that lay ahead would determine the fate of both Chryshaihem and Tiriyu-ud.

Tenrai looked upon his nephews, then back across the waters toward the capital.

"As Rion did before us, we shall fight with everything we have to defend these islands. If Tiriyuud succeeds, peace will endure upon these shores. If Tiriyuud falls, all shall be lost," said Tenrai.

"Our mother's realm may have fallen, but we will fight for the survival of our father's kingdom." Darshima dropped to his knee and bowed his head in the direction of the capital.

"We shall fight together as guardians and as family," said Khydius.

Khydius genuflected beside Darshima and bowed his head. Tenrai stood behind them and rested his hands upon their shoulders. He whispered a prayer asking for guidance, and his words faded into the wind. After a solemn moment, Darshima and Khydius rose to their feet and walked with Tenrai to the cliff's edge. They mounted their cloudboards and leaped into the skies.

Chapter 38

Darshima stood with his companions amid the lines of men and women in the courtyard of the Guardians' Shrine. Beams of moonlight gave the atmosphere an airy, almost dreamlike glow. Lanterns hanging from the peristyle illuminated the space, their flames casting a soft light upon the assembled crowd. The hour of their departure had arrived. The guardians would be fulfilling their sacred duty to defend Tiriyuud. It was a responsibility that Darshima took seriously, and the moment weighed heavily upon him.

Darshima waited in the courtyard amid the rising winds. He eyed the uniforms of the guardians ahead of him. The backs of their black overcoats bore Tiriyuud's glowing blue star and halo of eight golden crescents. The guardians scheduled for deployment had reported to the shrine as ordered.

They had come by the thousands, arriving from all corners of the kingdom. Fiercely proud of their origins, their uniforms bore symbols denoting their birthplace and ancestral clan, stitched prominently upon their shoulders and arms. They represented every village, settlement, and city upon the archipelago. Darshima looked down at his sleeves and saw lines of polygonal symbols depicting the history of Foseidem, the Nax clan's ancestral village. Darshima's heart filled with a sense of pride. He belonged there with them.

The air hummed with low, anxious whispers rising from the crowd. Under the displays of confidence, Darshima felt a palpable sense of anticipation among the guardians. Though it remained hidden behind his stern expression, Darshima's pulse thrummed, and his anxiety mingled with theirs. Their fight against Navervyne would begin at dawn, and their abilities would be tested. Darshima had survived the inflicted devastation of war, but this would be his first time waging war in kind.

"I'm glad we are fighting together." Sydarias nudged Darshima's shoulder.

"I wouldn't have it any other way," said Darshima.

"We will see each other again after the first missions," whispered Khydius, his eyes glittering with a hint of anticipation.

"I am counting on it." Erethalie nodded toward each of them.

Darshima stood with his companions and awaited further instruction. His fingers instinctively checked the straps fastening his cloudboard and his utility belt. At their commander's word, they would mount their cloudboards and fly toward their assigned vessels for the voyage to the allied dominions. The carrier ships for the mission had been fully readied with weapons, aircraft, and artillery and would depart once the crews of guardians and soldiers arrived on board.

With a loud groan, the large doors at the entrance of the courtyard parted. The din among the assembly fell silent, and they stood at attention. The Sages of Tiriyuud, dressed in their ceremonial robes, stepped onto the platform.

"Behold the exalted Anaidys Rexe, Oracle of Tiriyuud!" they shouted. Both sages and guardians fell upon their hands and knees, the collective thud reverberating throughout the shrine. Darshima and his companions knelt with them, and they anxiously awaited the oracle's command.

"Arise, Guardians of Tiriyuud." The oracle approached the podium, her voice echoing into the night. Darshima rose to his feet along with Erethalie, Sydarias, and Khydius. He lifted his head and glimpsed the oracle, illuminated by the starlight.

She wore a commander's uniform of black boots, trousers, and an overcoat embellished in leather ribbons and countless embroidered lines of golden Tiriyuusian script. She wore gauntlets upon both arms fashioned from plates of silver and glowing blue crystal. A golden crown sat perched atop her head. The winds stirred through the courtyard, and her blue cloak swirled around her. A profound hush fell over the courtyard as Darshima and the other guardians beheld her in awe.

She stood before them, her delicate features set in an expression of steely determination. She was a vision of power, and Darshima felt it deeply. She narrowed her glowing gaze and looked upon the vast audience. Though she had the gravitas of an oracle, the look in her eyes revealed her past as a guardian and a warrior.

She outstretched her hand over the audience and issued a stirring prayer. Darshima bowed his head as he listened to the words of her incantation. She asked for the strength of kai to guide them, preserve their health, and protect them against harm. She beseeched their victory in the battles that awaited them. Once the oracle concluded the prayer, she looked out over the crowd.

"Guardians of Gilded Moon, the unwelcome scourge of war is upon us. The invaders that brought The Vilidesian Realm to its knees have now arrived upon our shores. They seek to mete out the same fate to Tiriyuud, the last free territory in the known world." She gripped the podium with her hands. "The hour of war has arrived. Tonight ushers in a new era for our nation. Tonight will forever mark the occasion when we took the battle beyond the islands of our kingdom in defiance of those that threatened our sovereignty."

A cheer rose from the audience, and she continued as their voices settled. "Our enemies are powerful, but we Tiriyuusians shall never be dominated. Our ancestors thwarted the Vilidesians and ensured our peace and prosperity. It is now time to reaffirm our allegiance to these islands. Though our enemies are fearsome, they shall witness Tiriyuusian strength and resolve. They will learn what has made us indomitable, and we will defeat them." His heart rising into his throat, Darshima let out a cheer at her exhortation, his voice mingling with the other guardians.

"Guardians of Gilded Moon, I command you carry this battle to distant lands. May you march onward to victory and in defense of Tiriyuud." She extended her hands toward them, her voice resounding throughout the courtyard.

Darshima looked on in awe as the guardians and sages cheered raucously at the oracle's speech, their voices filling his ears. Her words struck like a bell in the hearts of the entire assembly. Her call to arms represented a significant moment for the kingdom and the Order. Darshima knew this mission would mark the end of Tiriyuud's centuries of isolation and usher in a period of unprecedented engagement with the wider world.

As the oracle and the Council of Sages departed the stage, the commanders issued their orders for deployment. Darshima, Erethalie Khydius, and Sydarias mounted their cloudboards along with their fellow guardians. Each row rose from the ground in a coordinated fashion and took to the skies. Before long, the courtyard stood empty, and the city swarmed with the guardians flying toward their awaiting ships.

Flying at a torrid pace through the night sky, Darshima, Sydarias, Erethalie, and Khydius carved a wide path above the capital. Flakes of snow stirred in their wake as they dashed over the spires and temples toward the lakeshore. Thousands of their fellow guardians surrounded them, making their way toward the rows of aerial carriers looming below the clouds. Their immense, sleek surfaces glinting in the moonlight, Darshima looked on in awe as they floated effortlessly over the rippling lake. As they drew nearer to the craft, their features became clearer.

Darshima remembered seeing these carriers soaring through the Tiriyuusian skies during their training exercises, but he now saw how sophisticated they truly were. They rivaled ships from both Navervyne and The Vilides in their sheer size and capacity. Their enormous angular frames stretched toward the horizon. A complex pattern of crescents imprinted in gold, reminiscent of the Order's traditional motif, wrapped its way around the gleaming black hull of each ship.

Their undersides were tapered and lined with enormous plates of crystals whose white lights pulsed rhythmically against the darkness. Two pairs of broad trapezoidal wings jutted out from both the stern and bow. As they approached the rear of the carriers, Darshima counted more than a dozen cantilevered decks housing fleets of Gilded Wing aircraft. He peered through his visor at the silhouettes of workers moving between the vehicles.

"The soldiers are arriving." Erethalie pointed in the distance as she sped beside Darshima. Ahead of them, Darshima eyed swarms of bright pulsating lights hovering among the ships and recognized them as the Order's soldiers. Each ship maintained multiple divisions that operated under the supervision of the guardians.

The soldiers flew upon boards fashioned of a single plate of a glowing white crystal wrapped by a band of grey metal. These small craft, known as zogura or airboards, were made from several unique materials found in Tiriyuud. When a current of electricity was applied to the crystal, the board floated against the force of gravity. Smaller than the saigura, the boards were light, durable, and swift. The soldiers used them as their primary mode of transport.

Darshima watch as divisions of soldiers arrived upon each carrier in coordinated swarms of glowing light. The low hum of their paired rear exhaust vents grew louder as they approached the vessels. Their enormous engines emitted glowing white plumes that illuminated the night. Darshima braced himself for blasts of hot air but was surprised to feel not warmth but cold blasts of wind rushing toward them.

"What kind of propulsion system is this?" exclaimed Sydarias.

"They use solid crystalline fuel. It doesn't give off heat like Vilidesian fuel, only propulsive energy." Erethalie pointed toward the exhaust vents.

Darshima remembered her mentioning that Tiriyuusian engines utilized a unique chemical reaction for propulsion. They obtained their fuel from a replenishable source, unique to the archipelago. Smaller versions of these engines were used in various types of Tiriyuusian aircraft. These engines generated significant quantities of light and propulsive force and minimal heat. A modest amount of fuel was enough to keep a carrier running for a months-long voyage.

Darshima looked on in astonishment as he drew closer to their assigned carrier. He always believed that the Vilidesians had the most superior technology among the four moons. Their time in Tiriyuud continually showed him how much they all had underestimated the kingdom's capabilities.

Darshima peered further afield as he approached the upper flight decks. Ahead of him, lines of guardians flew into formation, descending in preparation for their approach. Through the gusts of swirling snow, He exchanged glances through his visor with Erethalie and Khydius.

"Until we meet in Gavipristine!" shouted Darshima.

"We shall meet again!" yelled Erethalie. With a wave, Darshima and Sydarias saluted Erethalie and Khydius, and they veered in opposite directions toward their respective ships. His heart rising into his throat, Darshima kept their mission in mind and pushed his emotions aside. He looked forward to their next meeting when they would face the challenge of Fauridise together.

Chapter 39

Darshima's eyes scanned the brightly lit space as he and Sydarias walked with their fellow guardians along the gleaming deck. Rows of soldiers flanked their path. They stood at attention with their arms stiffly at their sides, their black and gold uniforms fluttering in the breeze. Their crew counted one hundred guardians, and they would each assume command of a unit of soldiers.

Darshima and his fellow guardians reviewed the soldiers, then headed toward the carrier's bridge where they would welcome the commander of their mission. As Darshima walked, he caught a glimpse of Sydarias, who stared straight forward. Sydarias caught Darshima's gaze and offered him a subtle nod. Despite his anxiety, Darshima was grateful to have Sydarias by his side. They arrived at an elevator bay and boarded a carriage, which whisked them to the uppermost deck and onto the bridge.

Darshima stepped into the enormous, brightly lit glass-lined room. The senior guardians directed them onto rows of low benches, where they waited for the commander. He and Sydarias settled beside each other on the hard metal surface and waited patiently with their fellow guardians. The bridge featured a vast array of glowing, clear crystal panels. Complex displays of images and maps moved along their shiny surfaces. A contingent of guardians from Gilded Wing stood before the images, intently facing the screens, toggling controls and manipulating the maps. The low but audible hum of the engines filled the room.

As Darshima took in the busy surroundings of the bridge, he felt a gentle thump from the ground beneath his feet. He felt the force of upward motion as it pressed him into his seat. His heart thudded as he realized they were on their way.

Darshima and Sydarias sat near the middle of the group, anxiously awaiting the commander to address them. They were aboard the lead ship in their carrier group, and Tenrai was at the helm. Though Darshima didn't expect to see him for the duration of their mission, he was glad to be in his uncle's presence.

Before long, the sound of thudding footsteps pulled him from his thoughts.

"Commander Nax has arrived on the bridge," announced one of the guardians. Tenrai strode into the room and came to a pause in front of the benches. Darshima, Sydarias, and their fellow guardians rose to their feet and offered Tenrai a salute as he stood before them. A group of senior guardians assisted him and carried stacks of black leather envelopes. Tenrai cast a stern expression toward the group, his gaze softening for a moment as he saw Darshima and Sydarias.

"Greetings, fellow guardians," said Tenrai. His assistants moved about the group and handed each of them an assigned envelope.

"These envelopes contain the details of your mission. The Order has done its utmost to guard their secrecy." Tenrai gripped a black envelope in his hand. "Each of you has been assigned a specific task to accomplish as we make landfall in Keverese and work to assume control of its territory. You each will be responsible for leading a unit of twenty soldiers."

Tenrai opened the envelope and retrieved a glowing pane of crystal. "This tablet contains the specifics of your mission along with details of the soldiers in your unit. You are responsible for making sure that your unit accomplishes the tasks herein." His gaze swept over them. "It is essential that everyone follows their instructions and works together if this mission is to succeed. Please familiarize yourself with the details and discuss them with the soldiers in your division."

With his envelope in hand, Darshima pulled his tablet from the envelope. With a touch of the finger, the crystal illuminated and displayed moving images, maps, and text explaining the details of his task. He and the other guardians pored over the information on their devices, asking for clarification where necessary. Tenrai and the senior guardians walked among the group, answering questions and ensuring they understood their duties.

Darshima and Sydarias sat shoulder to shoulder, looking over the dizzying array of images and information contained on their bright screens. They would be responsible for leading their units to the palace in Keverese, and securing the compound for Tenrai's arrival.

"I hope I am ready for this," whispered Sydarias, nervously biting his lip. He tapped his fingers upon the crystal as he read over details of his mission.

"We'll rely on everything we learned during our training. We are more ready than we think." Darshima patted him on the shoulder, and Sydarias' frown lessened.

For Darshima, the prospect of leading a unit into battle was both exciting and daunting. He had never thought of himself as a leader, but now as a guardian, it was expected of him. A sobering reality settled in the pit of his stomach as he studied his mission. During the past months of training, his mistakes and errors had been forgiven. He had always been given another chance to prove himself. His training was now over. Any of his mistakes could lead to serious if not fatal consequences for himself, his soldiers, or his fellow guardians. Bearing this in mind, Darshima studied his briefing closely, making sure he understood everything.

Chapter 40

Khydius Nax

The doors of the bridge sliding closed behind them, Khydius, Erethalie, and their fellow guardians made their way down the passageway toward their assigned deck. They marched down the brightly lit corridor in a single file line. Their meeting with Dydan, the leader of their carrier group, had adjourned. Khydius held his tablet in hand and mulled over his mission. He was now was on his way to meet with his unit of soldiers, and Erethalie was due to meet with the fellow pilots of her Gilded Wing fleet. There was a palpable sense of excitement among the guardians as they walked along the corridor. They had received their instructions and were now responsible for successfully carrying out their individual missions.

Though it was not evident from his serious expression, Khydius felt more nervous than the others. He was equally trained and skilled but worried about the soldiers under his command. Though he was a guardian and shared a part of their heritage, he did not look like an Omystikai. He wondered if the soldiers in his division would truly accept his authority.

Khydius cringed at the unimaginable thought. In his days as Prince of The Vilides, his status was never questioned. He was accorded respect and adoration simply by virtue of his name, wherever he traveled among the four moons. His lineage and status as heir to the throne meant that whenever he entered a space, he outranked every single person except the emperor.

He shook his head and chided himself. There was no longer a realm, and he was no longer a prince. His pulse quickened as his mind repeated the words. With time, he had come to accept his circumstance, but the truth was still hard to bear. Khydius walked faster through the corridor, refocusing his thoughts on the moments ahead of him. He was now a Tiriyuusian, part of the Order of the Gilded Moon, and charged with leading troops into battle. The idea of going to war both intrigued and terrified him.

Like all young members of the dynasty, Khydius had received basic martial training and been given a rank in the Vilidesian Army. Even so, he had only served basic missions on Ciblaithia. Leading troops into war was something he had never done in his life. His heart thudded as he pondered the gravity of the task.

During his time as prince, The Vilides had known mostly peace and a degree of decadence. His chest tightened as he contemplated both the excesses and the deprivation of that era, and what it truly meant. He now recognized that it had in fact heralded the realm's inexorable decline. Emperor Aximes and his usurped reign had been the final strike, ushering The Vilides to its doom.

Pushing his heavy thoughts aside, Khydius watched the other guardians as he walked with Erethalie. They made their way through a maze of bright hallways toward the soldier's living quarters in the aft of the carrier. He scoured the details as they made their way. It was his first time aboard a Tiriyuusian aircraft, and its level of sophistication stunned him. He saw hints of Vilidesian influence in its overall layout, but Tiriyuusian sensibilities prevailed its flight systems and accommodations.

Despite hosting large numbers of soldiers, each vessel was designed with ample room to house them comfortably. There were areas for training, rest, dining, meditation, and recreation. The guardians were assigned private residences aboard the carrier, but they were expected to spend most of their time with their soldiers. Khydius realized the importance of this and wanted to get to know them. He would make sure that his unit functioned as one.

During their training, Tenrai and Priest Dawn had told them about the soldiers they would one day be leading. Like the guardians, they hailed from all corners of the kingdom. Though intense, their training was not as extensive or lengthy as the guardians. Nonetheless, they were strong men and women who were experts at martial combat and weaponry. They had also been trained in the basics of eneri-kai and could interact with kai fields to augment their strength when needed.

As they reached the end of the corridor, Khydius and Erethalie lingered together.

"Take care, Erethalie. I wish you well." Khydius nodded toward her.

"Take care of yourself, Khydius." She moved closer to him and spoke in a whisper. "Despite your protests, you are still the Prince of The Vilides. You are right where you need to be as the Defender of Iberwight, leading the fight to free this moon."

"Thank you, Erethalie," said Khydius, his heart rising in his chest. "I will do my utmost to succeed."

"I know you will." She offered him a polite nod, then continued down the corridor toward the flight deck.

Khydius cleared his throat and suppressed his roiling emotions. Though time had passed since the invasion, he found himself easily triggered by the mention of his former title and the memories it brought forth. As Khydius watched Erethalie walk away, memories of her superior flying skills over the skies of Navervyne flashed across his mind. Erethalie had carried them all to safety, and he admired her more than he could fully express.

Khydius arrived at his unit's assigned sector and peered at his tablet to confirm the matching numbers. He stood for a moment, drew in a breath then slid open the door. He stepped into the brightly lit square room. Furnished with a bank of low desks, benches, and a large screen upon one wall, he found it serviceable. He stared at the opposite end of the room, whose walls were made up of large panes of cantilevered glass. He eyed the Chryshaihemese skyline, steadily shrinking in the distance, its reflection gleaming upon the lake below them. Khydius' heart thudded as the realization settled within him. They were on their way.

"Guardian Khydius Nax." The soldiers said in unison. Khydius turned toward the voices, and a group of young men and women greeted him. They rose from their seats, stood at attention, and saluted him. A flicker of embarrassment swept through him, but he maintained his composure.

Khydius greeted each one of them, offering a formal bow and learning their names. After brief introductions, they sat at their desks, and he stood at the head of the room. They each held a grey leather folder containing bright crystal tablets, much like the one he received. The screen behind him aglow with maps and images, Khydius led the discussion as the group went over the specifics of their mission.

"Our mission, like the others, will be critical to the Order's success," began Khydius, his pulse thudding with confidence. His soldiers nodded in unison, focusing on the images behind him.

Once their carrier arrived over Nyzhaiheb, their units would secure the streets around the city center. They would accomplish this task after the Gilded Wing fleets established control. After the fleets completed their initial aerial sweep, the units would depart from the ship and make landfall in the city. The guardians and their soldiers would establish control of the central hill, where many of Nyzhaiheb's civic institutions, temples, and shrines were located. The image on the board flashed a detailed map of Nyzhaiheb overlaid by a complex, multicolored grid.

Each unit was responsible for maintaining control of one square upon the map. The units would receive support from the Gilded Wing fleets should they need it. Khydius' division of soldiers was tasked with securing the road leading to the entrance of the ruler's palace. They would establish a path for the other divisions to enter and occupy the compound.

Once the capital was under Tiriyuud's control, Dydan and the senior guardians would have an audience with the Ruler and the Sages of Nyzhaiheb. Their sages would officially welcome the Order's forces into the territory. After their declaration, they would sign documents accepting Tiriyuud's control of their dominion.

Nyzhaiheb's leaders had informed Tiriyuud that most of Navervyne's remaining forces had abandoned their dominion to fortify their position in Fauridise. Nyzhaiheb had been declared an open city and was spared the onslaught of war. Even so, the Guardians of Gilded Moon were prepared for the unexpected. They were ready to face the enemy in the streets and the skies over the dominion.

Throughout the vessels of the squadron, guardians were having similar conversations with their divisions of soldiers. They exchanged information and arranged the details of their given tasks. Commanders also checked with their guardians to ensure they were prepared. Each division had a different mission, but their roles were equally important for the Order's success.

Several divisions of soldiers would be part of the first wave of Tiriyuusians into the capital and throughout the dominion. They would be responsible for neutralizing Navervyne's forces with aerial support from Gilded Wing. Subsequent waves of soldiers would secure the cities and villages throughout the vast territory, working to firmly establish a Tiriyuusian beachhead as the initial waves pulled back.

As the hour grew late, Khydius and his soldiers took a moment to rest before they arrived at dawn. They settled upon woolen mats arranged before the windows. The air filled with chatter as the soldiers swapped stories and traded banter, readying themselves for the crucial hours ahead. Khydius sensed their nervous excitement as they prepared their weapons and belongings.

Khydius looked at his soldiers as they gazed through the windows, taking in the starry expanse of sky. Through the cloudy veil, the ocean spread before them, its rippled surface glimmering in the moonlight. They had traveled beyond Tiriyuud's shore, and there was no land in sight. Even the more experienced soldiers paused to take in the view. Khydius realized that it was a vista that most of them had never seen before.

Until this evening, these young men and women had never left their kingdom. Tiriyuud's centuries of isolation had been forcibly broken, and they were answering their oracle's call to arms. Now they embarked on a mission that generations past would have never fathomed. Khydius vowed to give everything within him to succeed in their mission. He would accept no less than the complete liberation of Iberwight.

Chapter 41

Erethalie Danthe

Erethalie stood in a close huddle with her fellow pilots. She looked at the enormous screen hanging from the rafters of the hangar bay, the arrays of maps shifting as the vessel cruised forward. Guardian Eikan Faite looked upon them with a stern eye. She was in charge of their fleet and would be leading their mission.

Erethalie glimpsed behind her at the dozens of black angular aircraft arranged neatly in staggered rows. The gold paint on their wings shimmered in the subdued white light filtering from the glowing crystal panels in the ceiling. Teams of mechanics and technicians dressed in simple black cloth uniforms and split-toed boots swarmed around the craft, loading crystalline fuel rods and munitions. A long, gleaming metal runway stretched before the rows of aircraft leading to the hangar bay entrance. She peered through the gigantic doors, opened to the starry night sky. Powerful gusts of heated air from vents around the entrance kept the icy winds at bay.

"Our approach to Nyzhaiheb will be challenging, but we are ready." Eikan pointed toward the map behind her.

Cruising at full speed, the ship had already traveled a third of the way to their target. In a few moments, Erethalie and her group of Gilded Wing pilots would board their craft and take off, flying ahead of the ship to reach the dominion. Her heart pounded as she realized that her fleet would be the first wave of Gilded Wing to make landfall. She and her fellow pilots would neutralize Navervyne's military installations around the capital and surrounding villages. Their assigned aircraft were among Tiriyuud's swiftest, and they would lead their carrier group into battle. Subsequent waves would follow them and complete their specific missions.

The screen went blank for a moment, and then a detailed moving image came into view. Sweeping images of Nyzhaiheb's rocky shore flashed across the translucent panel. The expansive capital sat upon a line of steep palisades plunging toward the ocean. Erethalie's fleet would fly in formation toward the coast and fan out over the capital's main axes. They would do their utmost to protect the citizens on the ground and open fire upon any hostile aircraft that threatened them.

Each pilot had been given an individual list of targets to demolish, ranging from factories to warehouses and arms depots. When they destroyed these targets, the fleet would attack Navervyne's principal installation in the dominion, a series of aerial platforms positioned over the city. Navervyne had based much of their aircraft within these floating structures. Erethalie's fleet would be the first to attack, and subsequent waves would follow to ensure their destruction.

As Eikan spoke, Erethalie and her fellow pilots poured over their tablets and the screen in front of them, memorizing the specifics of their mission. Though they had individual tasks, they were arranged in concert to achieve the Order's goals. Erethalie saw the images and instructions before their meeting, but her pulse raced as she reviewed the details. She was responsible for destroying several of the airfields and roadways leading from the enemy bases on the outskirts of Nyzhaiheb's capital district. It would require precision and coordination from herself and her fellow pilots, who would then demolish the military bases.

"Our mission will not be complete until all enemy bases and lines of transport are destroyed," said Eikan, her voice rising above the engine noise. Eikan concluded the meeting with a salute. Erethalie and the other pilots returned the gesture.

Eikan walked toward the rows of gleaming aircraft. Erethalie, along with the other pilots, followed her. As she and the other guardians were now officially resident pilots of this carrier, they had been assigned new aircraft. Her eyes eagerly swept over the machines, neatly parked on either side of her.

A mechanic stood beside each aircraft and greeted the pilots. Individually assigned to each craft, the mechanics were responsible for maintenance. As Erethalie approached her aircraft, she heard someone calling her name.

"Salutations, Guardian Danthe." A short, uniformed woman with long black hair fashioned in a braid saluted Erethalie. Her sapphire eyes glittered as Erethalie approached.

"Greetings." Erethalie waved to her, then looked up at the nose of the craft. Her heart skipped a beat as she read the gold Tiriyuusian script upon the gleaming metal.

"Danthe-Pelethedral Erethalie, Order of the Gilded Moon, Guardian of Tiriyuud," whispered Erethalie. Her pulse thudded with a sense of pride as she read her name. She stood upon a small metal platform that whirred as it lifted her to the level of the cockpit. She stepped inside the aircraft and familiarized herself with the instruments. As she gripped the steering controls, her pulse slowed with a feeling of familiarity. A smile crossed Erethalie's lips as she peered through the windshield and into the dark skies. She was where she belonged.

Chapter 42

Darshima peered out into the night, his shoulder resting against the cold metal frame of the hangar bay door. Sydarias stood beside him, and their eyes searched the inky vastness spreading before them. Their vessel sailed above the wispy clouds. The expanse of ocean stretched far below, its glassy surface shimmering in the moonlight.

Darshima and Sydarias had met with their units. They would soon retire for the evening and then prepare for their dawn missions. A sense of anticipation filled the silence between them, and their gazes shifted between the stars and the ocean. Their tasks seemed daunting, but Darshima was confident they would succeed.

As they looked out upon the emptiness, the sound of footsteps caught Darshima's attention. He turned around, narrowing his eyes as they acclimated to the bright interior of the hangar bay. A smile crossed his lips as he saw Tenrai approach them. Darshima and Sydarias offered him a salute.

"There is no need for formalities at this moment," said Tenrai, suppressing a mild look of embarrassment. "I am your uncle before I am your commander." Tenrai rested his hand upon Darshima's shoulder and offered Sydarias a nod.

Darshima looked upon his uncle, and his heart thudded with a feeling of pride. Though he was the same Tenrai that he had come to know over the months, there was a distinctly different aura about him. Darshima imagined the weight of duty figured heavily upon Tenrai's mind.

"How are you both handling everything?" asked Tenrai, looking upon them with an air of genuine concern.

"We are doing the best we can," said Darshima.

"We reviewed our missions with our soldiers and are giving them time to rest." Sydarias gestured toward the interior of the ship. Tenrai nodded in approval as they described their meetings.

They stood together, the silence between them filled by the whipping winds.

"You both have been trained well, and I trust your judgment. You will make the Order proud," said Tenrai.

"We will defend Tiriyuud with all we have," said Darshima.

"I wish you both success and health. Please take care of yourselves and each other." Tenrai's eyebrows wrinkled in a look of concern. He rested his hands upon their temples and whispered a prayer, his eyes flashing with an intense glow. "I will be following the reports of your missions. Let me know if you find yourselves needing support. No request is too small."

Tenrai bade them goodnight and walked back inside, his footsteps echoing in the hangar.

Darshima and Sydarias moved toward the edge of the deck, further out into the night. They sat together on the heated metal surface and peered at the ocean below them. It had been hours since they left Chryshaihem, and though he studied the maps, Darshima marveled at how they had yet to come across a single trace of land. The kingdom's isolation became even clearer to him as they voyaged across the frigid Iberwightian sky.

"I never would've guessed when we met on that ship leaving Ardavia, we would've experienced so much together," said Sydarias, his voice thick with emotion.

"Who would've imagined?" Darshima looked at Sydarias, a lump forming in his throat.

They reminisced about the times that they shared since their very first meeting. From their fateful encounter in Ardavia to their toil as slaves, their friendship had grown. In their current journey above the clouds on the coldest, most isolated moon of the fallen realm, Sydarias remained at his side.

"I've never known a truer friend, Darshima," said Sydarias, his voice catching in his throat. He looked up to the stars and gathered his thoughts. "If something should happen to me during our missions, please tell my family that I love them."

"You are my best friend, and no harm will come to you." Darshima stared at him. "You will see your family again."

"I wish that I had more of your bravery." Sydarias hastily wiped away a tear with the back of his hand.

"You are one of the most courageous people I know," said Darshima. "We will succeed in this together. Tiriyuud is counting on us." Sydarias bowed his head and drew in a breath. Darshima placed his arm around

Sydarias' shoulder in a protective embrace, and they looked out over the ocean in silence.

Darshima mulled over his mission as they lingered amid the winds. He felt ready and knew that his soldiers were well prepared. It had been more than a year since they were rescued from their brutal toll on Navervyne. Since then, Darshima had recovered a great deal and felt more like himself. He had grown stronger and found a sense of peace among the Tiriyuusians. His father's people taught him not only how to live again but how to fight and how to thrive amid desolation. He owed his very survival to them.

During the most difficult parts of guardian training, when the task seemed insurmountable, Darshima was sustained by a vision of that hallowed day when he would fight back against the invaders, who had brought a cruel end to the world he once held dear. Darshima stood beneath the stars, the weight of his thoughts upon him. The sun etched a faint trace of light upon the arc of the horizon. Darshima felt the ground slow beneath his feet as the craft prepared for its descent. The time for war had come.

Chapter 43

Erethalie Danthe

Erethalie gripped the steering controls and narrowed her eyes against the receding darkness. She gazed to her sides, the rays of the rising sun glinting against the golden trim of her craft. Beside her, she eyed a dozen identical vehicles flying in formation, their wings nearly touching. Further afield, she spied several fleets, totaling more than one-hundred craft. She brought her focus back upon the horizon, her eyes peering through the blue crystal visor of her helmet. She pushed the controls forward in unison with the other pilots, and her craft's nose angled downward.

The craft dipped, and her seatbelt held her in position as she momentarily floated. A flash of white enveloped the canopy as she pierced through the thick layer of clouds. Erethalie leveled her craft and pushed against the throttle. She sank back into her seat as she raced forward. Her fleet tore ahead at a frightening pace, the rippling waters below a mere blur as she flew over the expanse of ocean.

She turned her attention to the glowing array of screens before her. Her fleet was approaching Nyzhaiheb and would break formation in a few moments. Each guardian would go on to fulfill their respective tasks. Once completed, her squadron would rejoin formation and destroy the chain of Navervynish platforms floating over the city. The Order's intelligence from Nyzhaiheb confirmed that the structures had been abandoned, and Navervyne was regrouping its fleet in Gavipristine. Erethalie hoped that the low risk of a counterattack would make this final task easier. After her fleet fired upon the platforms, the subsequent waves of aircraft would arrive on shore to complete the work of dismantling the enemy forces.

Erethalie's fleet raced over the ocean, the pale sunlight filling the cockpit. Her heart skipped a beat as she looked up at the sky. In the distance, she saw a series of jagged cliffs rising above the waters. Nyzhaiheb's palisades steadily grew upon the horizon as she approached. She narrowed her eyes and tried to make out the details of its domes and spires. She pushed the controls forward, the distance rapidly shrinking between her and the coast.

Erethalie nosed her craft downward, racing above the waters, toward the immense white palisades. The city rose before her in a line of impressive white brick towers abutting the edge of the cliffs. She looked at the display panels, keeping alert for the presence of enemy craft.

With a deafening roar, her fleet made landfall. She pulled the controls toward her, angling her craft upward. Her gaze alternated between the glowing maps and the intricate pattern of the city streets below her.

A crackle from the speaker broke the tense silence in her cockpit.

"Units, assume your positions." Guardian Faite's voice came through clearly. Erethalie's pulse thudded in her fingertips, and she gripped the controls. A fine sweat broke out upon her brow. The moment had arrived. One by one, the craft of her fleet veered in separate directions to carry out their specific tasks.

With an eye trained upon the moving maps in front of her, Erethalie flew in a wide circuit. She eyed the expansive rectangular grid of streets, low-lying brick buildings, and stout towers amid the snowy, forested plains. The capital spread out in all directions, stopping abruptly at the palisades abutting the ocean. Erethalie cruised over the city center, marked by a prominent hill with a cluster of towering monuments, temples, and shrines. Their slender rectangular forms rose into the sky, gleaming beneath the sun.

Her map guiding her toward the city's western edge, Erethalie pressed upon the control wheel and gained speed. A series of metallic structures in the shape of a broad bow floated above the forests in the distance. The immense objects caught the sunlight, reflecting stark rays upon the city. Her heart pounded as she recognized the features of the aerial platforms. Memories of her harrowing escape from the guarded platforms in Stebbenhour raced through her mind. She shook her head and guided her craft forward, looking warily upon the structures as she approached the edge of the capital.

Erethalie surveyed the snow-covered city below, comparing it with the moving maps in front of her. Her first target, a series of airfields upon the northwestern corner of the grid, came into view. She pushed the steering controls forward, and her craft descended below the clouds, the topographic details rapidly coming into view. Erethalie's craft tore through the sky at a blinding pace, shaking the ground beneath her. She held onto the controls as the gusts of wind buffeted the wings.

She eyed several dozen Navervynish aircraft neatly arranged upon an airfield. Their greenish, rounded frames glistened in the sunlight. Parked further afield, she saw rows of wheeled, armored surface vehicles used by their patrols. Snowdrifts blew over the black pavement between them, giving the impression that they had remained unused for some time. She gained speed, and the field came closer into view. Moments later, the screens in her cockpit flashed, alerting her that she was within striking distance of her target.

With a hand firmly upon the controls, Erethalie steadied the craft. She extended her finger toward a glowing icon in the control panel, took in a deep breath, and pressed it firmly.

Instinctively, she pulled upward on the control wheel, and her craft raced skyward. She held her breath for a few moments and awaited the result. A series of deep thunderous claps shattered the din of the cockpit as the pair of ikarifym bombs hit the ground. Her eardrums throbbed at the deafening noise. Blinding flashes of intense red and white light filled the windshield, briefly obscuring her view. She banked the craft sharply and flew in a wide circle to survey the damage. Her gaze cutting through the dense grey smoke, she looked below and saw that the fields were no more. All that remained was an immense flaming crater gouged into the frozen ground.

She let out a sigh of relief as she circled the destruction, flying in low and methodically taking out the roads leading toward the city. She angled her craft parallel to the ground and depressed a trigger upon the controls, a trio of cannons upon the nose cone raining a rapid volley of light upon the pavement. The heavy stones buckled and crumbled under the intense beams of energy, sending up a hail of rocks that pinged against her craft's fuselage. Erethalie circled the airfields, making several passes, strafing the roads until they lay in ruins.

Pulling back against the controls, she guided the craft through the thick columns of smoke and soared higher into the sky. All around her, hundreds of aircraft tore across the skies, carrying out various tasks. They destroyed warehouses and factories, leveled weapons depots, and bombarded airfields and garrisons. With her work finished, Erethalie flew toward the ocean to rejoin her fleet.

Her heart pounded with feelings of excitement and fear as she raced across the sky. Memories of the invasion of The Vilides filled her mind. She remembered watching helplessly as enemy aircraft invaded her city and rained fire upon them. Now here she was, carrying out what felt like a similar raid in a foreign city. Her stomach twisted in an anxious knot as she imagined a helpless child in Nyzhaiheb who felt the same fear she and Shonan felt those many months ago in The Vilides.

She guided her craft over the ruins and pushed her thoughts aside, reminding herself that Nyzhaiheb had asked the Tiriyuusians to free them from Navervyne. She was carrying out her duty and striking a blow against the enemy. She guided her aircraft over the ocean, her pulse slowing with a feeling of reassurance as she pondered this vital fact. Moments later, several aircraft from her fleet glided on either side of her. Pulling on her controls, she maneuvered her craft into formation for the final attack.

Chapter 44

Khydius Nax

The fierce winds whipping against his uniform, Khydius held his footing upon his cloudboard, carving a path through the snow squalls. Crouched upon their airboards, his division of soldiers flew behind him in a single line. They departed their carrier only moments ago and were on their way to the city center. His face toward the sky, Khydius peered through his visor, astonished by the scene unfolding before him.

In the distance, fleets of Gilded Wing raced through the skies, carrying out rapid sorties. Hundreds of aircraft swarmed over the capital, blotting out the sky in some parts. They dropped their payloads upon targets throughout the city, rattling the air in concussive blasts, sending up flashes of bright red and yellow light. Plumes of smoke rose from the cratered streets.

Amid the commotion, Khydius led his division down from their carrier toward the city. Flying in formation, they descended through the smoke and toward the streets. He and his soldiers kept alert for enemy soldiers as they made their approach. He looked off in the distance and spied hundreds of guardians and thousands of soldiers sailing across the skies toward their designated wards of the city.

During the voyage from Tiriyuud, Khydius and his fellow guardians learned that Navervyne had largely abandoned Nyzhaiheb. They were reorganizing what was left of their fleet to hold their position in Keverese and Gavipristine. Nevertheless, Khydius did not rule out the possibility of encountering any lingering enemy forces. He had warned his soldiers to remain alert.

Khydius' unit landed upon the city's central hill in a spray of snow. Slinging their boards upon their backs, his soldiers formed two lines behind him. They walked along the snow swept, tree-lined avenue leading to the ruler's palace. A grand, hexagonal brick structure with a series of crenelated towers at its vertices, the palace loomed over the city. Both the ruler of Nyzhaiheb and the Council of Sages administered the dominion from this edifice.

The emptiness of the city struck Khydius. He had once paid an official visit with Emperor Aximes during his childhood and had remembered it as a bustling city, bringing citizens from all parts of the dominion. The once-tidy homes, buildings, and shops lining the route appeared in a state of disrepair. Drifts of snow piled up along the litter-strewn streets.

Khydius led his troops down the avenue toward the palace, assessing the damage, and set about searching for any evidence of Navervyne's troops.

"We come in peace," announced Khydius. His soldiers knocked upon every dwelling they passed. The occupants cautiously opened their doors, staring fearfully at the Tiriyuusian soldiers and shielding their children behind them. When questioned, they denied quartering any Navervynish or Fauridisian soldiers.

Throughout the morning, Khydius and his soldiers searched all of the homes in their ward. They marked each door with a crystal disk bearing Tiriyuud's seal, signifying that the dwellings had been inspected. As the morning wore on, they moved down the avenue, scouring the alleys and securing the area for the patrolling sentries that would eventually take their place.

As Khydius led his troops, his pulse thudded with a familiar, foreboding sensation. He stood for a moment in the middle of the street, drawing in a breath to regain his composure. Khydius looked at his soldiers as they methodically surveyed their ward. He stared at the grey skies above, eying the frenzied activity.

Numbering sixteen ships total, the line of immense Tiriyuusian vessels hung motionlessly amid the clouds. Thin beams of sunlight filtered through the tight formation of carriers. The frozen ground beneath them lay cast in a mosaic of shadow and light. The carriers' long silhouettes spread across the city like the fingers of an unseen hand.

The twinge of anxiousness growing, Khydius made his way up the steps of a residence and propped himself against the doorframe. His mission was nearly complete, and his soldiers had secured every building in their ward. He was now awaiting word from their assigned ship of Dydan's arrival to the palace. Once he had arrived, Dydan would issue documents to the ruler, who would sign them and formalize the transfer of power to Tiriyuud.

As Khydius surveyed the scene, movement from the corner of his eye caught his attention. His pulse thudding, he turned toward the direction of the disturbance. His pulse thudded as he saw an approaching crowd making its way down the street. Khydius mounted his cloudboard and flew toward the group. His soldiers stepped on their airboards and floated closely behind him.

Numbering several dozen, the group approached them with pistols in hand. Their uniforms in tatters, the ruddy-faced, bearded men stared up at them as they approached. Khydius' stomach sank when he realized they were confronting a group of Navervyne's remaining troops. Khydius descended until he floated above the street. The Navervynish combatants stopped in the middle of the street and leered menacingly toward Khydius and his soldiers. They appeared starved and haggard, but the glint in their crimson eyes suggested that they were ready to fight despite their hunger.

"We come in peace," said Khydius, speaking in Vilidesian. "Surrender, and we will not harm you." He flashed his open palms toward the troops. The group engaged their weapons, filling the air with a loud flurry of metallic clicks. With a wave of his hand, Khydius signaled his soldiers to fall back.

After a hesitant moment, they followed Khydius' orders and floated further back, leaving him to face the group alone. His gaze squarely trained upon the men, Khydius rose above the ground on his cloudboard, and their menacing eyes followed him.

"Navervyne will not surrender Nyzhaiheb!" shouted one of the troops as he brandished his pistol.

"Look around. Your republic has already abandoned you. Surrender and no harm will come to any of you," reiterated Khydius.

The soldiers let out a shout, aimed their pistols then rush toward Khydius.

Heart pounding, Khydius instinctively floated higher upon his board. He placed a hand upon his chest and felt the surge of the surrounding kai fields. A fierce gust of wind filled the street, whipping the snow into a blinding, white flurry. The air around them crackled, and arcs of white electricity surged across the sky, illuminating the space in a flash of searing light. Khydius narrowed his gaze against the brightness. A series of concussive blasts shook the air, and the troop froze in place. Mouths agape, their eyes rolled into their heads. They fell to the ground in a heap of writhing, seizing bodies.

The winds died down, and they lay still. Khydius' soldiers dismounted their boards, rushed over, and assessed the fallen combatants. Khydius landed on the ground, refastened his cloudboard, and surveyed his unit. They shackled the Navervynish troops and sat them in a row against the street curb. A dazed look in their eyes, they stared at Khydius and his soldiers, murmuring incoherently, unaware of what had happened to them.

Khydius' soldiers radioed the ships above for assistance, and moments later, a fleet of large wheeled vehicles arrived in their ward. Their angular black and gold armored frames glinting in the sunlight, they traveled in a column down the road. The pulsating hum of their toroidal engines rose above the silence. The lead vehicle stopped directly in front of Khydius, and its paired doors slid open. Two guardians disembarked from the vehicle and greeted him. A spark of recognition flashed across his eyes as he remembered them from their training.

"We must be careful. There are still Navervynish troops within the city." Khydius pointed toward the line of shackled combatants as he shared the details of their capture.

"We have heard similar reports. Several units are neutralizing this threat and holding them captive," replied the guardian. She turned to her partner, who nodded in agreement.

The pair of guardians had captured the Navervynish prison in the city and freed Omystikai captives who were wrongfully held. Their units would transport the combatants and interrogate them on the whereabouts of any other enemy troops. Khydius' soldiers transferred the dazed troops into the awaiting armored vehicles.

The pair of guardians saluted Khydius, climbed aboard their vehicle, and departed. Khydius and his soldiers watched the column of vehicles steadily move back down the snowy road. He then turned around and faced his soldiers.

"Incredible, Guardian Nax," exclaimed one of the soldiers. They all looked at him, their hands raised to their visors in salute. Khydius was sure they were familiar with the guardians' advanced control of kai fields, but he imagined they had never seen it until today.

"Excellent work, all of you." Khydius returned their salute. Khydius knew that he wouldn't have been able to complete the mission without his soldiers' assistance. "Let us continue." He pointed toward the palace looming in the distance. Khydius and his soldiers resumed their work, patrolling their ward and awaiting Dydan's arrival.

Chapter 45

His feet planted firmly upon his cloudboard, Darshima cruised toward the steep shield of mountains ahead, his eyes scouring the rugged landscape below. He caught a glimpse of Sydarias flying beside him. In the shape of a large oval, the imposing, jagged peaks jutted up from the surrounding forests, far inland from the ocean. The city of Keverese lay cradled within the protective rocky basin.

A line of Tiriyuusian carriers made a steady circuit above the mountains encircling the city, the sharp angles of their fuselages glinting under the morning sun. Engines thundering, waves of Gilded Wing aircraft carried out sorties, soaring in the skies, before disappearing beyond the snow-capped ring of mountains.

Their soldiers trailing closely behind them, Darshima and Sydarias carved a path through the snow squalls toward the mountains. Forming lengthy columns, guardians and their soldiers descended upon the city.

Darshima and Sydarias were leading their convoy into the city to prepare the path for Tenrai's official meeting with the ruler of Keverese. They had received word that enemy forces in the city had been neutralized, and Tenrai had disembarked from the ship upon a smaller craft. They would secure the palace, and Tenrai would arrive for the handover of Keverese.

The peaks came into view as Darshima and Sydarias hurtled forward. He peered into the large valley as their divisions cleared the mountain range in a dramatic sweep. The skies above teemed with dozens of formations of Gilded Wing craft, skating around the steep edges of the mountains. They strafed enemy targets throughout the valley, their shadows sweeping over the ground. Staccato blasts shattered the air as the fleets discharged their incendiary payloads, trails of smoke rising from the smoldering rubble.

As Darshima and Sydarias approached the palace, a loud screech pierced the chaotic thrum. Darshima looked toward the horizon, his heart thudding in surprise as he saw the floating line of fire. Beyond the line of mountains, immense platforms in the shape of an arc hung motionlessly in the sky. Tongues of flame engulfed the alien structures, linked by spindly metal conduits. Smoke poured out of their slanted portholes and vents. Their metallic surfaces shimmered, warping as they melted, appearing as if they were a rainbow aflame.

Darshima's pulse raced as he recognized the structures as Navervyne's main base over Keverese. Several dozen craft from Gilded Wing swarmed the flaming structures, the air rattling as they bombarded them with idori-fym charges and rapid volleys of searing light. Without warning, the structures shuddered violently, groaning as the flames consumed them. With an earsplitting crack, the bases disintegrated into several enormous pieces.

The fragments of metal drifted downward, gaining speed as they approached the ground. Moments later, the remains of the platforms crashed into the far side of the ridge away from the city, sending forth an enormous wall of snow and debris. A sonorous rumble reverberated as the avalanche careened into the valley. Darshima pressed his hands to his ears as the waves of sound enveloped him.

The snows stopped at the sparsely populated edge of the city, and the air grew silent. Darshima exchanged a stupefied glance with Sydarias. He could not believe what they had witnessed.

"Tiriyuud is taking control." Sydarias raised his fist into the air as they descended over the valley.

"Gilded Wing has done its job. Now we must do ours," said Darshima. They raced toward the concentric circles of snowy streets spreading out below them. Darshima's heart thudded with a sense of hope as the scene of destruction replayed in his mind. He heard of the skill of the Gilded Wing fleets and was awed by their prowess. The Order's fighting forces were capable of inflicting a decisive blow. Thoughts of Erethalie crossed his mind as he imagined her undertaking a similar feat over the skies of Nyzhaiheb.

Darshima and Sydarias led their soldiers onto the central axis of the city, leading toward the palace. They descended upon the snowy ground, their soldiers landing behind them. Darshima and Sydarias marched at the head of their convoy toward the palace. Standing at attention, hundreds of Tiriyuusian soldiers waited on either side of the cobbled avenue. Stately grey stone buildings lined the streets, their doors newly marked with Tiriyuud's seal. Despite the chilly air, the windows of the grand edifices were flung open. Darshima looked up to see hundreds of pallid faces, both young and old, haggard by hardship, waving banners, cheering the passing convoy.

Darshima and Sydarias marched onward, their faces bearing solemn expressions. The Palace of Keverese came into view, its majestic wooden towers reaching skyward. Flags bearing the circular seal of Navervyne hung prominently upon a flagpole, fluttering in the wind.

Darshima's chest tightened as he recognized the familiar symbol. It was the same seal imprinted upon the uniforms of the Navervynish troops and their ships. It was the same symbol stitched upon the tattered clothes he had worn as a slave.

"After today, Navervyne will no longer claim this dominion." Sydarias glared at the banner, his eyes narrowing in a disdainful expression.

"The tide is turning." Darshima stared at the Gilded Wing fleets soaring over the city. He looked on in disbelief as Tiriyuud extended its aerial dominance, surprised at the lack of resistance.

"It is happening much faster than I imagined," mused Sydarias.

Their soldiers following them, Darshima and Sydarias walked along the paved stone path leading to the palace. As they approached, the gates opened, and a contingent of sages stepped out to greet them. They wore simple robes of green and grey that draped the ground and exposed their bare right shoulders. Their pale skin and angular facial features lent them a similar appearance to the Omystikai of Tiriyuud. However, their eyes were a deep shade of brown, and their scalps were shaven.

The sages stood in silence. They stared at Darshima and Sydarias, their eyes widening in bewilderment. Darshima had anticipated this situation and understood the priests' confusion. Though they wore the distinct black and gold uniforms of Tiriyuusian guardians, they did not look like Omystikai.

"I am Darshima Nax, Guardian of the Order of the Gilded Moon." Speaking in Tiriyuusian, Darshima nodded toward the sages.

"I am Guardian Sydarias Idawa." Sydarias offered a curt nod as he greeted them in Tiriyuusian. The sages' jaws dropped in astonishment as Darshima and Sydarias greeted them in an Omystikaiyn dialect.

"The Order of the Gilded Moon has come to the Dominion of Keverese at the request of your ruler." Darshima gestured toward the palace.

"Tiriyuud's forces are at work destroying Navervyne's presence within your city and dominion. The first phase of our Order's mission is nearing completion." Sydarias stared intently at the sages. "We are here to prepare for Commander Tenrai Nax's meeting with your ruler and the handover of Keverese to Tiriyuud."

"We understand, and we thank you," said the lead sage, offering Darshima and Sydarias a deep bow. He then ushered them into the palace.

Chapter 46

Tenrai Nax

Tenrai marched down the middle of the freshly cleared street, the heels of his boots scraping against the rough pavement. A retinue of senior guardians walked beside him. Lines of soldiers stood at attention along the path, saluting him as he passed. Flakes of powdery snow fell from the grey skies and clung to his overcoat, the layers sloughing off as he marched.

The steady din of applause filled the chilly afternoon air as crowds of Keveresians stood behind the rows of soldiers. Tenrai caught glimpses of them from the corner of his eyes. Throngs of men and women, both young and old, stood casting anxious gazes toward them. Some hoisted children upon their shoulders, who curiously looked on. Their clothes were in tatters, and they appeared weary, but the crowds clapped steadily.

Tenrai looked upon the palace, whose main tower rose before him. At its pinnacle, he saw Navervyne's orange and red flag fluttering as it was steadily lowered. Cheers rose from the crowds, and the applause reached a fevered pitch. Moments later, the black and gold banner of Tiriyuud, followed by the green and white banner of Keverese, climbed to the top of the pole.

Tenrai's heart pounded as he saw their black banner, with its blue star and halo of golden crescents waving atop the palace. The crowds erupted in an ecstatic cheer at the display. The guardians and soldiers of Gilded Moon came to a standstill in the middle of the street, saluted their flag, then marched on in silence. Tenrai's eyes widened in disbelief as he pondered the moment. He had been raised in a nation that had reluctantly engaged with the outside world. Never in his life would he have imagined a day when he would witness Tiriyuud's flag flying over the capital of an Omystikai dominion.

Tenrai approached the large iron gates of the palace. A group of senior guardians from Tiriyuud and several sages from the Order of the Forest Moon awaited him. The sages offered him a deferential bow, then ushered Tenrai and the guardians past the gates. They crossed the large courtyard, stepped through a pair of massive wooden doors, and entered the inner sanctum. A colonnade of thick, richly carved wooden pillars surrounded the circular space, soaring upward to form vaulted arches high above. The austere room glowed amid soft torchlight. Innumerable layers of jade-colored stones, intricately carved in the shape of trefoil leaves, covered the rotunda high above them. The tessellated patterns gave the appearance of a dense forest canopy. Tenrai walked across the wooden floor, inlaid with various shades of lustrous green and brown crystal, resembling a dewy field.

Green-tinted daylight from the crystal canopy flooded the space. A green marble platform sat in the middle of the floor. A large polished wooden throne festooned in emeralds sat atop the dais. The Ruler of Keverese and his council of sages waited before the empty throne. Darshima and Sydarias stood beside him. Tenrai's eyes swept over the Tiriyuusian soldiers standing at attention around the perimeter of the room.

Tenrai approached the throne, and Darshima and Sydarias offered him a salute. His heart thudded with gratitude that his nephew and his friend were safe and had completed their missions. He returned their greeting and stood before the ruler. Like the sages around him, the ruler wore elegant robes of green and grey. A shimmering jade cloak draped his shoulders, and a silver crown covered in emeralds and diamonds sat atop his head. Equal in height, the ruler gazed at Tenrai with piercing brown eyes. Considerably older than Tenrai, his square features were marked by worry and exhaustion.

"Commander Tenrai Nax, the Dominion of Keverese welcomes you. We thank the Order of the Gilded Moon for answering our pleas." The ruler offered Tenrai a bow.

"Lord Asan Indrade, Ruler of Keverese, I accept your welcome on behalf of Tiriyuud." Tenrai nodded politely.

Tenrai felt vibrations beneath his feet as intermittent blasts from ordnance in the distance rattled the building.

"Our people have suffered dearly under the grip of Navervyne. We have been rendered starving, defenseless, and destitute. Keverese is forever indebted to your Order for delivering us in our hour of need." Lord Indrade bowed his head.

"My fellow guardians and I come on behalf of the Oracle of Tiriyuud. Navervyne's presence within your city has been destroyed. Their warehouses and depots have been bombed, and their main airbase over your city has been demolished." Tenrai gestured beyond the palace walls as he spoke. "Our squadrons of aircraft are patrolling the skies over your territories and waters, rooting out what little remains of their forces. Your dominion has been liberated."

Lord Indrade paused for a moment as he digested the words. He clasped Tenrai's hand and bowed deeply. The sages around him fell to their knees. Hands clasped in prayer and eyes pointed toward the heavens, they issued a chant. Tenrai stood silently and observed their poignant ritual.

The sages rose to their feet and ushered Tenrai to a long wooden table placed before the throne. Tenrai, Darshima, Sydarias, and several of the senior guardians sat on one side. Lord Indrade and the Sages of Keverese sat across from them. A guardian handed Tenrai a black leather envelope containing documents issued from the Order of the Gilded Moon on behalf of the oracle, enumerating the conditions of Tiriyuud's control of Keverese. Lord Indrade and the sages glanced over them, murmuring as they poured over the script.

Another guardian brought a tray of golden pens and issued one to every member seated at the table.

With an elegant stroke of his pen, Lord Indrade signed the document. He drew a wooden seal from the folds of his robe and firmly stamped its pages. Tenrai then accepted the document, inked his signature, and stamped his wooden seal. The papers made their way down the table as every guardian and sage signed it. When it was completed, Tenrai placed the document into the leather folder, and Lord Indrade retained his own copy. Tenrai summoned his fellow guardians, and the entire table rose to their feet.

Lord Indrade and Tenrai walked together toward the entrance.

"Tiriyuud is prepared to assist Keverese in every conceivable way," said Tenrai, his voice echoing through the room.

"There is much work to do to restore our dominion. Keverese accepts whatever help you can offer." Lord Indrade looked upon Tenrai, humbly bowing his head. He shook Tenrai's hand and thanked him.

Tenrai looked upon the ruler and the sages, their sincere expressions striking him. The worn lines on their gaunt faces told the story of their suffering more than any testimonial ever could. Tenrai knew that the challenge of rebuilding this dominion would be great. He believed Tiriyuud would succeed.

Chapter 47

Dydan Waike

Dydan stood upon the grey stone floor of the rectangular atrium. A steady draft of wind swept through the space, tugging at his cloak. Khydius, several other guardians, and their divisions of soldiers stood with him. Somber expressions upon their faces, the Ruler of Nyzhaiheb and her large retinue of clerics and priests faced Dydan.

Dressed in a formal garment of white and blue completed by a long silver cloak, she stood silent amid the shattered yet opulent room. Her black hair, graying at the temples, was swept up in a bun. Her regal features bore an expression of resignation. Late afternoon light flooded through the fractured panes of rectangular windows encircling the room. An empty grey marble throne stood behind her. She peered through the glass, gazing upon the scene unfolding beyond the palace walls.

Tiriyuusian carriers formed a long, unmoving line over the city. The golden seals of the Order festooned upon their fuselages glinted under the sunlight. Formations of Gilded Wing craft tore across the skies, raining heavy artillery upon the city, their explosions rattling the windows of the palace. In the distance, Navervyne's aerial base hung in the skies beyond the city limit. Giant plumes of smoke and columns of flame rose from the linked platforms, setting the skies aglow. Dozens of craft swarmed around the failing structures, raining idorifym charges upon the failing platform, hastening its demise.

Dydan stepped forward and spoke, his voice breaking through the anxious silence. "Most serene Serith Arai, Ruler of Nyzhaiheb, Tiriyuud has responded to your plea. The Order of the Gilded Moon is working to liberate your dominion from Navervyne. We are clearing out the enemy from the capital, and our forces are securing your territory as we speak." Ruler Arai stepped forward and clasped Dydan's hand,

"Chancellor Wake, Nyzhaiheb is forever grateful for your efforts in freeing our dominion. We are thankful for Tiriyuud's mercy during what has been the most desperate hour in our people's history." A somber expression crossing her features, she bowed her head. "My people have borne a heavy load under Navervyne's yoke. We have suffered greatly and will rely on your kingdom's goodwill."

"Tiriyuud is prepared to offer full assistance to Nyzhaiheb in its efforts to rebuild," said Dydan. Ruler Arai bowed her head and whispered a prayer of gratitude.

Dydan and the guardians made their way to a stone table in front of the throne. They took their places in preparation for the handover ceremony. Dydan produced the documents detailing the transfer of power. The ruler reviewed them with her sages, signed them, and stamped them with her seal.

With a flourish, Dydan signed the documents with a golden pen. The documents made their way down the table, passing between the guardians and sages. At the end of the ceremony, Dydan rose from his seat, and the guardians joined him. Ruler Arai stood with Dydan and assured him of Nyzhaiheb's unwavering allegiance to Tiriyuud. They discussed the provisions of the document and the assistance that Tiriyuud was preparing for Nyzhaiheb.

As Dydan spoke, thoughts of the responsibility that Tiriyuud was undertaking in defending and rebuilding this shattered dominion raced through his mind. It took every fiber within him to believe that the events unfolding before him were actually happening. He was a Sage of Tiriyuud standing in the Palace of Nyzhaiheb, brokering the transfer of the sovereignty of this vast territory to Chryshaihem. Deep within him, he knew that Darshima was right. Tiriyuud was truly left with no other choice beside rescuing the Omystikai dominions and assuming complete and unquestioned control of Iberwight.

Chapter 48

Darshima crouched upon his cloudboard as he climbed further into the sky.

"Our missions are complete," said Sydarias as he floated beside him. He pointed to the landscape drifting below them. Darshima glimpsed to his side and saw fleets of Gilded Wing screeching across the valley, vaulting over the surrounding ring of mountains. Darshima flew with Sydarias through the plums of acrid smoke rising above the city. His heart thudded, and he drew in a breath as memories of the Vilidesian invasion flashed before his mind.

The Gilded Wing fleets had ceased bombarding their targets, and their craft approached their assigned carriers. In the distance, Darshima eyed a formation of carriers moving away from the city toward the snowy hinterlands.

"Keverese declared itself an open city, but I hadn't expected we would capture it so swiftly." Darshima shook his head in disbelief.

"From what other guardians are saying, Nyzhaiheb has also fallen fast to Tiriyuud. The Order has neutralized Navervyne's forces without much opposition." Sydarias gestured toward the immense, smoldering fragments of the shattered enemy platforms lying upon the soot-stained snow.

"Let's hurry back to our ship. We don't have much time before the journey to Fauridise." Darshima lifted his gaze toward the immense fuselages of the awaiting carriers, obscuring the skies as they loomed overhead.

He peered over his shoulder past his soldiers flying in formation behind him and saw the rows of buildings at the city center. The palace stood prominently amid the cluster of administrative buildings. Atop the tallest spire, Darshima eyed Tiriyuud's banner fluttering in the gusts of wind. Darshima turned back toward their carrier and soared higher, drawing in a nervous breath as he pondered the significance of this moment.

As events unfolded in the skies around them, Darshima learned from the transmissions echoing in his helmet about Tiriyuud's advancing position. Little more than two days had passed since the Order began its offensive. By the dawn of the third morning, Nyzhaiheb and Keverese had accepted Tiriyuud's rule. The Order's forces had neutralized what remained of Navervyne's installations, establishing firm control over the dominions' capital cities.

This morning, the first squadrons were departing the dominions' capitals to secure control of their sparsely populated but immense territories, each many times more vast than Tiriyuud's archipelago. The Order encountered minimal resistance from what remained of Navervyne's forces, whose soldiers were left starved and exposed. Ill-suited to Iberwight's harsh climate, the Navervynish equipment had suffered technical failures and stood vulnerable to Tiriyuud's swift advance.

The Order's rescue convoys carried much-needed food, essential medicines, heavy machinery, and other vital equipment to support the guardians, soldiers, and citizens as they voyaged to hinterlands.

"I hope that the people here realize that Tiriyuud is here to help," said Sydarias, pointing toward the scorched and scarred lands below them.

"I hope so too," replied Darshima.

Like with the Keveresians, the Order had faced no resistance from the Nyzhaihebans. Darshima heard astonishing reports from Order's guardians and soldiers. They were swarmed by the citizens in both dominions, thanking them for their bravery and begging them for help. As Darshima and Sydarias had experienced in the streets of Keverese, the Order's members traveling deeper into the dominions encountered equally troubling scenes. Like most Tiriyuusians, who previously had never ventured beyond their home villages, the dearth of essential resources and the decay of infrastructure amid the frozen wastes beyond the capitals was startling. The guardians offered what immediate assistance they could as the rescue convoys planned their campaigns.

As they approached the uppermost deck of their vessel, Darshima felt a subtle pulse in his limbs as the kai fields swirled around him. With a final push, he and Sydarias landed and dismounted their boards. They walked upon the metal plates of the hangar, their footsteps echoing amid the pulsating drone of engines and rushing wind. On either side of them, aircraft moved into position, extending their wings and readying themselves for sorties beyond the valley.

"I wonder how Tiriyuud will maintain its strength. Its responsibilities are growing by the hour." Sydarias walked beside Darshima. Darshima gestured toward the aircraft around him as he eyed the soldiers and mechanics rushing to complete their various tasks. He looked past the hangar bay doors and saw the lines of vessels flying toward the horizon, their golden script glinting in the sunlight.

"From what we've seen, Tiriyuud can and will provide." Darshima and Sydarias walked further into the vessel, toward their awaiting units.

Chapter 49

Standing at attention in the brightly lit hangar, Erethalie looked ahead to Eikan and her assistants. The large display screen depicted the vessel's current position upon the moving map. Her fellow pilots stood in rows before them, listening as Eikan relayed their next mission. Teams of technicians rushed between the craft parked behind them, refueling and readying them for the looming battle.

Their squadron had departed from Nyzhaiheb two days ago and would soon cross into Fauridisian territory. Their carrier had joined the eight squadrons that recently departed Tiriyuud, and their carriers were making their final preparations for battle. As Erethalie stood with her colleagues, images of her mission over Nyzhaiheb replayed in her mind.

Their victory had been so swift and complete. Erethalie's heart fluttered with a feeling of trepidation. She imagined the battle for Fauridise would be far more difficult.

"The latest intelligence gathered by the Order confirms that a significant challenge awaits us." Eikan gestured to the images behind her. Several fleets of Navervynish ships were en route from Gordanelle and Wohiimai and would arrive in Fauridise within a day. The window in which Tiriyuud could challenge Navervyne was rapidly closing.

Presented with this troubling information, the commanders of the squadrons beseeched the Order for more assistance. The oracle herself had personally ordered an additional five battle-ready squadrons to join them, and they were leaving without delay.

"There will be fifteen squadrons, for a total of sixty aerial carriers taking part in the battle." Eikan pointed to the screen as images of the vessels materialized. Erethalie and her fellow pilots murmured in surprise.

"Several dozen ocean-going vessels have already departed from Tiriyuud's southernmost naval base and will support Gilded Wing as we make landfall."

Despite the confrontation that awaited them, Erethalie took comfort that the Order would demonstrate a formidable presence in the skies and seas around Gavipristine.

She looked on as the map magnified Gavipristine's triangular plan. It depicted the Tiriyuusian squadrons arranging themselves into staggered columns at each corner of the city, steadily advancing toward an island at its center. Images of Gilded Wing fleets raced across the map, indicating strike targets within the city.

Eikan gestured to the map and reviewed the mission. Their biggest challenge would be to neutralize Navervyne's aerial presence over the city. As Gavipristine was their capital on Iberwight, they had built three floating bases several times larger than those found over Keverese and Nyzhaiheb. Serving as the home for most of their fleet on Iberwight, this would be Gilded Wing's most important target.

Erethalie and her fellow pilots would be the first fleet to attempt to destroy them. Given the sheer size of the bases, they would be backed by several aerial waves. They would repeat their strikes until the damaged bases lost their ability to stay airborne and fell to the ground. Other Gilded Wing fleets would support them, defending their position as they approached the bases.

Erethalie focused on Eikan's words as she spoke. She had led a successful attack upon the floating base in Nyzhaiheb and would lead her fleet toward the largest structure in the trio. Her decisive actions led to the destruction of the base in Nyzhaiheb. She earned the commendation of the guardians in her fleet, and they entrusted her with this critical task.

Though honored by the responsibility, she felt a lingering sense of unease. Her fleet had met no resistance over Nyzhaiheb and had swiftly destroyed Navervyne's abandoned infrastructure. This battle would be far more difficult. Their enemy had long fled to Fauridise and was regrouping.

Though their position had been weakened, first by Darshima's hand and then by Tiriyuud's forces in the allied dominions, Navervyne would show its strength. She knew it would be difficult for Tiriyuud to defeat them, even with the arriving reinforcements.

"Despite the strength that Navervyne presents, we may have an advantage if we work swiftly," said Eikan.

The vessels in Navervyne's fleets were traveling from Gordanelle and Wohiimai. Much of their previous fleet on Iberwight had been destroyed by Darshima. The Order determined that Navervyne's vessels would have spent much of their fuel completing the long voyage. They would require a stop at their aerial bases to refuel and restock for battle. Erethalie's fleet would destroy these bases before Navervyne's vessels had the chance to refuel. With no place to replenish their stores, Navervyne's spent fleet would face the onslaught of Tiriyuud's squadrons, with no chance of escape.

The pilots saluted Eikan as she finished her remarks. As Erethalie made her way to the awaiting rows of aircraft, Eikan walked beside her.

"You have performed well thus far, Guardian Danthe. Our squadron will call upon the best of your skills for this mission." Eikan faced her.

"Thank you, Guardian Faite." Erethalie offered her a salute.

"I sense your nervousness, but trust your skills. We all do." Eikan gestured toward the pilots around them, who offered nods of support toward Erethalie.

"I will do my utmost," said Erethalie, her pulse thudding at the unexpected praise. Eikan bid her farewell, then walked over to her aircraft.

With the details of the mission running through her mind, Erethalie boarded her craft and settled in the cockpit. She adjusted the screens and toggled the controls, and her sense of nervousness tempered. Despite the monumental task that lay ahead, her fellow pilots trusted her. Erethalie realized she needed to trust herself too. Nonetheless, she knew this mission would be wholly different.

The guardians had accomplished an unprecedented success in prying both Nyzhaiheb and Keverese from Navervyne's grip. Fauridise stood as Navervyne's stronghold on Iberwight. Gavipristine would be the most difficult city to liberate. She mulled over the possible outcomes of her perilous mission.

Her thoughts racing, Erethalie let go of the controls for a moment and sank back in her seat. She gazed upon the starlight glimmering over the ocean and drew in a breath. She closed her eyes and took a few moments to clear her mind. Gusts of frigid air from the open hangar bay swept across the deck.

Bracing against the cold, she nestled into her seat and buried her hands into her pockets. A cool, unfamiliar object greeted her fingers. Curious, she retrieved it. Erethalie immediately recognized it as the photograph that Shonan had given her before she left Chryshaihem.

The metal frame resting in her hand, she gazed at the image. She smiled as her eyes traced over Shonan's features and his distinct uniform. His young face stared at her with those ever-serious green eyes. Her gaze drifted toward his Tiriyuusian teacher, dressed in a similar consume, bearing an equally stern expression. Memories of their life together in Pelethedral and The Vilides came back to her. She blinked as tears formed in the corner of her eyes.

Her heart rose with a deep sense of pride as she thought of Shonan. He had adjusted to their new life better than she could have hoped. Erethalie drew in a breath and her doubts about the hours ahead dissipated. Her heart slowed with a tranquil sense of calm. Erethalie knew that her brother, the Order, and the entire kingdom depended on the success of her mission. Victory would mean enduring peace for all on Iberwight. She dare not contemplate defeat.

The relative silence of the deck broke under the sound of igniting engines around her. Erethalie slipped the photograph back into her pocket and set to work, preparing herself for the trying moments ahead. She secured her harness, and the glass canopy closed around her with a firm click and a mechanical hiss. Her sense of focus renewed, Erethalie gripped the steering controls and readied herself for takeoff.

Chapter 50

Their uniforms flapping in the fierce winds, Darshima and Sydarias stood silently on the brightly lit deck of the vessel. Their divisions of soldiers standing at attention behind them, they gazed out onto the moonlit vista below. They cruised far above the expanse of ocean, its glassy ripples broken by the wake of dozens of immense, trapezoidal vessels. Comprising some of the most advanced vessels from the Tiriyuusian navy, they sailed silently toward the horizon. Beneath the ripples, Darshima made out several dozen large fusiform shapes speeding ahead. A fleet of blade-like submarines charged stealthily past the ships floating upon the surface.

Darshima marveled as he saw the watercraft speed off into the night. As he learned from his guardian's dossier, the Tiriyuusians were the only people of the former realm to maintain a navy. The Vilides had given up manufacturing non-freight bearing, waterborne craft centuries ago as it expanded outward from Ciblaithia and conquered territory on the other moons. It had established aerial supremacy and had relied on that strength to secure its realm.

Darshima stared out over the waters, toward the horizon. Gavipristine's glowing skyline burned brightly against the night. The ghostly grey orb of Benai illuminated the skies to the east, its rings barely skimming the waters of the ocean. The other moons hung brilliantly over the city, casting its glass towers in vivid shades of gold, green and grey light.

In the distance, a series of long silver arcs hung motionlessly below the clouds. They blocked out the moonlight, casting shadows upon the city. The bases were much larger than the ones he had seen over the skies of Keverese. Though he had seen images of Gavipristine in his briefings, nothing could have prepared Darshima for the striking view of Iberwight's capital city.

Gavipristine was located at the northeastern end of Iberwight's largest content. It was built upon several dozen low-lying islands at the mouth of a torturous river gorge. An array of bridges and canals crisscrossed the vast city. Fashioned in the image of The Vilides, its islands were studded with a dense array of glittering towers of glass and steel that rivaled Vilidesian height and grandeur. Counting several million inhabitants, Gavipristine was the largest civilized territory on all of Iberwight. To its west lay a vast continent of ancient forests, desolate tundra, and snow-capped mountain ranges.

They approached the city's glittering lights, and Darshima kept a keen eye out for their enemy. They were in hostile territory, standing out in the open air of the cantilevered deck, but they were far from alone. He looked around them and saw the silhouettes of the squadrons joining them. They cruised in precise formation, the quiet drone of their engines audible above the gusts of wind. As Darshima looked around, he marveled at the sheer number of airborne and seaborne craft that Tiriyuud would wield in this mission. The Order would strike a formidable presence in the heart of Gavipristine.

Darshima and Sydarias reviewed their missions with their soldiers, huddled around them. As with their previous missions, they would be responsible for capturing the imperial palace and securing it on behalf of the Order. They would prepare the way for Tenrai and Dydan, who would present the articles of surrender to the sovereign. The Order's squadrons were expecting fierce resistance from both the Navervynish and the Fauridisians.

The skyline looming in the distance, Darshima eyed the glowing exhaust of the carriers ahead of them.

"The squadrons are making their final approach," said Sydarias as he lifted a hand to his visor.

"We are trained, and we are ready." Darshima instinctively gripped the straps securing his cloudboard. He felt their vessel decelerate underfoot as it prepared to make landfall. As they approached the capital, a pang of nervousness coursed through him. He couldn't help but think of Khydius. Darshima hadn't seen him since they departed Chryshaihem. He worried about how his brother was faring. Darshima drew in a breath and took a moment to clear his mind. Khydius was stronger than he appeared, and he had more than proven it.

In the distance, Darshima eyed the other carrier columns approaching the city from opposing sides of Gavipristine's triangular plan. The ocean-going vessels would support Gilded Wing and take control of the canals coursing between the islands. The aerial and naval fleets would work island by island to establish control. These maneuvers would take place as Gilded Wing squadrons destroyed Navervyne's aerial bases. When Tiriyuud's forces arrived at the central island, the Order's guardians would seize the palace and formally claim the dominion.

Darshima gave Sydarias a salute as the craft descended. They faced their soldiers and issued their orders. The ground below them shook, and the air rumbled with engine noise as subsequent waves of Gilded Wing craft launched from the decks below them. Their angular forms flew into the night, the glowing white exhaust of their engines streaking across the sky like comet tails. His heart raced, and his mind filled with the vision of the fight that lay ahead. Darshima and Sydarias secured their belongings and boarded their saigura. They offered each other a final salute and leaped into the night.

Chapter 51

Erethalie Danthe

The air rumbling around her, Erethalie gripped the steering controls as she tore through the skies above Gavipristine, fierce squalls of snow briefly obscuring the cockpit. Trails of searing light flashed above her as enemy artillery screeched past. She guided her craft between the volleys of fire, flying above the narrow canyons between the soaring glass edifices. She darted between rows of cylindrical gun turrets positioned upon the towers. Their barrels glinted in the fading moonlight as they rotated toward her craft, sending a rapid hail of missiles her way.

With a swift motion of the hand, she pushed the controls forward and ducked below the shower of metal. Her thumbs depressed a trigger, and she fired upon the cannons. Volleys of light shot from the nose of her aircraft, striking the guns. She pushed hard against the throttle and tore past the burning weapons. Showers of sparks cascaded upon the snowy streets below as the row of canons exploded in flashes of flame and smoke. Her ears filled with the earsplitting groan of stressed metal. The cannons slipped from their elevated perches and tumbled into the street.

Erethalie raced toward the soaring grey-blue glass spires at the city center. She tapped a glowing series of icons upon her display screen, releasing incendiary bombs and leaving a flaming wake of destruction in her path. In the distance, she saw the sleek, rounded profile of Navervyne's trio of immense aerial platforms. Floating in the skies beyond the city, they hung still amid the snow squalls.

She glanced toward the streets below, then across the sky at the fleets of Gilded Wing. The Tiriyuusian aircraft swept through the urban canyons, destroying Navervyne's defenses, leaving the streets aglow in a grid of flame. Several of the Order's fleets directly engaged a pair of Navervyne's aerial vessels in the skies ahead, exchanging rapid volleys of blinding fire. Her chest tightened as she saw Gilded Wing's agile craft swarm and strafe the enemy vessels.

The Gilded Wing fleet scattered as a lone Tiriyuusian aircraft screeched above them. The craft dropped a charge and then raced away. Erethalie's visor automatically tinted as the falling orb emitted a streak of golden light as bright as a quasar. The charge imploded between the two enemy vessels, vanishing into a pinpoint of blackness darker than night.

The oblong vessels succumbed to the gravitational wave, slamming violently into each other in a shower of sparks. The vessels crumpled inward, their stressed metal sighing in a deep groan. Their fuselages contorted into a grotesque intertwined shape, then imploded. The destroyed Navervynish carriers tumbled onto the city streets below, exploding in a stupendous ball of fire upon impact.

"That must've been a juurofym charge," murmured Erethalie. Her eyes widened in astonishment as she witnessed the devastating effects of the rare crystal. An image of Priest Dawn's demonstration at their training temple briefly flashed before her eyes. She glanced toward her display panel, her fingers sweeping over the icon for her loaded juurofym charges. Erethalie flew toward the perimeter of the city, strafing her assigned targets in a hail of fire. Her pulse thudded with confidence as she realized the immense power she could wield if necessary.

Toward the horizon, she saw Tiriyuud's carriers steadily making their way up each corner of the city's triangular grid. Several hundred Gilded Wing aircraft made repeated sorties from the vessels, racing across the skies over Gavipristine, striking targets seemingly everywhere. She set her course toward Navervyne's aerial installations.

The platforms grew larger as she approached, and she flipped a row of switches upon the instrument panel beside her. Her craft slowed as its wings articulated themselves forward. The click of engaging weaponry filled the cockpit as the machinery sprung into action. In the near distance, she identified her fleet. They fell into formation behind her when suddenly her craft began to shudder amid an unexpected downdraft. Startled, Erethalie gripped the steering controls and stabilized her craft. A sense of dread filled her as she looked upon the horizon.

In the distance, dozens of bright blue lights descended from the skies above and vaulted toward the platform. Erethalie made out the rounded, sleek forms of the Navervynish ships as they entered Iberwight's atmosphere.

"Navervyne's fleet has arrived sooner than anticipated. Prepare for attack." The speakers in the cockpit echoed with Eikan's voice. Erethalie drew in a sharp breath as she assessed the evolving scene ahead of her. She knew it would be a race against time to make it to the platforms before the Navervynish ships arrived. She approached the floating structures, the members of her fleet falling into formation behind her.

Chapter 52

Sydarias Idawa

His division of soldiers behind him in a single column, Sydarias flew on his cloudboard down a wide boulevard. His uniform flapped against him as he carved through the fierce winds. In close formation, they soared high above the street, stirring up swirls of snowflakes as they carved a path through the frigid air. In the distance, the straight boulevard terminated at a large hexagon-shaped central pond located at the heart of the city. The imposing space was flanked by soaring rows of towers, shimmered amid the fierce snow squalls. He eyed the metallic reflections gleaming in the surrounding dark waters.

In the center of the pond, the Sovereign's Palace sat upon the stone rampart of a heavily fortified hexagonal island. The palace's elaborate stone and glass spires cast an imposing presence. Three equally spaced drawbridges flanked the island, connecting it with the rest of the city. Sydarias eyed the raised spans hanging above the pond. Several wide canals sliced through the city and converged at the body of water.

Crouching low upon his cloudboard, Sydarias cast a wary eye over the scene before him. A phalanx of Navervynish soldiers at the opposite end of the boulevard marched toward them, their footsteps echoing throughout the steep canyon. Columns of four-wheeled vehicles flanked them on either side. In the skies above him, the shrinking forms of a Gilded Wing fleet swept high above the buildings near the pond. They strafed the gun turrets and cannons on the buildings lining the path before them, sending them into the streets below. The acrid smoke from their glowing remnants hung in the air, burning at his throat as they sailed through the newly cleared path.

While other squadrons bombarded the streets, avenues, and canals throughout the city, Sydarias' division was responsible for securing the thoroughfares adjacent to the pond. They were of critical importance to access the central island and could not be destroyed. Sydarias and his soldiers were tasked with neutralizing enemy forces in preparation for the ground-based reinforcements that would arrive. Once the divisions met at the pond, they would occupy the heavily guarded island and seize the palace. Apart from the destruction of Navervyne's aerial platforms, Sydarias realized that their task would be among the most vital operations of the entire mission.

Sydarias and his soldiers swept over the boulevard, skimming past the curtains of glowing glass. He descended toward the road and approached the Navervynish troops. Several rows deep, the marching lines of men and women moved forward, their weapons aimed skyward as they tried to track Sydarias and his soldiers. Sydarias glimpsed over his shoulder at his soldiers and signaled them to fan out behind him.

They followed Sydarias' command and crouched lower upon their airboards, readying themselves to engage. His eyes narrowed, Sydarias crouched forward, his limbs surging with bolts of energy. He navigated the surrounding kai fields, and the feeling intensified. The streetscape filling his visor, Sydarias rushed toward the ground.

Startled at his rapid approach, The Navervynish troops moved into formation. They aimed their pistols as Sydarias sped toward them. The sound of artillery erupted as they released their fire. Sydarias signaled his soldiers, and they scattered, dodging the hail of bullets.

Sydarias raced headlong into the troops, thrusting his hands out in front of him. He held his breath and focused his mind until time seemed to slow down. He felt a pulse of energy surge through him, and the Navervynish troops stopped marching. The rows of soldiers let out cries of pain, then convulsed in unison. Stunned, they collapsed upon each other, the clatter from their weapons echoing throughout the snowy street. The vehicles traveling beside them screeched to a halt.

Sydarias and his soldiers landed upon the street, and he faced them.

"Is everyone accounted for?" he asked, his heart racing as he remembered the fire they received.

"We are all here and unharmed," said several of the soldiers.

"Let's keep moving." Sydarias beckoned them forward, his pulse slowing with relief.

Sydarias walked through the chaotic scene, his eyes sweeping over the dozens of unconscious soldiers splayed out before him. His mind raced as he realized how close they had come to disaster. He knew that the contingent of enemy soldiers was large, but he hadn't realized there were so many.

"Your control of kai has protected us all," said one of the soldiers. Sydarias turned to them, and they offered him a salute.

"I did what was necessary," said Sydarias. Memories of his training with Tenrai, Dydan and Priest Dawn at the temple flashed before him. Back then, he hesitated to believe that someone like him, with no Omystikai heritage, would ever be able to channel kai. As he surveyed the scene, his lingering doubts evaporated.

Slinging their boards upon their backs, his soldiers knelt before the felled Navervynish troops, checked their condition, and disarmed them. Others extracted the unconscious troops from the enemy vehicles. They put shackles on the troops and sat them in lines along the curb. Their chins touching their chests, the troops remained unconscious, puffs of steam rising from their nostrils. Sydarias' soldiers took up positions at the entrance of the buildings, and he looked around the deserted section of the boulevard. The booming echo of Gilded Wing fleets roaring through the skies overhead punctuated the tense silence, their angular shadows sweeping rapidly over them.

Moments later, the sound of tires crunching over the littered streets echoed against the damaged edifices. Sydarias eyed a column of Tiriyuusian armored vehicles approaching him. A team of guardians and their soldiers disembarked, offered Sydarias a salute before taking custody of the captured troops. Another team of guardians occupied the boulevard, taking control of the roads, disabling the enemy vehicles, and securing the buildings. Sydarias surveyed the handover until it was complete.

With the snow falling around him, Sydarias stared down the boulevard. In the distance, he could make out the spires of the palace. It seemed close, yet it remained far. Despite his exhaustion, he felt the urge to push forward, attributing it to the sovereign strength. Sydarias and his soldiers needed to press onward. They mounted their boards, took to the skies, and continued their march toward the central island.

Chapter 53

Khydius Nax

Khydius and his soldiers moved across the flat surface of the tower's summit. Powdery flakes of snow fell from the darkening late afternoon skies, covering their footsteps as they made their way toward the edge. With Gilded Wing aircraft strafing targets around them, Khydius' unit, among several others, had landed upon the towers supporting the drawbridges connecting the central island to the rest of the city. Their task involved overriding the machinery and lowering the roadways to allow the Order's forces to cross onto the island and seize the palace.

Khydius approached the edge of the tower, and a group of his soldiers moved into formation behind him. He looked across the waters and signaled the other guardians. Based upon Khydius' briefing, the drawbridges were controlled by a complex set of gears near the stout bases of each tower. When they destroyed this mechanism, the drawbridge would lower, thereby connecting the island to the rest of the city. Khydius and two other guardians were responsible for lowering the trio of bridges so Tiriyuud's forces could reach the island and occupy the palace.

Khydius stood at the edge of the tower and looked around him, assessing the scene. Directly below him, the dark waters of the hexagonal pond rippled under the steady snow squalls. The waters spread out before him, abruptly ending at the embankments of the outer islands. The waning sunlight shone against the fractured edifices.

"Half of my soldiers will stay atop the bridge and survey the area. The other half will follow me to the base." Khydius pointed toward the island.

"As you wish, Guardian Nax." Khydius' soldiers offered him a salute. They divided into two groups, the ones accompanying him unfastening their airboards.

With a wave of the hand, Khydius signaled his soldiers. They ran across the tower, and in one great stride, leaped off its edge. Eyes narrowed, Khydius' gaze cut through the fierce winds at the rapidly approaching water. Against the tug of gravity, he deftly reached behind his back and grabbed his cloudboard.

His descent immediately slowed as his feet made contact with the gleaming metal surface. Khydius maneuvered the board beneath him. He stood upright and carved a path through the air. Out of the corner of his eye, he could see his soldiers floating closer to him.

Khydius sped down the immense leg of the tower, the ground rapidly encompassing his field of vision. He spied groups of Fauridisian troops patrolling the tower base, weapons in hand. Eyes closed, he focused his mind upon them as he approached. Unaware of his presence, they stared out upon the pond.

Khydius placed his hand out in front of him, and he felt a distinct yet familiar pulse of energy coursing through him. Within moments, the group of soldiers clawed at their necks in spasms of agony. They lost consciousness and fell to the ground, stunned before they could fire a single shot. Khydius' soldiers landed ahead of him. They placed cuffs upon the felled soldiers and positioned them against the stone rampart surrounding the tower base.

Concealed in the shadows of the tower, Khydius craned his neck upward at the immense superstructure. Several of his soldiers fanned out upon the area, the heavy snow on the ground muffling their footsteps. With a wave of his hand, he directed them to their positions, and they hurried to secure the perimeter of the tower. The snows falling around them, Khydius cast his eyes upward. He scanned over the gears, pulleys, and wires, searching for a way to disable the mechanism.

His eyes closed, Khydius recalled the diagrams of the bridges that the reconnaissance teams had prepared. His eyes fluttered open, and he searched the length of the towers. His pulse thudded as he recognized a series of six large metal panels halfway up the span. They were the electromagnets that held the drawn span upright, and they would have to be destroyed. The weight of the span alone would be enough to lower the bridge. He confirmed this finding with his soldiers, stepped upon his cloudboard, and hovered toward the bridge.

His feet squarely planted on his board, Khydius soared up the side of the bridge tower. His eyes locked onto the series of metal panels as they glinted in the sunlight. He tilted the nose of his board upward and slowed to a stop. Khydius hovered between the narrow spaces separating the bridge pylons from the raised roadway.

Not much bigger than the length of his cloudboard, the silver panels were bolted to the tower's stonework. They were paired with identical panels affixed to the sides of the bridge span. Eyeing the devices, he placed a hand upon the smooth, cold metal.

"We should be able to disable the mechanism with explosive charges," he said aloud. The speakers in his helmet crackled to life with the sound of the guardians stationed upon the other bridges.

"We will use ikarifym charges. They will disrupt the electromagnets long enough for the bridge span to come down," said another guardian.

"I agree." Khydius turned to his soldiers. "We will place charges on the panels and detonate them simultaneously."

Khydius retrieved a glowing white crystalline orb from his utility belt. He reached out and deftly placed it in the center of the panel, the crystal emitting a high-pitched whine as soon it made contact with the metal. He distributed the remaining crystals to his soldiers, who floated around the span, placing an orb on each panel. Khydius grasped a vibrating black, dekafym crystal in his right hand. Brittle in nature, the crystal would deform nearby kai fields when broken. It amplified the intrinsic resonance of nearby crystals and would function as a detonator.

Khydius and his soldiers placed the charges, then drifted away from the tower. The air around him rumbled with the sound of engines as the Gilded Wing fleets surveyed the central pond. Their wingtips glinted in the rays of the late afternoon sun as they made their circuit. Their cannons fired intermittently, strafing the ground around them with rounds of artillery fire. A feeling of reassurance filled Khydius as he saw them soar overhead, protecting Tiriyuud's gains.

Khydius looked past the pond toward the main thoroughfares slicing through the clusters of buildings. His pulse thudded in surprise as he saw vessels from Tiriyuud's navy sailing up the wide canals toward the central island. Their angular hulls carved the surface of the water, leaving behind a turbulent wake. Fin-shaped control bridges atop their hulls exchanged fire with Navervynish forces on the ground and in the air. Their paired cannons rotated into position and launched potent taibifym charges, vaporizing their targets in a flash of searing orange light.

Khydius turned his attention toward the boulevards, where massive columns of Tiriyuusian vehicles and soldiers advanced toward the pond. They approached the embankment and made their preparations to seize the island.

"Our charges are placed. Prepare for detonation," the voices of the other guardians echoed in his helmet.

"My unit is ready," said Khydius, his voice reverberating in his speaker. Holding the detonator in his hand, Khydius awaited their word. They would count down together and activate the charges simultaneously.

"All soldiers, take cover." Khydius radioed the members of his unit, stationed both atop the tower and at the base. Gripping the crystal detonator, Khydius counted down, the voices of the other guardians echoing in his helmet. As they approached zero, his speaker crackled to life. "We must pause the detonation. There is a problem down here," reported one of his soldiers.

His heart thudding, Khydius gripped the detonator, his hand trembling.

"Our tower will pause detonation," said Khydius, communicating their predicament to the other guardians. He looked over to the other towers and saw their silhouettes floating upon their cloudboards, waiting to detonate their charges.

"What problem have you found?" asked Khydius.

"There is a ratchet mechanism on the span's pivot. The bridge will not collapse unless we disable it."

"What do you need to disable it?" Khydius shook his head in frustration at the unanticipated finding.

"We can remove it, but we must do this before you detonate your charges," replied the soldier.

"How much time do you need?" asked Khydius.

"We need a few minutes, but all the bridges have them," reported the soldier.

"We don't have enough time. We must detonate the mechanism," Khydius replied. He knew it was a risky move that may damage the pivot and the roadway, but they were running out of time. He looked past the pond as the Order's forces neared the embankment.

Khydius drifted toward the tower's base and joined his soldiers to understand their problem. They worked feverishly and placed charges upon the circular, toothed mechanism securing the span's axis. Khydius reported their findings to the other guardians, who instructed their soldiers to place charges in the same positions.

With their task completed, Khydius led his soldiers from the tower's base, and they floated back to the summit.

"Good work." Khydius nodded approvingly at the soldiers who had solved the problem. In the distance, Khydius saw the other guardians and their units waiting atop the other bridges.

"On my word, we will detonate both sets of charges, and the spans should fall," said Khydius.

"We will await your word," echoed the voices of the other guardians.

Khydius floated closer to the edge to get a better view of the other bridges, and his soldiers moved behind him. Khydius momentarily closed his eyes and drew in a breath. He held the crystal in his right hand.

"Ready," said Khydius. He lifted his hand, then hurled the crystal down past his feet. It collided into the top of the tower, shattering into black splinters, which emitted rays of intense violet light. The air filled with a deafening rumble, and Khydius watched as the bridge began to sway.

Chapter 54

Tenrai Nax

Tenrai stood upon the bridge of his carrier and gazed through the windows, surveying the chaotic scenes unfolding before him. Fleets of Gilded Wing craft fanned out over the grid of streets, defending their newly annexed territory. In the canals below, the vessels of the Tiriyuusian navy sailed between the islands toward the palace. The reports delivered to him from his squadron were encouraging. The Order succeeded in capturing the islands of the city and its environs. He looked down at the circular array of glowing control screens in front of him. The rotating maps and images flashed black and gold in many quadrants, indicating the Order's positions throughout the city.

Tiriyuud's army continued its steady march toward the center of Gavipristine. Though they had encountered stiff resistance, their forces were making significant progress. In little more than a single day, they had succeeded in destroying much of Navervyne's defenses, securing the capital street by street. A group of senior guardians standing behind him relayed instructions to the units of their squadron.

Tenrai looked toward the darkening horizon. His heart thudded as he eyed the green forms of Navervyne's ships break through the clouds. Tenrai's eyes narrowed as he surveyed the immense fleet approaching their aerial bases. Though the Order had enough firepower to pose a serious challenge to Navervyne, Tenrai had not anticipated directly engaging their fleet.

The Order had intended to attack the aerial platform before they landed, then destroy the spent vessels. They now had no other choice but to engage them directly. As Tenrai mulled the predicament, a display screen hanging before the bridge flickered to life. He looked toward the panel and saw Dydan's moving image.

"The Navervynish have arrived earlier than we anticipated, Commander Nax," said Dydan, his voice echoing through the speakers in the panel. He clenched his jaw in frustration. "Tiriyuud's hold on Gavipristine will not last if we fail to destroy those platforms."

"We must confront them with everything we have, Chancellor Waike." Tenrai nodded, his confidence growing. "We will guide our squadrons toward the fleet and fire upon them."

"We are outnumbered, and they will overwhelm us before we even have a chance." Dydan shook his head in disbelief.

"We have more of an advantage than we admit." Tenrai steepled his fingers as he thought of Darshima and Khydius. Their rare abilities with kai would be crucial, and he needed to coordinate a strategy with them.

"Whatever you decide, my squadron will fight alongside yours," said Dydan. His image vanished from the screen, and the panel dimmed.

"Full speed ahead." Tenrai gestured toward the enemy ships.

Tenrai relayed his plans to his senior guardians, who stood beside him. Their hands swept over the control panel as they toggled various moving icons and switches, aiming their squadron toward the line of enemy ships.

Tenrai stood firm as the carrier move beneath him. He looked out over the city as they raced through the columns of oily smoke. Fleets of Guided Wing darted in the skies ahead of them, strafing targets in the city center.

He glared at the approaching line of Navervynish ships and lost count at one hundred. Tiriyuud was outnumbered and would soon be outflanked.

Navervyne's ships traveled in broad lines extending from the horizon and were halfway to the platform. A lump formed in Tenrai's throat as he thought of his nephews and their companions fighting for Tiriyuud amid the chaos. His heart thudded as he saw their hold upon Gavipristine slipping away. If the Order failed at this mission, they would surely lose Iberwight and Tiriyuud would fall. He needed to do something. Tenrai closed his eyes and set his thoughts upon his nephews. Their abilities with kai were needed now, more than ever.

Chapter 55

Darshima crouched upon his cloudboard as he dashed through the acrid plumes of smoke. His lungs burning with each breath, he raced toward the trio of bridges, his soldiers flying closely behind him. The air vibrated around him with a concussive force, rattling his chest.

"Guardian Nax, look ahead!" shouted several of his soldiers. Darshima looked up at the skies, his pulse racing in fear as he recognized Navervyne's familiar ships.

The ghostly, rounded silhouettes descended through the clouds, the winds whipping violently around them. Navervyne's vessels maneuvered into a broad line and made their approach to the aerial platforms. Darshima glimpsed the canals below and saw Tiriyuud's naval craft sail into the city center. They patrolled the waters of the pond, aiming their cannons at the palace island and toward Navervyne's approaching fleet.

Fleets of Gilded Wing craft screeched overhead, their exhaust jets glowing through the night like comet tails. Darshima watched as they formed a coordinated swarm around the platforms, strafing them with repeated payloads of their incendiary bombs. The skies erupted in a stupendous blaze of fire and showers of sparks, the dissipating shockwaves jostling his board. Darshima's heart froze as the smoke cleared, and the platforms remained aloft, unshaken by the relentless assault.

A dozen more Gilded Wing aircraft roared toward the platforms, raining juurofym charges upon the platforms. The structures shuddered and swayed as the golden points of light imploded in blinding flashes, but the platforms held their position.

"We have to do something," said Darshima, looking toward his soldiers, his voice lost amid the bomb blasts. "Tiriyuud will not succeed if those platforms remain aloft." He shook his head in disbelief as he saw the frenzied activity around the central island. His soldiers were tasked with making a way for Tenrai once the bridges were lowered, but he couldn't conceive of a way to get them there safely.

The Navervynish vessels drew nearer to their circular berths tucked in the sides of the floating platforms. If they had the opportunity to refuel, they would mount an attack against Tiriyuud's forces and recapture the city. Darshima's stomach sank as he realized the Order's chances of victory were vanishing before his eyes. With his soldiers behind him, Darshima drifted down toward the city.

As they neared the pond, several thunderous explosions shook the air around them. Darshima snapped his gaze toward the palace island and saw a series of flashing charges raining sparks onto the waters below. Dense columns of white smoke wafted up from the drawbridges surrounding the island. A deep rumbling groan filled the air, followed by the click of churning gears. The spans opened simultaneously, extending outward like fingers toward the pond's embankment.

"Excellent work, Khydius," whispered Darshima, remembering his brother was one of the guardians responsible for securing the bridges. Columns of Tiriyuusian soldiers and their wheeled convoys moved through the streets below, toward the newly lowered spans.

Darshima looked above him and saw four long columns of Tiriyuusian carrier ships speed toward Navervyne's fleet. Darshima guided his troops through the skies, past fleets of Gilded Wing craft, and around the enemy vessels. He navigated the hail of screeching fire, extending his hand before him and deflecting volleys of projectiles in their path.

The skies around him were a chaotic battlefield, and he was unsure where to lead his soldiers. He looked toward the bridges and let out an anxious sigh. Amid the commotion, he saw vehicles and Tiriyuusian soldiers rushing onto the island. With the early arrival of Navervyne, his mission seemed like a futile effort. They would surely take back all of Tiriyuud's gains.

"Let's head toward the palace." Darshima waved his troops forward, then descended toward the pond. As they raced toward the towers of the palace, Tenrai's voice echoed in his head.

"Darshima, Khydius, you must hand off your missions. I have other teams that will perform them. There is a task of vital importance that you both must complete." Darshima stopped in mid-air, his troops rearing up behind him.

"What must we do?" asked Darshima, his voice barely audible amid the bomb blasts. A shiver coursed through him as Tenrai's voice echoed in his head, and his speaker remained silent.

"You and Khydius are our last hope in stopping Navervyne's advance. You must work together," said Tenrai, his voice fading in the wind.

"Where are you, Darshima?" asked Khydius, his voice ringing Darshima's ears. The speakers in his helmet remained silent, and Khydius' voice was coming from somewhere else.

"You're able to communicate like Tenrai," exclaimed Darshima, his voice wavering with fear and exhaustion.

"So are you," responded Khydius. Darshima drew in a breath as he realized his lips were not moving. He was indeed speaking with no words and using his mind like Tenrai.

"How is this possible?" exclaimed Darshima.

"We don't have the time to ponder it. Meet me above the bridge tower ahead of you," said Khydius. Darshima looked toward the pond. He saw brother's silhouette in the distance, perched upon his cloudboard.

Darshima angled his cloudboard toward Khydius, and his soldiers followed.

With the winds whipping around them, Darshima and Khydius hovered beside each other above the palace. Darshima looked on in muted fear as Tiriyuusian, and Navervynish vessels exchanged fire, lighting up the night sky.

"Tiriyuud's deflectors will not hold the Navervynish off for much longer." Darshima pointed to the missiles as they spiraled away from the Order's carriers.

"How are we going to defeat them?" Khydius looked around, his terrified expression illuminated by the surrounding explosions.

"I will try and take the platforms. You must find a way to incapacitate the troops aboard their ships." Darshima pointed toward Navervyne's fleet, which neared their berths.

"But how?" Khydius shook his head in confusion.

"Remember what you did in the Outer District. You must do it again," said Darshima, pointing toward the approaching ships.

Darshima floated upon his board and faced Khydius through the haze. Khydius glared back at him, when suddenly his eyes widened in an expression of utter disbelief. Khydius looked over Darshima's shoulder and opened his lips to speak but said nothing.

"What's happening?" yelled Darshima. Khydius looked toward the advancing ships and then back to Darshima. Darshima's heart froze in disbelief as Khydius' eyes briefly flashed in a brilliant blue glow.

Khydius tilted his cloudboard toward the enemy ships, and the air around them erupted in a flash of lightning. Khydius dashed forward, racing faster than Darshima had ever seen. Darshima looked on in astonishment as Khydius hurtled away from him and their soldiers. He traveled in a burst of raging light, appearing as if he were riding atop the bolts of lighting.

Khydius' silhouette shrank as he flew toward the lines of Navervynish vessels. Bolts of lightning arced across the sky, striking him as he drew nearer. His hands extended, Khydius zipped between the first row of vessels, bolts of electricity surging between him and their fuselages. One by one, the vessels slowed their approach. They shuddered and veered off course. Several vessels crashed into each other, sending showers of sparks and smoke into the sky as they fell to the ground.

Before Darshima fully understood what was happening, a silhouette materialized before him, its vivid sapphire eyes burning through the smoke and the darkness. Every fiber within him tingled as the kai fields surged around him. The figure drew nearer, its features enveloped by scintillating sparks of silver and gold. Darshima's heart froze as he looked through the light and glimpsed Rion's spectral figure floating before him.

"Father," stammered Darshima, his heart pounding in fear as Rion's ghost glared at him. He appeared in a guardian's uniform, and his features were exactly as Darshima remembered from the day of the invasion. He expected to feel fear, but a strange sense of calm flooded his senses. The sounds of explosions and racing engines faded to a muted din.

"You know what you must do," said Rion. His lips were closed, but his voice came through as a deep whisper amid the winds. He cast a glowing, determined gaze upon Darshima and pointed toward the platforms.

"Please, show me how," pleaded Darshima, his heart rising into his throat.

"It is you who will show us all, Darshima," said Rion. His eyes flickered, and a hint of a smile formed upon his lips. The curtain of sparks reemerged around him in a vortex of light, and he disappeared into the darkness.

"Wait!" shouted Darshima as he reached toward the open air. His pulse thudded with a mixture of disbelief and sadness. There was so much more he needed to know. "This can't be happening," murmured Darshima, stunned by his father's apparition.

A series of explosions rattled the skies above Darshima, snapping him from his trance. He saw Khydius hovering over the remaining vessels, his hands extended as they clumsily veered off course. They collided into the edifices surrounding the pond, erupting in flashes of fire and broken glass.

"We must hurry, Guardian Nax!" shouted Darshima's soldiers, frantically pointing toward the platforms ahead of them.

"I know what I must do." Darshima pulled his gaze from the pond and glared at the floating structures. He dashed forward, cutting through the stiff winds and squalls of snow, beckoning his troops to keep up with him. The line of platforms grew larger, appearing as a series of glowing structures hovering above the burning city. Tubular spans radiated from the central platform, linking them in a broad arc.

His right hand outstretched, Darshima seized the open air, slowly tightening his grip. His mind focused on the scene before him. Like the times before, a familiar sense of strength and lightness rose from a place deep within him. Darshima narrowed his eyes and extended his right arm out in front of him. A surge of electricity surged through his hand as the sovereign energy roiled within him.

Darshima closed his fist even tighter, and a force like nothing he had ever felt bolted through him. He felt as if every sinew in his body was on fire.

"I don't know how much longer I can hold on!" yelled Darshima through clenched teeth.

"You must!" shouted Khydius as he raced toward him.

Darshima drew in a breath to stifle the pain, and he held his grip. The earsplitting screech of twisting metal, exploding munitions, and the boom of colliding aircraft shook the air around him. He narrowed his eyes against the bright flames, and the platforms steadily deformed under his grasp. They strained under his immense force, imploded into a hulking twisted mass of glowing steel. The remnants burned brightly against the night sky, casting the entire city in its brilliant glow. The platforms erupted in a series of explosions. Tongues of flame flared from its sinking remnants.

The destroyed bases drifted downward under their own weight, and with a flick of his wrist, Darshima cast the wreckage past the edge of the city. The remainder of Navervyne's fleet broke into a chaotic swarm, steering clear of the destroyed platforms. Several of them exploded as they were struck by the hail of fiery debris.

Without warning, the skies above Darshima, Khydius, and their soldiers burst into a fury of light and smoke. Tiriyuud's fleet fired upon Navervyne's remaining vessels. Wave after wave of rockets sailed across the skies above them, exploding in flashes of thunderous sound and searing light as they collided with the enemy craft. Tiriyuud's naval vessels fired mortar shells upon the Navervynish aircraft, methodically knocking them from the sky. The enemy craft went into a tailspin, exploding in flashes of light as they crashed into edifices throughout the city.

The Order's aerial and naval ships unleashed even more fire upon the retreating Navervynish craft, which fled the city in haste. The remaining ships collided with each other in a thunderous clangor of scraping steel and wrenching metal. They rained sparks onto the river gorge beyond the city in their fiery descent. Within moments, the remnants of their burning fuselages crashed into the snowy forests, setting the surrounding woodlands ablaze. Fleets of Gilded Wing flew toward the craft and surveyed the area.

Darshima looked upon the fiery carnage surrounding them. The air grew tranquil as the explosions abated, and the crackle of burning fires and sirens filled his ears. Faint rays of sunlight glimmered over the horizon.

"I did what Rion showed me," whispered Khydius, his voice wavering with emotion.

"You saw him too?" Darshima shook in disbelief.

"He pointed toward the ships and disappeared in a flash of lightning, and I somehow did the same." Khydius shrugged his shoulders. "I felt every one of those enemy soldiers lose consciousness, then die as their ships crashed." A shudder coursed through Khydius as he relived the memory.

"Rion spoke to me," stammered Darshima. "He said that I must show everyone."

"You heard his voice?" Khydius' jaw dropped in disbelief.

As Darshima was about to answer him, the speakers in his helmet crackled to life.

"All units report back to their carriers for further instruction." Darshima and Khydius exchanged glances as they received the same message. They summoned their soldiers and journeyed back to their carriers.

Chapter 56

Darshima, Sydarias, Khydius, and Erethalie walked side by side amid the canyon of towers. Ahead of them, Tenrai and Dydan led the way. Their soldiers marching behind them, they crossed the span onto the palace island. The snowflakes falling around them, Darshima glimpsed the cloudy skies and drew in a breath. His thoughts raced as he contemplated the improbable moments ahead.

They were on their way to meet the Ruler of Fauridise and orchestrate the terms of surrender. On either side of the street, rows of soldiers stood at attention, saluting them as they passed. Darshima felt a peculiar sense of calm enveloping him. He could hardly believe the scene unfolding before them, let alone what it signified.

As they approached the palace, evidence of the days-long siege lay all around them. Bullet holes, craters, artillery shells, and charred stone littered their path. Darshima looked toward the palace and its trio of towers, Tiriyuud's banner fluttering boldly atop their spires. His ears filled with the sound of marching footsteps and the roar of Gilded Wing fleets making routine sorties over the captured island.

All around them, Tiriyuud's forces were ever-present. Formations of aircraft soared overhead, blotting out the morning sky. The waters teemed with navy vessels and submarines plying the adjacent canals and central pond. Their sleek black hulls glided silently along the water's surface, steadily slipping underneath the trio of bridge spans leading onto the island.

Darshima and his companions arrived at a broad staircase leading to the gates of the palace. He looked up at the towers surrounding him. The palace and the island reflected in their fractured facades appeared as a wounded mosaic.

"It feels like a wintry version of The Vilides," exclaimed Erethalie.

"The similarities are uncanny," added Sydarias.

"They planned it this way." Khydius looked around them, his eyes narrowing in an appraising stare.

"Let us continue. We have much to accomplish." Tenrai beckoned them forward.

They marched up the stairs and onto a stone plaza where lines of Fauridisian sentries met them. Their weapons placed their feet, the men and women stared at Tenrai and Dydan. The rows parted as Tenrai led them past, and Darshima glimpsed their tattered red uniforms. He exchanged direct gazes with them, their gaunt faces bearing expressions of resignation as they stared back.

A pair of sentries opened the wrought iron gates and ushered them into an oval courtyard. A trio of Fauridisian sages, dressed in sweeping red and white robes emblazoned with triplets of silver crosses, stepped through the parted ranks.

Tenrai and Dydan approached the sages, who offered them a curt bow.

"I am Commander Tenrai Nax, and we are guardians of the Order of the Gilded Moon." He gestured to his companions.

"I am Chancellor Dydan Waike, and we come on behalf of the Oracle of Tiriyuud. Your forces have been defeated. We have come to outline the terms of your surrender." The sages stood in silence as Dydan spoke.

"Tiriyuud's forces are traveling throughout your dominion and neutralizing what remains of Navervyne's installations," said Tenrai.

"We understand," said the sage standing in the middle of the group. "Please come with us." The sages ushered them into the palace. They traversed a circular courtyard and stepped through a pair of enormous doors fashioned from thick slabs of quartz.

Tenrai and Dydan walked side by side down the central aisle of the throne room, its floors paved in a smooth opalescent stone. A clear crystal dome capped the cavernous chamber. Beams of sunlight filtered through its translucent ceiling, giving the room an ethereal white glow. Darshima looked toward its oculus, decorated with innumerable angular dagger-like shards of crystal, pointing precariously downward.

They followed the sages past rows of immense white crystal pillars lining the path toward the throne. The structures rose from the ground in natural geometric forms, supporting the heavy canopy high above. Rows of Tiriyuusian soldiers stood in formation, saluting them as they moved through the chamber. The throne appeared as a collection of imposing quartz shards, jutting from the dais at oblique angles.

The Sovereign of Fauridise sat upon the throne, his auburn eyes narrowing as Tenrai and Dydan approached. His square face was marked with lines of fatigue, and his lips were wrinkled in a resigned frown. His greying black hair was parted in the middle and hung over his shoulders. Wearing frayed robes of red and white, he waited in silence.

Dozens of prelates, priests, and magistrates, sat at the foot of the throne. Darshima looked toward the perimeter of the chambers and saw hundreds of Tiriyuusian soldiers flanking the columns. A long table fashioned of white crystal sat before the throne.

The sovereign rose from his seat and walked toward them. Slightly shorter in stature, he looked at the assembled guardians for a moment, then offered a reserved bow.

"Our dominion has fought with everything we have. Our capital has been laid waste, and our ally, Navervyne, has abandoned us amid their defeat. We have neither the resources nor the resolve to continue this fight. Fauridise has no choice but to surrender to Tiriyuud."

"Mose Hireyed, Sovereign of Fauridise, we have come to your dominion on behalf of the Oracle of Tiriyuud, of the Order of the Gilded Moon," said Dydan, his voice echoing in the chamber.

"We have laid siege to Gavipristine not by choice but as a last resort." Tenrai gazed at the sovereign as he spoke, his eyes glowing intently. "Your dominion's alliance with Navervyne has caused untold turmoil and strife in our world. There was once peace and stability among the four moons. There is now death, slavery, and destruction."

"Tiriyuud's sole aim is to restore peace on Iberwight. We must protect our kingdom and uproot the evil that you have ushered forth." Dydan pointed toward the sovereign and his court.

"Our dominion was deceived by the Navervyne Republic. Despite outward appearances, Fauridise, like the other dominions, has languished under Vilidesian Rule. We sought prosperity on this harsh moon, but struggled." The sovereign shook his head, and a resigned frown formed upon his lips. "We covertly engaged in diplomacy with Navervyne but never anticipated our exchanges would have led to such an unfortunate circumstance."

"With time, The Order of the Gilded Moon will discover the truth about your collaboration. Both Fauridise and Navervyne will be held accountable for their crimes," said Tenrai, his voice echoing in the chamber.

Darshima listened to the sovereign's explanation, his pulse thudding in disbelief. Though the sovereign admitted to Fauridise's collusion with Navervyne, he avoided taking direct responsibility for the invasion. Darshima clenched his jaw, trying to stifle his emotions. The sovereign's admission only scratched the surface of Fauridise's true relationship with Navervyne. Darshima was grateful that the Order would seek justice. He would make sure of it.

"The terms of your surrender are clear." Tenrai handed a black leather envelope to the sovereign. "Tiriyuud claims provisional control over Fauridise's lands, waters, and skies. Tiriyuud will assume the governance of your citizens. Fauridise agrees not to challenge nor contest Tiriyuud's rule over Keverese and Nyzhaiheb, their people, and territories."

"We will not challenge Tiriyuud's claims." The sovereign gripped the envelope, his hand shaking in a subtle tremor.

"With your surrender, you relinquish your authority as sovereign. The Order of the Crystal Moon and its dominion will submit to Tiriyuud's rule of Iberwight," said Dydan.

The court stared intently at the sovereign, whose expression dissolved into sullen resignation as he processed Dydan's terms.

"I accept your terms," said the sovereign, his voice barely above a whisper. "I never fathomed a day like this."

The silence of the room was deafening. As Darshima looked at the solemn faces around them, he could imagine their surprise. For generations, Gavipristine had been the source of power and influence on Iberwight and beyond.

Tenrai summoned the guardians, and the sovereign summoned his sages, who rose from their seats. The two parties met at the long crystal table before the throne in preparation for the handover ceremony. Tenrai and Dydan and their accompanying guardians sat beside each other on the opposite side of the ruler. The sovereign and his party took turns signing and witnessing the document before passing it to the opposite end of the table. Tenrai and Dydan signed, followed by Khydius, Erethalie, and Sydarias.

The document made its way to Darshima, and he scanned the delicate parchment. His thoughts racing, he signed his name beneath Tenrai's. He drew in a breath and passed the document to the guardians at the end of the table. A shiver coursed through him as he realized what this moment represented for Tiriyuud. Long viewed as backward and isolationist, it had achieved the unfathomable. Tiriyuud had defeated Navervyne and liberated Iberwight.

Chapter 57

Darshima looked out upon the city, aglow in the afternoon sunlight, and soared above the glittering surface of the lake. Flying upon his cloudboard, he carved a meandering path toward Chryshaihem. The towers and spires of the skyline loomed at the shore in a dense arc. Khydius, Sydarias, and Erethalie flew beside him on their boards, their path guided by the surrounding kai fields.

The skies had cleared after a heavy snow shower, leaving the air with a clarity that made everything seem more vivid than he remembered.

"We're almost there." Erethalie pointed toward the Guardian's Shrine in the distance.

"What an incredible journey," said Sydarias, his voice mingling with the winds.

"We all have earned a much-deserved rest." Khydius pulled alongside Darshima.

"It feels good to be home." Darshima looked at the city below, barely able to contain his smile. He never felt more thankful to be returning to a familiar place.

Darshima and his companions raced through the skies amid a wave of several hundred of their fellow guardians. Several thousand of the Order's soldiers flew with them. Gilded Wing fleets and squadrons of aerial vessels glided beside them, accompanying them into the city. They had won the battle of Gavipristine only two days prior and were returning to Chryshaihem to great fanfare.

Darshima peered through his visor at the capital below them, his heart fluttering with a rare feeling of joy. He briefly closed his eyes as the feeling settled within him. Joy was not an emotion he was accustomed to, but he allowed himself to experience the moment. He and his companions flew over the city, the harmonious peal of bells ringing over the roar of aircraft engines and the rush of wind.

Darshima and his fellow guardians descended from the skies toward the dense southern tip of Chryshaihem's main island. Through the snowflakes clinging to his visor, he eyed throngs of cheering crowds flanking the main boulevard. Darshima and his companions landed in one grand swoop, strapped their cloudboards to their backs, and marched in lockstep toward the shrine.

The crowds issued rousing cheers and applause as the guardians filed past.

"Can you believe it?" asked Sydarias, shaking his head in disbelief.

"I certainly can," said Erethalie. A smile formed upon her lips as she surveyed the throngs of people celebrating their return. Enormous Tiriyuusian flags unfurled upon the grand edifices lining the boulevard, the black and gold fabric fluttering in the chilly breeze. The crowds' cheers grew louder as they neared the shrine. Darshima's ears rang with their words of praise and gratitude.

Darshima's thoughts raced as he marched with his companions. He remembered the moment when Tenrai brought him and his companions into the city under cover of darkness. Back then, they were refugees from conquered lands. Now they marched as heroes along that same boulevard, to the sound of cheers and the peal of bells. Darshima looked toward his friends. From their overwhelmed expressions, he could see that they felt the same way he did.

They made their way up the boulevard, the spires of the Guardians' Shrine and Oracle's Palace looming high above them. They were expected at the shrine, where the oracle would welcome their return. Though Darshima was thankful to be back in Tiriyuud, his chest tightened with a twinge of sadness. Not all of the guardians had returned with them to Chryshaihem. With Tiriyuud's victory, the Order had new obligations that now spanned the entire moon. The guardians would maintain a continual presence throughout the territories, skies, and waters of Keverese, Nyzhaiheb, and Fauridise, in addition to their duty to protect Tiriyuud.

Darshima, his fellow guardians, and their soldiers filed into the shrine. They sent up a deafening roar of cheers as they stepped beneath the arches and into the courtyard. They formed into neat lines as they awaited the oracle. Darshima looked around him as he stood in a row with his companions. Memories of the night that they departed the shrine filled his mind. Back then, he remembered the feelings of anticipation and worry. Now he felt a palpable sense of victory and responsibility, reflected upon all of their faces.

Darshima waited patiently, smoothening the wrinkles from his uniform, trying to put aside his fatigue from the long journey. The sound of chanting rose above the murmurs. The sages marched out onto the dais at the opposite end of the courtyard.

"Behold, the Oracle of Tiriyuud!" they proclaimed in unison. The assembled crowd fell prostrate onto the ground in a sonorous thud. The courtyard fell silent as they waited for her summons.

"Arise, guardians and soldiers," she commanded. Darshima rose to his feet and looked toward her as she stood behind a podium. Dressed in voluminous robes of black, embroidered with rays of gold, she gazed upon the guardians.

"Guardians and soldiers, welcome home," she said, her words absorbed by the cheering crowd. Darshima and his companions cheered with them, their voices rising with joyous commotion.

"You have achieved a victory for the ages. As your oracle, I commend you. Your kingdom offers its utmost gratitude. Your achievements on the battlefields, in the skies, and the oceans of Iberwight have secured our sovereignty." Peals of applause thundered as she spoke.

The oracle paused for a moment, then continued. "You have won an eternal place in our history." Her voice echoed throughout the courtyard, its walls barely able to contain her words. "Our victory has not come without a price. The Order's thoughts and support are with the guardians and soldiers who have been injured in battle. Though the will of kai protected their lives, it is my vow to hep them heal." Overcome with emotion, several of the guardians bowed their heads, nodding at her words. Darshima stood rapt as she spoke, the emotion of the moment palpable.

"For most of our recorded history, Tiriyuusians have been an isolated people. Our ancestors were exiles, refugees from Ciblaithia. They came to this frigid moon with nothing. With their will, traditions, and faith, they fashioned these rocky islands into what became the oldest civilization on Iberwight." She gazed over the crowds, her eyes narrowing in a contemplative expression.

"Over the ages, we did all that was necessary to protect our kingdom, our culture, and our way of life from the outside world. We defended ourselves from external threats and formed necessary alliances to maintain peace." She raised her hands as she emphasized her point. "When confronted with the Navervynish, we had every reason to capitulate. The Vilidesians and their realm succumbed to their relentless forces, thus ending their centuries-long rule over the four moons. We Tiriyuusians were not resigned to this fate." Rapturous cheers from the courtyard interrupted her words." She offered a solemn nod, acknowledging their reaction. "Your skill, your untiring efforts have ensured that Tiriyuud remains a free nation."

She stepped from behind the podium and toward the assembled crowd.

"Guardians and soldiers, you have demonstrated to the people of Iberwight and the moons beyond the strength, skill, and determination that dwells within the Tiriyuusian heart. You have shaken Iberwight to its core, and the known world has taken notice. This moon has been freed from the grip of Navervyne and is now under Tiriyuud's sole rule." She raised her hands, and the crowd erupted.

The oracle lowered her hands, and the crowd grew quiet. Darshima and the other guardians fell to their hands and knees, and she issued a prayer of thanksgiving.

Darshima followed along with her words. A lump formed in his throat as the emotion of the moment struck him. In his previous life, he would've never believed in an unseen force like kai or its purported ability to influence both the seen and the unseen, but the evidence abounded. Despite the fierce fighting, Tiriyuud had not lost a single man or woman in battle. The injured had been rescued and were being cared for in hospitals throughout the kingdom. Like his fellow guardians, Darshima believed that the Oracle's prayers had protected their lives.

She continued her words, asking for the sovereign strength to protect the Kingdom of Tiriyuud and the dominions beyond. After her prayer, the guardians rose and cheered as she was escorted away by the sages. Darshima lingered in the courtyard with his companions. He saw the other guardians reuniting with friends and family in emotional gestures. He could feel the energy in the air as the men and women milled about, catching up with each other and swapping stories from the battles in the dominions.

Twilight fell, and the guardians, visibly exhausted from the voyage home, made their way toward the exits of the courtyard and to their quarters. Darshima, Sydarias, Khydius, and Erethalie walked together through the crowds, greeting familiar faces and embracing fellow guardians.

They passed through the dark corridors of the monastery and up the flights of stairs to their suite. Darshima threw open the doors, and they entered the space. They rested their cloudboards beside the door and collapsed onto the floor, letting out sighs of contented exhaustion.

"After what we saw in Gavipristine, I never thought we would make it back here," said Sydarias, shaking his head in disbelief.

"I had faith in our talents." Khydius removed his overcoat. "We are trained guardians."

"We accomplished something remarkable together." Darshima turned to his companions. "We surpassed any challenge they could've given us during our deferred final test."

"Oh, I forgot about that, amid the bombs and enemy aircraft." Erethalie playfully rolled her eyes.

"Though we are the newest class of guardians, I would wager that we were undoubtedly the most tested." A studied frown crossed Sydarias' lips.

"You're both right." Darshima turned to them, heartened at their responses. He felt a sense of maturity and ease among them.

Despite their fatigue, Darshima and his companions were filled with energy from all they had seen and done. They shared harrowing tales from the battles and skirmishes that they and their soldiers had fought. Darshima, Sydarias, and Khydius were particularly interested in Erethalie's stories as a Gilded Wing pilot. It was widely acknowledged that the battles fought throughout Iberwight would not have been won without the decisiveness of their fleets.

"How did you manage to attack so many of their craft?" asked Sydarias.

"There was a method to it. I won't bore you with the details, but we were ready." Erethalie casually shrugged.

"Word has already spread about how good of a pilot you are," said Darshima.

"I flew you three back from Stebbenhour, so you already knew about that." A wry smile crossed Erethalie's lips. "The guardians only needed time to see it."

"I can't argue. You are the best." Darshima let out a playful sigh, and they all laughed with him. They listened to every detail as she spoke, marveling at the feats and close calls she encountered over Gavipristine.

During the battles, the other guardians beyond Gilded Wing learned of her prowess as a pilot. Several of the missions she led had given Tiriyuud an advantage and secured its gains during the fierce aerial battles.

After the laughter died down, Darshima turned to Khydius, who had remained silent.

"Is everything okay?" Darshima turned to him.

"Tiriyuud is a different nation now." Khydius looked through the windows, the city lights glittering against the night sky. A pensive frown formed upon his lips.

"How so?" Sydarias shook his head in confusion.

"Chryshaihem is now the center of power on Iberwight." He steepled his fingers.

"That is a good thing," said Darshima. His brow wrinkled in puzzlement as he tried to decipher Khydius' statement.

"The Tiriyuusians will learn difficult lessons, as did the Vilidesians," said Khydius. "Chryshaihem has gone from governing a minor archipelago to ruling an entire moon."

"I believe they will succeed," countered Darshima. "They are different from the Vilidesians."

As Khydius opened his mouth to speak, a soft knock at the entrance interrupted him. Darshima rose to his feet and approached the door. He pulled the handle, and slid open the door to see Tenrai and Dydan. Erethalie, Sydarias, and Khydius jumped from their seats and joined Darshima.

"Welcome back to the shrine," said Tenrai.

"We are glad to be back home." Darshima stood for a moment, simply grateful to be in the presence of his uncle.

"The four of you have accomplished so much during your months in Tiriyuud. Tenrai and I are immensely proud of what you have achieved."

Dydan looked at each of them. "It is late, and you need your rest. We have an important day tomorrow."

"We are ready," said Darshima, his colleagues nodding in agreement.

"We will greet you at dawn for the service at the Sapphire Temple," said Tenrai. He and Dydan wished Darshima and his companions a good night and then returned to their quarters.

"We have a full day tomorrow," exclaimed Sydarias as they walked back to the center of the room. The kingdom had planned a week of celebration to commemorate the Order's victory. The festivities would begin with a religious service at the Sapphire Temple, the oldest temple in Tiriyuud, presided over by the Seer of Chryshaihem. Afterward, the guardians would report to the Oracle's Palace for her official address, to be broadcast to the entire moon.

"I'm interested to hear what the oracle and the seer have to tell us," said Darshima.

"I'm sure they're going to explain Tiriyuud's next steps." Erethalie turned to Darshima. "As Khydius said, Tiriyuud has burgeoning responsibilities."

"Tiriyuud may have won the war, but the kingdom's success will require a monumental effort," added Sydarias. Darshima nodded in agreement at his friends' observation.

Darshima smiled to himself, remembering that Vilidesians were deeply interested in politics and power, owing to their legacy of hegemony. As an Ardavian, he was less interested in those discussions, but he realized it was necessary. He needed to grow familiar with these concepts. Tiriyuud had assumed an immense responsibility and had much work to do, even after its astonishing victory. The four stood together for a moment, bid each other goodnight, then to their rooms for the evening.

Chapter 58

Darshima, Khydius, Erethalie, and Sydarias marched in lockstep with their fellow guardians down the broad tree-lined axis, its grand stone edifices festooned in black and gold bunting. The dawn sky faded as the sun rose above the skyline. Dressed in their finest, the ranks of guardians struck an imposing presence as they approached the Sapphire Temple. Despite the early hour, the streets were lined with innumerable rows of citizens standing and waiting to observe the procession. Despite their fatigue from their long journey, Darshima and his companions were ready for the events and festivities that lay ahead.

As Darshima walked along the road, he recalled Khydius' description of today's events. The oracle's procession to the temple was an ancient tradition imbued with meaning. The seer's address to the temple was an occasion reserved for religious occasions or significant events. As the guardians arrived at the temple, they took their positions at the gates of the building, forming opposing lines along the avenue leading to the entrance. Darshima, Khydius, Erethalie, and Sydarias stood together beyond the gates and waited for the oracle.

Darshima looked down the road to see a procession of dignitaries make their way along the avenue. Numbering in the hundreds, they marched toward the temple. Their affiliations and rank within the Order were clearly displayed upon the folds of their robes, in an array of crests, elaborate symbols, and flowing script. From tradesman to priests, merchants to scholars, all members of the Order had been called to attend this address.

As the dignitaries filed into the temple, the air filled with the peal of bells. Darshima looked up toward the octet of soaring blue obelisks surrounding the main temple. He caught glimpses of the temple assistants stationed in the belfries, sounding the bronze bells atop the towers. Darshima's ears hummed with the resounding notes. He realized that the harmonies were distinct from anything that he ever heard.

Darshima felt the air stir around him, and he looked toward the skies above the temple. A fleet of imposing vessels soared above him. The craft escorted a large vessel, whose deltoid fuselage bore Tiriyuud's seal. The convoy disappeared behind the steep walls of the compound. As the engine noise dissipated, Darshima and his fellow guardians entered the temple. They marched past the enormous wrought iron gates, up the broad, blue staircase, and into the cavernous building.

In the shape of an octagon, the Sapphire Temple was the largest house of worship in Tiriyuud. One of the most important institutions in Chryshaihem, the temple held immense significance for all Tiriyuusians. As the oldest temple on Iberwight, it was constructed on the site where the first Omystikaiyn exiles conducted the earliest religious rites. Their ancestors had inaugurated the windswept islands of Tiriyuud as their permanent home, and their descendants had performed rituals at that location ever since.

As time passed, the encampment evolved into the city of Chryshaihem, and the location grew in importance. Constructed of enormous blocks of blue marble and lustrous sapphire, the temple's immense colonnades were adorned in carved friezes and religious script. Its complex array of multi-tiered sloping tile roofs were adorned with a glittering coat of blue and white crystal. The temple stood boldly against the forest of wood and stone towers and spires that had risen around it during the centuries of Chryshaihem's growth. Its magnificence and artistry were renowned and had been a source of inspiration for all Omystikai temples on Iberwight.

Darshima, Sydarias, Erethalie, Khydius, and their fellow guardians, made their way into the temple toward their designated section. Darshima was awestruck with its opulence. He eyed the interior colonnade of blue pillars forming a ring around the periphery of the temple. A crystal canopy opening into a gilded oculus sat high above their heads. The thick walls encased large panes of blue stained glass, casting space in vivid colors. Braided chains of gold crisscrossed the air above, suspending golden censers, which released fragrant smoke. Dozens of elegant tapestries and banners bearing the emblems of Tiriyuud's many regions hung from the walls.

Darshima and his companions settled upon a row of low-lying benches arranged in semicircular rows before the throne. Darshima looked at the oracle's throne, which sat in the center of the temple upon a black stone dais. Fashioned from a solid ingot of gold, its artistry rivaled the throne in the Oracle's Palace. Bathed in the sunlight filtering in from the oculus above, it shimmered brilliantly amid the shadows of the temple.

Darshima looked behind him to see the soldiers, priests, and other members of the Order seated in tiered balconies surrounding the center of the temple. Murmurs rose from the crowd as they awaited Seer Ryte, who would deliver the address, and the oracle, who would perform the religious rites. There was a palpable sense of excitement in the air. There was no precedent for an address such as the one they would hear. Given the magnitude of challenges that Tiriyuud had faced in recent months, the seer's speech was expected to be a prelude to the oracle's address later that evening.

The chatter among the pews fell silent as the Sages of Tiriyuud, led by the seer, entered the shrine. The members of the Order rose to their feet as the sages took their seats beside the throne. They issue the familiar chant signifying the presence of the oracle.

Darshima joined the assembly and fell to his knees as she walked down the aisle. Flanked by her retinue of priests, she wore her traditional black and gold robes. A shimmering black cloak bearing Tiriyuud's emblem draped her shoulders, following her in a flowing train down the aisle. Her crown sat upon her locks and gleamed amid the shadows. She assumed her seat upon the throne, and her priests sat in a row behind her.

The sound of an unseen choir filled the silence, and the assembly rose to their feet. Darshima recognized the chant as a melody reserved for the oracle. He listened intently to the choir as their powerful voices soared through the haunting harmonies. As the music faded, Seer Ryte rose from her seat and approached the pulpit, her red and gold robes shimmering in the light. She wore her hair in a tail that flowed down the nape of her neck. A solemn expression crossed her features as she cast a vivid blue gaze toward the audience.

Seer Ryte outstretched her hand, and the crowd again resumed their seats.

"My fellow Chryshaihemese, fellow Tiriyuusians, many of whom have traveled from afar, Members of the Order of the Gilded Moon, I would like to welcome you to the Sapphire Temple on this most auspicious occasion." She rested her hands upon the podium. The sober expression on her face hinted that she had much to discuss. She cleared her throat and continued. "I extend my congratulation to the guardians and soldiers for their valiant effort. You are the guarantors of our peace. Your skill and sacrifice underwrite Tiriyuud's freedom and stability."

A round of applause broke through her discourse, and she resumed. "This day is more than a celebration of victory. It shall forever mark the beginning of a new era for Tiriyuud." The audience looked on intently as she spoke. "We are no longer a remote island kingdom in the middle of a vast and windswept sea. We are no longer ensconced in the splendid isolation of our geography and the ancient tenets of our culture." She paused again, taking in the reaction of the audience, who clung to her every word.

"The attempted invasion of our kingdom by Navervyne shook our sense of stability to its very core. The guardians' unwavering defense of these islands has forever won them a hallowed place in our history. Their formidable offense against the enemy and their resounding victory have changed this kingdom and this moon forever." She paused for a moment, her expression growing somber. "We Tiriyuusians have been an insular people for all of our recorded histories, but our victories have accorded us new duties and responsibilities from which there is no retreat. We are called upon to gain a new sense of ourselves."

The audience nodded at her pronouncement, and she continued. "Tiriyuud's very nature must change if we are to maintain peace on Iberwight. Our ancestors were exiles. Among the rich heritage they bequeathed us, they left us with a survivalist mentality that still endures. When faced with external challenges, they retrenched deeper within these islands. They built more ramparts, tunnels, and fortifications to keep the outside world at bay. This strategy worked for centuries." A pensive frown formed upon Seer Ryte's lips as she spoke.

"When our kingdom was faced with an enemy so powerful that it conquered the once-mighty, Vilidesian Realm, several of our guardians were brave enough to challenge our prevailing logic. They forced us to see the dangers of our isolationism. They pushed us to defend our kingdom beyond its own shores to the distant lands of this moon. These ideas would have been unthinkable only a generation before."

Seer Ryte paused for a moment amid the silence, a thoughtful expression crossing her features. "I openly admit that I was one among many who doubted these new guardians. I erred in disregarding the truths they told. I believed that the old ways would continue to protect us." The assembled members of the Order bowed their heads at her admission.

Seer Ryte drew in a breath, then continued. "The steady guidance of our exalted oracle convinced us all to believe in them." A brief round of applause interrupted her words. "Because of their insistence of a new way forward, Tiriyuud endures. These brave men and women are the first to undertake the long task of dismantling the walls that have surrounded our kingdom and culture for too long. We all must adopt their way of thinking if we are to lead as a kingdom." Peals of applause filled the cavernous space.

Seer Ryte rested her hands upon the podium and stared at the audience." I challenge everyone in this temple not to fear but embrace Tiriyuud's new role in this fraught world. We are no longer a reclusive people from a forgotten land, long lost to the ages. We are no longer the tribe spurned by the rest of the world for its unyielding orthodoxy. We can no longer be a nation that has resisted the tide of progress. On this day, we must become the Tiriyuusians that discarded these outmoded ways of thinking, of doing things. We must be the pioneers of this new era."

The seer continued, her voice resounding throughout the temple. "We must be confident of our kingdom and its larger place in the world. As the leader of Chryshaihem and a faithful member of this Order, I will do my utmost to serve our kingdom through this challenging new period." She raised her hands amid the peals of applause and spoke through the noise.

"Tiriyuud has liberated the conquered lands of Nyzhaiheb and Keverese. Tiriyuud has defeated Fauridise and Navervyne. Tiriyuud now rules sovereign over this moon."

As the applause faded, she continued. "We mustn't entertain any illusions. Tiriyuud has an enormous task ahead. We must rebuild and restore the dominions of this moon, devastated by conquest and war. We must begin the hard task of reuniting the Omystikai tribes." A somber frown formed upon her lips as she enumerated the work ahead of them.

"As many of you are aware, much of Iberwight beyond our shores lay in ruins from neglect and war. We must work hand in hand with the other Omystikai tribes to restore lost infrastructure and civic institutions." The seer spoke louder, the intent in her voice ringing clear. "To foster a new sense of unity and purpose among the people of Iberwight, they must see The Kingdom of Tiriyuud as more than a military presence within their borders and more than a source of immediate assistance. They must see Tiriyuud as a beacon of stability and hope. Tiriyuud must now be an arbiter of peace and an underwriter of prosperity. They must realize that they hold an important stake in this new order."

A tide of murmurs rose from the audience as she spoke. Seer Ryte looked unflinchingly toward them. "Our aims can only be achieved if Tiriyuud is seen as the guarantor of peace. The other Omystikai must see our kingdom, our oracle as their leader and their protector."

The audience nodded in unison as Seer Ryte continued. "With this awareness, for the sake of unity, and in the name of restoring peace to this moon, the Sages of Tiriyuud have decided to confer a new title upon the oracle." The temple fell silent as her words echoed. "I present to the members of the Order of the Gilded Moon, our leader."

Seer Ryte stepped from the podium. Two of the sages rose at either side of the throne and unfurled two large scrolls of silken black cloth embroidered in golden script bearing the oracle's new title. The seer's voice rose again. "Members of the Order, citizens of Chryshaihem, sons, and daughters of Tiriyuud, behold our leader, the Most Serene Anaidys Rexe, The Oracle of Tiriyuud, The Defender of Keverese and Nyzhaiheb, The Sovereign of Fauridise, The Empress of Iberwight." The sages approached her slowly, bearing a new crown upon a cushion. Fashioned of resplendent gold, the crown was festooned in diamonds, rubies, and other precious gems. An eight-pointed sapphire star sat at its apex, ensconced in a delicate, glowing white crystal orb. They uttered a solemn prayer and gently placed it atop her head. The assembled crowd genuflected before the throne, then rose to their feet.

Darshima stood amid the thunderous peals of applause, his eyes widening in disbelief.

"What an unexpected speech." Darshima turned toward his friends. The incisive words of Seer Ryte replayed through his mind, and part of him was heartened at her acknowledgment of him and his companions.

"Can you believe it?" Sydarias shook his head as he applauded.

"I don't know what to say." Erethalie's brow raised in astonishment as she gazed at the throne.

"Iberwight's last ruler was a Vilidesian emperor, and now its new ruler is a Tiriyuusian empress." Khydius folded his arms across his chest and looked toward the throne. "The world is changing before our very eyes."

The applause settled, and the oracle approached the pulpit. Seer Ryte stepped back, bowed deeply toward her, and resumed her seat. The oracle looked upon the audience, casting her piercing sapphire gaze upon the thousands of faces. She outstretched her hand, and the crowd bowed their heads as she issued the first incantation.

Chapter 59

Darshima and his companions walked through the streets, the crowds cheering as they departed the temple. Chryshaihem hummed with activity as ceremonial festivities took place throughout the city. Worshippers filled the temples, taking part in religious rites to celebrate Tiriyuud's improbable victory over Navervyne. Markets teemed with people preparing celebratory feasts for their returning soldiers and sentries. Though the ceremonies at the Sapphire Temple had been open only to ranking members of the Order, Seer Ryte's stirring address and the oracle's incantation had been broadcast throughout the city and kingdom. Their words echoed throughout the shrines, buildings, and streets of every city and village.

The day was treated as an official holiday, and the streets of Chryshaihem were alive with activity. Seemingly every neighborhood and quarter held a parade or procession celebrating Tiriyuud's victory. Though usually a staid people, the Tiriyuusians enjoyed a good celebration when there was a reason, and they could think of none better. Amid the chaos and flurry of excitement, the members of the Order made their way to various engagements and ceremonies marking the day. Among the most important events was an official ceremony recognizing the Guardians' service to the Order and their outstanding achievements during the war.

Wherever the guardians and soldiers traveled that day, they were cheered and hailed by Chryshaihemese of all sorts, wanting to express their gratitude. Civilians who saw them passing offered them food, drink, and invited them into their homes for rest. For the members of the Order who hailed from the hinterlands, the crowds, hospitality, and excitement were unlike anything they had ever experienced.

Darshima, Sydarias, Khydius, and Erethalie walked with the other guardians down the grand axis toward the Oracle's Palace. They marched in formation beneath the snowfall amid the deafening cheers and flurry of waving flags. Overhead, the skies rumbled with the sound of Gilded Wing aircraft roaring over the urban canyons, tipping their wings to the guardians parading below.

People extended their hands as Darshima and his companions passed by, and they clasped them, offering thanks for their prayers and support. Fathers and mothers hoisted their children upon their shoulders to get a better look at the young heroes as they walked. The scenes of celebration and revelry gave Darshima pause. A sense of duty filled his heart as they approached the palace. Their sacrifice had protected this kingdom, and the citizens were showing their gratitude.

Despite their enjoyment of the festivities, Darshima's happiness was tempered by the realization that many of his fellow guardians were stationed in the far-flung regions of Iberwight, maintaining peace. He knew that his time to serve again would come soon. He would take Seer Ryte's words to heart and work with his fellow guardians to rebuild Iberwight's destroyed cities, forge new alliances and build new friendships. They would do it with conviction and purpose in the months to come, but today, Darshima and his companions would take a moment to enjoy themselves and their accomplishments.

Chapter 60

Dressed in their finest, Darshima, Khydius, Sydarias, and Erethalie stood in a line before the throne. Darshima wore his engraved gauntlet upon his right arm, and Khydius wore his breastplate. Sydarias wore a golden greave wrapped around his right shin in recognition of his superb skill upon the cloudboard. Erethalie wore a golden band upon her forehead in acknowledgment of her wisdom and decisiveness as a pilot. Before the ceremony, Tenrai presented them with these gifts in preparation for the day's ceremonies.

Tenrai and Dydan stood with them before the throne. Tenrai wore his engraved epaulets, and Dydan wore an engraved headband similar to Erethalie's. A dozen other guardians stood along with them. Hundreds of people sat in a semi-circle, dressed in their uniforms and ceremonial ornaments.

Darshima cast an eye around the room as he took in the scene. Rays of sunlight set the opulent interior aglow as they filtered through the gusts of swirling snow beyond the windows. The city below bustled with traffic, its skies teeming with fleets of military and merchant vessels. The once tranquil lake stirred with formations of naval ships traveling between the lake and the ocean. Darshima marveled at how much had changed since his last visit to these chambers, just after the attempted invasion. The oracle's clear voice interrupted his thoughts, and he looked toward the throne.

"Every guardian in this room deserves recognition for their service to the Order and the Kingdom." She led the room in applause and continued after a moment. "Our recognition also includes the Order's newest class of guardians. Though circumstance prevented them from submitting to the traditional test of their ability, they have been tested more on the battlefield than any generation before them." The oracle gestured toward the audience. "Tiriyuud's new guardians have proven themselves, and they are among the most talented people our Order has ever known." The audience erupted in cheers, and she applauded along with them.

"The men and women standing before me have been chosen by their superiors for their valor. They have served Tiriyuud with distinction and must be recognized. They stand before me as recipients of the Order's highest commendations." She then called the guardians one by one to the throne. They knelt before her and received her praise along with uproarious applause.

The oracle handed them various medallions and pennants, sharing the history behind them. They received their medals and rejoined the guardians seated behind them.

The line of guardians thinned out until Darshima, Khydius, Erethalie, and Sydarias, along with Dydan and Tenrai, were the only ones who remained before the throne.

"I have saved the most distinguished medals for the six of you standing before me. Please come forward." Tenrai and Dydan exchanged a look of surprise, then ushered Darshima and his companions toward the throne.

"Rarely has there been an occasion in Tiriyuud's history where a group of individuals has made an impact so large, a sacrifice so great, that it forever changes our destiny. More than sacrifice alone, these individuals chose to act differently. They followed their instinct and chose a course that defied our sense of tradition. They did this not when it was convenient, but when it was most difficult and when the opposition against them was the fiercest." The oracle looked around the room, her eyes glowing softly.

"Because of their courage, our kingdom triumphed over a merciless enemy. The six individuals standing before me are heroes of the highest order." Darshima stood still with his companions, taken aback by the generosity of her words. Before they had time to reflect, she called them to the throne.

"I call upon Guardian Erethalie Danthe to approach the throne." Erethalie froze for a moment, unsure of what to do, and Dydan nudged her forward. She walked to the throne and knelt before the oracle. "Your skills as a guardian and as a pilot have become legendary. When the tide turned against our forces, you did not retreat, but you advanced, leading your fleet toward its targets and completing the mission. You achieved this with every sortie, and your commanders have recognized for your efforts over Nyzhaiheb and Gavipristine." Erethalie bowed her head at the oracle's praise.

The oracle continued. "I call upon Guardian Sydarias Idawa to approach the throne. Sydarias stepped forward and knelt beside Erethalie. "Your skill and dexterity on the saigura are renowned, and you have become the most adept guardian at this Tiriyuusian art. You were able to lead your soldiers and perform critical missions in Keverese and Fauridise. Your efforts cleared a safe path toward the palace in Gavipristine, helping the Order advance our forces." Sydarias nodded as he listened to her words, his eyebrows raised in astonishment.

"I request Guardian Khydius Nax to approach the throne." Khydius walked toward the oracle and knelt beside Sydarias. "Khydius, your contribution to the Order's efforts have been lauded, and your feats have spared us cruel defeat. When Navervyne attempted a second attack within our borders in the Outer District, you channeled kai to stop their troops from carrying out an evil act. As our Order struggled in Gavipristine, you lowered one of the bridge spans, and our forces gained control of the palace island. Even more astoundingly, you called upon kai to incapacitate the crews of the enemy ships threatening our squadrons." Khydius bowed his head at her words, a surprised expression forming upon his lips.

The oracle then turned to Darshima. "I call Guardian Darshima Nax to approach the throne." She beckoned him. Darshima took his place beside Khydius. "Darshima Nax, you hold a rare power lost to the ages, once wielded by our ancestors. You must be commended for saving Tiriyuud during its time of crisis. When Navervyne's ships breached our borders, you used your divine hand to control the flow of kai and destroy the enemy's fleet and spare our kingdom from a cruel fate. Your act of defiance gave us time to prepare a counteroffensive. You were the first guardian in this kingdom to turn the tide against Navervyne."

The audience applauded at the oracle's assessment, and she continued. "When no one dared to speak up and convince me of the necessity of liberating the foreign dominions and the need to take the fight beyond our borders, you were the only one to stand and speak your mind." Darshima bowed his head at her words, his heart rising into his throat at her recognition. "When our forces were unable to destroy Navervyne's platforms over Gavipristine, you used your gift to destroy them, assuring Tiriyuud's victory."

Darshima's pulse raced her words, astounded at the accuracy of her account. As he knelt before the throne, memories of his former life raced through his mind. During his days on Ardavia, when he felt like little more than an outcast boy with no purpose, he would've never imagined that he would one day become a battle-tested warrior, kneeling before an empress and lauded as a hero. A shiver coursed through him as he relived the pain, joy, struggles, and triumphs that he had experienced up until this moment.

"For your efforts, I award each of you one of the Order's highest honors, the Sapphire Star of Chryshaihem. I also bestow the title, Knight of Tiriyu-ud upon you, and all of the rights and privileges that it accords." She ordered them to rise. The four exchanged glances of surprise and awe as they rose to their feet. The title of knight was bestowed to the most courageous of guardians and was a great honor. The Tiriyuusian Knights were among the most elite members of the Kingdom, and Tenrai had served as one. The oracle stood before each of them. She retrieved the medallions from a golden platter held by a priest standing beside her. She affixed two distinct medallions to their uniforms. The first was a large sapphire hewn in the shape of a star, encircled by eight engraved gold crescents, and the second was a small silver filigreed shield denoting their rank as a knight.

"The four guardians standing before me have taught the entire Order and myself more than we could've ever imagined. They have shown us that neither heritage nor lineage defines an Omystikai. Through their grace, sacrifice, and bravery, these four have become among the most talented guardians in our Order. They have proven themselves loyal Tiriyuusians and are true Omystikai." The oracle led the audience in applause. Darshima and his companions bowed deeply at her gracious words, then took their seats among their fellow guardians.

Tenrai and Dydan stood beside each other, their heads bowed.

"Chancellor Dydan Wake, please approach the throne," said the oracle, her voice echoing amid the silence. Dydan walked toward the throne and knelt before her. "You have served valiantly as chancellor, and your actions leading your squadron over Nyzhaiheb and Gavipristine assured our kingdom's victory. More importantly, you worked closely with Commander Nax and the guardians when everyone else doubted you. Despite your role as a sage, you cast aside the doubts of the Council and risked your reputation to assist him in training these four young guardians."

The oracle looked around the room as she spoke. "After the first attempt at invasion, you fully embraced Tiriyuud's struggle and engaged in battle, more than any sage in living memory. You did what was necessary to serve this kingdom, and for that, I commend you." Dydan bowed his head in recognition of her comments, then rose to his feet. "For your contribution, Dydan Wake, I award you with the Shield of Tiriyuud" A large diamond set in an engraved shield of gold, she fastened the medal upon his uniform. The award was only bestowed upon one sage every generation. He bowed once more, then took his seat among the guardians.

The oracle then faced Tenrai, who stood as the sole guardian in front of her.

"I request Commander Tenrai Nax to approach the throne." She beckoned him, and he knelt before her.

"The guardian before me is perhaps the most outstanding of them all." Tenrai looked up as she spoke. "Commander Nax has been the guardian, the Tiriyuusian who has sacrificed the most to defend this kingdom." Hushed murmurs rose from the audience as the oracle spoke. "Tenrai challenged the belief that only the sages and myself could see the future. He remains the only Tiriyuusian to have divined the invasion of the realm and the attempted invasion of Chryshaihem."

The oracle paused to collect her thoughts and continued. "Commander Nax was the one, who despite fierce criticism, followed his vision and scoured the fallen realm in search of our salvation - Rion Nax's sons, his nephews. Against all odds, he carried out the difficult voyage to Navervyne and rescued them." She moved closer to Tenrai and looked at him, her eyes narrowed in an earnest gaze.

"Commander Nax was the one who, despite intense scorn and ostracism from both the Guardianship and the Council of Sages, brought five Vilidesians, five foreigners into the heart of this isolated kingdom. Facing much resistance and against all doubt, he trained them in our ways and made them into exemplary Tiriyuusians and talented guardians of our Order. His sacrifice, vision, and wisdom have guided this kingdom through the most profound challenge it has ever known. With this award, I acknowledge his sacrifice and the debt that our nation owes him. To Commander Tenrai Nax, I award the Heart of Tiriyuud." The oracle nodded toward Tenrai.

The Heart of Tiriyuud was the rarest honor in the Order. The medal was reserved for a guardian who had risked or given their lives to save the kingdom. The Order had given it posthumously to Rion Nax after his defense of Chryshaihem against the Vilidesians.

"Arise, Commander Nax." The oracle beckoned Tenrai, and he stood before her. She affixed the medal to his uniform. Fashioned of a large red ruby set amid eight engraved gold crescents, it glittered brightly upon his uniform. Overcome by the moment, he looked up at the oracle. She leaned closer to him.

"You have earned this accolade Tenrai. You deserve far more than any award could ever grant you. Your time has come, and you must step from beneath Rion's shadow." She whispered into his ear.

"As you command, most exalted one," said Tenrai. He exchanged a poignant gaze with the oracle and bowed toward her. The entire room rose to their feet and applauded. Tenrai turned toward his fellow guardians, the applause growing louder. He stood amid the adulation, his eyes filling with tears. Darshima looked at his uncle, and his eyes grew damp. He understood the significance of the moment, and his heart stirred with a sense of pride.

Chapter 61

The ceremony concluded, and the oracle was escorted from the chambers by her retinue of priests. Darshima and his companions, newly decorated with their medallions, filed out of the chambers with their fellow guardians.

"Congratulations on your achievements. I am proud of you all." Tenrai walked alongside them, gazing at their awards.

"We couldn't have done any of this without you." Darshima gestured toward himself and his companions.

"You all would've found a way with or without me," said Tenrai, a smile forming upon his lips. "I will see you all this evening for the oracle's address." He joined Dydan, who walked ahead of them.

Darshima and his companions stepped back into the afternoon air and walked toward the Guardians' Shrine. They looked forward to a moment of rest amid a busy day. For the remainder of the afternoon, the members of the Order shuttled between the Guardians' Shrine and the Oracle's Palace attending celebrations and banquets commemorating the Tiriyuud's victory. They met with long-separated friends and colleagues, sharing harrowing stories about the war. Amid the revelry, many discussed the challenges and opportunities that Tiriyuud's victory would bring. They awaited the oracle's address, which would take place later in the evening in the throne room and be broadcast to the entire moon.

As they walked down the boulevard toward the shrine, Darshima eyed enormous screens hanging from the edifices.

"It seems as if everyone will be viewing the oracle's speech." Darshima pointed toward the rows of enormous crystal panes.

"Her words will be heard by billions." Khydius gazed upon the screens, his eyes narrowing in contemplation.

"I thought it was only going to be broadcast on Iberwight." Sydarias shook his head in confusion.

"Today's dossier said that the Order will broadcast her speech to the four moons." Erethalie tapped her coat pocket, and the slips of paper crinkled. Darshima's brow raised in surprise as he remembered reading the same details.

In preparation for the event, the Order erected enormous viewing screens upon edifices throughout Chryshaihem and in public squares throughout the kingdom. The guardians stationed in the dominions enlisted their engineering corps to patch into the existing communications networks, previously built by The Vilidesians. Though equally sophisticated, Tiriyuusian technology was different and required ingenuity to adapt to the former Vilidesian standards. Furthermore, Navervyne had disrupted the communications systems during the invasion, and the Tiriyuusians had put much effort into restoring the system.

To Darshima and his fellow guardians, the significance of this evening's speech was not lost on them. The kingdom's victory was still new, and the novelty of Tiriyuud's heightened influence even newer. Their kingdom had achieved the unthinkable, and these facts were beginning to settle within them. They had defeated Navervyne, and now their oracle was the Empress of Iberwight. This victory cemented Tiriyuud's role as a newly dominant power and Chryshaihem as the center of influence upon the moon.

Beyond the walls of Order's palaces and temples, many ordinary Chryshaihemese were vaguely aware of the profound effect that Tiriyuud's victory had on the worlds beyond the skies of Iberwight. Their triumph had upset Navervyne's imposed order, and word of their defeat spread among the peoples of Wohiimai, Ciblaithia, and Gordanelle.

People were stunned that their forgotten kingdom remained the last unconquered territory among the four moons. Many wondered how a small island nation had achieved such an improbable victory amid large-scale plunder and ruin. They marveled that Tiriyuud had successfully marshaled its resources and assembled a fighting force that liberated an entire moon, and handed a crushing defeat to Navervyne's mighty army - the same force that toppled The Vilides and its realm.

This fact was not lost on the Order. They realized whether they were prepared or not, Tiriyuud's success had drawn the attention of untold billions upon the other moons, still subject to Navervyne's rule. The Tiriyuusians kept no illusions about their current situation. Though they had chased Navervyne from Iberwight, their enemy still existed and remained an ever-present threat.

The Order realized that they must communicate directly with the peoples of the fallen realm. They would achieve this aim by broadcasting the oracle's speech throughout Iberwight and to the cities and villages of the other moons. Sending a message to the wider world about their victory was their first step in demonstrating that Navervyne, though powerful, was not invincible.

Chapter 62

Darshima and his companions stood behind Tenrai, General Heede, and several other guardians in the staid ambiance of the anteroom. He looked over their shoulders and glimpsed the Sages of Tiriyuud, led by Seer Ryte and Dydan, along with a retinue of priests and prelates. The Oracle stood in the middle of the crowd, a few paces ahead of Darshima. Dressed in robes of shimmering black, embellished with gold thread and sapphire, she struck a powerful presence. A flowing blue cloak bearing the star and eight-crescent seal of Tiriyuud, surrounded by a glowing ring of white crystals, hung from her shoulders. As Darshima understood, the crystal ring symbolized Tiriyuud's new relation to Iberwight. The new crown atop her head glittered in the rays of sunlight.

The priests threw open the golden doors, and the procession moved into the chambers. Darshima and his companions walked into the opulent space with the group. The throne room glittered brilliantly in the late afternoon sun. Rows of Tiriyuusian flags hung from the ceiling, their golden seals gleaming as they fluttered. The harmonious tones of a choir filled the air. Darshima felt his heart rise into his throat as he remembered his first visit to this rarified space. Back then, he felt like an anxious outsider, but now he felt welcome, and a part of something greater than himself.

They walked past their fellow guardians, dressed in full regalia, standing at attention in neat rows. Several dozen seats, reserved for the seer, Council of Sages, guardians of the highest rank, and the oracle's guests, sat on either side of the throne. Ranks of priests and prelates in their ceremonial robes stood in rows behind the guardians. Hundreds of soldiers dressed in full uniform stood throughout the chamber. The rulers of Keverese and Nyzhaiheb waited in a line before the throne, accompanied by their sages. A group of priests representing Fauridise stood with them. Darshima looked at the representatives from Fauridise and tried to suppress his emotions. He learned that Fauridise's deposed sovereign and their sages remained under custody in Tiriyuud, awaiting a fair and objective trial. He knew the outcome would be closely watched by all.

Darshima noted the surprised expressions of the assembly as the oracle proceeded toward the throne. He imagined their appearance as the oracle's guests would surprise many. Dydan and Seer Ryte, followed by the Council of Sages, led the procession toward the dais. They stopped at the reflecting pool, faced the crowd, and lowered their hoods.

"Behold the Oracle of Tiriyuud, Empress of Iberwight," announced Dydan. They issued a harmonious prayer and then a chant. The entire room fell onto their knees as the procession followed her over the footbridge onto the dais. As he approached the throne, Darshima eyed the clear lenses of cameras positioned around the room, ready to film the speech. A smile briefly crossed his lips as he imagined the event being broadcast to people far beyond the kingdom.

Darshima settled beside his companions at the foot of the throne. The oracle looked out at the audience, maintaining a solemn expression amid their murmurs. As he looked out upon the assembly, Darshima contemplated the oracle's request for their presence beside her. She had already commended them for their efforts during the war, but he wondered what others would think.

They were now Tiriyuusian, even if they didn't outwardly appear so. Darshima shook his head and dismissed his doubts. He and his companions had demonstrated loyalty and strength like any other guardians. Tiriyuud was their home now, and they would find acceptance, no matter their appearance.

The sound of the choir faded, and Seer Ryte rose from her seat.

"To the citizens of Chryshaihem and the Kingdom of Tiriyuud. To the Omystikai of Iberwight, to peoples of the moons beyond our own - Ciblaithia, Gordanelle, and Wohiimai. I present our leader, the exalted Anaidys Rexe, The Oracle of Tiriyuud, The Defender of Keverese and Nyzhaiheb, The Sovereign of Fauridise, The Empress of Iberwight." The audience broke into rapturous and sustained applause, and Seer Ryte resumed her seat.

The oracle looked around the overflowing room and settled in her throne.

"To the people of Tiriyuud, the battle is now over, and we have secured a resounding victory." She then turned her gaze toward the rulers seated in front of her. "To the people of Keverese and Nyzhaiheb, the people of Tiriyuud send you their warm greetings. We welcome you into the dawn of your new freedom. To the people of Fauridise, we now set down the weapons of war and offer you an open embrace in the hope of a new friendship. We seek to establish an everlasting bond between our peoples, free of the enmity and strife that have marked generations past."

The oracle then looked beyond the audience and cast an eye toward the camera lenses. To the surprise of all, she issued her words in both Omystikaiyn and Vilidesian. "To the subjected peoples of Ciblaithia, Gordanelle, and Wohiimai, the Kingdom of Tiriyuud has delivered the moon of Iberwight from Navervyne's grip, and it is now free. We will fiercely defend our liberty against this merciless enemy. We beseech the peoples of these conquered moons to rise against your masters and do the like." The room filled with thunderous applause at her words. Darshima applauded her statement, tears forming in his eyes as he thought of the ongoing suffering elsewhere.

The applause faded, and she continued. "Tiriyuud's responsibilities have grown, and we now must defend the entirety of Iberwight." She paused to collect her thoughts. Her eyes narrowed as she continued. "The invasion of The Vilidesian Realm, accomplished by Navervyne and abetted by Fauridise, has taken a disastrous toll on the entire world. Iberwight has perhaps suffered the least as a result of the enemy's conquest. We understand your plight. We share your anguish, sense your despair, and shed tears at your suffering. Please know that the prayers of the Tiriyuusian people are with you."

She continued over the ensuing applause, her voice taking on a distinctly somber tone. "After the attempted invasion of the Tiriyuusian islands, we learned the true nature of Fauridise's link to Navervyne and the untold damage it had done to the world beyond our shores. The betrayal of The Vilidesian Realm by the Order of the Crystal Moon is an unforgivable act that Tiriyuud rebukes. Families, societies, and cities have been destroyed. The ties that once united the peoples of these moons and the Omystikai of Iberwight have been ruptured. We must be the ones to repair them." She steepled her fingers as she spoke.

"To rebuild Iberwight, to heal the wounds torn open by invasion, enslavement, and betrayal, Tiriyuud must open a new era in the history of these moons. As decreed by the liberation pacts signed by the Rulers of Keverese and Nyzhaiheb and the articles of surrender signed by the deposed Sovereign of Fauridise, the peoples of this moon will be from this moment forward united in freedom, prosperity, and peace under my rule as Oracle of Tiriyuud and Empress of Iberwight." Peals of applause erupted, and she took a moment to reflect. The oracle looked again upon the crowd, her sapphire eyes burning with intent.

"Tiriyuud does not seek to establish an empire of hegemony," she said. Hushed gasps escaped from the crowd, and she continued. "We seek an empire of peace. We seek neither to impose our culture, faith, nor our ways of life on those beyond our shores. We Tiriyuusians are dedicated to maintaining peace, encouraging prosperity, and fostering a new sense of unity among the Omystikai of Iberwight and the peoples beyond this moon who long for freedom." The oracle spoke in exact terms, laying out proposals and plans for rebuilding Iberwight. She noted her intention to visit the dominions and observe their progress.

The oracle concluded her speech to a standing ovation by the entire assembly. Her speech had given the Order and kingdom much to contemplate. However, one word she expressed hung at the front of Darshima's mind – empire. He had come to understand that Tiriyuusians long disdained the idea of empire. Their history was one of rebellion against foreign empires seeking to impose sovereign rule upon their islands. The notion that Tiriyuud now ruled its own empire posed existential questions for the kingdom as a whole.

As intended, the oracle's words and moving image were transmitted beyond the walls of the palace, to the most remote corners of Iberwight and the moons beyond. Despite Navervyne's attempts to block the speech, it had been broadcast everywhere and was widely viewed on every moon of the fallen realm. As Darshima sat amid the applause, he imagined the peoples of the other moons listening to her words and anticipated their potential reaction.

From the snow-swept mountain villages on Iberwight to the pastoral hamlets on Wohiimai, the jungle encampments on Gordanelle and the stately domes and spires of Ardavia, to the towers of steel and glass framing the busy intersections of The Vilides, to the nomadic settlements amid the dunes of Ciblaithia, Darshima imagined her message resounding clearly.

Like Darshima, most peoples of the realm had never met an Omystikai, let alone given much thought about Iberwight and its isolated dominions. He imagined the peoples of the other moons and their reaction to the grandeur of the Oracle's Palace. The ancient pageantry, the rich vestments and unique costumes on display, and the sheer numbers in attendance evoked a unique sense of foreign power and might that would stir even a reluctant heart.

Many people had only heard occasional murmurings of a hermetic kingdom on Iberwight, but most were unfamiliar with this unique tribe of Omystikai. As Darshima had learned from the guardian's dossier, word of Tiriyuud's liberation of Iberwight had spread. Darshima imagined that seeing her image and hearing her words would make the victory feel real and tangible on all of the moons.

Her honesty about Fauridise's egregious sin and their defeat at the hands of Tiriyuud gave Darshima pause. He hoped that Tiriyuud's presence in their dominion would neutralize the threat they posed. Her pronouncements gave him confidence that Tiriyuud could bring balance and peace to the fractured Omystikai tribes and stability to the wider world.

Beyond Chryshaihem, her hopeful words glimmered through the despair enveloping the moons since the fall of The Vilides. Most were astonished by the people seated in her company. The broadcast images of the young, brown-skinned guardians, seated before the throne amid the sea of pale faces, were greeted with elation and disbelief. Billions contemplated the impossible circumstances that brought these children of the fallen realm to a faraway, once-forgotten kingdom where they had assisted it in its crusade for freedom.

The streets of The Vilides erupted into a cataclysm of disbelief and raw, unfettered joy. Millions of people viewed screens throughout the city and in their homes and saw the image of their former prince, Khydius, seated beside the empress. Long presumed a casualty of the invasion, Vilidesians reacted to his image as if they had seen his ghost. His moving image brought a sense of hope that all had not been lost after the invasion.

Though not as widely celebrated but equally joyous, three families - one in The Vilides, one in Ardavia, one in Chryshaihem who cared for a Pelethedran boy as their son, sat at home crowded around their viewing screens in disbelief at the proceedings. They were overjoyed to see their sons, brothers, and their sister alive and well. The sight of Darshima, Khydius, Erethalie, and Sydarias seated before the empress, dressed in Tiriyuusian regalia amid foreign opulence, brought forth a flood of emotions. For a brief moment, the peoples of the four moons overlooked the despair consuming their lives and felt a sense of hope.

Chapter 63

His legs folded, Darshima sat amid the tranquil silence of one of the inner sancta of the Guardians' Shrine. He had shed his elaborate costume for simple black prayer robes. He closed his eyes against the soft blue glow of the crystal ring etched in the stone platform beneath him. He released a sigh and cast his thoughts adrift.

The oracle's address had concluded earlier that evening and was followed by the finest banquet he had ever attended. He enjoyed an evening with his companions, full of entertainment showcasing the best of Tiriyuusian musical and theatrical traditions. Darshima was humbled that the Order and the Kingdom had done so much to show their gratitude for the guardians' service.

He yawned as feelings of exhaustion and something he couldn't quite place settled within him.

Darshima closed his eyes and tried to focus his thoughts. A sense of restlessness stirred in the corners of his mind. The past two years had brought significant changes to his life, many of which he could barely comprehend. He had seen and accomplished more than he would have ever imagined as a young boy on Gordanelle.

He had experienced the scourge of slavery and the gift of freedom. He had learned of his true Omystikai heritage and gained the legacy of a legendary father. He had found a new family with his uncle Tenrai and brother Khydius. He had developed close, unshakable bonds with his two companions, Sydarias and Erethalie. He had borne witness to the fall of a mighty empire and the awakenings of a new one. He had come to learn and master the primeval sovereign strength that he wielded with his right hand. At times, Darshima felt much older than his twenty years.

He looked through the clear windows surrounding the sanctuary and into the starry sky. The brilliant orbs of Ciblaithia, Gordanelle, and Wohiimai hung beyond the sharp edge of Benai's faded rings. He stared past them and into the void, trying to peer through the darkness to Navervyne. Despite Tiriyuud's victory and the re-establishment of peace on Iberwight, he still felt a sense of disquiet. The moon of his childhood, Gordanelle, and the others remained under Navervyne's rule, riven by strife, poverty, and conflict. His thoughts drifted back to the oracle's speech, and a hesitant smile formed upon his lips.

Darshima learned that the Order had broadcast it widely, and the people of these moons had listened to her words and seen her image. He understood that her exhortation had been well received, and there were protests and mass gatherings in celebration. He prayed The Vilidesians and the peoples of the other moons would heed her call and fight for their freedom, like the Tiriyuusians.

Darshima's thoughts drifted between the past and the present as he meditated. The sound of a sliding door broke through the silence. He looked up to see Tenrai, dressed in similar black robes.

"I don't mean to interrupt you." Tenrai took a seat in front of Darshima. The sight of his uncle cheered him up, and his restlessness eased some.

"You left the celebrations far too early. Is something the matter?" Tenrai's eyebrows arched in concern.

"I was feeling a bit tired and wanted some time to myself." Darshima lowered his gaze.

"I can sense your restlessness," said Tenrai. Darshima sat in silence as he gathered his thoughts.

"What will we do next?" asked Darshima, shrugging. "Since you rescued us, I have grown accustomed to preparing for the next moment. I can no longer remain in one place."

Tenrai smiled at his words and rested his hand upon Darshima's shoulder. "We have all worked hard and deserve some time to rest."

"How can we rest when there is still so much suffering?" Darshima cast a forlorn gaze toward his uncle. "There are still slaves on Navervyne, toiling with no hope." Darshima's voice grew heavy with emotion.

"We must trust that the oracle's words have made an impact on the other moons. We are a free people and will support the aspirations of those who seek their liberty." Tenrai looked toward the skies, his gaze lingering amid the stars.

"What do you mean?" Darshima shook his head in confusion.

"We must follow her lead. She will do what is right," said Tenrai. "I sense you want to continue the fight against the enemy, but this is no longer our fight alone. We must work with the Order." Before Darshima could respond, Tenrai continued. "Tiriyuud was able to save itself and capture this moon, but we must face the harsh reality of the present."

"Though we know peace here on Iberwight, the fact remains that so many people beyond this moon continue to suffer under foreign rule. I have heard no concrete plans for Tiriyuud to continue the fight," said Darshima, his voice rising in exasperation.

"I understand your frustration, but we must consider the stark situation our nation now faces." Tenrai drummed his fingers upon his knees.

"I realize that things are different now," said Darshima.

"Thanks to you and your brother, Tiriyuud had an extraordinary advantage over Navervyne. You and Khydius demonstrated a powerful control of kai that helped the Order gain control of this moon." Tenrai leaned closer to Darshima.

"I understand, but even so, Tiriyuud's forces were formidable," said Darshima. They sat together in silence, the soft chants from the shrine filtering into their sanctuary.

"Yes, but remember that every victory has its price." Darshima remained silent as Tenrai continued, "Though Tiriyuud now rules Iberwight, we remain an island kingdom with enormous responsibilities. Our military and our civilian apparatuses are extending their capabilities to defend and rebuild this moon."

"Tiriyuud is capable and can handle the added responsibility," said Darshima, remembering the Order's impressive mobilization in the dominions.

"The battle has only finished, and the dominions have been rendered destitute. At the moment, Tiriyuud is at capacity. Our farmers are the sole providers of food on all of Iberwight. Our mines, mills, and factories are the only active source of the materials and machinery needed to rebuild the dominions."

"I understand." Darshima glared at the floor as he pondered Tenrai's words. He had been swept up in the momentum of war and had not fully realized the scale of Tiriyuud's newfound responsibility. It was the only civilization with the capacity to rebuild what was destroyed. Tiriyuud's power had limits that he needed to consider.

"The oracle has stated her purpose in encouraging the other moons in their struggle. I pray that they heed her call," said Tenrai. Darshima looked through the window at the other moons, his thoughts with the people there still suffering.

"I wanted to ask you about the night of the final battle in Gavipristine." Tenrai folded his hands in his lap.

"What do you want to know?" Darshima's heart thudded as he recalled the bomb blasts and flames.

"I've spoken to Khydius about what he experienced when he incapacitated the crews of those Navervynish ships. He reported seeing your father's spirit. What did you see?" A pensive frown formed upon Tenrai's lips.

"He appeared before me through the smoke, and then he spoke," said Darshima, his voice growing heavy as he remembered his father's apparition. "There was so much I wanted to ask him."

"You heard his voice?" Tenrai's eyes widened in disbelief. "What did he say?"

"It is you who will show us all," said Darshima, slowly repeating Rion's words. Tenrai bowed his head in thought, placing his fingers upon his temples.

"Is something wrong?" Darshima tried to catch his uncle's gaze.

"Rion has appeared to me over the years, but his spirit has never spoken to me." Tenrai looked up at Darshima, his eyes glowing with a startling intensity.

"Though he was with me, his voice was far away." A shiver coursed through Darshima as he recalled the sound of Rion's disembodied voice amid the whipping winds.

"Only a few Omystikai each generation have the gift of hearing messages from our okainym or departed ones." Tenrai's brow wrinkled in thought.

"I read about it in those books during training," said Darshima, remembering how some sages listened to the spirits of the past for guidance.

"Rion was only one of two people in our generation to hear the okainym." Tenrai held Darshima's gaze.

"Who else heard the spirits?" Darshima shrugged, taken aback by Tenrai's intensity.

"Our oracle, Anaidys Rexe." Tenrai bowed in deference. He looked up at Darshima and searched his eyes.

"There is no way that I could share such a destiny." Darshima backed away from Tenrai, vigorously shaking his head as he pondered the incredulous notion. "I don't believe it."

"Only you truly know what your future holds." Tenrai drew nearer and rested his hands upon Darshima's shoulders. "I believe that your future is limitless, but you must believe it too."

Darshima sat in silence, Tenrai's words weighing upon his mind. He was only growing used to his abilities with kai and what that meant for him. Now he realized that a more improbable future possibly lay ahead of him. He didn't know if he was ready.

Tenrai looked upon his nephew. "We've spent enough time here for one evening. Let us rejoin the others." He cast a poignant gaze toward the moons that hung seemingly beyond the window. He continued softly, "In a world as turbulent as ours, moments of happiness are fleeting. Let us go and enjoy ourselves."

"You are right, uncle." Darshima mustered a smile and pushed aside his roiling emotions. They stood up together and left the sanctuary.

Chapter 64

Darshima followed Tenrai through the narrow hallway. Torches emitting jets of flame lit the dark path. Even amid the shadows, Darshima knew the familiar twists and turns. The sounds of muffled conversation and laughter echoed against the walls. His heart lightened at the familiar voices of his companions. They approached a doorway at the end of the hallway, a sliver of bright light escaping from its threshold.

Tenrai placed a hand upon the door to his quarters, and it gently slid apart.

"We wondered where you went." Sydarias waved to Darshima. He and Erethalie sat upon plush rugs around the glowing hearth. Darshima's heart thudded in surprise as he saw Shonan seated beside Erethalie, dressed in his school uniform.

"I missed you, Darshima!" Shonan leaped to his feet. His eyes lit up as he saw Darshima, and he rushed over and embraced him. Shonan had grown in stature since Darshima last saw him. He looked more like an adolescent, bearing only a passing resemblance to the boy he met back in The Vilides.

"It's been too long." Darshima hugged Shonan. "How are you?"

"I am doing well." A smile formed upon Shonan's lips.

"The Byx family says that he's practically Tiriyuusian now." Erethalie looked at her brother and chuckled. "He finished his classes for the day, and I couldn't wait to see him." Darshima followed Shonan back to the hearth and joined his companions.

"Are you okay, Darshima?" asked Dydan, looking concernedly upon him.

"It's been a long day. I'm sure he needed some rest," said Erethalie, her lips curling into a sympathetic smile. She turned her gaze to Khydius, who reclined upon a stiff woven mat away from the hearth, his eyes closed.

"Don't worry, I'm okay." Darshima nodded to his companions. He and Tenrai joined them around the hearth and warmed themselves. Darshima looked over Dydan's shoulder through the large windows to the city below and the lake beyond, its ripples glowing with undulating reflections of starlight.

This evening marked the first time they were in the same place, under less dire circumstances. Darshima was grateful for the moment.

"Have you enjoyed the day's festivities?" Tenrai looked to Erethalie and Sydarias. Hearing their voices, Khydius had awoken and joined them at the hearth.

"It's truly been spectacular, Tenrai," said Erethalie.

"The Tiriyuusians know how to celebrate." Sydarias smiled to himself.

"There are a few more important events, one of which is the fireworks display." Tenrai pointed toward the windows. "We will have an excellent view from my terrace."

"I can't wait to see it." Shonan's gaze drifted toward the window.

"What else is happening tonight?" asked Erethalie, scooting closer to the hearth.

"Wait, and we will show you." A rare smile formed upon Dydan's lips.

The low rumble of distant mortar shells and explosions interrupted their conversation. Darshima looked through the window and saw the night sky erupt in a blaze of dazzling light and color. He and his companions stood up with Tenrai and Dydan and followed them to the terrace. Tenrai slid open a glass door, and they stepped out onto the space. Darshima drew his robes against his shoulders amid the chilly air and looked up to the skies, ablaze in a shower of festive sparks.

"The Vilidesians never had such a display," exclaimed Erethalie.

"I've never seen anything like it." Sydarias pointed toward the brilliant show of light.

"The Omystikai invented these festive displays when they came to Iberwight," said Dydan. "They discovered crystals that could set the night ablaze, and we have used them ever since."

"Our ancestors used these crystals as an occasional source of merriment and color to enliven the snowy skies." Tenrai looked up at the display, a subtle smile forming upon his lips.

"It certainly warms the heart on a cold night." Darshima looked up at the skies in wonder. He followed the trajectories of the luminous shells toward the lake. Cannons stationed upon ships in the harbor sent up round after round of shells, the multi-hued explosions filling the night air with smoke and light. The boom of the shells echoed through the sky, rattling the windows and thudding against his chest. He spied the brilliantly backlit silhouettes of Tiriyuusian aerial vessels gliding through the skies. They let out a round of applause as the show concluded and stepped back indoors.

Tenrai and Dydan excused themselves, and Darshima and his companions rewarmed themselves around the hearth. Moments later, they returned, carrying dark lacquered wooden cases engraved in Omystikaiyn symbols. Curious, Darshima and his companions turned from the hearth to see what they were doing. Tenrai and Dydan settled upon the floor and opened the cases. Each contained a set of styluses with delicate golden handles and sharpened green crystal tips of various shapes and sizes. A dozen small glass jars containing various colored inks sat below the styluses, exuding a subtle luminescence that cast their faces aglow.

"What are you doing?" asked Darshima. He stood up from the hearth and sat beside Tenrai to get a better look. Erethalie, Khydius, Sydarias, and Shonan joined him. Tenrai and Dydan stayed silent, and their brows were knit in concentration. They methodically spilled the substances onto metal palettes and carefully mixed them, producing a variety of glowing shades and hues.

"This is an ancient tradition that is dear to the Omystikai of Tiriyuud." Tenrai looked up at them and offered a smile. "Erethalie, Sydarias, we would like for you both to take part in one of our most sacred rites." Their eyes sparkled with curiosity as he spoke.

"Though you were not born into a Tiriyuusian family, you know our ways and are members of our Order. You are Omystikai of Tiriyuud, and we want to give you your proper markings," said Dydan.

"We have divined your symbols. They reflect your talents, your spirit, and your relationship to the sovereign strength. They are indelible and will represent your eternal bond to these islands, our people, and our faith." A solemn expression formed upon Tenrai's face.

Erethalie and Sydarias sat still and exchanged astonished glances. Tenrai and Dydan looked at Erethalie and Sydarias, who returned with stunned expressions.

"Will you accept these markings along with the everlasting bond they represent?" asked Dydan.

"Without question, I accept these markings." Sydarias bowed his head.

"On my honor, I will accept them," said Erethalie.

Dydan sat next to Erethalie. She pulled her wavy locks back in a long tail, exposing her temples. With a damp cloth, Dydan prepared the skin behind her right ear. He withdrew a stylus from the kit with one hand and held the palette of colors in the other, and set to work placing the intricate design upon her temple. Sydarias lay upon the ground, with his chest pressed against the soft rug. He rested his face in his arms, and his right pant leg was rolled up to the knee. Tenrai sat beside him and applied a cloth to the bare skin of his calf.

Darshima and the others looked on in silence as Tenrai and Dydan sat focused, their styluses moving methodically. Their abstract lines turned into beautiful, tessellated designs, their multi-hued lines casting a subtle glow. Darshima watched in amazement as he witnessed the tradition. Though he and Khydius had experienced childhoods that were worlds and classes apart from each other, they had both looked upon those once strange markings gracing their skin with the same mixture of fear and curiosity.

As Darshima learned more about his Tiriyuusian heritage and the ancient meaning behind those sacred symbols, he grew to revere them and what they represented. Witnessing the skill and artistry that Tenrai and Dydan employed in marking his friends was a moment that he would never forget. Darshima sensed that Erethalie and Sydarias occasionally felt as if they did not belong in Tiriyuud. He was glad to see that they too would bear the markings that all Tiriyuusians bore.

When Dydan and Tenrai finished their work, Erethalie and Sydarias stood up and examined their markings. Dydan presented Erethalie with a handheld mirror. The ink still fresh, she studied the intricate lines and symbols curving along her temple and behind her ear.

"It's stunning," she said as she traced markings. "It almost feels like it was always there, but I never noticed it." A look of calm spread upon her features.

"You will feel your connection to them grow with time," said Dydan.

"Thank you." Erethalie reached over and embraced him.

"What do you think?" Erethalie turned to Shonan.

"They suit you." He looked upon the symbols, his eyebrows raised in astonishment. "I hope to get markings one day."

"I know you will." Tenrai patted Shonan upon his back.

With his markings complete, Sydarias stood up and looked down at the freshly-inked design upon his calf. The angular lines and symbols glowed softly against his smooth dark skin.

"It's perfect." He smiled to himself as he saw it and exchanged a glance with Darshima.

"As you are so talented upon the saigura, I could think of no better mark," said Tenrai.

"Thank you." Sydarias turned to Tenrai and hugged him. Sydarias and Erethalie looked to Darshima and Khydius and resumed their seats around the hearth.

Darshima looked toward his friends, his eyes growing damp with emotion. Since they had arrived in Tiriyuud, his friends had done their utmost to practice the culture and learn the language. They had developed mastery of kai and of the cloudboard that rivaled the best guardians in the Order. Their courage on the battlefield had cemented their loyalty to the kingdom.

Though they were treated as equals, Darshima often worried that Erethalie and Sydarias felt different. They did not benefit from a deep ancestral link to the kingdom, like him and Khydius. Darshima looked to their new markings, impressed with their artistry. His heart thudded with a feeling of pride. They were Tiriyuusians.

Chapter 65

The week of celebrations drew to a close, and the guardians resumed their duties to the Order. Tenrai had assigned Darshima and his companions to training duty. They would be responsible for teaching the newest recruits in the ways of the guardianship. Despite his anxiousness at the task, Darshima took comfort in knowing that Priest Dawn would be there, waiting at their training temple to assist them.

As they prepared themselves for the months ahead, Tiriyuusians resumed their daily patterns. The guardians stationed in the dominions continued the difficult task of assessing and repairing the damage done by Navervyne's occupation and the subsequent war. Tiriyuud's factories continued their record production of aerial vessels, vehicles, materials, and machinery to meet the Order's demands.

Chryshaihem's treasury issued silver coins for the dominions, readily converted to the gold and gem coins used in Tiriyuusian currency. Their economies largely moribund from Navervyne's wide-scale plunder, the dominions utilized this new currency to restore economic patterns, ridding themselves of Navervynish coin. As teams cleared the debris, reestablished supply lines, and laid plans for infrastructure, the Omystikai cautiously gained confidence in Tiriyuud's leadership. Tiriyuud's merchants made plans to fill in the void and open new enterprises in the dominions. Tiriyuud's farmers increased their production to match the dominions' demand for provisions. The Orders engineers sought to establish their unique pyramid greenhouses throughout Iberwight. Long dependent on Wohiimai for food, the Order sought to make the dominions self-sufficient.

Their successes on the battlefields and their new responsibilities on Iberwight gave the guardians increased stature and influence. Wherever they traveled, they garnered praise and respect. Even so, there was much work to be done. The guardians recruited young men and women throughout the kingdom to join the ranks of guardians and soldiers.

In a break with tradition, the guardians in the foreign dominions drew up plans to train the local young men and women as soldiers. Though the Order employed them in clearing the debris and rebuilding the cities and villages, the guardians knew that Tiriyuud's forces were finite. If the Order were to maintain peace, it would have to enlist the citizens of the dominions. To Tiriyuud's relief, its Order was not greeted as an imposition but was seen as a force for peace and goodwill. The peoples of Keverese, Nyzhaiheb, and even Fauridise sought to learn more about the Tiriyuusians and their way of life.

The Tiriyuusians had been reluctant to accept the idea of their new-found power ever since the oracle's speech. Nonetheless, evidence of empire was accumulating all around them. Chryshaihem was transforming from an isolated capital into the center of power on Iberwight. Chryshaihem's civil engineers and architects drew plans for new buildings to create space for the increase in the Order's administrative duties.

In a surprise move, the Order had permitted unrestricted travel to and from the Outer District. The Order allowed envoys from the dominions to enter and reside within the kingdom while they helped orchestrate Tiriyuud's rebuilding of their territories. Omystikai families with means moved to Tiriyuud and reestablished their lives. Others sought to send their children to the schools and universities in Chryshaihem and other cities to continue their studies, interrupted by the invasion. Slowly but surely, the Order began the challenging task of breaking down the ancient barriers that had shielded their kingdom for so long.

Chapter 66

Darshima and his companions walked in a line along the rocky beach. In the distance, he spied the weathered piers, and the long sleek watercraft moored to them. The morning sun rose above the waters, and the city slowly revealed itself in the daylight. Despite the early hour, Darshima was far from tired, and a sense of energy coursed through his veins. Though it had been barely a month since Tiriyuud's victory, he still felt twinges of excitement.

The Order had succeeded in recruiting many young men and women for the guardianship throughout Tiriyuud. Several recruits came from Nyzhaiheb and Keverese, answering the oracle's call.

"It's not much further." Darshima pointed toward the pier.

"How could we forget?" Khydius shrugged and let out a chuckle. Erethalie and Sydarias laughed along with him. Darshima smirked at his brother as they moved along the beach. They were on their way to training islands to prepare for the newest class of recruits who would arrive in the coming days. Tenrai and Dydan would meet them there. They would supervise the setup before turning the responsibilities over to Darshima and his companions.

As Darshima marched upon the frozen soil, he marveled that not long ago, they were the ones walking this trail behind Dydan and Tenrai, full of worry and anxiety. Now here they were, the four of them, making the trek on their own, preparing to train an entirely new class.

He walked in silence, his mind racing with memories of their struggle and sacrifice, failure and triumph during their own training.

"We have so much to teach these new recruits," said Sydarias, his words coming out in puffs of steam.

"They will learn from our experience." Erethalie looked up to the sky and let out a sigh.

Like the other members of the Order, Darshima was excited to meet the new class. He and his fellow guardians had much to teach them beyond the traditional Tiriyuusian arts of saigura and eneri-kai. They had gained

400

skills and knowledge during the war that would make the Order much stronger, more modern, and more agile.

As they walked toward the pier, the low rumble of a struggling engine broke through the tranquil silence. Darshima craned his neck toward the sky, narrowing his eyes in surprise as he saw a large fleet of Gilded Wing craft fly overhead. Dozens of black and gold aircraft escorted a greenish aerial vessel, whose rounded lines and elongated hull distinguished it as a Navervynish vessel.

"What's happening?" Sydarias pointed to the craft, his lips trembling in fear.

"It's a Navervynish ship, but it's in poor condition." Erethalie lifted her hand to her brow. Darshima eyed its peeling paint and failing engines, leaving a trail of acrid smoke as it crossed the sky.

"It is clearly in no condition to attack," said Khydius. "There is something highly unusual about this." His eyes trailed the convoy as it flew in the direction of the Outer District.

"Even so, Gilded Wing is ready for them," said Erethalie. She reached for her cloudboard strapped to her back.

"We have to investigate." Darshima and his companions boarded their saigura and took to the skies. They raced across the lake and above the encircling mountain range. Darshima pulled his visor over his eyes as they neared the convoy. Bits of the failing craft disintegrated, hurtling past them as they approached. Amid the buffeting winds, they cleared the mountains and ventured over the ocean. Gilded Wing escorted the craft over the Outer District toward an airfield perched at its edge.

Darshima, Erethalie, Khydius, and Sydarias reached the island and landed near the airfield. They walked among dozens of their fellow guardians, standing at the ready. They waited at the edge of the field, and Darshima's heart thudded in surprise as he recognized several familiar faces.

"Guardians Nax." Lleidas Vowe offered Darshima and Khydius a polite bow.

"Guardians Danthe and Idawa." Seibu Reede nodded toward Erethalie and Sydarias.

"What is happening?" Darshima pointed toward the approaching fleet.

"The Order's network of satellites identified this foreign craft breaching Iberwight's atmosphere," said Lleidas.

"We tried to establish contact, but the ship's communication system is non-functional," added Seibu.

"Whatever their aims, Gilded Wing has intercepted them," said Erethalie.

The sound of engine noise grew louder as the lead vessel of the convoy descended upon the airfield. The enemy craft sputtered along, barely maintaining control. As it neared the ground, its nose suddenly slammed into a snowdrift, sending sprays of flakes skyward. Darshima and his companions stood firm as the ground trembled beneath their feet.

The Gilded Wing aircraft hovered to a landing around the enemy vessel. Darshima watched as Guardian Eikan Faite descended from the lead aircraft, its stairs telescoping to the ground.

"We must seize them all, but no harm shall come to them," she said. Eikan led her unit toward the dilapidated aerial ship. Darshima, Khydius, Sydarias, Erethalie, and their fellow guardians approached the craft as the engine noise died down. The cargo bay doors at the vessel's aft opened, and a metal gangway extended to the ground.

The guardians rushed up the plank and entered the craft. Darshima stood at the ready, in disbelief at what he was witnessing. Moments later, Eikan and her unit returned from the aircraft's interior. They marched the occupants down the plank with their empty hands held above their heads toward an awaiting Tiriyuusian vessel.

Chapter 67

Steady snow showers fell from the grey skies, covering the courtyard of the Guardians' Shrine in a layer of white powder. Darshima, Erethalie, Khydius, and Sydarias stood at the front of the courtyard. Hundreds of other guardians waited with them and trained their eyes upon the captives. Tenrai and Dydan stood at the head of the group, along with Eikan, and surveyed the scene.

Dozens of gaunt men and women stood still, their tattered clothing fluttering in the steady breeze. Though they had received overcoats to protect them against the cold, they shivered in the unfamiliar climate. To Darshima and everyone else's surprise, the ship's occupants were not Navervynish enemies. They were refugees from the fallen realm. Amid the sea of pale faces, their black, brown, red, and tan hues stood boldly against the falling snow, representing virtually every tribe and people from Ciblaithia, Gordanelle, and Wohiimai. Darshima looked at each of them, reading the fear and wonder written upon their expressions.

They had not long been transported from the Outer District to the Guardians' Shrine, and details of their remarkable story were becoming clearer. They had survived the initial invasion of the realm. Some had fled their homes, fearing capture by the invading forces. Others had managed to avoid the conquering armies and escaped enslavement on Navervyne, unlike untold numbers. Nevertheless, they had suffered. Many toiled in Navervynish mines and quarries on Ciblaithia under extreme conditions. They had lost everything and had been rendered destitute by the harsh circumstances.

The men and women had wandered the moons of the fallen realm, seeking refuge. They eventually found their way to Wohiimai, where they had worked together in the fields, for one of Navervyne's agricultural concerns. They worked in near servitude, barely eking out an existence. The oracle's message had been broadcast in their camp, and it had given them hope. With nothing to lose amid the ruins, they banded together and plotted their escape. They commandeered an old Navervynish ship and fled

Wohiimai only three days prior, making the perilous voyage to Iberwight and seeking refuge in Tiriyuud.

The silence of the courtyard was deafening. The guardians looked upon the refugees with a mixture of suspicion and wonder. Before long, the sound of footsteps broke through the silence. Dydan and Seer Ryte led the Sages of Tiriyuud into the courtyard, and the guardians snapped to attention.

"Behold the Oracle of Tiriyuud, Empress of Iberwight!" shouted Dydan. Darshima's heart thudded in surprise when he realized the oracle was present. The assembled crowd fell to their hands and knees, the thud reverberating against the walls. Unsure of what to do, the young refugees clumsily genuflected.

Upon the oracle's word, the entire courtyard rose to its feet and beheld her. She stood among the crowd, the snowflakes accumulating upon her crown and within the folds of her robes. She looked upon the refugees, her eyes narrowing. Seer Ryte, Tenrai, and Dydan moved beside her.

"Who amongst you leads this group?" asked Tenrai. After a moment of hesitation, a man and a woman stepped forward. Tenrai looked at them, his stern gaze belied by a spark of curiosity in his eyes. "Why have you come to Chryshaihem?" he asked, in impeccable Vilidesian.

"We are refugees from the invasion. We seek shelter within the Tiriyuusian Realm. Please have mercy on us," said the young man, shivering amid the cold weather. His curly black locks draped over the deep brown skin of his forehead. The young woman stepped forward, her long black hair, copper skin, and amber eyes standing out vividly against the snow.

"We heard the empress's words. We seek to learn the ways of the Omystikai of Tiriyuud so that we too may fight against Navervyne." She offered a bow.

Another refugee stepped forward and spoke. "The Tiriyuusians are the only ones who have been able to defeat the enemy. Please teach us."

The refugees before them recounted their struggle for survival on the war-torn moons.

They shared stories of strife, injustice, and brutality at the hands of the Navervynish invaders that made even the most seasoned guardians shudder. Darshima stood silent as he listened intently, his heart thudding as he remembered his own toil.

Darshima looked on as the oracle stared at the refugees in the courtyard. He had hoped her words would reach the people beyond Iberwight and encourage them to fight the Navervynish. Darshima would never have fathomed that men and women of the fallen realm would flee their world and arrive upon Tiriyuud's shores seeking to learn the ways of the Omystikai. His mind stirred with the possibility of having even more Vilidesians here in Chryshaihem.

The men and women stared at the oracle, the toll of the strife and suffering etched upon the worn lines of their young faces. Darshima had contemplated how Tiriyuud's influence had changed, and now there was indisputable evidence that it extended beyond Iberwight. Tiriyuud was a source of hope for people throughout the conquered moons. As he watched the oracle standing before the refugees, Darshima could feel the weight of history upon them all.

The crowd parted as the oracle approached the group, and they instinctively genuflected. She cast an appraising glance upon every one of the refugees, clasping their hands and greeting them. She then stood at the head of the group and spoke. "These men and women have heeded our call. They shall find refuge within this kingdom. We will train them in our ways. They will join our ranks with the intent that they will one day rise to fight and reclaim the freedom that is rightfully theirs."

Chapter 68

Darshima looked out upon the water as their craft skimmed over the ripples of the lake. A chilly mist obscured the horizon. Dawn had broken, and the sun's rays etched a faint but strengthening path across the sky. Chryshai-hem's skyline receded as they moved further away from the shore. With a hand on the rudder, Darshima kept a keen eye on the path ahead. Khydius, stationed at the helm, kept an eye toward the training islands.

Through the mists, Darshima spied the familiar shape of the enormous arch at the entrance of the training islands, its graceful lines looming over the waters. He eyed hundreds of similar craft on either side of them speeding through the mists. Seated in the ships around them were young Tiriyu-usians heading to the training grounds. Joining them were the refugees from Wohiimai. Darshima looked ahead and saw Tenrai and Dydan directing a ship. He looked behind him to see Erethalie and Sydarias doing the same.

Darshima's gaze shifted to the two passengers seated ahead of him, his heart thudding with a mixture of curiosity and awe. One was a young man from Gordanelle and the other a young woman from Ciblaithia. Drawing their overcoats against their frames, they shivered in the cold and peered all around them, their eyes wide as they took in the strange surroundings. As he looked at them, thoughts of his own voyage to the training grounds came to mind.

Darshima anticipated that they would be training the next class of guardians, but he never would've imagined that their recruits would be refugees like himself. The prospect set his imagination afire. He had secretly worried that Tiriyuud's victory would mean the end of their fight against Navervyne. However, the arrival of these refugees gave him cause for hope. He was humbled that the oracle had welcomed them with open arms and sought to train them to carry on the fight. Though it remained unsaid, Darshima believed that he and his companions had paved the way for the refugees sailing with them.

Darshima steered their ship beneath the arch, its script glinting in the sunlight. His mind raced with memories of the struggles he faced and the triumphs he achieved. He pushed aside his thoughts, and looked upon his recruits. It was their time now. Darshima made a silent vow to teach them everything he knew. Like the misty waters ahead of them, the future had never been more uncertain or full of possibility. Tiriyuud had boldly staked its claim in the unforgiving world around it. Darshima and his companions would fight with everything they had to defend Tiriyuud's enduring peace and its newfound realm.

Beneath a veiled sky, its doomed specter cast
Remnants of worlds, from noble eras past
Conquest of empires beyond heaven's shroud
Legacy of ages, all heirs wear proud
Glittering cities rise on gilded sands
Faulted foundations fracture hallowed lands
Ordained scepters rule a starry expanse
Unto sovereign voids, stained shields advance
A new dominion, its reign established
Eons quake, as old nations fall vanquished
Innocents perish on a bloodied shore
An enlightened land fades to ancient lore
Sage tribes exiled to history's refrain
Fire transcends ice, hope's virtues sustain
Allied orbs bear hegemony's decline
A realm shattered in destiny's resign
Cryptic clans prosper in frozen embrace
Ancient cultures preserve a concealed face
Hidden islands maintain a sacred pledge
Unyielding might beholds a kingdom's edge

The End
-Dustin R. Cummings

Also by Dustin R Cummings

Exiles of a Gilded Moon
Exiles of a Gilded Moon Volume 1: Empire's Wake
Kingdom's Edge

About the Author

Dustin R Cummings is an author who lives in New York, NY. Originally from Michigan, he is an avid fan of science fiction and fantasy. In his spare time, he enjoys reading, piano, and long walks. He is an assistant professor of surgery in New Jersey.

The first installment in his epic fantasy series *Exiles of a Gilded Moon Volume I: Empire's Wake* chronicles the incredible life of Darshima, a young, inquisitive man finding his place in the world, who faces the unexpected - the invasion and destruction of his homeland.

He can be found on Twitter @dorenavant2020 or at dustinrcummings.com

Made in United States
Troutdale, OR
08/19/2023

12196055R10236